ROMANTIC TIMES READERS'
CHOICE AWARD NOMINEE
LISA CACH

". . . weaves a story rich in humanity and emotional intensity!"
—*Romantic Times*

". . . shows a tremendous amount of promise!"
—*All About Romance*

". . . is fast showing herself to be an author of ingenuity!"
—www.TheRomanceReader.com

". . . is quickly moving toward auto-buy status."
—*The Romance Journal*

". . . demonstrates the enchanting creativity which, combined with her ever improving writing skills, should attract and satisfy fans of regular and paranormal romance alike."
—*Romance Reviews Today*

"[Her book] *Of Midnight Born* passes my CODPIECE test . . . Creative, rather Original, Dramatic, Poetic, Intensely Emotional, Comedic, and best of all, Entertaining."
—*Mrs. Giggles*

THE HAND OF DESTINY

"Is that the real reason you want to do this?" she asked.

He didn't answer for a moment. There were a host of reasons he wanted to take the ship. But one was strongest. He beckoned her closer with his fingertips. With visible reluctance, she came.

"Anne," he said softly. "If we let Chartier bring us to a port, what will happen then? I'll end up back in England, or perhaps back with John Company. You will go back to service as someone's maid, or perhaps you will be 'fortunate' enough to find yourself back with Miss Godwyn—if she is still alive. Or you'll go back home if someone will pay your way.

"What of your dream, then? You would have come all this way for nothing, suffered the shipwreck for nothing, roamed a pirate ship with a monkey on your shoulder for nothing but a story to tell your family."

"You said it would make a very romantic story." She bent her head down and closed her eyes for a long moment, and when she opened them he caught a glimmering sheen of tears that she blinked away.

He lifted a fingertip and gently, ever so gently so as not to startle her, stroked the softness of her cheek. "But it's only half the tale. Can't you feel that? You left England to pursue a vision. Can you turn away now, when the Hand of Destiny has set you on a path to reach it?"

Other *Love Spell* books by Lisa Cach:
THE MERMAID OF PENPERRO
OF MIDNIGHT BORN
BEWITCHING THE BARON
THE CHANGELING BRIDE

THE WILDEST SHORE

LISA CACH

LOVE SPELL NEW YORK CITY

*To Sarah Wescott and Kathy Preuss, two who dream of
wilder shores.*

A LOVE SPELL BOOK®

October 2001

Published by

Dorchester Publishing Co., Inc.
276 Fifth Avenue
New York, NY 10001

ISBN 0-505-52454-6

The name "Love Spell" and its logo are trademarks of Dorchester
Publishing Co., Inc.

Printed in the United States of America.

Visit us on the web at www.dorchesterpub.com.

THE
WILDEST
SHORE

Oh mistress mine! where are you roaming?
O, stay and hear; your true love's coming,
That can sing both high and low,
Trip no further, pretty sweeting;
Journeys end in lovers meeting,
Every wise man's son doth know.

What is love? 'tis not hereafter;
Present mirth hath present laughter;
What's to come is still unsure:
In delay there lies no plenty;
Then come kiss me, sweet and twenty,
Youth's a stuff will not endure.

—William Shakespeare

Chapter One

Aboard the English East Indiaman Coventry
Indian Ocean, 1811

"Sails on the horizon. Perhaps it's pirates," Horatio Merivale said to Miss Godwyn, widening his eyes in an affectation of terror.

The woman giggled and raised her chin as she tried to look out over the sea without rising from her seat on deck. "You should not jest about such things," she said. "Anne, go look. I don't believe there are any sails at all."

Anne smothered her irritation and marked her place in her book with a ribbon. She'd been reading aloud to her mistress, and had been quite enjoying the story. Now that Mr. Merivale had joined them, though, she would have to sit and endure while he flirted with Miss Godwyn, complimenting her dark hair, her porcelain skin, her sky-blue eyes, her wit, her grace, her vast comprehension of world affairs, her remarkable musical talents, her way with injured animals and orphaned children, her trilling, tinkling laugh. . . .

She set the book on her chair and staggered down the rolling and pitching deck to the lee rail, Mr. Merivale following close behind. She already had heard the lookout call his sighting of the sails to the first officer, an event which Miss Godwyn had failed to give notice.

"You see . . . that tiny square of white?" Mr. Merivale said, pointing. They were the first words he had ever directed to her. As a lady's maid, she was not the social equal of an officer in the East India Company, and she assumed she was generally beneath his notice. She'd be surprised if he knew her name.

She followed his line of sight, and found the sail of which he spoke. She nodded.

"You see it?" he prompted, apparently not happy with a silent nod.

"Yes, sir." From the corner of her eye she could see him looking down at her. He was a tall man, with dark brown hair and blue-green eyes that were set under down-sloping lids, giving him a mournful gaze that was at odds with his light-hearted manner. She had yet to see him without a smile playing around his lips, and she was not surprised that Miss Godwyn chattered constantly of him when they were alone. He possessed a certain charm, and if the gossip was to be believed, he had used that charm to break many a female heart.

There was one advantage to being beneath notice as a maid: She was enough of an outsider to clearly observe the follies of her betters. Miss Godwyn might fall under the spell of Mr. Merivale's fawning flattery, but she, Anne Hazlett, could see the shallowness of the man, and the hints of his insincerity.

"You don't seem worried. It could be that dastardly French privateer, Philippe Chartier. Aren't you afraid?" he asked, that same smile teasing his lips.

"No, sir," she said. It was infinitely more likely that the sail on the horizon was the East Indiaman *Neptune* than a pirate ship. The *Neptune* had left Cape Town at the same time as the *Coventry*, bound like them for India, and yesterday had fallen behind, dropping out of sight beneath the horizon in the same manner in which this ship was now appearing.

Mr. Merivale turned and leaned his back and elbows against the rail beside her, craning his head like a bird to get a better look at her face. She tucked her head down, the brim of her little jockey-style hat blocking her eyes from his view.

"No, you don't look scared. Not of pirates, anyway," he said.

He meant she was shy of him. She felt a flush of embarrassment heat her cheeks. She nodded once in his direction, then turned and staggered back up the deck to the awning under which Miss Godwyn sat. Her shoulders were tight with the sense of being watched, and she knew Mr. Merivale was observing her awkward retreat.

"Well?" Miss Godwyn asked. Her mistress's voice was sharp, and Anne knew she hadn't been expecting

Mr. Merivale to follow her to the rail. The one thing Miss Godwyn could not abide was attention focusing on any woman but herself.

"There are sails," Anne confirmed.

"What was Mr. Merivale saying to you?"

"Very little, Miss. He asked if I was afraid of pirates."

Anne heard Mr. Merivale come up behind her, and Miss Godwyn's face relaxed into a warm smile that was not meant for her. "Are you trying to frighten my maid?" she asked.

Anne picked up her book and resumed her seat, keeping the brim of her hat between her eyes and Mr. Merivale's face. She examined his white pantaloons, the very latest fashion, with their straps that slid under each foot in its neat black shoe.

"Would a gallant man stoop to such a thing?" Mr. Merivale asked. "I frighten neither children nor servants—only ravishing young ladies sailing to exotic shores, in hopes that they'll leap into my arms for safety."

Miss Godwyn giggled. "You wouldn't have had much success in frightening Anne, anyway. She is a veritable stone! She does not even start when surprised."

"Is that so?" Mr. Merivale asked.

Even through her hat brim Anne could feel him looking at her. She held motionless, realizing as she did so that she was acting the very stone Miss Godwyn claimed. Her mistress had not yet deduced—and likely never would—that her stillness when surprised was not the result of bravery. Like a small animal, she froze when confronted.

Her mind skipped through modes of escaping this unwelcome attention—excusing herself with mention of a chore; suggesting that Miss Godwyn change for dinner—but speaking aloud seemed worse than sitting still and allowing these two sponge-brains to tire of her and move on to other topics.

"We could use someone like you in my regiment," Merivale said. "Can you wield a sword?" he asked, to Miss Godwyn's continued giggling. "Fire a gun? Ride a horse and chase down rebels, screaming a war cry as you go?"

Resentment simmered inside Anne. Did he think her fair game for his jests because she was a mere servant?

She raised her narrowed, angry gaze to his. Their eyes met and he blinked, his head jerking back. Perhaps he was astonished to see that she was human and possessed of ears and understanding, was not the emotionless stone Miss Godwyn believed.

His playful mouth unexpectedly settled into a somber line, the angle of it for once matching the mournful cast of his eyes. With the smile gone, there was something in his gaze that brought up a moment of empathetic sadness inside Anne. The man looked lost.

"My apologies," he said softly to her.

"Tsk. Apologies? For what?" Miss Godwyn asked. "You don't mind a little teasing, do you, Anne?"

Anne looked to her mistress and smiled stiffly for her benefit, as if no harm had been done.

A cold gust of wind swept over them, and the bright sunlight beyond the awning dimmed, the decks going grey. Anne shivered, and Mr. Merivale stepped out from under their shelter and looked up at the sky.

"Perhaps it is the weather we have to worry about more than pirates," he said.

Anne clasped her arms across her stomach, a sick feeling coming over her. It had nothing to do with the pitch and roll of the ship, and everything to do with the approaching storm. The shadow that had moved over them felt like the shadow of death.

"This isn't going to be like the last storm, is it?" Miss Godwyn asked, her voice quavering. The ship creaked and groaned around them, the running footsteps of sailors heard overhead, as sails were reefed and hatches covered.

"Would you like a few drops of laudanum so that you can sleep through it?" Anne asked. They were in their cabin, one of only four that were in the relatively luxurious roundhouse. The roundhouse was high in the stern of the boat, the poop deck overhead, the dining saloon and the captain's cabin just down the passageway. They were fortunate in having portholes whose glass remained uncovered, free from the threat of waves in even the foulest of weather, although they could still hear the water rushing by below. Those who lodged in the great room the next deck down were less fortunate, the water not only rushing by but, from all reports, occasionally rushing *in*, even through the deadlights. Mr. Merivale was down there, as was Miss Godwyn's brother, Edmund.

"Two or three drops. Perhaps four. I don't like storms, Anne. I don't like them at all."

"We'll come through all right," Anne soothed, although her own belly was twisting with a sick certainty that this time such would not be the case. She'd been terrified through each and every storm they'd endured since leaving England some three months earlier, and had only retained her wits because the work of tending to Miss Godwyn kept her distracted from her fears.

But this time, it was less a mere fear than a queer certainty that disaster was roiling towards them across the turbulent seas. Since she was a child she had had a fear of dark, confined spaces, and being trapped in a cabin all through a stormy night, the ship in danger of foundering, was enough to make her want to down Miss Godwyn's entire bottle of laudanum.

She brushed out another lock of Miss Godwyn's black hair and rolled it in a rag, tying it to the young woman's crown. It was nearly ten o'clock, and they would have to blow out the lamp soon. There was danger from French warships and privateers even here in the Indian Ocean, and the ship would be safest from attack if it were invisible in the dark, no lights shining from its portholes.

"What of those stories Captain Butters was telling, of ships breaking in half under the force of waves?"

"Shhh," Anne soothed, and tied the last roll of hair in place. She met Miss Godwyn's eyes in the small mirror that was bolted to the vanity, the vanity in turn roped to staples in the floor. "I imagine he was amusing himself at your expense, is all. He wants to sink no more than we do, and he will do his utmost to keep us afloat."

Anne poured a small glass of water and mixed in

three drops of laudanum, then added two more for good measure.

Miss Godwyn took it from her and gulped it down. "I wish we were there already," she said. "I don't know how much more of this boat I can take." She handed back the empty glass. "Sometimes I feel quite certain that we will never reach India."

"A month from now you will have forgotten all about this night. You'll have parties to attend, and a basketful of suitors vying for your hand." Even more powerful than laudanum was the mention of men for soothing and distracting Miss Godwyn.

"Do you truly think so? I thought Edmund had been exaggerating about how many eligible bachelors there are in India. I don't suppose they have many opportunities for finding a wife, do they?"

"They'll be tripping over themselves in their rush to woo you," Anne agreed, feeling like a doctor pulling a favorite cure-all potion from his bag. *Apply two mentions of men to patient. If patient does not immediately improve, apply third mention and offer compliments on the complexion.*

"As Mr. Merivale does now, like an eager puppy trying to please me. What do you make of him as a potential husband? His family has money, but I think perhaps I could do better. After all, he is twenty-five and still only a lieutenant, which does not say much for his ambition. And I gather he has a most frightful reputation for being a flirt. Edmund tells me he jilted a girl back home, and that in Cape Town there was at least one angry Dutch papa who was glad to see our ship leave port." She sighed, pouting at her reflection in the mirror. "Still, he is the only amusement to be had on board. If I were not talking to him, I would have no one to entertain me but you and Edmund. What a bore that would be!"

"Indeed."

"Now don't sulk, Anne. You know I meant nothing against your company, and I am very happy you chose to accompany me to India. Can you imagine me with an Indian maid? She wouldn't understand a word I said! No, I could never find another who knows me as well as you do."

Anne gave a tiny smile and tried to let the words roll off her back. She knew they were, in Miss Godwyn's self-absorbed way, kindly meant, and yet they had the effect of making her feel like a pillow or an old pair of shoes: an item present only for the comfort or use it could give, capable of no thought of its own. Miss Godwyn seemed to think that she had no inner life, no interests beyond tending to Miss Godwyn herself.

Mama perhaps had been right; Anne was not suited in her temperament for life as a lady's maid. Mama said she had a mind too bright and a heart too sensitive to be happy being ordered about by another, especially when that other was a bird-wit like her employer. Anne's father was the gardener at Suffington Hall, Miss Godwyn's home, so Anne had ample opportunity in her twenty years to watch the spoiled antics of Pamela Godwyn.

She'd had her own reasons for seeking the position of lady's maid, and accompanying Miss Godwyn on her husband-hunting expedition to India. Mrs. Godwyn had been delighted to hire her to accompany her irresponsible daughter, assuming, no doubt, that Anne's quietness bespoke dull reliability and lack of imagination.

Anne helped Miss Godwyn into her bed, holding the swaying cot steady as she climbed in. The narrow bed hung from ropes attached to hooks in the deck overhead. Anne was to have had an identical bed, immediately above Miss Godwyn's, but her mistress had protested that it made for too much furniture in the room, and blocked the light from the porthole. The cot had been removed, and each evening Anne unfolded a hammock just as the sailors used, and strung it up on the other side of the cabin.

"I don't know why Mr. Merivale was trying to talk to *you*, though, Anne," Miss Godwyn said, her voice sounding sleepy as the laudanum took effect. The little frown between her brows smoothed out as the drug worked its magic. "I'm sure it meant nothing. He was only amusing himself." She yawned and pulled her blanket up under her chin. "Tomorrow I'll wear the blue silk. My eyes always look lovely when I wear the blue."

"Sleep well," Anne said, but as she started to put away the toiletries, Miss Godwyn's brief musing on Mr. Merivale's motives revived questions of her own.

Why *had* Mr. Merivale tried to talk with her? Why had he noticed her today, when he never had before? It surely had been simple bored mischief on his part, like Miss Godwyn said. Yet, she could not forget that moment when their eyes had met, and he had seemed to see more in her than a mere maid, just as she had, for an instant, seen something other than an empty-headed fool in him.

The boat heeled sharply to port, and Anne stumbled into the small sofa that had been tied to the floor. She plunked down on the seat and clung to its arm. Miss Godwyn's cot stayed level on its ropes, but the cabin tilted weirdly under it, giving the illusion that Miss Godwyn was about to be rolled out of her bed.

With one hand constantly gripping a piece of furniture for support, Anne got up and dug out her hammock. She succeeded in attaching it to its hooks only after being thrown into the bulkhead twice by the ship's movements. The pitching and rolling were getting worse, more violent, and she was anxious to climb into the relative safety of the hammock.

A soft rap came on the door, and then she heard Kai, the Chinese cabin boy. "Lights out, Missy," he said, then moved on. He was little more than a child, and he often assisted the steward, his long black braid swinging across his back as he worked. He'd helped her as well, bringing water for laundry and washing, grinning at her with the high spirits of a youth who liked to have fun. She'd wanted to ask him about his home country, how he liked working aboard an English ship, but hadn't yet mustered the courage to inquire as to such personal things.

Courage: that was something she was going to need a lot of tonight. She blew out the candle in its hanging lantern and climbed into her hammock, the maneuver well-practiced after months at sea. She was still fully dressed, having removed only her stockings and slippers. She'd taken up the habit during the worst storms; it made her feel a little safer to be clothed.

The wind whistled through the shrouds above decks, the canvas of the sails ruffling and snapping as they were caught in a gust. She heard shouts and orders, then a great crashing boom which made her flinch, her eyes open wide in the dark cabin as she listened with straining ears for sounds of distress. None came, so as the minutes passed she began to relax. Likely it had been something coming loose and falling to the deck, like one of the longboats. She only hoped it hadn't been a sailor falling from a yardarm.

The movement of the ship was less noticeable in the hammock, and despite her nervousness she began to feel her eyelids grow heavy. The sounds of wind and water, and of creaking timber, all began to blend together in a queer sort of lullaby, and she drifted off.

The dream came to her as it had every night for as long as she could remember. She was flying through the sky, looking down on miles and miles of blue-green water, the sun bright overhead. In the distance was a bank of thunderclouds, immense, towering, majestic. She flew towards them.

As she approached she dropped down closer to the water, flying like the figurehead of a ship across the waves, her hair streaming behind her. Beneath the bank of thunderclouds was an island, a jade carving set upon turquoise water, its inland mountains disappearing into the underbelly of the clouds. And somehow she knew that this was *her* island, her world, the place where she belonged.

The island grew larger, filling her horizon, and between the water and the green of the jungle she could make out the brown squares of small wooden houses, perched on stilts above the shore. Long, thin, brightly painted boats bobbed at their moorings, and a small brown child with black hair stepped out of one of the strange houses, onto the decking in front. The child shielded her eyes with her hands and looked out over the water, her gaze meeting Anne's.

Lightning cracked out of the sky overhead, the juddering clap of thunder so loud that Anne could feel it in her chest. She jolted awake to the dark of the cabin, and to the sound of something immense being dragged across the deck overhead. Through the roar of wind and pounding water she could hear the shouts of sailors, their voices tinged with panic and desperation.

Her own heartbeat thudded in her chest, the frantic calls of the sailors infecting her with their fear. She could see nothing, the cabin black as tar. The very air around her felt distorted, the sound of her own movements wrong. She reached out one arm, brushing it through the air, and hit her hand on a wall slanting above her to the left.

She touched it for a moment, confused, and then something heavy slid across it on the other side, and she realized it was the deck overhead that she was feeling. The ship had heeled so sharply to port that her hammock had swung to within two feet of the ceiling.

The ceiling came suddenly closer, and she heard the rush of a wave crashing over the ship.

Listing this far over, the ship was in danger of being unable to right itself. In her mind's eye Anne had a sudden vision of the sails dipping into the water, waves washing over them and holding the ship pinned upon its side.

There came the rhythmic chopping of an axe from above, and more shouts. She remembered the crashing boom of thunder in her dream, and guessed now that it had been a mast that had splintered and fallen. The sailors were trying to cut the lines and free the ship from its dragging weight.

Another wave washed over them, and the chopping sounds stopped. She listened, but they did not start again. The entire ship gave a great groan, its timbers cracking and popping.

Her body moved before thought had time to direct it. She flipped out of the hammock, hanging on to its ropes for support. Her feet found purchase on a wobbling board, and a moment of exploring told her it was the side of Miss Godwyn's cot. She reached into the bed with her bare foot and jabbed at her mistress with her toes.

"Miss Godwyn! Wake up!"

Pamela Godwyn mumbled and shifted. Anne jabbed her again, harder, then shook the woman's entire body with the sole of her foot, fear coursing through her veins like quicksilver. "Miss Godwyn!" she screamed.

"What?" the young woman asked, coming half awake. "Anne?"

"Wake up! We are wrecked!"

"Wrecked?"

Anne shook her again with her foot. "Up! Get up! We must get to the longboats!"

"Where . . . Anne? I cannot see. Anne?"

Anne lowered herself from the hammock to Miss Godwyn's cot, which was tilted up against the outside bulkhead. "Here, I'm right here," she said as her mistress's hands clamped onto her arm.

The cabin door above came suddenly open, lantern light spilling down on them.

"Pamela! God's sake, get out of bed! We've got to abandon ship!" It was Edmund, her brother, straddling the opening to the cabin, his feet on what had previously been walls.

"There's water! Oh, Edmund, there's water!" Miss Godwyn wailed, coming fully awake, and Anne felt the cold touch of the sea seeping through the porthole and the floorboards. "I cannot reach you!" Miss Godwyn cried, gazing up at the doorway so wrongly above their heads.

Anne's eyes lit on the sofa, still roped to the staples on the floor. "The sofa, Miss Godwyn. We'll climb up the sofa."

"Anne, help her," Edmund ordered. "God's sake, girl, don't just sit there!"

Anne shoved at her mistress, forcing her to stand on the tilted bulkhead. Water sloshed over her feet, and together they climbed over the tilted cot. Anne gave Pamela Godwyn a boost up to the arm of the sofa, pushing on her rear end to help her up onto the small ledge, then pushing her again to climb onto the upper arm that was closer to the doorway.

"Edmund!" Miss Godwyn cried, stretching against what had been the floor and reaching upward.

Edmund set his lantern down and got to his knees,

bending down through the doorway to grasp his sister's hand in one of his. He pulled her up, his sister's feet scrambling at the deck for footholds that weren't there.

Hurry, hurry, hurry, Anne mentally screamed, the fear in her blood urging her to climb up herself, over Miss Godwyn if necessary, and escape this coffin.

Edmund got his sister to the passageway, the young woman sobbing audibly now. Her muscles weak with fear, Anne climbed up onto the top arm of the sofa and reached up.

"I've got to get Pamela to one of the longboats," Edmund called down to her, picking up the lantern. "You're strong, you can climb up."

"No!" Anne cried. He vanished from view, and a moment later Miss Godwyn's dangling feet disappeared from the doorway.

"Wait! Don't leave me!"

Her employers' retreating lantern light cast a faint glow in the passageway, the doorway a dim rectangle, and then that light, too, was gone.

"Miss Godwyn!" she screamed. "Miss Godwyn! Don't leave me!"

There was no answer, only the roar of the storm all around her, and the groaning death throes of the *Coventry* as timbers shuddered and began to collapse.

She was alone, and in utter darkness.

The ship rolled, and she crouched atop the side of the sofa, clinging to the wooden legs. She stared stupidly at where she knew the doorway was, as if someone would appear and help her.

A wave crashed over the ship, and a moment later

cold water poured onto her face from above. She shrieked, clinging more tightly to the legs of the sofa until the cascade of water stopped.

She crouched, bracing herself with her arms extended against what had been the floor, her balance precarious. When the ship rolled slightly to starboard she stretched upwards against the floor, feeling for the doorway. The vessel was hit by another wave, and a new rush of water flooded over her hands and head in the dark, splashing salt water into her mouth and nose and making her gag as she hunched again on the side of the sofa, her body quivering with the certainty of approaching death.

The *Coventry* lurched and then Anne's feet were covered in water. It wasn't pouring down the passageway this time: It was welling from beneath. The glass in the portholes must have broken, flooding the cabin.

Going down with the ship, was this how she was going to die? Drowned in a cabin, alone in the dark, left behind like an old shoe.

Images of her dream island suddenly flashed through her thoughts, white clouds and green mountains, more real than the blackness around her.

The dream had been what lured her from the safety of home. Deep inside her was an absurd certainty that the island existed, and that it was waiting for her to find it and take her place on its wild shores. It was ridiculous—insane, even—to believe that such could be true, but deep inside she did believe it, and had hoped to somehow find the island by coming with Miss Godwyn to India.

The water rose up her shins. Had the dream meant

nothing at all? Had everything been simply a way to pretend she was more special than a gardener's daughter in a small, unimportant village?

"Bloody hell!" a voice swore.

"Help!" Anne cried.

"Goddamn it, I knew I should have shipped on one of the newer boats!" the man griped, his voice moving closer.

"Help me!" Anne shouted, the water now up to her thighs. She carefully stood on the end of the sofa, leaning against the floor, reaching for the doorway.

"Here now, who's that?"

"Down here! I cannot reach the doorway!"

"I can't see a bloody thing!" There was a stumbling sound. "Christ! I almost fell down there myself!" he said. "Here, grab my hand."

She batted her hand through the darkness, searching, then at last connecting. The man's hand was warm and strong as it clasped her own. With a great heave she was suddenly up in the passage.

"We have to get out of here!" she gasped. Her rescuer was no more than a darker shade among shadows.

"Actually," the man said, "I was hoping to stay a little longer and enjoy the atmosphere." Giving a brief chuckle, he took hold of her arm and started dragging her with him towards the stern of the boat, away from the dining saloon to which she had thought to exit. "What are you still doing in here? Don't you know we're sinking?"

"Don't I . . . Where are we going?" she asked, stumbling along behind, water beginning to fill the passage as well, making their steps slow and heavy.

"The gallery. The saloon is flooded, everything has come loose, cannon, table, all jumbled in a heap—it's impossible to climb through."

Ahead there was a faint square of charcoal blue, only a fraction less dense than the blackness around them. It was the window in the door to the gallery at the stern of the ship.

"There won't be any boats this way," Anne said.

"That's not an optimistic way to look at it."

"It's realistic!"

"You can stay here, if you'd rather," he said, releasing her arm.

"No!" she cried, and grabbed hold of his coat. The water was rapidly rising, past her knees, inching towards her waist.

They were almost to the door. As they approached, a wave hit the boat from the stern, smashing open the door and letting in a rush of water. Her feet slipping, her skirts pulling at her, Anne grabbed her companion; he clung to something on the wall.

"That was fortunate," he shouted above the raging wind and water. "I was worried about getting the door open and look! It's been opened for us."

Anne blinked at him in the darkness. He was beginning to sound almost cheerful. He took her arm and dragged her with him to the open doorway.

"Can you swim?" he asked, shouting to be heard over the roar of the storm.

"No!"

"Neither can I!"

"What will we do?" she cried.

"We'll think of something," he answered. With that, he boosted her over the side of the doorway and out onto the small porch that was the gallery.

Any protest she had was drowned in a mouthful of sea water as a wave poured in over her. She scrambled for handholds and grabbed on to the banisters of the gallery balustrade, across the narrow deck that she had once stood upon with Miss Godwyn, waving goodbye to England. With the ship tilted on its side the banisters made a ladder, and she climbed them as high as she could go, feeling her companion bumping into her from behind, urging her upward.

Soon they were out in the open air, the wind and water wild in the night around them, deafening and disorienting. Hardly any light came from the moon, blanketed as it was in heavy clouds. The only thing Anne could see was the paleness of sails in the water a dozen yards away, and even that only for a few seconds at a time, for the ocean continued to buffet and wash over the ship. She and her rescuer were slightly protected by the gallery itself, but that would not last long.

"There! We can float on that!" the man yelled.

She assumed he was pointing at something, but she couldn't see what. "Where?"

"Ready?" he asked, wrapping his arm around her waist.

"No!"

"This is it!"

"No!" she cried again, but her hands lost their grip on the banister as he dragged her with him to the outside of the balustrade and then threw them both into the raging sea. They were immediately torn apart, and by instinct Anne kicked her legs and flailed her arms, the fear in her veins going wild, shooting panicked energy through her limbs. She didn't know which way the ship was, or the fallen mast with its entrapping lines and sails. She didn't know where her companion had gone. Her skirts wrapped themselves around her kicking legs, and both rain and sea water slashed at her face, making her gasp and cough as she inhaled it, her arms still slapping futilely at the water that refused to hold her up.

A hand grabbed her by the back collar of her gown and yanked her up against something hard. Her flailing arms hit the thing behind her, and with one arm she grasped hold, spinning round in the grip, grabbing onto the smooth, rounded surface.

"It's a spar," her companion's voice shouted at her from the other side of the floating timber. "Hold on to my arms."

She dug her fingers into the material of her rescuer's coat, and felt his own hands come around to grip her upper arms. Their arms made a bridge across the spar, easier to grasp than the slippery log between them.

"What do we do now?" Anne shouted.

"Now?" the man asked, and laughed. "Now, we hold on!"

A storm like this could last for days. She doubted she could last an hour, clinging to the spar. She looked in terror around her at the roiling darkness, then closed her eyes and wedged her cheek between her shoulder and the wood. Again the image of the island came to her, like a green promise of life from across a sunlit sea. She dug her fingers a little more tightly into the man's coat sleeves.

Time went by, creeping in painful inches. Her companion let go of her left arm, and her head came off the spar. "What are you doing?" she cried, panicked.

"Hold on. Can you do that for a minute, without my help?"

"Why? Where are you going?"

"Just hold on! Can you?"

"Yes," she said, her voice weak and lost in the tempest.

"What?"

"Yes!" she screamed at him, terrified.

"Good girl!" he said. Then he was gone.

Her weight felt suddenly heavier on her arms, her hold less secure. The spar rose and fell with the huge waves, rolling under her grip, and it was desperation only that gave her the strength to continue to cling to it. The cold of the water was slowly sapping away her energy. Each second was filled with disappointed hope as she waited for the man's return, each shadow and shifting patch of dark becoming his head in her imagination, then disappearing as nothing. Where was he? Would he come back at all? She didn't want to be alone. She wouldn't be able to hang on.

Then suddenly he was beside her, reaching around with a length of rope. "I'm going to tie you to me and to the spar," he shouted against the wind.

She nodded, even though she knew he could barely see her. Her relief at having him back had stolen her voice. It took him several minutes of fumbling to get her secured before she finally relaxed her aching arms and rested against the support of the rope. He climbed over the spar to the other side and tied himself in place across from her. The storm raged on.

In time the sky gradually began to lighten, shapes coming out in shades of grey. The wind became slightly less fierce, and Anne began to drift off to sleep.

"Ahoy!" her saviour shouted, startling her awake. "Ahoy there!"

"Ahoy!" came an answering cry from somewhere behind her. "Who's there?"

"It's Merivale," the man called. "And Miss Hazlett."

Anne gaped through the twilight at him. Mr. Merivale, the fawning, foolish puppy. He had been the one to save her. And he knew her name. In her befuddled state, she could not decide which was the more unbelievable.

"Ulrich, here. And Kai, and Ruut."

Anne turned to watch as a strange, lumpy shadow slowly moved towards them, disappearing in the darkness of a wave trough and then suddenly looming in silhouette above them, on a crest. Then she realized that they were not moving towards her; she was moving towards them. There was a rope stretching between the spar and the lumpy shadow, and someone from the other end was pulling on it, the rope going taut and snapping out of the water a few inches from her shoulder.

The lumpy shadow drew closer, and Anne saw that it was made up of chests, barrels, broken timber, and miscellaneous bits of wood furniture, all haphazardly lashed together. Three men were atop the makeshift raft, working together to pull the rope tied to the spar.

"You must have been tangled with us all night," one of the men said, a young, slender fellow with pale blond hair. "We did not know you were there."

"Thank God you found us," Merivale said. Climbing over the spar to Anne's side, he began to unlash her. "You've got to get out of the water," he admonished.

She nodded as if she understood, but her thoughts were foggy. When she was free of the rope and tried to pull herself up onto the raft, her arms refused to lift. "I can't," she said, exhausted now past even fear. She felt the need to cry tight in her throat, and yet even that emotion was distant, a physical sensation lodged in a body that was separate from herself.

"Give hand, Missy," Kai said from above.

"Don't give up now, Anne," Mr. Merivale said from beside her. He grasped her by the wrist and raised her hand for her. Kai's small hands closed around hers, and then another of the men joined him, taking her other hand. Together they hauled her out of the sea, Mr. Merivale pushing from behind.

She flopped across a sea chest, her body too heavy to move. She was vaguely aware of the men helping Mr. Merivale up onto a nearby barrel, and then, as if the hard, rough chest were the finest mattress of feathers and down, she fell deep asleep.

Chapter Two

Life, Horatio Merivale thought to himself, had a way of taking you by surprise. One day you were flirting with pretty women, wishing that something exciting would happen to relieve the tedium of your voyage, and the next you'd give your left leg to be back in your dank and smelly cabin, vomiting into a chamber pot.

Horatio gazed up into the sky, patches of blue showing through the clouds as the storm blew away. All things considered, he actually felt pretty good. No broken bones, no serious cuts. A few minor bruises: That was the extent of his injuries. On consideration, he felt better than he had while being seasick in his cabin during the storm, so perhaps he could keep his left leg. The future might not be looking particularly bright at the moment, but he was still alive, and as long as that was the case there was hope.

He looked over at Anne, the mouse-like lady's maid. She was asleep on her stomach on a piece of sailcloth lashed across two chests, her straight blond hair half-covering her face. Every time he had seen her aboard ship her hair had been discreetly covered in either a cloth cap or a bonnet, with only the barest hint of the glossy treasure that lay beneath.

He remembered the furious look she had given him when he had been making those asinine jokes about her joining his regiment. She had been so quiet, he had made the mistake of assuming that nothing was going on in her head. Locking gazes with those dark blue eyes had disabused him of the notion.

How had she gotten separated from Miss Godwyn? Had she wasted time getting dressed instead of damning modesty and trying to save herself? He himself was clothed only because the storm had rendered him too seasick to undress—and too seasick to notice the boat was sinking until water sloshed over him in his cot. Fortunately, he'd had the wit to grab his sheath knife before trying to find his way abovedecks. The knife had been what allowed him to cut the ropes he'd found dangling from the spar, and that he'd used to tie both himself and Anne to the piece of wood.

"We die out here," Ruut said, his tone mournful. He was a Dutch sailor in his forties, skin roughly red and weathered by years at sea, tall and sandy-haired. His body was thick as a log, and Horatio had already decided his personality mirrored his physique: cheery and uplifting as a piece of waterlogged timber.

"You complain too much," Kai said, squatting on a chest with his knees up near his shoulders. Horatio envied the young man's ability to sit that way for hours. He'd seen the Indians do it, and had tried to copy the pose himself with no success, always falling backwards onto his behind. "Always Ruut complain. Nothing good enough for Ruut."

"I not complaining; I speak truth. We die out here."

"The Hand of Destiny would not do that," Ulrich commented from his perch on a pile of tangled furniture. He was a young Norwegian, fluent in English, and with his blond hair and delicate features he looked more like a poet than a sailor. He was the only one amongst them who could swim.

"Hand of Destiny!" Ruut sneered. "Hand of Destiny put us here, for slow death."

"It saved us," Ulrich quietly insisted, his blue eyes calm.

"I alive. I happy," Kai said.

"Hear, hear!" Horatio agreed. He caught Ruut's eye and nodded meaningfully at Anne's sleeping form. "You don't want her to hear you saying we're going to die, do you? Do you want to scare her like that?"

Ruut's heavy brow came down in a frown as he looked at Anne. "Truth is good," he said.

The young woman stirred, nuzzling her face against her arm in a childlike, vulnerable way, and then her eyes slowly came open, only to shut again against the bright sunlight. Horatio looked expectantly at Ruut.

The big Dutchman crossed his arms over his chest, his thick red lips pouting, but he remained silent.

Anne rose up on her elbows, her head down, her hair curtaining her face. He guessed she was trying very hard to remember where she was.

"Anne!" he said brightly. "Good morning! Did you sleep well?"

She lifted her head and squinted at him, then at the three other men scattered over the bobbing, undulating crates and barrels. As the last bits of confusion were swept from her mind she sat quickly up, turning in all directions as she searched the bare ocean around them. "Oh, God . . ." she said.

"It's a beautiful day, don't you think?" Horatio asked. "The clouds are all but gone, and the wind"—he paused to suck in a deep breath of air—"is fresh and sweet." He smiled at her.

She looked at him as if he had lost his mind, which was fine with him. Let her think of other things than the fathoms of water beneath her, and the lack of either land or boat. "Where are we?" she asked.

"Somewhere off the coast of Madagascar, I should think."

"How far?"

"I imagine we'll drift there within a day or two," Horatio said. A day or two might be a rather large understatement, but he couldn't swear it wasn't possible.

"How can you know that?"

"After all we've been through, you don't trust me?" he asked. The confused look she gave him made him grin. "The winds and currents all head west in this part of the ocean," he explained. "We simply have to wait for the trades and the tide to carry us to the coast."

"You are sure of that?" Ulrich asked.

Horatio blinked at him, taken off guard by a question from that quarter. "Yes, of course. But surely you knew that?"

"I'm a sailor. I set sails, not the course," Ulrich said matter of factly, as if this was common knowledge.

"Captain and first mate only know charts," Ruut confirmed.

"Kai?" Horatio asked.

The Chinaman shrugged his shoulders.

"Incredible," Horatio murmured. Three men who had spent their lives at sea, and they hadn't been taught the first thing about prevailing winds or currents. What a waste! And here he had thought himself ignorant in England, when he set about learning what he could of sailing and navigation.

"Has there been any sign of the longboats?" Anne asked. Her eyes were wide, her pale eyebrows scrunched up in worry.

"The one with your mistress, I know it got safely away," Ulrich said.

"Is bad storm for little longboat," Ruut said darkly. Horatio gave him a warning glare, and Ruut's lower lip went out mutinously.

"There were sails in the boats, so I should think they're making good progress. I doubt we will see them," Horatio said. "They're probably tying up at a dock at this very moment."

"I can take the truth. He was right," Anne said, nodding towards Ruut. "If the storm was strong enough to sink our ship, what chance do longboats have?"

"What chance did we have?" Horatio asked. "But we're safe, and doing quite well." He watched as the wind tugged at her hair, blowing a strand across her cheek. She tucked it away behind her ear, but it was promptly pulled free again by the breeze. He didn't know if she had heard him, her eyes focused on some spot a thousand miles away. "How did you get stuck alone in the cabin? Where was Miss Godwyn?" he asked, to bring her back.

She made a noise halfway between a laugh and a sob, turning those deep eyes towards him, their midnight blue now filmed with tears. "Her brother came and helped her out of our cabin, then left me to escape on my own." Her lower lip began to tremble.

"Bastard!" Horatio said.

"Dirty English dogs!" Ruut said. "They leave you like garbage. They not care."

Anne's mouth turned down at the corners, the trembling in her lip growing more violent. "They won't come back to look for us, will they?"

Poor little mouse, she was scared to death. She'd probably had nothing in her life to compare to this. He at least had had the chance to look death in the face once before—and as for being treated like useless refuse, life with his father had been one long lesson in that.

"Do you know our shipmates?" he asked lightly, to change the subject. Without waiting for an answer he started making the introductions, hoping to distract her from her thoughts of gloom and doom. The prospect of a weeping female was obviously as unsettling to Kai, Ruut, and Ulrich as it was to him, if the overbright smiles they were quick to put on their faces were any indication.

"I have been sailing on East Indiamen since I was

fourteen," Ulrich said, once he had been introduced. "My family in Bergen think I should be working the fishing boats, but I wanted to see more of the world."

"Ulrich, Kai, same," Kai said. "I go to sea, want to see world." He frowned. "See ship, ship, ship. Water, water, water. Not much world. Kai want to see ladies of world." He raised his brows and gave a wolfish grin, the expression especially comical given his half-shaved head. Anne put her fist up to her lips, covering a smile.

"You go to sea, you not leave," Ruut said. "It is in blood. I at sea thirty year. I go home once, leave in one week. No live on land. Sea is dangerous, but sea is home."

"I envy you, Ruut," Anne said, lowering her hand from her mouth. "I should very much like to feel at home right now."

"You'll have a marvelous tale to tell when you do reach home," Horatio pointed out. "Think how romantic this will sound when you tell everyone about it."

"Mr. Merivale, I sincerely hope that I have the chance to do so."

" 'Horatio,' please. We're going to be as close as sister and brothers for the next few days."

She smiled uncertainly.

"Much wine," Kai said, slapping a barrel. "No worry about water. Have good trip to land, much to drink." He grinned.

"Is there any food?" Anne asked.

"Maybe we will catch some fish," Ulrich said.

"No food," Anne translated. "If it's only going to take

a few days to reach Madagascar, then I suppose we can survive on the wine." She looked to Horatio for confirmation, her eyes asking for reassurance.

"We'll be drunk and happy by the time we arrive," he said, and hoped to hell it was the truth. He was beginning to feel a sense of responsibility towards the little mouse, as if it were up to him to bring her safely to shore.

Strange, that. It had been longer than he could remember since he had felt responsible for anything at all. His service so far in the Indian army was without distinction, his father had long considered him a disappointment, his mother was disgusted with his flirtations that had led nowhere near marriage. All round, he was used to being regarded as a waste of breeding and education. He was used to having nothing expected of him, except that he fail.

Anne Hazlett, this frightened lady's maid, was a different story. He had saved her life. He, Horatio Merivale, had saved someone's life! He'd done something right for a change.

He liked the feeling. And he liked her for giving it to him.

Chapter Three

Her face was hot and tight with sunburn, but she was too drunk to care. The sun was setting on their second day drifting on the waves, and there was no sign of Madagascar on the horizon, not even so much as a seagull in the air to say that land was near.

She tried not to think about it. The wine helped her not to think about it, but when a stray thought did pop into her head her plight seemed all the more poignant. The wine also made all of them need to relieve themselves frequently, which was another thing she was happier not thinking about. She'd squatted awkwardly with each foot on a separate crate while the men turned their backs, but the strain of maintaining her balance—not to mention the sheer embarrassment of the situation—had made it impossible for her to go. In the end she'd followed Kai's lazy example of slipping into the water and holding onto one of the ropes until she could force her bladder to release. At least her wet skirts had felt a little cooler in the sun, upon climbing out.

"Kai, don't you think that's enough for now?" Horatio asked.

Anne looked over at where Kai was shifting the wine cask, the bung out and his red-stained mouth ready for another round of intimacy with the hole. "Plenty wine," Kai said.

"Plenty, perhaps, but you'll roll off your crate and get eaten by a shark if you drink any more of it."

Kai shrugged, and put the bung back in the hole, rapping it into place with the heel of his hand. "Nothing to do, only drink," he said.

"Drink and cook in sun," Ruut said. "And starve."

"A week ago you would have given a month's wages, I'll warrant, if you could lie around all day drinking," Horatio said. "You would have thought it a fine holiday."

Anne looked at the officer, his teeth white in his beard-stubbled face, his hair tousled by the wind and standing up at strange angles, stiff with salt. Even through her muzziness his good cheer gave her pause. Was the man out of his mind? He looked as though he were thoroughly enjoying himself, and had not a moment's care for their fate.

"Holiday!" Ruut said, and snorted. "It slow death. You fool if you not see that."

"We will not die," Ulrich argued in his melodious voice with its lilting Norwegian accent. "The Hand of Destiny will not let us."

"What Hand of Destiny?" Anne asked.

"Ulrich believes that Destiny meant for us to be saved," Horatio said. "Otherwise we would not still be here."

"Do you believe that, too?" she asked.

He smiled. "Of course!"

For a moment, she almost believed it herself. Destiny. Hadn't that been what she had been pursuing when she first set foot on the *Coventry*? Her destiny, as foretold in the dream?

"Tell me more," she asked, then gave an unladylike belch, grimacing against the sour taste of wine and bile in the back of her throat. She vaguely realized she was too intoxicated to be embarrassed.

Ulrich changed position, moving onto his stomach on a crate so that he could face her, chin propped in his hands. The movement reminded her, with a pang of homesickness, of her sister Violet and how she would lie on their bed and gossip while Anne dressed.

"We do not know where the Hand of Destiny will carry us, but we end up where we were meant to be."

"It want me sitting on barrel in middle of ocean?" Ruut asked.

"Maybe," Ulrich agreed, turning to the Dutchman. "Maybe there is a purpose to your being alive and being here with us."

"Maybe we eat you," Kai said, "when very hungry. You big enough for many meals. I cut nice rump roast off you."

"I like to see you try!" Ruut cried. "I eat you first, I break you little chicken arm!"

"Enough!" Horatio ordered. "Behave yourselves. You are not children."

Ruut fell silent, glaring at Kai. Kai made an exaggerated "I'm so scared!" face, and shook his hands at either side of his head as if quaking with fear.

If Destiny decreed the ship should be wrecked, perhaps it was merely finding a way to divert her from reaching India. Maybe, her muzzy mind suggested, her dream island was somewhere near Madagascar.

Even as she thought it, something inside her said *no, go east, go east*. The opposite direction.

She turned to Horatio, the wine in her blood making her willing to speak where otherwise she would remain silent. "Do you believe there is a reason we are together?"

He raised his eyebrows at her, grinning.

"All of us," she amended. "On this raft."

He winked, flustering her. "You never know how an event will change you . . . or your course. I spent most of my time with my regiment, drilling Indian troops, marching them back and forth and over hills. It seemed a good enough way to pass the time, and get paid for it.

"Then there was a rebellion in one of the neighboring states, and my regiment was called in. At last! Excitement, battle, a chance to prove myself." He gave a little snort. "Within five minutes I had taken a ball in the lung, and my glorious battle was over. They floated me down the river for four days, lying in the bottom of a shallow boat, feverish and half out of my mind.

"And it's strange, but it's that trip down the Brahmaputra that I remember better than the battle. Despite being feverish, despite the laudanum I was given to dull the pain, it is the hot, white-blue sky overhead that has stayed with me, the gentle rocking of the boat, the voices of Indians soft around me."

In Anne's mind a dreamy, hazy picture of the scene played out, Horatio in the bottom of a boat. The rocking of the raft on the swells confused her for a moment, making her think she was there with him.

"By the time we reached our destination I felt as if I had been reborn a child of the East, baptized anew by the waters of the river. My soul was no longer entirely that of an Englishman.

"They sent me home to recuperate . . . gave me four years in which to do so. My mother and father were all for marrying me off, and perhaps getting me to stay in England. All I could think of, though, was returning to the East. Not to my fort and the tedium of drilling soldiers, but the Far East. I wanted to mount a voyage of exploration and trade."

"I thought you were returning to your regiment," Anne said. "Isn't that why you were aboard the *Coventry*?"

Horatio grinned. "I was. Father refused to finance my adventure, and I couldn't find any other backers. It was either stay at home and be herded into the matrimonial pen, or come back to India. I kept praying that something would happen to surprise me, to keep me from ending up back where I'd started. And look!" he said, gesturing at the empty sea around them. "The Hand of Destiny has willingly complied. The chances of my returning to John Company by the end of my furlough are almost nonexistent, and if I miss the deadline I will be forced to resign my commission." He grinned. "What a great pity! I suppose I'll just have to find something else to do, won't I? Like take ship on a trader, as a common sailor if I must." He cast a look at their raft-mates. "No offense to present company."

Ruut snorted.

"You're that certain we'll survive?" Anne asked.

Horatio shrugged. "There's no use in thinking otherwise, is there?"

It was hard to argue with that. She lay back on her crates, the thin streaks of clouds overhead tinged orange and pink against a deep blue sky as day slipped into twilight. Perhaps these days adrift, drunk on wine, would become etched in her mind in the same way as had Horatio's trip down the Brahmaputra with a bullet in his lung. What would be the change in her person when she landed on the shores of Madagascar? Would she have become a part of the sea, in her soul?

"Every night I have the same dream," she said. "A dream of an island set in turquoise waters, thunderclouds towering above. It's my island, and it is waiting for me to come claim it. I am its queen."

She heard Kai laugh.

"It is silly, isn't it?" she asked, rolling her head sideways until she could see him. "Me, a queen on a tropical island." She stared back up at the darkening sky, the brilliant colors of the clouds fading under a dusting of charcoal night. "It's just a dream, a lovely, lovely dream. And yet. . . ." As long moments eased by, the images came to her again, the child on the porch of the stilt house, the jungle rising up behind.

"And yet?" Horatio prompted.

"And yet it feels so real. It's why I came with Miss Godwyn. I thought there might be a chance I would find the place, somewhere near India. Although I think it may be in the East Indies. There are thousands of islands there. Maybe one of them is mine."

"You crazy, Missy," Kai said.

She smiled up at the falling night, too drunk to be offended. She was crazy, wasn't she?

"You came all this way just because of a dream?" Horatio asked.

"It seemed a good idea at the time," she said, and then started to laugh. After a moment the others joined in, except for Ruut.

"You all crazy," Ruut said. "Crazy fools!"

Kai and Ulrich kept laughing, but Horatio's laughter faltered, then stopped. All of a sudden he climbed to his feet, balancing awkwardly on a chest. "Ahoy!" he shouted, and waved his arms wildly above his head, then tried to jump up and nearly lost his balance. "Ahoy!"

Anne turned her astonished gaze from Horatio to where he was facing. There, on the southern horizon, just visible in the last light of day, were the sails of a ship.

Anne scrambled to her feet, as did Kai and Ulrich, big Ruut managing only to get to his knees astride his barrel. She began waving her arms and shouting as frantically as Horatio, knowing even as she did so that no one on the ship could possibly hear. Their only hope of being seen was by a man on lookout up in the rigging, and that was assuming he had a spyglass. The knowledge did nothing to stop her heart from leaping in wild hope.

The Hand of Destiny might be upon them, after all.

Chapter Four

Anne sat huddled with her knees pulled up to her chest, wide-awake and silent with the others, waiting for the darkness to give way to the first lightening of dawn. Night had fallen before they could know if the ship had spotted them, and with the fading of the light had gone most of Anne's optimism.

She knew it well, this weird magic of the darkness to steal hopes and set free hidden monsters of worry and fear. She had never known it to be so fierce, though, tightening every muscle in her body despite the fading traces of wine in her blood.

They haven't seen us, her dark-infected mind told her. The ship will be gone when morning comes. We won't be rescued. We'll still be alone.

Almost worse than that were the moments of hope, scattered amongst the dark like stars in the night sky, brilliant flashes of light that were smothered one by one under her growing blanket of doubt. To believe for even a moment that she would again be safely aboard a ship was to invite the pain of disappointment.

"This is very romantic, don't you think, Anne?" Horatio asked out of the darkness.

"Romantic?" Anne asked, frowning at him. His face was planes of grey shadow against the night. "I do not know what is romantic about this."

"The stars! The moon! The gentle lapping of the sea against our crates and barrels! And then there is my own company to consider."

"Ha!"

"Wouldn't your friends at home consider this a romantic tale?" he asked, unperturbed. "Adrift with a handsome young man who has saved you from the clutches of death, sharing soulful secrets, waiting together for the sign of sails in the morning that will herald our deliverance—wouldn't they wish to be in your place?"

"I only hope I shall live so long as to be able to tell the tale, and tell them as well what an utter lunatic you are."

"You see no romance in it whatsoever?" he asked, his voice aggrieved.

She squinted at him in the dark. He was joking—wasn't he? Was he at all serious? He was kinder and more decisive than she had originally thought, but he was also considerably more strange. What man in full possession of his senses could keep up such a cheery outlook in these circumstances? Was it all a façade? She had no notion of what he was truly thinking, or why he was acting flirtatiously towards her.

"The stars are indeed lovely," she finally answered, "but I would prefer to view them from the deck of a ship."

"And my own handsome presence, would you be happy to have it beside you?"

Was she supposed to say "yes" or "no" to such an outrageous inquiry? "Why are you making fun of me?" she asked crossly. She hadn't the wit at present to work through his tangle of meanings.

"I learned my lesson about teasing you. I would not do so again."

"You are doing so right now," she said.

"Nonsense. Why is it you cannot answer my question? Do you perhaps have a fondness for me, of which you are too shy to speak?"

"Not if you were the last man on earth!"

"At the moment I am the last but for three others, and as the only one from your native shores, I should think that gives me an advantage."

"I should rather live in China with Kai than choose you!"

"No, Missy," Kai chimed in. "My parents not like you. You make bad daughter-in-law."

Horatio burst into laughter. "See? Come now, I wouldn't be such a bad choice, would I? What do you find unsuitable?"

Anne muttered a few choice thoughts under her breath.

"What was that?"

She was not about to repeat what she really thought, that he was nuttier than a walnut tree. There had been moments these past few days when she had found herself perilously close to admiring the man— being saved from a watery grave had a way of doing that, she supposed—but clearly he was an unstable personality. "I should think that your parents would find me no more acceptable than would Kai's," she said.

"My parents approve of very little that I do. No, I think that you and I would sail away and find the island in your dreams, and live there as king and queen."

"I should never have told you about that."

"I quite like the story," Horatio said, then his voice lost some of its levity. "You must think the island exists, if you came out to India in hopes of finding it. If you had the chance, wouldn't you want to search for it?"

"It's just a dream," Anne snapped. She was regretting the impulse that had led her to share aloud something so private.

"I think it's out there," Horatio said. "I think you'll find it, if you look."

"I won't. And it doesn't exist," Anne said.

"You'll find it, and then you can laugh at Miss Godwyn, who will be married to some poor sod of a soldier in India while her lady's maid has become a queen. You'd like that, I think."

Anne didn't reply, but she could easily imagine Miss Godwyn's expression of displeasure upon hearing such news, and a shameful smile of anticipated gloating crept onto her lips.

"I think I should very much like to be an Oriental

potentate, myself," Horatio went on. "I could lie back on cushions all day, smoking my hookah, while boys dressed in cloth-of-gold fanned me with peacock feathers. You could kneel by my side, Anne, dressed in veils and feeding me peeled grapes."

"I would be the potentate, not you, and I could order you beheaded."

"I'd much rather be your kept man."

She couldn't help it; she laughed.

"You could put a gold collar around my neck and lead me by a silken cord."

"You'd have to perform tricks for visiting dignitaries," Anne said.

"And wear stockings tied with pink garters. I think that would be a nice touch," Horatio said. "Maybe a pearl earbob? Gold bangles on my wrists?"

"I cook," Kai piped up. "Head of royal kitchen."

"Yes, that would be excellent," Anne said. "And you, Ulrich, what would you like to be?"

"Court poet and singer."

"I be admiral in royal navy," Ruut said. "No one put cat-o-nine to back of admiral."

"I have beautiful wife," Kai said, "who think me god."

Ulrich snorted at that.

"That type of nonsense won't be allowed on my island," Anne said. "If you marry, you will have to wear a collar like Horatio's, with the name of your wife inscribed upon it."

"Then we'll be married, will we?" Horatio asked her.

"Queens don't need to marry. I will do as Elizabeth did, and rule alone."

"That sounds lonely."

"It's the price of power, but I am willing to make the sacrifice."

"So ours will be a secret liaison," Horatio said.

"Such persistence will win you only a place in the dungeons, sir," Anne said.

"I will write a ballad to the queen and her ill-fated lover," Ulrich said. "It will be very tragic, and girls will weep."

"The more tragic, the better," Anne said.

Ruut started droning about his future fleet, and Anne's mind wandered, going against her volition to Horatio, still a dark shadow on the chest a few feet away from her. She didn't know quite what to make of his joking. It was rare for someone to joke about something unless there was a grain of truth to it, somewhere. Did he *want* to be her lover? It was too ridiculous to contemplate.

On the other hand, he was a ridiculous man, and she was the only female in sight. It wouldn't matter if she were fifty years older and had a hairy mole on the end of her nose, he'd likely still play with the thought.

Her eyes went again to Horatio, remembering the way he looked in daylight, perched on his crate, his coat folded beneath him, the neck of his shirt open to reveal a vee of tanned skin, a few curls of dark hair showing. His shoulders were remarkably broad, his forearms beneath the rolled sleeves of his shirt thick and strong, defined by a dozen sets of muscles and tendons she had never seen moving beneath her own skin.

A sense of hunger moved through her that had nothing to do with food. For Horatio Merivale? She had been on this raft much too long. The sun had damaged her mind. The wine had made her stupid.

"Is that the ship?" Ulrich suddenly asked, interrupting Ruut's nautical fantasy and shaking Anne from her thoughts.

"Which way?" Horatio asked.

"There," Ulrich said, and as he held his arm out Anne belatedly noticed that the sky held the first faint promise of dawn. They had talked themselves through the night, and somewhere along the way her fears of being missed by the ship had been replaced by musings on Horatio's forearms.

She craned with the rest of them, searching the sea for a shadow lighter or darker than the water that might signify a ship. Their raft rose up over the crest of a wave, and just for a moment she thought she saw a hint of paleness in the distance.

They were all five silent, their eyes trained upon that distant hope, willing it to mean rescue with the force of their minds. Anne felt perfectly in tune with the men: Their thoughts were hers, and they waited with muscles tensed as the sky shifted from charcoal to blue.

"There!" she cried, the sails suddenly clear as they crested a wave.

"They're heading right for us! They must have seen us!" Horatio said.

"Are they English?" Anne asked.

"Too soon to tell, but it doesn't matter, does it? At this moment, I'd be grateful to see Napoleon, himself."

"Too small for East Indiaman," Ruut said a minute

later, as they rode the crest of a wave and caught another clear sight of the ship's rigging.

"Whatever she is, she will pick us up," Horatio said. "No mariner would ignore castaways."

Ruut and Ulrich grunted their agreement, but Anne noticed that Kai didn't look quite so certain of their welcome. It made her wonder what treatment he had received at the hands of European strangers. Chinamen were not, as far as she knew, held in particularly high regard. Kai was even smaller than she was, and she felt a sudden empathy with him, surrounded by men twice their size, and knowing that those aboard the unknown ship might have less than friendly intentions. He caught her looking at him, and seemed to read the thoughts in her eyes, answering them with the barest wrinkle of concerned brow before turning his gaze back to the approaching sails.

As the ship came nearer Anne rose up on her knees, Ulrich and Kai to their feet, all of them shouting and waving their arms, any thoughts of possible danger from Frenchmen or pirates overcome by the excitement of being rescued from the very real and present danger of the sea. Anne saw, as well as did the others, that the ship flew no colors, which could either be a precaution in these times of war, or a sign that she had no colors to fly. Her decks were low and sleek, painted black, the molding posts canary yellow, and nine cannon poked their black and deadly snouts through gun ports down each side. Swivel guns were mounted along her rails.

There came an answering holler from the ship, indecipherable except for its tone of excited reassurance.

They whooped in joy, Kai nearly falling off his barrel when Ruut slapped him on the back in comradely high spirits. They all whooped a few more times, then, spent and feeling slightly ridiculous to keep it up, settled down to await the ship.

"Ruut," Horatio said quietly, after a few minutes of silence had gone by. "Have you heard of a ship called the *Cauchemar*?"

"Aye," Ruut said, the glee now notably absent from his tone.

"What of it?" Anne asked, picking up the undertone of tension. "What is the *Cauchemar*?" She understood enough French to know the name translated to "Nightmare."

"It is Philippe Chartier's ship," Horatio answered.

And then she remembered. Philippe Chartier was the French privateer Horatio had joked about before the *Coventry* sank. He was infamous, having captured more than twenty English merchant ships over the past two years.

"And that's the ship about to pick us up?" she asked, her voice rising.

"I've never seen her, but she is legendary, and the ship approaching fits her description." Horatio smiled at her. "But have no fear, Chartier is reputed to be quite civilized, and to hold a special respect for women."

She failed to find that reassuring. "Special respect" could mean many different things. "I'm not finding this to be very romantic," she said nervously.

Lisa Cach

The ship was now but a few hundred yards off. It hove to, and a longboat was lowered from its side. A small group of sailors began to row towards them, their craft appearing and disappearing between dark blue waves.

For better or worse, they were about to be rescued.

Chapter Five

"*Capitaine Chartier, á votre service, mademoiselle,*" Captain Chartier said to Anne, bowing over her hand and kissing the air just above it.

"*Je suis enchanté á faire votre connaissance,*" Anne said in her rudimentary French, hoping she was correctly expressing her pleasure at making his acquaintance. She'd learned a smattering of the language from the parish school teacher, who had been only too happy to teach it to a bright and willing pupil.

Anne curtseyed, and felt it was passing strange to be doing so, barefoot on the deck of an enemy ship. The entire scene had a sense of unreality to it: the scruffy sailors who looked little better than her own bedraggled group; Captain Chartier in his elegant, be-ruffled clothing, hair greasy, reeking of perfume; the solidity of the boat around her, after the unsteadiness of their raft, where the chest beneath her had wobbled with every shifting of her weight. None of it could be real.

Something greyish-brown, the size of an infant, scrambled down a mast and galloped across the deck towards her, its thin tail held high. She blinked at it in atavistic horror and stumbled back.

"This is Mango," Captain Chartier said, switching to English. "He is my monkey."

"Your—" Before she could finish, Mango lept up onto her arm. A shriek slipped from between her lips, and she shrieked again as the monkey climbed up onto her shoulder and wrapped his arms around her head.

"He likes you!" Chartier cried, as she subdued the impulse to scream. With her free hand she pried at the monkey arm across her eyes. Mango bit her hand, and she cried out.

"Please, get him off me," Anne called, her voice trembling, her wounded hand clenched to her breast. She had always hated monkeys, both in stories and as toys, and the real thing was proving itself much worse. Mango had a nasty animal stench to him, and she could almost feel his fleas crawling into her hair.

"He loves you!" Chartier said. "Mango, you love the lady! Good monkey!"

"I say, I'm afraid the lady doesn't return his regard," she heard Horatio say from behind her, then felt his hands on her, trying to separate Mango from her head. The monkey gave an outraged shriek, and then Horatio gave a shout. "Damn thing bit me!" A string of blue curses followed, and a renewed tug-of-war on her head, making her stumble.

She heard laughter from the sailors, but Captain Chartier was not amused.

"Unhand my monkey, dirty English dog!"

"Dirty! Your monkey stinks worse than my—"

"Get it off me!" Anne wailed.

"I've just about—" Horatio said, and then the monkey gave a tortured howl and fell from her.

"English scum!" Chartier cried.

The monkey continued to howl in short high-pitched shrieks that pierced the ears. It grabbed Anne's skirts and started again to climb.

"Keep your damned beast off her!" Horatio shouted. "I'll skewer the thing if I have to!"

She saw the flash of Horatio's sheath knife, and then Mango's shrieks reached a new pitch of monkey agony as it dropped from Anne's skirts and scampered away, one paw held to its chest in parody of Anne's own wounded hand.

"Ungrateful pig! I rescue you from the sea and you try to kill my Mango!"

"Obviously your reputation as a gentleman is false, if this is the treatment you offer a lady!"

"Your pardon, sir! I will not stand for such insults upon my own ship! Georges! Henri!" Chartier called, and two of the larger ruffians stepped forward from the gathered crew, grabbed Horatio, and threw him to the deck. One kicked him in the side, and the other grabbed a belaying pin.

"Captain!" Anne cried, startled by the sudden turn. All her limited French left her. "Please! Captain Chartier, please!" She stood motionless, not knowing what to do, how to stop it, watching as Horatio took another kick, this time to the chest, the thud thick and heavy, before he grabbed the man's foot and yanked him to the deck. The sailors roared in appreciation.

"Attack my Mango, will you? Ungrateful pig!" Chartier said.

The man with the belaying pin raised his arm, and as Anne watched in horrified disbelief he brought it down. Horatio released the first man's foot just in time to roll to the side and cover his head, taking the blow on his arm.

"Buggering French frogs!" Horatio cried.

She felt a surge of movement from Ulrich and Ruut behind her, and just as quickly an answering swell in the ranks of heavily armed sailors, weapons being drawn, a warning that it was futile to fight.

"Captain Chartier! He tried only to help me!" Anne pleaded. "He did not understand."

A third sailor joined the two who tussled with Horatio, kicking him in the back.

The man with the belaying pin struck again, hitting Horatio's ribs, and swung again and again while Horatio tried to fend off the kicks from behind. The man he'd felled rolled onto his knees and began using his fists to pummel him, striking his face, cutting Horatio's lip or breaking his nose, Anne could not tell which, only that suddenly there was blood.

"Stop it! Please, Captain. Please!" she pleaded, grasping Chartier's arm. The touch drew him from his eager observation of the beating, and his face softened when he looked at her.

"But my dear, you are distressed!"

"Please stop them," she said, her whole body cringing with each thudding kick and punch.

"*Assez!*" Captain Chartier said. "*Assez!*"

She knew he was saying, "Enough!" And then he gave another order in French, and Georges and Henri grabbed Horatio by the armpits and began to drag him away, leaving a trail of blood from his wounded face. Just before they reached the hatch, Horatio lifted his bloodied head and met her eyes. And winked.

"*Chère mademoiselle*, your hand, it is bleeding!" Chartier said, as if just noticing. "Your friend is not so good with his knife, to cut you like that."

She wanted to say it had been his awful monkey that had done it, but would not dare, not after the demonstration she had just witnessed. She pressed her fisted fingers more tightly against her chest. "I would bandage it, if I could," she said, struggling to keep her voice level. She hoped she was showing as little of her fear as Miss Godwyn always claimed.

"But of course." He took her good hand and tugged her to his side, then slipped her hand into the crook of his arm, turning her so that they both faced the other castaways.

"You three, you are seamen, yes?" His tone was urbane, but Anne felt her own tension mirrored in the others, and a similar wide-eyed concern for Horatio. Chartier played at civility, but it was a game meant only for the surface of things.

"Yes, sir," Ulrich answered, and told Chartier each of their home ports in a passably calm voice.

"You like to sail for the English?"

"We sail for the sea, sir," Ulrich said.

"The English, they have the cruel mates, yes? They

are not the gentle masters. Maybe you would like to sail with a Frenchman who knows how to treat his crew, and how to divide a prize. You would like that, yes? To be rich men?"

Chartier's crew did not look rich, but if Horatio was right about his successes upon the high seas, there were doubtless chests upon chests of goods and treasure in the hold. Anne watched the faces of the three sailors as closely as she knew that Chartier did. They could not fail to understand that to decline the privateer's offer to join his crew would be to volunteer to follow in Horatio's wake, or worse. She hoped for their sakes they chose expediency over honor; not that they had any particular reason to feel loyal towards the English to begin with.

"Would we be equal to our shipmates? Have you articles to sign?" Ulrich asked.

Chartier barked out a laugh. "You know of articles! Maybe you have been hoping to join a privateer all along, eh?"

Ulrich shrugged. "Perhaps the Hand of Destiny has brought me here."

Anne frowned. Ulrich seemed to find a lot of convenient uses for the Hand of Destiny. Ruut was frowning, too, but Kai just looked scared. His usual jauntiness was gone, replaced by a stonelike stillness similar to her own. She couldn't imagine him wielding a knife and brace of pistols, clambering aboard an enemy ship and laying bloody waste to any who opposed him. Ruut maybe, but not rambunctious Kai.

"Gianni!" Chartier called. "Gianni, *apporte les articles!*"

A dark little man broke away from the circle of on-lookers and headed for the small doorway under the poop deck that no doubt led to the quarters of the captain.

Chartier laid his hand over hers where it rested in the crook of his arm and gave it a squeeze, turning to look down at her. "*Maintenant, ma chère*, what shall we do with you?"

She parted her lips to respond, but no words came out. She hadn't noticed before, but the pupil in one of his brown eyes was twice the size as in the other, giving him a strangely disturbing gaze, as if part of his soul was forever trying to leap forth through that one dilated eye. A chill ran down the back of her neck, and she sensed that she would not want to be any-where near when Chartier's dark side came fully out. The violence to Horatio may have only been a hint of what this man was capable of.

"You need fresh clothes, yes? And perhaps a little something to eat?" he asked, leading her towards the door through which Gianni had disappeared.

"That would be most welcome, yes," she said. No, what she wanted was to know what was to become of Horatio, and of herself. She wanted to stay with Ulrich, Kai, and Ruut. She wanted a hundred things other than to go through that door on the arm of Phi-lippe Chartier, with his evil, distorted eyes.

To protest would be pointless, that much was clear. Let the man feed her if it would make him happy. She would deal with what else he might have in mind as it came.

"And the bandage. We cannot forget the bandage, *ma chère*."

"No, we cannot forget that," she said weakly. With that, she stepped through the portal and into darkness.

Chapter Six

"In Amsterdam there lived a maid," Horatio sang, sitting chained to a post in the darkness belowdecks.

"Mark well what I do say,
In Amsterdam there lived a maid
And she was mistress of her trade—"

He paused. That last bar, he'd had the notes off.

"In Amsterdam there lived a maid
And she was mistress of her trade," he sang again. Much better. His voice reverberated nicely off the wooden bulkheads and decks, if he did say so himself. *"I'll go no more a-roving with you, fair maid."*

He really should change the words next time through. The fair maid should be from Stowe-on-Tyne, where Anne was from. At least, that had been Miss Godwyn's home, so he assumed it had been Anne's, as well. He would have to ask her the next time they spoke.

"A-roving, a-roving," he belted out with renewed energy. *"Since roving's been my ruin . . ."*

It wasn't roving that had been his ruin, it had been that damn monkey. Vicious, nasty little monster. Foolhardy or no, he hadn't been able to stand idly by while it mauled Anne. He was only sorry he hadn't done the smelly creature to death, although if he had he supposed he'd be dinner for the sharks by now, instead of merely sporting a wide array of cuts and bruises from those apes Georges and Henri. Chartier did appear to be fond of his little beast.

If that didn't prove the French had cheese for brains, he didn't know what did.

Mango! He'd like to make a paperweight out of his head. Or an inkpot. Now that was a nice idea—he could dip his nib into monkey brain every time he wrote. He'd have brown glass eyes put in, perpetually opened wide in surprise, monkey lips pursed in an "o" of disbelief.

"I'll go no more a-roving with you, fair maid.
Her eyes are like two stars so bright,
Mark well what I do say. . . ."

Anne, Anne, Anne. Her eyes were more like the night sky behind the stars, than like the stars themselves. He hoped his little mouse was doing all right, and wasn't too frightened. It was her state of mind he worried over more than her physical safety: There had never been a word spoken against Chartier's treatment of female captives, and with the number of English merchant ships he had captured, there had been plenty of opportunity to treat an Englishwoman ill if the captain had so desired.

Was she worried about him? Perhaps he flattered himself to think so. She seemed to regard him as someone who had misplaced his wits, and who regrets the loss about as much as a child who has misplaced a toy for which he has no particular liking or use. Once or twice, though, she had looked at him as if he were the only person in the world upon whom she could rely. The memory of those looks stirred up latent chivalrous tendencies he had not known he had.

Pity he was chained to a post on a lower deck, surrounded by crates and barrels, the smell of bilge heavy and unpleasantly ripe. There wasn't much he could do to impress her from here.

"Her eyes are like two stars so bright,
Her face is fair, her step is light—"

A dim light appeared at the end of the open deck. He leant forward, squinting to see better. Someone was coming his way, carrying a lantern.

"I'll go no more a-roving—"

"Horatio?" he heard Anne say.

"Anne?"

She ran towards him, and now he could see that she was accompanied by a short, chunky young man with the curling black hair of an Italian. "No, no. No talk!" the man said, running after her. His hand rose to touch Anne on the shoulder but then fell short, as if he was afraid to be so impertinent as to touch a woman.

Anne knelt down beside Horatio, reaching out to lightly touch his cheek, her face a mask of distress. He was tempted to turn his head and kiss her pink little knuckles, and the bandage around her hand. He

71

restrained himself, just as the Italian had. He didn't want her to flee down the passageway, shrieking like she had with the monkey on her head.

"Are you in pain?" she asked in a fervent whisper, as if such a question were the height of espionage.

"I'm quite comfortable, actually," he lied. "I have this entire deck to myself, which is a considerable improvement on my cabin aboard the *Coventry*. Certainly it smells no worse. But how are you doing? How is your hand?"

"It hurts, but the bleeding has stopped. The wound was much smaller than I'd expected, after I washed it off."

"Is Captain Chartier treating you well?"

She gave a snort of laughter, more sardonic than he would have expected from his mouse in a sober state. "He has sent me to sift through trunks of clothing. He entreats me to indulge myself. As if a dress is going to make me forget that he is a French pirate!"

"Privateer. There is a difference."

"Are you defending him?"

"No talk," the Italian tried again, his hand inches from her shoulder.

Anne cast the man a pleading expression. *"S'il vous plaît?"*

Horatio suspected she could do as she wished and the man would feel powerless to stop her, but well-behaved as she was she was still seeking the man's permission. Silly mouse.

"No," the Italian repeated.

Anne continued to look at him. Her lips pulled

down in unhappiness. The Italian shifted, looked away, then shrugged his shoulder.

The face Anne turned back to Horatio was pure and innocent, as if she had not just manipulated her guard into giving her her way. "I don't think he's very happy on this boat," Anne whispered, tilting her head towards the Italian. "I don't think he's much of a pirate, at heart."

"Are there others who feel the same?" Horatio asked, feeling a quickening of interest.

"I don't know. I haven't had the chance to speak with any. Ulrich seemed strangely eager to sign on with them, though."

"And Ruut and Kai?"

"They signed the articles, but neither looked as complacent about it as Ulrich."

"Don't be too hard on him," Horatio said. "He made the only choice he could, and having those three as members of the crew might be of advantage to us."

"Advantage? What do you mean?" she asked, her voice rising. "You're not going to try something, are you?"

"Shhh," Horatio shushed her. "Your friend."

Anne directed a big-eyed look at the Italian, and Horatio barely kept himself from striking his own forehead. She did not make much of a conspirator, his mouse.

"Captain Chartier told me that he would ransom you back to the English as soon as we reach port," Anne whispered. "He said he would release me, as well. Why make trouble?"

"I didn't say that I would. But if an opportunity should present itself . . ."

"You'll get us all killed," Anne said. "You've nearly gotten yourself killed, already. Don't try anything. Please, Horatio. I've had about as much excitement as I can stand."

He took her hand, making her start. When she didn't pull away he gently rubbed the side of her hand with his thumb. "Don't fret yourself. After all, I'm chained up. What trouble could I possibly cause?"

Her midnight eyes met his and held, as if she were seeking to read his heart. The worried look did not leave her face. He grinned and patted her hand. "We'll be all right. Would the Hand of Destiny let us down?"

"Destiny may not have the same idea of what should happen as you have," she said.

"But it all works out in the end. You'd better go now, before your Italian gets impatient."

She stood up, still looking troubled. "Have they given you anything to eat or drink?"

"Water and some sea biscuits. It was just what I needed—anything more substantial, and I wouldn't have been able to keep it down." God forgive him for fibbing. A hunk of salted pork and boiled peas would have been heaven. The biscuits had been riddled with weevils, which was no surprise aboard a ship. He'd entertained himself by flicking them against the bulkheads, their carapaces making minute thuds against the wood when they hit. Maybe he'd hunt them down and eat them later, if he got hungry enough.

"I'll try to come back and talk to you again," she said.

"If you can, but don't cross Chartier. Stay on his good side."

"I have every intention of doing so."

"Good girl."

She held his eyes for a few moments longer, then turned back to the Italian and nodded. He led her away down the deck, then down another hatch to a lower level.

Horatio sat back on his pile of ropes and began humming "A-Roving" under his breath, a whole host of thoughts and schemes dancing along with the melody.

It was a relief to know that Horatio was not seriously harmed; and apparently unconcerned about his incarceration, as well. The suspicion crossed Anne's mind that his jolly singing and good humor were an act for her benefit, but she couldn't quite believe it. He couldn't be that good of an actor: Only someone with a genuinely blithe spirit could remain cheerful through shipwreck and imprisonment. A blithe spirit, or a madman.

Anne followed Gianni down another companionway into the bowels of the boat, the air warm and humid, cooler than topside, but laden with rich and sickening odors. The smells were little different than those aboard the *Coventry*, and she decided there must be a scent that was universal to sailing craft, comprised of bilge water, tar, spoiled food, animal refuse, human effluvia, and God only knew what else. Aboard the *Cauchemar* those smells were overlaid with spices, making the stench both more bearable and more disturbing, as if Satan were trying to wear perfume to cover the stink of Hell upon his skin.

Or was that her imagination going wild? She sniffed the air again, and the hint of spices was all but gone. Then, as she followed Gianni between the stacks of lashed-down chests and crates, the scent of flowers came to her, pure and sweet, so heady it made her sway against a stack of crates for support. The dim storage deck faded out of her vision, replaced by a tunnel of deep green trees, vines of purple and yellow flowers cascading down their branches to trail in a clear green river. A brilliant red and gold kingfisher flashed through the air, alighting on a branch above the water.

The vision faded, the dank storage deck returning, and Anne found herself staring at where the strangely colored kingfisher had been. All there was was a chest, with nothing to distinguish it from the others.

"Ça va?" Gianni asked, holding up the lantern, looking back at her with concern.

"I'm all right," Anne said, pushing off the stack and coming forward. Her stomach was fluttering, her knees weak. She'd never had a vision like that before, coming unbidden in the midst of her waking day. She had the dizzying sense that something was happening to her, something beyond her control, as if some change had been set in motion within her, and she could do nothing to stop it.

For a moment she felt distanced from her own body, watching herself from above and behind. Who was this girl? Who had she been before the shipwreck? She couldn't remember.

Then suddenly she was herself again, the monkey bite on her hand throbbing, her skin itching with salt, her clothes damp and uncomfortable. An overwhelming weariness washed over her, the excitement of the past few days draining away all her energy.

Gianni said something in Italian, then opened one of the chests beside the one where the imaginary kingfisher had landed. She stepped closer and looked down at folded waves of turquoise and lavender, cream and willow green. She was too tired to take pleasure in choosing dresses, as Chartier had instructed her to do, and was distastefully aware that these garments had been stolen. She pulled one out at random, the lavender, and then reluctantly pawed through the chest for undergarments, finding them at the bottom.

Gianni was busy opening other chests, tugging out dresses and chemises so that they spilled over the sides in silken abundance, his demeanor that of a proud shop clerk displaying his wares. Ignoring him, she reached out and lifted the lid of the kingfisher's chest. Inside, in a tray divided into compartments, were a dozen spheres the size of cannonballs, each one coated in thin scales. She leaned closer and touched one, and saw that they were not scales, but faded flower petals. She sniffed, smelling something acrid and foul. What in heaven's name were they?

Gianni made a sound of complaint, his open hand gesturing at the clothes. He started talking, and the meaning was clear enough, despite the Italian words: Why are you looking at that? Look at these beautiful dresses! Take more! Enjoy! Admire!

"What is this?" she asked in French, as it seemed the language they had the most in common.

He mimed drinking something, smiled dreamily, then lay his head on a crate and pretended to be asleep. She frowned at him, then looked again at the balls. Could it be opium? She'd never seen it before, only having come across it when it had been dissolved as laudanum. It would make every bit of sense to find it amongst the spoils of a pirate, especially in the Indian Ocean: The substance was heavily traded by the English.

She nodded in understanding and shut the lid, wondering if that vision with the kingfisher had been related to the chest.

Gianni abandoned his opium-induced stupor and said something, holding up another dress.

She shook her head, no. Gianni spoke again, and she understood by his expressive gestures and tone more than by his words that it was what the captain wanted, that Gianni had been told to see her well-garbed, that there was no one to wear the clothes but her. With no energy to argue, she pulled more dresses at random from the chests, the silks and cottons heavy in her arms.

Gianni frowned at her, then took the load from her, picked up the lantern and shooed her back towards the companionway, muttering under his breath. Somehow she'd failed him, disappointed him, and she wanted to make it right, only she was so very tired . . .

She was almost at Horatio's post before she noticed the quiet humming and realized where she was. She stopped, but when Horatio said nothing she let Gianni coax her onward.

She went back to the saloon beneath the poop deck, off of which the captain and two senior crew members had their tiny quarters. One of those cabins, little more than space for the hanging cot and a stand with a basin, had been given over to her use. She sat down on her cot, then despite Gianni's presence she lay her head upon the hard, musty pillow, brought her legs up, and was instantly asleep.

Voices and the sounds of movement woke her slowly. Soft yellow light spilled in stripes through the louvered wooden door of her cabin, and for a moment she thought it was sunlight coming through the trees of her jungle, the kingfisher flashing in gold and red from branch to branch.

Consciousness gradually asserted itself, the jungle fading away. As she came back to reality she winced against the hot tightness of sunburn on her face, and the throb of the bite on her hand. Without total exhaustion and hunger to distract her, other discomforts were being allowed to claim her attention.

She lay a moment longer, wishing she were still asleep, then jolted upright as she remembered her fellow castaways, none of whom were in such comfortable circumstances as she. Ruut and Ulrich, were they getting along with the privateer crew? And Kai? And then there was Horatio in his chains—how fared he?

An open sea chest protruded from beneath the bunk, the dresses and undergarments she had chosen lying within. She got out of bed and went to the basin on the stand, peering at herself in the small mirror that hung above it. The cabin was too dim to see herself well, but what she could see was not encouraging. She looked like one of the witches from *MacBeth*, only with the puffy pink face of a boiled pig.

Using her fingers as combs she smoothed out the worst lumps and snarls in her hair, then pulled it all back and twisted it into a knot. There were no pins she could see, but her hair was snarled and rough enough with salt that the knot held on its own. She washed her face—fresh water, what luxury!—then quickly stripped off her mangled gown and changed into the new clothes, nervous that the moment she was unclothed someone would open the cabin door.

The lavender dress had been made for someone several inches taller and broader, but the drawstring around the neckline allowed her to cover herself decently, even if she did feel like she was wearing a largish bag. She had to wear her own damp short corset, but a new chemise between it and her skin made that bearable. She still had no shoes, but the hem of the gown was long enough to conceal such a lack. Most of the sailors went barefoot anyway, so what did it matter? And the tops of her feet were as burnt as her arms, face, and chest, so she was just as happy not to wear shoes.

The only voice she heard now was Chartier's, saying something softly in French, cooing almost. She took a breath, rested her hand over her heart as if she could still its frantic beating, and opened the door.

The saloon was warm with the candlelight from the glass lantern hanging above the table, the leading and faceted glass throwing shadows of light and dark around the room. Chartier favored deep reds in his furnishings, and between that and the dark wood-work, the saloon was as cozy and snug as a rabbit warren.

Only, no rabbit warren boasted a filthy monkey wearing a miniature admiral's hat and jacket. Mango was sitting in one of the chairs at the dining table, face serious under the pointed brim of his black headgear. He saw her and let out a loud "Eeep!" Then he leapt to the back of his chair and bobbed his head in ex-citement.

Chartier, who had been leaning close to his monkey and enjoying some form of monkey-human commun-ion, frowned at his little companion and then when Mango continued his obnoxious noise, turned to see what was causing it.

"Ah! Mademoiselle! Finally, you are awake!" he said, standing and coming around the table towards her.

"Good evening, Capitaine Chartier."

He took both her hands in his, holding her arms out so he could better see her choice of attire. The contact and the gesture embarrassed her, and made her even more wary.

"And you have found something that becomes you, *bon!* You look like a queen," he said.

The comment took her off guard, coming so close as it did on the conversations from the raft. "You are the first to ever tell me so, monsieur," Anne said care-fully.

"But surely not? One such as you?" He put his fingertips to the bottom of her chin, forcing her face upwards. "Such a regal bearing."

"Regal?" she repeated, her voice a high-pitched whisper.

"Do not try to keep the secrets from Philippe Chartier. I have heard the rumors. The other castaways, they know who you are, you cannot hide."

Anne met his eyes, and saw there a fiery energy that would hear no opposition. One of the others must have spread the rumor that she was a real queen of a tropic island, perhaps in hope of protecting her by making her seem more valuable than she was. She could not see how anyone could believe such an obvious falsehood, but for whatever twisted reason, Chartier seemed to want to.

There was no benefit she saw to spoiling his fantasy, and insisting he had been lied to could only cause trouble for the others. He was nuttier than Horatio, and a hundred times more dangerous.

"Indeed, Capitaine, I have been travelling incognito," she said, trying to sound confident. It helped to bring Miss Godwyn's imperiousness to mind as a model. "My country is small and poor—just a tiny island east of Sumatra," she improvised, "but I am proud to call it home."

He smiled, his one large pupil seeming to grow even larger with his pleasure. "Come, sit. Eat." He led her to a place at the table, and pulled out the chair across from Mango. She sat, taking extreme care with her lavender silk skirts, as if they were the ermine-lined raiment of a true queen.

Chartier jogged back to his place at the head of the

small table, and beamed at both her and the monkey, his queen and his admiral come to dine.

Cold meat, cheese, and bread had been laid out, as well as wine and a large bunch of yellow, finger-sized fruits that she recognized as bananas. She had tried them when the *Coventry* had laid over in Cape Town. Miss Godwyn had gorged on the sweet, creamy fruit, and ended up severely constipated, which meant an unpleasant three days of listening to her mistress bemoan the state of her bowels. There were some things even a lady's maid did not care to hear about.

"This, it is good French wine," Chartier said, pouring her a glass.

She smiled her thanks, privately grimacing. After the time on the raft, she could have done quite well with never again having wine pass her lips.

"Admiral?" Chartier asked Mango, holding up the bottle. The monkey jumped back down into his seat, and Chartier poured him half a glass. The monkey had his own place setting, as well.

"Now, we will have a pleasant meal away from the low people, yes?" Chartier said, serving both Anne and the monkey and then sitting back, looking pleased. He was treating Mango as if he were a true admiral, and it suddenly made a twisted sort of sense that he would prefer that she pretend to be a queen.

She wondered what Chartier thought of his country's revolution, and the new power of the "low people." He sounded too fond of titles to be a true son of the new France, with its guillotined aristocracy.

"Your new crew members, how do they fare?" Anne asked, nibbling on a piece of cheese.

"Good, good," Chartier said, waving a hand dismissively. Apparently the low people were not a desired topic of conversation.

"I do feel responsible for those beneath me," Anne said haughtily, without trace of apology, then cast a quick look at Chartier to see how he took it. Was she overdoing it? Perhaps keeping Miss Godwyn in mind was not such a good idea. . . .

But Chartier only nodded, ceding the point. "The duty of those who rule. It is a great burden, to shepherd so many sheep."

"When shall I see them?"

"Tomorrow, tomorrow. Tonight we enjoy each other's company. I do not wish to bore the Admiral with such things."

Mango, as if aware that he was the topic of conversation, made a chirruping noise and climbed onto the table. With both paws he lifted his wine glass and drank, spilling only a little of the burgundy onto his tan fur and gold-braided jacket. The little beast had a bandage on his right paw that matched the one on Anne's own hand. She was unpleasantly aware of her similarity to the creature, both of them pretending to be something they were not.

Mother would never believe her, if she ever got back home to tell this tale. Could anyone possibly think this romantic?

She wanted to ask how long Horatio would have to stay chained below, but decided she had pushed her luck far enough by inquiring after the crew. "The *Cau-*

chemar is a beautiful ship," she said instead, testing the effectiveness of flattery.

Chartier smiled with pride. "She is incomparable, *non?*"

"Indeed. As is Capitaine Chartier, scourge of the English."

"You flatter me!" he said, pulling in his chin and feigning embarrassment.

"Yes, you are a scourge. Your fame is even greater than that of your ship. All the English know and fear you. I think it is the Admiral and I who are honored to be supping in such company."

If Miss Godwyn hadn't noticed when Horatio had laid on the flattery so thick, perhaps Chartier would not, either. They had something of the same nature, Chartier and Pamela Godwyn: Perhaps they would have made a good couple. Anne bit the inside of her lips, smothering a nervous giggle at the picture of the two together.

Chartier stared at her, his expression unfathomable. A sick feeling that she had indeed gone too far began to roil her stomach. Unable to hold his stare any longer, she turned her eyes to Mango and sucked in a breath of surprise.

The filthy monkey was sitting right beside her plate, picking through her food, his admiral's hat slightly askew as if he'd been on a drinking binge. Which he had, judging by the overturned wine glass that had had no wine left to spill. Mango took a bite of her cheese, then looked at her, and like a toddler with a half-masticated biscuit, held out the remainder of the cheese for her to eat.

"No, thank you, Admiral," she said. "You go ahead."

Mango stepped into her plate and sat down, knocking her knife from the edge of the plate and planting his rump atop her cold roast beef. He was still holding the cheese towards her mouth.

"It is *incroyable!*" Chartier said. "He has never shown such favor to anyone but me. Never has he loved a woman like he loves you. The Admiral has found his mother!"

Mother? To *that?*

Mango pushed the cheese, soft and warm from monkey paw, at her lips. She tried to lean away, her lips tight together. Mango gave one of his shrieks, threw the cheese at her, then jumped onto her, his hind feet digging into the neckline of her dress, one of his paws on her nose, the other gripping her ear.

Anne held frozen, afraid to move and agitate the beast further. The rear paws clawed at her chest, loosening the drawstring, then Mango was up on her shoulder, paws in her hair, pulling down her knot.

"Admiral!" Chartier cried.

Thank God! He was going to do something this time.

"You are correct, Admiral," Chartier said. "A queen needs a crown!"

She blinked open her eyes as Chartier pushed back from the table and stumbled over to a chest against the wall. It was in his erratic gait that Anne got her first inkling that the man was much further into his cups than she had thought. He opened the chest and started digging through it, then lost his balance and tumbled head-first into the open container.

Anne stared at his upended buttocks, and the motionless legs. Long seconds went by, where the only movement in the room was the sway of the lantern overhead and Mango's paws picking through her hair. Then, finally, there was a grunt from the depths of the chest and Chartier moved, slowly seesawing back to a horizontal, then to a somewhat vertical position.

"Here it is," he said in French, coming out of the depths holding a wooden box. He fell back to the deck on his rump, landing with the box in his lap. He opened his stretched-out legs and let the box drop to the boards between them, then lifted the lid. Shards of light sprayed from within.

Anne's eyes went wide, and she forgot for a moment that she had a loathsome monkey on her shoulder. The box held every child's imagining of a pirate's treasure: diamonds and sapphires and rubies, gold and pearls, emeralds and chains and brooches. Chartier poked around in them as if they were nothing but bits of rope, annoying in their tangled multitude.

"Ah, this!" he said, pulling out a diamond and ruby tiara. He shook it a few times to get rid of the string of pearls caught on its points. "This is a crown for a queen!" He put it on his own head and smiled at her. "You like, yes?"

"It is . . . lovely. Stunning, truly." For an unsettling moment she could picture Captain Chartier as a woman in jewels. A very ugly woman.

"It will look better on you, yes?"

"Perhaps," she said weakly.

Chartier took the tiara from his head and struggled to his feet. He could be no older than forty, yet the grunts and groans he made were of an old man.

He came over to her and slapped the tiara crookedly atop her head. She caught it before it slipped off, pushing it back into place. It needed pins to stay put, or at least a different arrangement of hair. Mango grabbed at it, and she held it in place against his tugs.

Chartier fell back into his seat. "There. You are crowned as you should be." He nodded at her, then raised his glass, his attention shifting to her shoulder. "We do not get many chances to dine with queens, do we, Admiral?" he said a little sadly.

Mango gave up on stealing her crown and leapt back onto the table with a shriek, taking Anne's wine glass and lifting it to his mouth, as if in answer to the toast. Chartier chuckled, and Anne sat motionless, wondering if this was going to be the pattern of her nights aboard the *Cauchemar* until they made port. She looked at her plate, at the bits of monkey hair and monkey dirt scattered over cheese and meat. She'd end up hungrier than Horatio with his biscuits and water, if that were the case.

Mango finished off her wine, ate a piece of cheese off Chartier's plate while the captain cooed in French, then dragged himself across the table back towards her, obviously the worse for alcohol. She sat back in her chair, vainly trying to put distance between herself and the monkey as he began to climb off the table onto her lap. Her eyes went to Chartier, but he was smiling like a fool, his lids at half-mast. Mango dropped into her lap, grabbed a handful of dress as if it were his favorite dolly, and snuggling close to her belly shut his eyes to go to sleep.

Anne's nostrils flared at the foul animal scent of the

beast, hair and faint hints of feces. She saw a flea move across his forehead.

"You take the Admiral to bed with you," Chartier said.

"Oh!" Anne said, looking up. "Oh, no, Captain, I couldn't. Surely the Admiral has his own quarters?"

"Heh!" Chartier laughed. "He is a monkey. Did you forget? Mango needs his mother. He will stay with you."

"Oh. Well, then, I'd be honored. Of course," Anne said, and forced a smile to her lips. It felt like the hardest thing she'd done this entire impossible week.

Chapter Seven

"Horatio! Horatio, are you awake?"

Horatio stirred, waking slowly. Dream images filled his mind, mostly of his teeth falling out, his gums left exposed and coated in a brown ruffly fungus. He woke to the stench of the ship, made even more foul by the bucket of his own waste that had not been emptied for two days, his mouth tasting as bad as it had looked in his dream.

"Horatio!" Anne whispered, and he saw her moving slowly forward, a lantern in her hand.

"Arrr," he gurgled, barely restraining himself from hocking up the phlegm in his throat. A sick shame filled him that she should be near him when he was in such a disgusting state. He wished he had a way to hide the bucket. "What?"

"You're all right?" she asked, kneeling down beside him.

"Fine. Couldn't be better," he grumbled.

She was silent for a moment. He could see her now, the light from her lantern illuminating her face from beneath. "You don't sound like yourself," she said at last. "Has Chartier hurt you again?"

He sighed, and sat up straighter, trying to look strong and well. "I'm fine. No one has hurt anything but my pride, and I'm filthy. As filthy as that damn monkey, I should imagine. You don't want to get too close, unless you feel like losing your breakfast. Or should it be dinner?"

"Breakfast. It's about eleven o'clock in the morning."

There was a frantic 'eeep' sound, and then Anne fell backwards.

"Anne!" he cried, lunging forward to the end of his chains, and then he saw in the flickering candlelight that Mango had latched onto Anne's gown, and was scampering up onto her shoulder as she rolled to her side and struggled to sit up again. "Dirty monkey! Let go of her!" he roared.

Anne had her arms raised as if she would shield her face, but as she managed to sit up and Mango continued to sit quietly on her shoulder, she let them fall.

Horatio noticed for the first time that she was wearing different clothes—a light colored dress that fit her rather poorly. And, most strangely, she appeared to have a crown on her head.

"Anne? What's that on your head?"

"Mango. Or don't you recognize him?"

"What do you mean, don't I recognize him? How

many monkeys does Chartier have on board, anyway?"

"Just the one." She scooted closer.

He took a closer look at Mango. "He looks different. He looks . . . fluffier."

A small smile curled her lips. "Smells better, too."

"What did you do, give him a bath?"

"Got him drunk first, then scrubbed him as if he were my baby brother."

"Wonderful," Horatio said glumly.

"What's the matter?"

"Now even the monkey smells better than I do."

"You're not doing very well down here, are you?" she asked softly, laying her fingertips gently over his, where they rested against the floor.

"I'm fine," he said, trying to put some energy into his voice. He didn't want his mouse feeling sorry for him. He was supposed to be her hero, not a pathetic rat hiding in the bilges. "I've been thinking, actually, of how romantic this situation is."

He saw her roll her eyes.

"Here we are, two lovers separated by an evil pirate—"

"You said he was a privateer—"

"—separated by an evil pirate and his monkey henchman, pining for each other, dreaming of the day when we might be reunited."

"We're not lovers."

He lifted her fingers in his hand, stroking the knuckles with the pad of his thumb. "Aren't we?"

"Mr. Merivale!" she said on an indrawn breath, pulling her hand away.

He could have been imagining it, but he thought she was blushing. Good. She wasn't thinking about his sorry state. "Horatio," he reminded her. "Lovers use their Christian names."

"If you're trying to make a jest, I don't think it's funny."

"No jest, my darling." And he almost wondered if that was true. Locked up in the dark, he had been spending an inordinate amount of time thinking about her. He also thought about plans for taking over the ship, but one could scheme only so many hours out of the day.

His favorite fantasy was one where he sat behind her in a chair, combing out her hair as she sat on the floor in front of him. He would set aside the comb, using his hands to spread her silken hair over her shoulders. He'd let a few strands drop over her collar bones, then follow them lightly with his palms, down her chest, down into the bodice of her gown to cup her breasts. She'd sigh and lean back against him, the back of her head resting against his groin, his flesh growing hard and hot. She'd turn her cheek against it, opening her mouth, then he'd—

He'd better stop think about it, that's what, as long as she was sitting right there. He should be talking to her, not fantasizing about getting up her skirts. Or having her go down his breeches. Or—

"Why are you wearing a crown?" he finally managed to ask, shoving erotic fantasies to the side. For God's sake, he smelled like a London gutter. He shouldn't dirty her with his touch even in his mind. But once he had a bath . . .

"Oh, this," Anne said, touching a point of the crown. "Chartier makes me wear it. He thinks I'm a queen, or at least he pretends to himself that I am."

"He what?"

"Maybe Ulrich or Ruut put the idea in his head. I don't really know what he believes, but he seems to enjoy pretending he's having a queen at table with him. And an Admiral," she said, tilting her head towards Mango.

"Is he mad?"

"I don't know," she said, plainly unhappy with the idea. "Maybe he's just eccentric? I think he wishes the Revolution had never come to France, and that he could be an aristocrat, himself."

"So if he can't be one on shore, he becomes one on the high seas. He doesn't make you pretend to do anything else, does he?" he asked, disturbing imaginings coming to mind.

She grimaced. "Well, there is the one thing—"

"What?" he demanded, his heart beginning to thump.

She curled her lip, and leaned her head away from Mango, who was stroking her hair. "He likes to pretend I'm Mango's mother."

He gaped at her. "Mother to Mango? What. . . . What does that entail?"

"Mostly, enduring his presence," Anne said. "It gave me the excuse to wash him, though, so it isn't all bad. I may even be allowed to discipline the little monster. Mothers do that, after all." She grinned, and there was something hard and disturbing in her look. "Mothers

94

can be quite stern with naughty children, especially when their fathers have been lax."

"Don't upset Chartier," he said, suddenly worried. Anne's dislike of the monkey seemed to have surpassed his own. He had vivid enough memories of his mother's occasional rages, and wouldn't like to be in Mango's monkey suit if Anne got into one of those moods.

"Of course not. I'm not stupid." She grinned again, her teeth looking preternaturally white. She was like a shark with a crown. "It's not as if I would leave any marks."

A change of subject appeared in order, otherwise he'd start worrying about just what she did have in mind for the beast.

"It seems an odd coincidence, Chartier being so eager to call you a queen. Most people would not have believed a rumor started by a seaman."

She fidgeted. "I know. It does seem strange, doesn't it? I've even wondered if that's all the dreams foretold, that I would end up here, like this."

"Then where's the island?"

"Chartier has an island he goes to, somewhere off the coast of Madagascar. Maybe that's it. Maybe I'm supposed to be a pirate queen." She sounded saddened by the prospect.

"It doesn't feel quite right."

She shrugged.

He smiled at her, hoping to lift some of her gloom. "Perhaps Chartier's game is really the Hand of Destiny, telling you that you are on the right path. Perhaps it's a sign."

"Perhaps."

"I don't think it's a pirate island we're meant to find," he said, then caught himself. We? Where had that come from?

"No," she agreed. "It doesn't. . . . I don't know. You're right that it doesn't feel right. And Madagascar is in the wrong direction, anyway."

"It is? How do you know that?" He had not thought she had any idea of which way to go.

She waved her hand to the side, as if giving general directions. "I don't know. Something inside says I have to go east, farther east."

"Then this queen-in-a-crown nonsense is a sign on the way, and not a destination."

"It may not have been the only sign."

"No?"

"I saw a red kingfisher. Down below, amidst the crates."

"How did it get down there?"

"It wasn't real," she explained, as if speaking to a child.

"Oh."

"It sat on a chestful of opium. I don't know what it could have meant, or even if the contents of the chest were what was important. And there was jungle all around. It was like I was standing in the middle of a shallow river, and—"

"Opium, did you say?"

"A chestful. Like cannon balls. It smells terrible. I never knew it smelled so bad—I'm sure it must taste awful, eaten plain."

Horatio heard her as if from a distance, his mind

running away with the possibilities presented by a chest of opium. He had come up with numerous haphazard plans for taking over the ship, but with each there had been major flaws. With opium, though . . . The plans that were unfeasible fell away like shattered glass, leaving behind the one pure plan that would reverse their situation, putting Chartier in the bilges— or worse—and he himself in charge of the *Cauchemar*.

"Anne, you've got to steal one of those balls of opium, then find a way to drug the crew—everyone .but those you think would be willing to mutiny."

"*What?* I will do no such thing!"

"It's perfect! We can take over the ship!"

"We will not! We're perfectly safe as we are. I know you're not comfortable down here, but at least you are in no danger."

He waved her protest away. "Of course we're perfectly safe, but what about the English ships that will fall prey to Chartier and his crew? Should we just let him go his merry pirating way when we have a chance to strike a blow for England?"

"I care more for my own skin right now than for the fate of an East Indiaman that has its own cannon to protect it."

"For shame, Anne! Where is your patriotic spirit?"

"I think it quite patriotic enough to try to keep myself alive. And to keep you alive, as well! You were the one who not five minutes ago reminded me to stay on Chartier's good side."

"You only need to humor those who have power

over you. Wouldn't you like to be rid of that damn monkey?"

"That is entirely beside the point. We're not going to try to take over the ship."

"Well, I admit I won't have much to do with it. It will be mostly up to you," he said.

"Oh, no." She inched away from him, shaking her head back and forth. "No, I can't do anything. I'd get caught, and then what would Chartier do?"

"You could talk your way out of any suspicions he had. You're a queen! You're Mango's mother! And he would never risk his reputation as a chivalrous man."

"No. There's no reason to create danger. We're lucky to be alive as it is."

"And what of the kingfisher?" he asked.

"I don't know what it meant," she said, setting her mouth in a stubborn line.

"It meant *some*thing. Just like your dreams mean something. Anne."

She frowned. "Yes?"

"Anne. I know you're frightened. I wouldn't ask this, though, if I hadn't thought it through. Chartier won't hurt you; it would go against everything he believes about himself. And look, I'm still alive, even after stabbing his monkey."

"This is no way to repay him for rescuing us."

"And he wouldn't do the same, were the positions reversed? We're at war. The *Cauchemar* is a terrible danger to our ships."

"Is that the real reason you want to do this?" she asked, meeting his eyes, her gaze peering into his very soul.

He didn't answer for a moment, his own motivations shifting and falling, rearranging themselves in his heart until he found the truth. "Well, no."

She waited.

There were a host of reasons he wanted to take the ship. Chartier had let his monkey hurt Anne. The man, for all his airs, was nothing but a greedy, heartless peasant in fine clothing and the *Cauchemar* was too fine a ship to be under the command of a filthy Frenchman. Chartier was a threat to English shipping, and a blight upon the seas.

But worst of all, the pirate had humiliated him in front of Anne. He had set his henchmen upon him, letting them kick him while he lay on the deck, watching gleefully as he was beat nearly senseless. Horatio had been all but helpless, able only to pull one man to the deck. Not much of a showing for an army officer, was it? Now Anne worried about him, pitied him perhaps, but there was nothing to admire in a man covered in bruises, chained to a post in the stinking bowels of a ship.

He would have rather they been left to drift slowly to Madagascar on their raft, relying upon themselves for survival. For humiliating him in front of Anne, he would gladly take Chartier's ship, and without qualm repay rescue with treachery.

But there was a reason stronger than all those, for taking the ship.

He beckoned her closer with his fingertips. With visible reluctance, she came. "Anne," he said softly. "If we let Chartier bring us to a port, what will happen to us then? I'll end up back in England, or perhaps back with John Company. You will go back into service as someone's maid, or perhaps you will be 'fortunate' enough to find yourself back with Miss Godwyn if she is still alive. Or you'll go back home if someone will pay your way.

"What of your dream, then? You would have come all this way for nothing, suffered the shipwreck for nothing, roamed a pirate ship with a monkey on your shoulder for nothing but a story to tell your family."

"You said it would make a very romantic story."

"But it's only half the tale. Can't you feel that? You left England to pursue a vision. How can you turn away now, when the Hand of Destiny has set you on a path to reach it?"

She bent her head down and closed her eyes for a long moment, and when she opened them he caught a glimmering sheen of tears that she blinked away.

"I don't know that I am pursuing anything but a fantasy," she said. "Sometimes I think I have been fooling myself, believing something that soothed my vanity because I hated the thought that all I should ever be in this life was servant to another. My dreams are a comfort to me, but perhaps no more than that."

"But you want to chase them."

"Do I?" she asked. "And what if I chase them and they turn out as false as I fear? What if they mean nothing at all? I wonder if it might be better to keep the dreams as dreams. Reality might shatter them forever."

He lifted a fingertip and gently, ever so gently so as not to startle her, stroked the softness of her cheek. Her breathing was ragged, and even Mango seemed to sense that all was not well, for he made a little gurgling trill deep in his throat, clutching tightly to her hair. He didn't know what to say to such a statement, didn't know what might make her feel better.

"Then don't think of it as pursuing your dream," he tried. "Think of it as helping me to pursue mine. I've always wanted my own ship, and to explore the islands of the East Indies. Wouldn't you like to help me do that?"

She pulled her face away from his stroking finger, and made a few hiccoughing noises that he realized after a few seconds were laughs. "You never give up, do you?"

"Should I?"

Her laughter trickled away. "No, I suppose you shouldn't. I don't know how you manage it."

Voices came from the far end of the deck, and she turned her head, watching to see who approached. "I had better go," she whispered, turning back to him. "Is there anything you need? Anything I should try to get for you?"

"Just the key to these chains."

The voices were getting louder.

"I've got to go," she said, and lifted her lantern off the floor, disappearing in the opposite direction from the approaching men.

Sailors moved past his post a moment later, kicking at his legs as if he were a dumb animal to be teased. They made a few rude comments in French, then when he did not respond went on their way.

He leaned back against his post and rested his heels against a nearby crate, pounding softly, feeling the weights of the chains as a constant reminder of his humiliation.

Frustration upon frustration, to be powerless to act when escape and command of the ship were there for the taking. Ideally, he would be able to slip free of his shackles and drug the crew on his own. Ideally, he would do it all himself, without help, and certainly without having to ask the assistance of Anne. But she was the only one he could rely upon.

He couldn't count on their fellow castaways to help: He'd seen both Kai and Ulrich a few times, but they had been too nervous to do more than offer a brief query as to his well-being. Ruut had at least brought him a few extra sea biscuits and bits of salt pork, but he, too, had been wary of being seen fraternizing with the monkey-stabbing prisoner.

Horatio couldn't blame any of them. They had their own skins to look out for, and likely felt their situations to be even more precarious than his own. At least he was worth something in ransom; they could be tossed overboard and not be a loss to anyone.

But Anne was right. He wasn't one to give up, and he would persuade her to help. She was frightened, but she was stronger than she knew. Despite her hesitation over taking part in his uprising, she had shown already that she was not as weak as she let on. She'd taken ship to India, leaving hearth and home, after all. She'd survived a shipwreck. She seemed to be dealing well with Chartier, and even had the upper hand on the pirate's monkey. Whatever her doubts about her abilities and courage, he had every confidence she could pull off the drugging of the crew, if only she could be persuaded to try.

His mouse had a dream to pursue, and he would make her do it.

Chapter Eight

Anne hated Horatio Merivale. He was a feather-headed nitwit, greedy, selfish, a man with no sense of honor, a flirt, and a devil-tongued sneak. He was shiftless, and he had no proper sense of responsibility.

The ball of opium slipped from her grasp and thudded to the deck of the hold.

"Blast!" she cursed. Mango gibbered, scampering up onto a crate, jabbering at her as she bent down to pick up the ball.

Horatio Merivale was not fit to walk upon this earth. Those chains were too gentle an imprisonment for him: He should have been down in the bilges, that's where he should have been, down with the sludge and the rats. He was a bad man, and she should never have listened to him.

The narcotic sphere was tacky to the touch, despite its layer of petals. She wrapped it in a dress she had taken from one of the other chests, her heart thudding hard and fast, perspiration soaking her underarms and beading on her forehead. If someone should catch her, she would say she was choosing another gown. And if they somehow found the opium, she would say she needed it for her wounded hand.

As if they would believe that! Who needed three pounds of opium for an already-healing monkey bite?

Nothing was worth being scared out of her wits like this. Why had she let Horatio sway her? Why? When she had walked away from him, she had been certain in her mind that she would ignore his plea.

"Preposterous plan!" she'd said to herself. "Fool-hardy!"

And then, not fifteen minutes later, she had found herself climbing down the companionway to the lower hold, ready to risk her life to please that idiot with the sad-eyed grin.

She knew why she was doing this, as much as she wanted to pretend she didn't. It had been the way he stroked her cheek that had done it, as if she were precious. Not precious in the way Chartier pretended, with his crowns and silken gowns, but precious like someone who was cared for. She had really believed he wished to comfort her in that moment, and not only that, but that he felt some element of tenderness for her.

Stupid, stupid, stupid!

It was all undoubtedly calculated to persuade her to do as he asked. She knew that in her head, but her heart cherished those gentle strokes upon her cheek. What's more, she wanted to be worthy of his belief in her. He seemed to think she had more courage than she actually did, and she wanted to live up to those expectations.

He was a wily one, was Horatio Merivale. If they came out of this alive, she intended to make him suffer. Somehow. She would spend many blissful hours considering exactly how.

If they came out of this with the ship in their possession, would he hug her in gratitude? Would he hold her so tightly that her breasts would flatten against his chest? Might he kiss her, even?

She gave a little groan of disgust with herself. Of all the things to be thinking about when she should be concentrating on returning safely to her cabin with the opium! And what did she care what Horatio Merivale thought of her, anyway?

Still grumbling under her breath, she made her way back up the companionway, Mango scampering at her feet, nearly tripping her. "Bad monkey!"

She passed by Horatio's chained figure without stopping.

"Anne?" he said.

She didn't answer, didn't even look at him. She didn't want to hear his satisfaction at her having done his bidding: At the moment it felt too much like he had won a victory over her. She also was not certain that she would have the courage to do anything with the opium once she got it to her cabin. There was no sense in giving the fool false hope.

She was up on deck and halfway to the captain's cabin when she spotted Kai, the shaved front of his head sprouting short black stubble. He was stirring a bucket of tar, a brush tucked bristle-end up in the waist of his loose breeches. A bosun's chair lay on the deck, its rope extending up into the rigging.

"Kai!" Anne whispered, leaning on the rail and trying to appear like she was more interested in looking out to sea than talking to him.

He looked up and smiled when he saw her. "Missy Anne! You queen now?"

She laughed softly, meeting his eyes, guessing that he might have been the one to spread the lie. "If only I were! Are you well?"

Kai took out a stirring-stick full of tar and dropped it back into the bucket, making a sloppy splash. "I steward, not sailor. Tar ropes not my job."

"Monkey mothering is not my job, either," Anne said, as Mango took her stillness as an opportunity to climb her like a tree, taking his favorite perch on her shoulder.

Kai used his tar-covered stirring stick to make teasing pokes at Mango. The monkey screeched, swiping his hand at the sticky prod.

"Stop it!" Anne said. "He'll get it on his hands, and then it will be in my hair and all over my clothes, and I'll have to give the beast another bath."

"Sorry, Missy," Kai said, then took one last mocking stab at Mango before putting his weapon back in the bucket.

Anne could feel Mango's hands tightening in her hair, and then he hissed at Kai, baring his long teeth, his fangs visible from the corner of her eye. "I'd drown him in that bucket of tar if I thought I could get away with it," Anne agreed, "but I can't. Kai, there's something I need to tell you." She looked around, noting the other sailors at work upon the deck and in the rigging. A few of them were watching her, but none with any apparent suspicion. She knew it would be hard for anyone's eyes not to be drawn to the only female on board, wearing a ridiculous crown and a monkey. She hoped that none who could speak any English were close enough to hear her.

She lowered her voice. "Kai, I might cook something special for the crew."

"You cook, Missy?"

"Yes, maybe. If I do, it is important, very important that you do not eat any of it. Nor Ulrich nor Ruut. Do you understand?"

Kai frowned at her for a moment, then raised one eyebrow. "You very bad cook?"

"Maybe. Maybe very, very bad." She moved aside one edge of the gown she carried, pretending to be displaying the fabric, so that Kai could see the edge of the opium ball hidden inside.

Kai peered at it, then shrugged, a questioning look on his face. Obviously he could not tell what it was. Anne didn't dare try to reveal any more. "Just trust me, Kai. If I cook, do not eat it. All right? Not you, not Ulrich, not Ruut."

"Aye, aye," Kai said, and smiled. "Missy Anne bad cook." He winked at her, and went back to his tar as she moved away.

She wondered if the boy had understood more than he had let on. She got the feeling that there was a lot more going on beneath the surface with Kai than most people knew. Come to think of it, Ulrich was that way, as well. It was only Ruut who seemed to be entirely what he appeared: bad-tempered yet steadfast, although she suspected the steadfastness was more a result of stubbornness than strength of character.

"Anne, *ma chère*," Chartier said from behind her.

Her breath caught in her throat, and she slowly turned.

"What is it you have here, heh?" he asked, tugging on the edge of the dress bundled in her arms. He was smiling, but there was a sly, calculating look in his eyes. He smelled even more strongly of perfume and body odor than usual, and the lace at his wrists was stained with food and wine. His face shone with oil, and a few thin strings of his hair were plastered to his forehead, having escaped his wig.

"A dress, Capitaine," Anne said, her voice cracking.

The pirate tugged again on the cloth, pulling out a half yard of the skirt. Anne clung tight to the opium ball as it turned within the confines of the gown, a cold liquid rush of fear washing down her body.

Chartier pulled the free material up towards her face, holding it there while he cocked his head to one side, examining. "What do you think, Mango? Is it a good color for our queen?"

Mango made an indifferent chirrup.

"No, I do not like it either," Chartier said, flinging the hem back into Anne's arms. "Find something else."

She straightened her spine as if an offended royal, but her heart was thudding and she felt like she could not breathe. "I really do not see why I should have to climb down into a dark and smelly hold for my clothing," she said, in her best Pamela Godwyn voice. "I should think it more proper for the trunks of clothing to be brought to me."

Chartier stated at her for a moment, and then grinned, showing yellow teeth spotted with grey. He gave her a sweeping bow. "*Naturellement*, Your Majesty. My apologies. You are correct."

Anne gave a haughty sniff of agreement, then without further ado turned on her heel and swept herself away to the poop deck cabin. Safely inside her own chamber, her knees gave way and she sank to her bunk, every muscle quaking, tears starting in her eyes. With weak hands she stuffed the dress and opium under her covers, then curled into a ball and hugged her lumpy pillow to her face to absorb her sobs. Mango pulled at her hair and chattered in simian impatience.

Whether her tears came from relief, terror, or anger at Horatio for getting her into this, she didn't know. All she knew was that she couldn't go forward with his plan. She didn't have it in her.

I don't *have* to go through with it, she told herself. She was in her cabin, kneeling on the floor as she used a pilfered dinner knife to cut off small bits of the opium ball then knead sugar into them. When each little piece was as laden as she could get it, she rolled it in yet more sugar to coat it thoroughly. She had obtained the sugar by demanding it, repeatedly, for her tea. The one-legged cook probably thought she had a fondness for drinking warm syrup, the way the sweet kept disappearing from its little bowl.

The opium had a bitter taste that was impossible to

mask entirely, but sugar seemed to help. She'd had to cautiously taste tiny bits, and her eyeballs were feeling fuzzy as a result. Her fear had diminished in proportion to the increase in her eyeball-fuzziness, but was still strong enough to make her sweat.

She kneaded yet another bit of opium, then shaped it as she had the others into the likeness of a raisin. She would cook the false fruits into several puddings for the crew, then top it off with a lemon-opium sauce. If that didn't do the trick, nothing would.

If, that is, she went through with it. She didn't have to. She could dump her raisins and the opium ball overboard and forget the plan entirely. That thought was all that kept her kneeling on the deck, kneading and sweating and cursing under her breath.

Only, she knew she couldn't back out of the plan . . . not really. She would have no respect for herself if she did, not now, and it had nothing to do with wanting to please Horatio.

Late this afternoon, sails had been spotted on the horizon. Chartier had changed course to pursue, darkness falling and the ship wisely dousing its lights before he could come close enough for an attack. He had, however, been close enough to tell that it was an English East Indiaman. The crew had been ecstatic, having gone several weeks without the chance to pillage and plunder and increase their share of the *Cauchemar's* prizes.

It had been impossible for her to sleep knowing that several sailors would soon be slaughtered in defending their ship, and she had lain awake restlessly peeling sunburned skin off her face, her mind racing within the same tight circle of dread.

She had never given any particular thought to feelings of patriotism, despite Horatio's attempts to sway her on that score, but now that the issue had been brought from theory to reality, and was about to play out before her eyes, she found herself identifying with those unknown men on the horizon who, whatever their nationality, sailed under the English flag. She felt more thoroughly English at this moment than at any other time of her life. How could she stand by and watch an English ship being attacked? How could she watch Englishmen murdered?

Chartier, expansive as ever over supper with herself and the Admiral, had explained how he would fly English colors and approach the East Indiaman with half his gun ports closed, to look less dangerous. The East Indiaman, twice the size of the *Cauchemar* and with half again as many guns, would not sense the threat until it was too late.

One of Chartier's favorite techniques for boarding, he explained, was to come up alongside the ship at such a close angle that the rigging of the two boats would entangle, allowing his crew perched on the yardarms to drop grenades onto the enemy ship, then climb aboard with the ease of monkeys leaping from tree branch to tree branch. Such an approach usually left his victims in too much surprise to react effectively, and their guns would be too high and too close to hit the *Cauchemar*, which sat low in the water and would be nestled up against the ship's side.

It was also his practice to have his men fight with

the madness of drink in them. They were so ferocious in battle that they had once taken a ship of 250 men with only sixty of their own.

It was mid-morning now, and she did not know how much time she had left before they would attack the East Indiaman. It had been out of sight at dawn, but the *Cauchemar* was fast, and if the East Indiaman had not altered course during the night they would be upon her before the day was out.

She heard the ship's bell toll. She counted the rings, recognizing that it was eleven o'clock. The first shift of crew would be eating dinner in an hour. She could never bake a pudding in that time, what had she been thinking? Foolishness, to be making raisins! She was going to be no help at all!

She scooped up her false raisins and dumped them into a reticule she had found in one of the chests of clothes, a whimper forming deep in her throat. It was hopeless. If she hadn't waffled over the past few days, she might have been able to do something. Now she'd have to watch innocent sailors slaughtered, and all because she was too much of a coward to act when there had been opportunity. It was too late now, too late.

Feeling sick to her stomach, she stumbled out of her cabin, Mango screeching with delight when he saw her. She pushed him away when he tried to climb up her dress, and he screeched again, then grabbed at the reticule. The drawcords were around her wrist and would not give but the seam did, the reticule ripping down its side, and her false raisins spilled out onto the floor.

113

"Damn you, Mango!" she cried, then knocked the monkey off her with both hands, too upset to care what damage she might do to the beast. She dropped to her knees, brushing up the faux fruit as Mango leapt from chair to table to bureau and back again, screeching angrily. Under his yowls she heard Chartier's voice out on deck, just beyond the door.

She had most of them, but then Mango was down beside her and grabbed the last two. She reached for them, but the monkey jerked back his paws like a greedy child, then with a sneering look at her popped them in his mouth.

Anne's jaw dropped, and after two quick chews Mango's jaw dropped as well and he let out a yowl. He shook his head back and forth, then stopped long enough to reach into his mouth with his long fingers, prying at the gummy black narcotic stuck to his teeth. He got some of it out, then went wild, racing round the floor, dropping to his side and kicking his legs, his head shaking violently in an attempt to dislodge the bitter gum.

"Serves you right, you dirty little bugger," Anne muttered, getting to her feet. Her language had deteriorated badly since the shipwreck, but at the moment she didn't give a bloody damn.

The door opened just as she reached it, and Chartier was standing there. She shrunk under his gaze, intense and lit with an unstable, erratic energy that she intuitively recognized as bloodlust. She could feel the tension coming off him like heat from a fire, her own muscles tightening with fear as they absorbed it, and making her feel a sudden need for the chamber pot. If it wasn't for the opium dulling the edges of her fear, she thought she might just collapse to the floor unconscious.

He opened his mouth to speak, but then his gaze shifted away from her, caught by Mango and his antics as the beast flew between the pieces of furniture, shrieking. "What is wrong with the Admiral?" he asked. The intensity of his gaze was briefly lessened by concern for the animal, and it was only that which gave her the courage to meet his eyes when he looked at her again.

"He tried to eat soap," Anne lied, saying the first thing that came to mind.

Chartier's frown deepened, and her legs began to feel weak. "Soap? Why would Mango eat soap?"

She shrugged and tried to look innocent, her hands shaking so badly she had to clasp them before her.

Chartier watched the monkey a few moments longer, then made an eloquent facial shrug that said such comprehension was beyond him. He turned his attention to her, his eyes roving over her hair and attire. She had to restrain herself from reaching up to tuck away stray strands of hair: She knew she looked a wreck, her face damp with perspiration, her ill-fitting gown crumpled and dark with sweat under her arms and in a patch below her breasts.

"It is warm, yes?" Chartier asked.

"Yes," Anne agreed. The saloon was stifling, the hot sun of the equator already baking the deck above their heads.

"Perhaps you should get air. Later you will stay below decks."

Anne nodded, understanding what would be happening then. As if she were a marionette controlled by an inexpert puppeteer, she moved with jerky motions out the door, her breath tight in her chest. Mango raced past, careening off her legs and nearly knocking her off balance.

The light on deck was blinding after the darkness of the saloon, and she squinted her eyes down to slits, moving as if in a dream towards the forward companionway that led down to the cook's tiny domain. The breeze of the ship's forward motion dried the perspiration on her skin and soothed the hint of nausea that roiled her belly. She saw Kai as she came to the forward companionway, and met his eyes for a long moment, trying to communicate to him what, against all her better sense, she was about to do.

"Missy, you all right?"

"I'm going to check on dinner," she said, and clasped the reticule to her chest. Kai's eyes went to it, and he gave a scarely perceptible nod. It crossed her mind to have him take the raisins to the galley to be disposed of, but there was no reason for Kai to carry a reticule, and if caught she knew he would suffer a far worse fate than she would.

"Missy stay out of sun. Not look good," Kai said.

"Not feel good," Anne said. No, she did not feel good at all.

"Horatio! Wake up!"

"Ruut?" Horatio said in disbelief, sitting up as he felt Ruut grab hold of his wrist, working a key in the lock.

"Yes! Quick. Need help."

"What is it? What's happening?"

Ruut grunted, pulling Horatio off the floor, his chains falling to the deck. Horatio stumbled, his unused muscles protesting. He felt dizzy for a moment, seeing stars.

"Not all quiet. Need help."

"*What* is going on?" Horatio demanded as Ruut dragged him down the deck.

"Dinner. Stew. Anne use opium."

"She did?" Horatio asked in surprise. "Good for her!" He felt the strength coming back to his legs, a grin stretching his face, his heart lightening in a way it hadn't for the long days he had sat in the dark without a visit from her. "Damn me! I knew she had it in her!" She deserved a medal, did his mouse!

Ruut nudged him, then slapped a heavy belaying pin into his hand. "Not all quiet," he said again, and Horatio understood. They could hear voices raised in argument, confusion in their tones. They came to a companionway up to the next deck and climbed.

The sailors—the cook and the man Horatio recalled as Georges—were in the forecastle, the crew's quarters that abutted the galley, the sweltering temperature of which undoubtedly had done nothing to improve the moods of the arguing sailors.

Horatio felt the familiar narrowing of attention that came before a battle, extraneous thoughts slipping away as his senses became focused, taking in information with unnatural clarity, his mind seizing upon the correct approach as if without effort.

The attack was brief and only slightly bloody, surprise on their side. The cook took two conks with the pin before he went down, red seeping from beneath his hair, but both he and Georges were still breathing. Horatio followed Ruut through the rest of the ship, staying belowdecks and searching out the sober. Several sailors were still awake, but their eyes were glazed, their movements listless if present at all, most of them either sitting or lying down. Horatio stepped over a pair of sprawled legs, smelling vomit, but that sailor, like the others, appeared in danger neither of protesting nor of dying.

It was less than ten minutes before they had searched the ship, knocking only a few more heads to ensure "quiet," as Ruut put it, and then they came up on deck. Horatio shielded his eyes, and then made out Kai and Anne working together, dragging crew to the rail and piling them there like contented, drowsy puppies. Ulrich was doing the same, showing far less compassion as he pulled a confused sailor by the feet, the man's head dragging across the deck and bumping into the corner of the deckhouse. The sailor let out a noise of protest, but then seemed to settle into a detached bemusement at his novel mode of travel. Horatio noticed the discarded belaying pin several feet away, a smear of red on its smooth surface. Not everyone up here had been so agreeable.

"Horatio!" Anne cried, seeing him and running over. To his astonishment she flung herself against him, and he closed his arms around her in reflex, happy enough to have her clinging to him. Her arms were surprisingly strong, like bands around his chest, and he doubted he could have pried her off even if he had wanted to. He patted her back, fighting off the temptation to reach down and give her buttocks a squeeze.

She held him a moment longer, then stepped back. He met her eyes, and saw that her pupils were dilated, almost covering the midnight blue of her eyes. She looked fairly alert, yet not entirely present within herself, and he suspected that some of the opium had found its way down her throat.

"I did it! I did it!"

"I see you did." He put his hands on her shoulders and squeezed. "Good job! I knew you could, I knew you had it in you."

"No, I don't." She giggled. "It was the opium."

There was no time to argue the point. "Where's Chartier?" he asked.

She smiled and took his hand, then pulled him to the cabin. He ducked inside the low door, coming down the three steps, and heard a terrible, phlegmy sound. A moment later he made out Chartier, sprawled in his chair at the table, snoring. Brown stew was spilled down the white of his cravat.

"He had been drinking half the day," Anne said. "The opium hit him harder than most of the others."

Horatio noticed two other places at the table, one with food splattered all around it, the other with a spoon laid neatly at the edge of the deep plate. He couldn't tell how much of the stew in that plate had been eaten, although the spoon had gravy in its bowl. Anne went to that place setting and played with the spoon, using it to move around chunks of meat and potato, then lifted it to her lips and before he could reach out to stop her, she had put it in her mouth, the silver coming out clean of gravy.

"Anne, what are you doing?"

She made a face. "It tastes terrible." She scooped up another spoonful of drugged gravy, and had downed it before he could stop her.

"Christ, Anne," Horatio said, and took the spoon from her, flinging it onto the table. He pulled her unresisting out of the cabin and back into the bright sunlight on deck. His mouse apparently had all the makings of an opium fiend.

Ruut and Ulrich were unlashing the ship's boats that were stored with spare spars atop two deckhouses. Horatio dragged her towards them, then released her so he could help them lower the boat from the roof of the deckhouse where it was stored. "How many crew are there?" he asked.

"Almost seventy," Ulrich said. "We will need all the boats."

"Unless we want to feed them to the fishes," Horatio answered.

Ulrich gave him a long look from his light blue eyes, as if this were a proposition he was more than willing to consider. "Do you wish to?"

"What I wish and what I will do are not one and the same. No, I'd rather not murder the bastards. They gave us a chance—let's give them one."

"That is what Anne said."

Horatio grunted in acknowledgement, having expected no different. They rigged the first boat to ropes and a pulley attached to a yardarm, and hoisted it over the lee rail. The sails were already hove to, putting the ship as motionless in the water as it could be, drifting slowly to the side. It was no more than ten feet from the deck of the *Cauchemar* down to the surface of the water—still too far to simply drop a living body, but not so far that there would be any trouble in lowering crew one by one with a rope around their middles.

"They'll need water and food," Anne said, coming up beside him, peering over the rail at the empty longboat. "Kai and I can fetch it."

He nodded, somewhat surprised she was still functioning as well as she was. It made him nervous of the state of the sailors—how far were they from being equally as capable? Perhaps she had had nothing to drink, as they surely had. "Be careful below. If anyone stirs, have Kai take them out," he said, handing her a belaying pin.

"I took everyone out," she said, smiling.

"Well, nearly."

"Out, out, they're all out," she said in a sing-song, then wandered off towards Kai, lifting her skirts with exaggerated care to step over an unconscious sailor.

Horatio shook his head, but there was too much to do to worry about her state of mind.

It took over an hour for them to get crew and supplies into the boats and set adrift, the three boats connected by ropes. The seas were calm enough that the boats should be in no danger of capsizing before enough of the men came sufficiently to their senses to properly handle them. Slurred queries as to what was going on were met with the soothing answer that they were all going ashore to visit a whorehouse.

After consideration Horatio had added a compass and old chart to their supplies, tucking them in beside the still-snoring Chartier, presumably the only one who would know how to use them correctly. The boats had oars as well as a single sail each, and it was not inconceivable that the lot of them would make landfall in one piece. Neither was it a given, but there was no other alternative for dealing with them. There were too many to try to control once they had come to their senses, and as far as he knew there was no island they could reach within a few hours to maroon them. And he wanted Chartier out of his sight.

Gianni, the short, stocky Italian man, they kept aboard. Anne was of the opinion he would be happy to leave the privateering life, and as they would need all the hands they could get to sail the boat, Horatio was content to let him stay. The others had deferred to him without question, as if it was assumed that he was captain now.

The longboats finally drifted away, and Ulrich, Ruut, and Kai started hauling sails as Horatio went to the wheel, unlashing it from its position at hard to port. He put the ship on an ENE heading, which was as directly east as the winds would allow. His tiny crew slowly trimmed the sails, and his skin began to cool in the breeze of their forward passage.

They were moving at a measly four or five knots, but doing so in a ship that was now their own. The reality of that spread slowly through his senses, and a shout of pure joy rose up from within. He set it free into the clear blue air, howling and whooping, the others turning to stare.

The stink of his confinement seemed to wash away with the breeze, even the memory of the last several days vanishing under the bright sunlight. The endless horizon of the sea was no greater than the horizon of possibilities he now felt spreading before them. He had a ship, a crew, goods in the hold, and no one to tell them which way to go. It was a freedom unlike any he had ever known.

And Anne was safely with him, happy and proud of herself.

God, he felt like getting drunk!

He laughed aloud, surprised by the thought. He was not a drinking man by nature, but his body seemed to want a drink to match the intoxication of his heart and mind.

The sheets now tied off, the men forward along the deck were catching some of his enthusiasm. With hands idle for the first time that day, Horatio saw them look at each other, at the ship, and then back at him. He grinned and gave another shout of joy. After a moment of stiffness, the three of them echoed his cry. Ulrich linked arms with Kai and spun the smaller man in an exuberant dance, releasing him, laughing, to fall into a coiled rope. Ruut stood to the side with his arms crossed over his chest, a grin cracking his heavy face.

He heard Anne emerge from the cabin behind him. "Anne!" he called over his shoulder, then saw that she had something in her arms. He frowned against the glare of the light, then felt his heart sink at what she was holding.

"The boats are gone?" She asked, her tone both confused and distant. "But we forgot about the Admiral."

Horatio glared at the sleeping devil in Anne's arms.

Damn monkey! "Throw him overboard! Maybe he can swim."

Anne looked down at the creature in her arms. "Oh, I couldn't." Instead, she released half her hold on him so that he dangled by one long arm from her grip, his other arms and legs dragging on the deck. She seemed to forget then that she held him, and dropped him to the ground, walking past his limp body without so much as a glance.

"Is he still alive?" Horatio asked.

Anne ignored him, her attention focused now on mounting the steep stairs to the poop deck. Kai came aft and poked a foot at the monkey, answering Horatio's question for her. "Still alive. Maybe meat for supper."

"I not eat that," Ruut said, coming aft with Ulrich. Gianni was still passed out near the forward deck-house.

Anne crawled onto the poop deck but seemed unable to rise to her feet, plopping down onto her rump with her legs stretched out before her, her feet sticking out over the edge. Her crown had slipped back on her head, hanging on by the grace of one tress of hair wound through it.

"Where are we heading?" Ulrich asked.

"East!" Anne said, raising an arm and pointing, with unnerving accuracy, due east. "The birdie says east!" she said, giggling, and dropped her arm. She gave a sigh, then collapsed to her side, unconscious.

"East," Horatio said. "Ruut, will you come take the wheel while I put Anne to bed? We'll talk about our destination after she wakes up: I don't think it would be right to discuss it without her. Agreed?"

There was a murmur of assent. "Missy very brave," Kai said.

"I think so, too," Horatio said, as Ruut took the wheel. Ulrich helped him to lower Anne from the poop deck.

Horatio hoisted her inert figure into his arms, ducking down to step through the doorway that Ulrich held open for him. He found the cabin she had been using, the dresses under the swaying cot marking it as hers, and laid her gently down on her side. He noticed a lump, and digging under the covers found the ball of opium off which she had cut a sizeable chunk.

He untangled the crown from her hair and set it on the washstand, then tried to look at Anne with objective eyes. He was not locked up in the dark now with nothing to distract him but his imagination. He should be able to see her clearly.

Her skin was blotchy with healing sunburn and peeling skin, unattractively pink in several places. The hair around her face was dark with sweat, sticking to her skin. She needed a bath. Her figure, hinted at by the oversized gown as it draped over her, was . . . quite tempting, actually. There was a lovely dip from hip to waist, and her breasts were full enough to be rounded, yet small enough that he was sure they would sit high upon her chest.

Her skin would heal in a few more days, and if he could find some balm for those pink cupid lips, the chapping would disappear. He could wash her hair for her, comb out the snarls, wash her body as she sat in a tub, allowing his hands to gently soap her, running over smooth limbs and down into . . .

He felt the tightening of his breeches across his loins as his erection grew. The same thoughts weren't the reason that the others were fond of her, were they?

He sat down on the edge of the cot, his hip against the small of her back, and leaned over her. She was twisted slightly, her face turned up, her lips parted. He reached out and stroked her cheek as he had when she had come to him below decks, feeling the softness, and feeling as well an astonishing upwelling of protectiveness. He suffered a belated rush of dread over what might have happened if the drugging had gone awry.

None of them had been hurt, though. They had succeeded, and now could look for Anne's dream island. Ulrich and his talk of the Hand of Destiny might sound far-fetched, but it almost seemed as if this had all been meant to happen. He had, he realized, been certain all along that his plan with the opium would work.

Poor brave mouse, though: She hadn't had such certainty. He wanted to lie beside her and hold her in his arms, whispering assurances into her hair. He wanted her to turn to him and press herself close, relaxing in the security of his embrace, her sweet smile saying that she knew he would let no harm come to her.

Anne stirred a longing in him to be more than he was, to be other than a man who slipped from one experience to the other as if by accident, useful to none, no purpose or plan to his life except to pursue idle pleasures. He wanted to be her hero.

He ran his fingertips lightly across her forehead,

brushing back the damp strands of hair, wondering at the dreams that played behind her closed eyes. He bent down and gently kissed her cheek, shutting his own eyes as he inhaled the scent of her, warm and musky, touched with the tang of salt. Her scent curled around his heart, her vulnerability in sleep ineffably precious, and he knew in that moment that he would do anything in the world for her. He would make her dreams come true.

Chapter Nine

Anne adjusted her hat, a sailor's oiled canvas she had found in a sea chest in the forecastle and had donned in hopes of saving her skin any further abuse by the sun. She was sitting on the quarterdeck, along with the other members of their ragtag group, Ruut at the wheel while Horatio spread a chart on the deckboards, weighting down the corners to keep it from rolling up or blowing away.

They were all cleaner than they had been for weeks: Everyone had had a bath this morning, and Gianni had pointed Horatio to the chests in the hold that held men's clothing. There wasn't much, but at least there were sufficient linen shirts that all except Ruut could have something new. The Dutchman was too big for anything in the chests, which had sent Kai into a long stream of jokes at his expense. In the end Ruut had found a semi-fresh shirt in a sailor's chest, but his grumpy expression said he would have preferred the fine linen of the others.

Mango was presently high up in the rigging, Kai and Gianni having joined in a game of swat-the-monkey early in the day, chasing him up and down the deck with mops. Apparently no one in Chartier's crew had been able to stand the beast, either, and Anne almost would have felt sorry for Mango if not for the thick scabs on her hand.

"My best guess is that we are somewhere near here," Horatio said, stabbing his finger at a point in the middle of a vast sea of charted nothingness. "Chartier, whatever his faults, kept a careful log, and we can't have gone too far since we got rid of him. I'm fairly certain we are in this vicinity."

They all peered at the map. Anne's gaze was drawn to the eastern edge, where the island chain of the East Indies began. In that direction was where her island was, if it was anywhere at all. She had woken knowing that.

"Will we head for India?" Ulrich asked.

Horatio looked up and met Anne's eyes. "That depends."

Anne broke his gaze, her cheeks heating. Last night had been filled with unusually vivid dreams brought on by the opium she had consumed. The dreams had felt so real that they had remained in her memory as if they had been lived in her waking life, and one of them had been of Horatio lowering himself over her, the both of them naked as the day they were born. She had felt the hair on his chest against her breasts, the black curls tickling her nipples, and she had felt his hand slipping between her thighs, urging them to open so that he could lie between them.

It didn't help that he was looking better than he ever had this afternoon. He had shaved, his skin where the beard had been paler than the rest of his face. His hair was clean and glossy, ruffled by the wind. His linen shirt was open at the neck, displaying a hint of the hair that had played such a naughty role in her dream. To make matters worse, he seemed to be naturally fitting into the role of captain, and she was finding his assumption of authority attractive.

Ulrich spoke again. "We have cargo. It would be a good place to sell it, and the ship. You can go back to John Company. Anne can find her mistress."

"Do you think the Hand of Destiny brought us this far simply to return to where we started, a few pounds richer?"

"Not few pounds," Kai said. "Much pounds."

Horatio looked up at Ruut, standing at the wheel. "And you, Ruut?"

"Money good." He shrugged. "But sea good, too. Money is for land."

Anne saw that Gianni was watching the talk with quick darting eyes, trying to follow. She had "talked" with him earlier today, the two of them using an improvised sign language and a smattering of shared French, and she'd been pleased at how well they seemed to understand each other. He was happy to be free of Chartier, but still somewhat uncertain about his fate amidst this new crew.

"If not India, where?" Ulrich asked.

"I think we should ask Anne that," Horatio said.

Five heads turned to her. She parted her lips in surprise, not having expected to be put on the spot like this. "Ask me? Why?"

Horatio cocked his head, his lips crooking in a smile. "You are the one with the destination."

It took her a moment to understand, and then she couldn't believe he meant what he was saying. "My island? But I could not ask others to search for it. India is the place to go, to sell the ship and the cargo, and that chest of jewels. You all would have enough money to start a new life, however you wished. I would, as well."

"Do you still have the dreams?" Ulrich asked. His blue eyes caught and held hers, so serious that a fluttering of nervousness came to life in her belly. He was looking at her as if she were a seer, holding a truth upon which he would decide his course.

"This is too much to ask of any of you," she said. "I cannot take the responsibility of setting your course. You know the island of my dreams may not exist; it may be nothing more than fantasy." The thought of these men devoting the next several months of their lives to her chimerical quest was too much for her.

She was a lady's maid with a foolish notion, not King Arthur in search of the Holy Grail. She was not anyone special, and it would be sinful to even pretend to be so, or to think she had a right to direct the lives of others.

Ulrich was still looking at her, as was Horatio. And Kai, and Ruut. Even Gianni was staring at her with interest, sensing that she was at the center of a crucial question.

"It is only a dream!" she snapped.

"And yet you yourself have come halfway 'round the globe in search of it," Horatio said. "The cargo can be sold elsewhere than India, and the jewels can be divided now or later, it makes no difference. When will you ever have a chance like this again, to point your hand in a direction and have a ship follow?"

"It is a chance, certainly, but I will not take it at the expense of others."

"I am not returning to my regiment. I have wanted for years to explore the East Indies, and the East India Company has nothing to offer me that compares with that. Ulrich, do you have plans?"

"I put my trust in the Hand of Destiny," Ulrich said, with a crooked grin.

"I'm sure you do," Anne said, "but surely there is something you would rather do?"

"I want to sail, to see the world. I think it is better to do so on this ship than to return to an East India-man. Your pardon, but Captain Chartier was correct: The English, they are not good to sail under."

"Kai?" Anne asked, seeking help from that quarter. She couldn't have them helping her like this, it was too great a gift.

"This good ship, good crew. Maybe good wine in hold. I go with you."

"Ruut?" she asked in increasing desperation. Surely ill-tempered Ruut would decline.

"Crew too small. Captain is not sailor. Maybe sink in next storm, maybe kill by pirates." Anne felt her hopes rising, but then he shrugged and patted the wheel beneath his hands. "Kai right. Is good ship.

Have food, have water, have cargo. Why not find island?"

"Very well put, Ruut," Horatio crowed.

Anne looked helplessly to Gianni, but the little Italian's eyes were bright with interest and excitement. He would agree to anything anyone suggested.

"It's decided, then," Horatio said. "We go in search of Anne's island."

There was a murmur of assent, and a release of the tension for all except Anne herself. She felt as if she had just been set adrift alone. "I don't know where it is!" she cried. "I cannot lead you there. Do not make me try." Her throat was tightening, tears stinging her eyes at the pressure.

Horatio was frowning at her. "Anne, what is it? I thought this was what you wanted."

"You expect too much. What if there is no island?"

Horatio shrugged. "There are thousands of islands. If we do not find yours, we will find others, and if we can find one with no Portuguese or Dutch, we will establish trade with them in the name of England. I do not think that any of us are acting against our own wishes." The others made sounds of agreement. Horatio cocked his head to the side, examining her before continuing. "We all have our own reasons for choosing as we do."

Some of the pressure eased off her heart. He was right: They each had their own reasons for wishing to remain aboard the *Cauchemar*. This journey was theirs as well as her own. She remembered Horatio's story of being shot and drifting down the Brahmaputra. The effects of an event were not to be predicted, and it would be arrogance to assume that these men sailed to fulfill her destiny, rather than their own.

She looked down at the chart and started, then relaxed. Her red and gold kingfisher was resting at the edge, using his beak to clean his feathers. What more of an omen did she need?

"Then it is east we go," she said, then stabbed her finger down next to the kingfisher's tiny black feet, where it stood at the edge of the East Indies. It looked up at her, then flitted away, invisible to all eyes but her own.

"East," Horatio said, and grinned. "As if there was ever any question."

Anne stood in the bow of the boat, leaning her side against the base of the bowsprit, feeling the wind reach its cool fingers into her hair. Behind her the sun was setting, but it was east she faced, east where her future lay. The horizon before her was a rich dark blue, and high in the heavens the first jeweled stars of the night shone in silvered brilliance.

She felt strangely light—giddy, even—now that she had accepted that they would pursue her dream of the island. For the first time in her life, she felt like she was truly following her own course. She was not doing what others expected of her; she was not fulfilling some duty as a daughter or a sister or a servant. Her course was being determined purely by the wishes of her own heart, and it was both thrilling and terrifying.

The wind tugged at her hair, whipping strands free of her knot, and then the entire mass came down, fluttering behind her like a flag. The dream image of skimming above the ocean surface came back to her, and she almost felt as if on the morrow when the sun rose she would see her emerald island before her, with its thunderclouds towering above.

She didn't know when or where this journey would end, but her heart was telling her that the exhilaration she felt now, with all its uncertainties and wild hopes, was worth every bit of trial and tribulation she had gone through to get to this point. She was finally on her way.

"Is it golden palaces you see, deep in the jungle?" Horatio asked from behind her.

She turned, surprised by his presence, feeling a quick fluttering of embarrassment. He was looking too attractive for her own good, and if she didn't try to ignore that she would be stumbling all over her words, unable to treat him in any normal manner. He stepped up right next her, bracing his hand on the base of the bowsprit. He was so close that if she leant in his direction they would touch. She shivered, her body wanting to close that distance. He was looking at her with a half-amused expression, and she belatedly remembered he had asked a question.

"Not golden palaces. Strange long houses, holding dozens of families, built of wood and dried leaves and bamboo."

His amusement was replaced by interest. "I thought you said you saw houses on stilts in your dreams."

"I did, on the coast. The long houses are inland." She gave him a crooked smile of her own. "Last night I had the most vivid dreams, thanks to the opium."

"This doesn't mean you're going to be consuming

it nightly, does it? For the dreams it brings?"

She would not think of the other dreams, the erotic ones. She would not! Yet she was almost tempted to dose herself nightly if it meant such luxurious sensations in her dreams, however mortifying they might be upon waking.

Only she wasn't truly mortified; she was aroused. She wanted to reach out and touch Horatio's skin where it showed at the open neck of his shirt, run her hand inside, feel the crispness of the black hairs. Her breath got short, and her breasts were tingling. Mentally she urged him to press against her, to let her feel the length of his body against hers.

"Anne? You're not going to become an opium fiend, are you?"

"What?" Why couldn't he just stand silent and let her fantasize? "Oh. No. I don't think that is going to be a problem."

"I feared I'd have to dump the chest overboard, to keep it out of your reach."

She saw that he was at least half joking, and smiled. "Don't do that. It may come in useful if we need further direction. My dreams last night—they were wonderfully detailed, and at times almost frightening."

"Tell me."

As if she would dare to tell them all! "I don't know that they make much sense. I saw much of the jungle, birds in brilliant colors, strange animals, insects as big as my fist, plants with leaves half the size of my body. And the people! They were nearly naked, dark, tattooed, and had earlobes that had been stretched by heavy jewelry until they brushed their shoulders."

Horatio made a face.

"No, don't think like that. They were beautiful, they fit their world perfectly. It seemed somehow right that they should be so different. It's as if the island is magic at its heart, a place not of the world that we know."

He lifted his hand to briefly touch her cheek. "You have a good heart, Anne Hazlett."

"Only an average one."

"No, you're special. You have a"—he paused, spreading his hands wide, struggling to find the right word—"an openness about you, a warmth that welcomes others, when you let it show and are not hiding behind a hat brim, or pretending to be offended."

"I don't pretend to be offended," she protested.

"You're doing it now," he said, meeting her eyes.

Her cheeks heated, and she tried to break his gaze, but couldn't.

"There is so much more to you than you let on," he wondered.

"No more than to anyone else." She laughed nervously, then felt like a silly schoolgirl the moment she did. She suddenly did not know where to put her hands, or how to stand still.

He leaned closer, his head tilting slightly to the side. Her eyes widened, her lips parting, her heart beating rapidly in response to his closeness.

"What do you suppose your parents would think if they knew you were sailing into the unknown with five unattached men?" he asked softly, his mouth coming closer to her own with every word.

"They would fear for my reputation and my future."

"Would they feel better about it if you were married to one of them?"

She blinked. He couldn't mean married to him, could he? Former officers in the East India Company who came from wealthy families did not make offers for the hands of lady's maids, not unless they wanted to be cut out of their inheritances and snubbed by their peers. "Likely they would be happier if that were the case," she said uncertainly.

"Then perhaps you should marry."

He was so close now that she could smell the soap on his skin, the linen of his shirt, could feel the warmth of his skin. He seemed so much bigger when they were close like this: His size was deliciously over-whelming, making her feel that he could wrap her in his arms and she would be unable to do other than submit. And she wanted to submit. "Should I?" she whispered.

With his fingertips he gently stroked the side of her neck, then traced over her breastbone. He pressed his palm flat against her chest, and she knew he could feel her heart thudding against his hand. He looked down into her eyes, his gaze steady and intent, and she felt a delicious sinking in her belly, as if warm water had been poured over her, waves of arousal making her aware of a growing dampness in her sex.

His hands came up to cup both sides of her head, his thumbs at the edge of her cheekbones, and then his lips came down to meet her own. The first touch was gentle, his lips touching against her own, his breath mingling with hers. He brushed his lips against hers, the friction slight enough to send sparkles of sensation across her lips. She raised her hands and gripped the front of his shirt.

"Marry me," Horatio said against her lips, and then took them firmly with his own, pressing hard. When she began to respond he urged her to open to him, to let him dip his tongue inside her mouth, touching it lightly against her own. Her knees went weak at the intimate invasion, and his arm came down to hold her around the waist, pulling her up against his body, his other hand digging into her hair as he deepened the kiss further yet.

She felt as if she were being consumed, not just in body but in soul, her sense of who and where she was subsumed by the hunger of her body. She had heard his proposal, but had been unable to process it in her mind. Nothing had meaning but his mouth on hers, his arm around her waist, the feel of his firm body against her own, the ridge of his hardening arousal pressing into the softness of her belly.

His lips left hers. "Marry me, Anne," he said again, then moved his kisses to the side of her neck, running his tongue into the small space behind her earlobe, using his teeth to scrape small bites from the skin in the bend of her neck, then fastening his mouth there and sucking, his tongue working her skin. She lost all strength in her muscles, becoming helpless in his arms.

He lifted his head until he could see her face. She stretched towards him, wanting his lips back on hers, but he held her slightly apart. "Say yes, Anne. Say you will."

She blinked. Say yes? She forced herself to think, to

let the coursing, aching desire in her veins subside to a hum. He was gazing intently at her, waiting for her answer, and finally she understood that he had asked her to marry him.

It made no sense. In her confusion she tried to push away from him, her hands on his chest. "Marry you? I cannot marry you."

"Yes, you can," he said, refusing to release her, using his free hand to gently brush strands of hair back from her face.

"But I hardly know you!"

He smiled his sad-eyed smile, and for a moment looked so vulnerable she felt guilty for not saying yes immediately. "You should, by now. We've been through more together in the past two weeks than most people experience in their lifetimes. We're good together, Anne. You shouldn't be out here alone, you need a husband to look after you."

"No . . . Horatio, marriage—" She took a breath, trying to gather her jumbled thoughts, knowing that to marry him would be wrong for them both, but not yet clear on how she knew it. "We don't know what the future is going to bring. Marriage is for the rest of our lives. Being here on this boat, this is temporary. I don't know what my life is going to be when—and if—we find the island. You don't know what yours will be."

"We'll work it out."

"Would we? Why? I don't love you, Horatio, and you do not love me," she said, hoping he would deny it. She wanted to believe he loved her, although she knew that what she felt for him was only a mild infatuation, that there had been no time for anything deeper to grow. The perversity of human nature, to want what it was not willing to give! "We are from different worlds—you are gentry, I am a servant. What reason would we have to build a life together?" She wanted him to convince her, to allow her to say yes even when all her instincts told her that this was not the time, that the proposal was lacking some basic underpinning and to agree would be disaster.

His hold around her waist loosened, and she stepped back, still within the circle of his arm but no longer pressed against him. She already missed the contact of his body.

"We're no longer in England," he said. "I don't know that I'll ever go back, so what does it matter what we were there?"

"It matters because it is still who we are *here*," she said, tapping her chest.

"The longer we are out here, the farther we will go from what we once were. I've lived abroad long enough to know the truth of that. Even now, if you were to return home, you would find that you could not fit in the way you once did. Your life as a lady's maid would feel too small to you, your family's interests too limited, their views too narrow."

"Perhaps. But that doesn't mean we should marry." She looked at him pointedly. "Why did you ask me?"

"You need protection."

"I have you and four sailors to protect me."

"Your reputation—"

"Who is going to report home on me? Who out here knows who I am? Enough has happened already that tales would follow me, were the last weeks known.

141

Shipwrecked, and then treated as a queen by a French privateer! Even a mere lady's maid would gain attention with such a story following her."

He closed again the distance between them, putting one foot between hers, his leg between her knees as she leaned back against the base of the bowsprit. "There are other benefits, besides protection," he said, touching her cheek. "Benefits that we could not share outside of wedlock."

Her heart caught in her throat. "Indeed!" she said, flustered, and then annoyed. "And would those benefits be largely for yourself?"

"You would enjoy them as well."

"So that is what this is all about, at the heart of it?" she asked, getting angry. "You want to marry me so you can claim marital rights?" The more she thought about it, the more upset she became. Here she had been allowing thoughts of the beginnings of love to play with her heart, and all he had been thinking of was guaranteeing himself a bed partner for the long journey ahead. She suddenly felt like she did not know him at all, and as if he did not know her. All he surely saw when he looked at her was a pair of breasts and two legs that could be parted for his benefit.

"I meant what I said: We are good together. You make me want—"

She brushed his hand away from her face and shoved at his chest, getting him to step back. She moved away from the bowsprit, and from him. "I don't want to know what I make you want. I'm not going to marry a man for his convenience."

"I don't know when marriage is ever a convenience for a man!" Horatio snapped, and she heard the anger rising in his own voice. "You didn't let me finish. I was going to say that you make me want to be a better man."

She stopped where she was and met his eyes. He looked angry and defensive, and she realized she had hurt him with her rash assumptions. "I'm sorry, Horatio," she said quietly, recognizing her error. "But I still don't feel it would be right."

"Why?" he asked, his voice softening as hers had. "And give me a better reason than that you used to do Miss Godwyn's hair."

"I don't know why not. I just know it isn't right."

"Will you only marry if you are madly in love?" he asked lightly, and she could tell he was trying to defuse the tension and save face as well.

She gave a small smile. "No. I've always thought a deep friendship would be enough, that and a sense that there would be security for the future. We've none of that now; all we have is a stolen boat and a madwoman's quest."

"And the beginnings of a friendship and affection. We do have that."

"Yes, we do," she said quietly.

He mustered a smile that did not reach his eyes. "Perhaps I'll ask again in a few weeks. By then you may find yourself overwhelmed by my charm."

She laughed as she began to move away, the sound as forced as his smile. "You will have forgotten your

143

intent, and I'll be wondering at the inconstancy of your heart as I wait for my proposal."

She was several feet away when she heard his answer, brought to her softly on the breeze, "There's no chance of that, my little mouse."

Chapter Ten

Four weeks later

"Land ho!"

The excited cry startled Anne out of her weary daze. She blinked and looked around the deck, then the cry came again.

"Land ho!" It was Kai, up in the rigging, where he had been replacing worn ropes with Ulrich.

Anne shielded her eyes and followed where Kai's outstretched arm was pointing, her tiredness falling away under the anticipation of sighting land at long last, but whatever Kai had seen was still below the horizon from where she stood. It took only a moment to abandon the pots she was scrubbing and the hunk of saltpork that was soaking in a barrel of seawater. She hiked her skirts—skirts shortened already to above-ankle length by a knife—tied them above her knees, and went to the ratlines.

It was Kai who had first goaded her into climbing up the ladderlike rigging that went from the ship's rails to the masts. Since he himself had initially hated going into the rigging, but then grown to enjoy it, he had apparently thought she might have the same response. Horatio and the others had protested, voicing concerns about her safety, but there had been so little to amuse or entertain any of them that they had given in without too much trouble, and given her repetitious advice on how to proceed.

All very silly, for climbing a rope ladder, she had thought. Then she had climbed it, and at fifteen feet above the deck had halted and gone no further. Fifteen feet above deck was twenty-five feet above the water, and the higher she went the more it was as if she was at the end of a pendulum, swaying back and forth with the motion of the ship. She had clung tight to the tarred ratlines, grinned hard-jawed at the men whooping at her from below, and refused to go another step.

Those first fifteen feet had become familiar ground to her since, though, and climbing up above the deck gave her some of the few moments of peace and pleasure to be had aboard the *Cauchemar*. From even that relatively low height, the world opened up, becoming sea and sky instead of the dreary drudgery to be had on and below decks. She had begun to dislike the boat intensely, with its constant motion and demands, its foul stinks and incessant creaking and groaning.

She and Horatio had perhaps been the only ones

who had not fully understood what they were taking on when they dumped Chartier and his crew into the longboats and took over the ship for themselves. Six people were enough to keep the ship moving, but only just. Raising sails was a slow, laborious process for so few people, and adjusting them for any change in course took a similar group effort. Although the *Cauchemar* could, with a full crew, sail at more than ten or twelve knots, with just six to run her she dawdled along at less than half that speed, making course corrections only when absolutely necessary.

Nor had Anne realized what constant upkeep a ship required, constant tending, constant repair. It was as if the ship were trying to rot and crumble beneath them, and it took all their energy to keep it in a state of equilibrium.

Add to that the business of keeping six humans and a monkey fed, and it felt as if the *Cauchemar* was her own personal bad dream. Cleanliness was a luxury to be indulged in the spare moments that were not devoted to sleep, and any worries she had had about unwise intimacies with Horatio had proved groundless. They didn't have either the time or the energy to do anything but run the ship.

She swung herself up onto the rail and then began to climb, her now-callused hands and feet comfortable on the ropes, the strap of her canvas hat tugging at her under her chin as the wind caught and buffeted the brim. Mango scampered along the rail, then raced up the ratlines at her side, his natural nimbleness making a mockery of her hard-won ease. At her fifteen-foot limit she wrapped her arms through the ratlines and gazed out to the east. There, as a thin strip barely visible on the horizon, she saw what could only be Sumatra.

Or Java. Horatio had admitted to being less than certain of the accuracy of his navigation.

The original plan had been to sail through the Straits of Malacca, on the north side of Sumatra. There had been two minor storms that had both scared the wits out of them and also confused the accuracy of Horatio's dead reckoning. Then Horatio had discovered a consistent error in his calculations with the sextant, their alternate method of navigation, and he had declared that they were farther south than expected. Now, if all went well and further navigational errors had not been committed, they planned to sail down the coast of Sumatra to the Sunda Strait.

Or up the coast of Java to the Sunda Strait, depending upon where they actually were.

The Sunda Strait would take them directly through the long barrier that Sumatra and Java made together. From where the strait let out, they could go farther east to the Spice Islands, or north to the South China Sea. The great island of Borneo would be dead ahead.

Before they set off in any direction, though, they planned to stop for supplies in Batavia, a Dutch port on the northern end of Java. They might manage to find a few deck hands, as well. And if a chance arose before then, they fully intended to refill their casks of fresh water. The water they had now, while still potable, had taken on a green and disturbing color and drinking it required straining the algae against one's teeth.

She savored the distant sight of land a moment longer, then turned to look astern, to where Horatio was at the wheel. He had a wide grin on his face, and she laughed, realizing that he had not been even half as confident of his navigation as he had let on. He'd probably worried that they would be at sea forever, perhaps sailing in circles until their food and water ran out and they had to eat Mango for dinner.

She climbed back down the ratlines and leapt lightly to the deck. Ruut and Gianni were belowdecks, asleep, and she considered waking them to share the news, but decided against it. Sleep had become more precious than gold for all of them.

Mango jogged along beside her on top of the ship's rail as she made her way aft. She had trained the little fiend to stay off her shoulders, but with Chartier gone Mango had attached himself to her more firmly than before, as if he were a frightened child abandoned to the world. Sometimes he would hold his tiny admiral's hat and chirrup sadly, his dark brown eyes soft and forlorn, and Anne would feel her heart partially melt. Partially, but not entirely. She had the vivid pink scar on her hand to remind her not to trust him.

She crossed the quarterdeck to Horatio, moving over the pitching deck with the confidence of a long-time sailor.

"You saw it?" Horatio asked, the pride and excitement vibrating in his voice.

"I certainly did, Captain Sir!"

"Thank God," he said, laughing.

"Are you certain it is not Africa we see before us?" Anne asked, teasing.

"If it is, I'll claim that's where I was headed all along. I should hope that even I could keep a boat headed towards the rising sun."

She put her hands on the wheel and nudged him aside. "Go on, go take a look."

He nodded his thanks. "Course east-southeast," he said, and left the wheel to her, going to climb up the same ratlines she had used. She watched him, helpless not to, sparing only the occasional necessary glances at the compass in the binnacle, and at the sails, to check for hints of luffing.

Horatio's skin had darkened to a Spaniard's cast, a rich dark tan that made the whites of his eyes and his teeth brilliant in comparison. These past four weeks she had watched him struggle to put the knowledge of sailing he had known only in theory into practice, and she was proud of his success, and of the way he let Ruut and Ulrich tutor him in the basics of setting sail and tending the ship. It was not every son of a well-to-do family who would admit his ignorance before common sailors, and bow to them as his superiors in knowledge and experience.

There was ease and grace in Horatio's movements now, and a confidence that had not been there before. She looked at him up in the rigging, easily balancing barefooted on a yardarm, one hand carefully holding to the safety of a line as Ruut had warned him to always do. He seemed sure of himself, and more mature than he had been aboard the *Coventry*. He still made light of any difficulties they encountered, and still was optimistic to the point of foolishness, but she was sensing the beginnings of something steady at the heart of him.

Not that it was strong or steady enough to make her regret her rejection of his proposal, that first day the ship was theirs.

They hadn't talked about it, had almost pretended it hadn't happened except for odd times when Horatio made joking comments about their future wedding. She never knew how much his comments were in jest and how much in seriousness, and to this day did not know for certain why he had made his initial proposal.

She had theories aplenty. He wanted a bedmate. He was feeling ecstatic and impulsive, and wanted to share the mood. He wanted to do her a favor. He wanted to make a statement of rebellion and freedom from past restraints. He felt responsible for her.

She didn't know what the truth might be. She only knew her own rationale for refusing, which was that marriage required more than a passing fondness as its foundation. Horatio was not a man who could be re-lied upon in the long run. The rumors she and Miss Godwyn had heard of his fickle heart seemed all too likely to be true. And even beyond that, his choice to go adventuring proved that he was not ready to be a husband. One did not marry an adventurer, however charming.

And she herself was not wife material: Over the past few weeks she felt she had become as much of an adventurer as he, albeit a much more cautious one. She had no intention of settling into maternity and domesticity until her island was found, and the mean-ing of her dreams revealed.

The very misery of sailing the *Cauchemar* had made the quest itself more valuable. She'd invested too much, come too far now to go back to a mundane life, and that's what marriage meant: the end of adventure and exploration. The end of freedom. Horatio might be happy enough to let her climb rigging with her skirts tied up while she was her own person, but she had seen amongst friends and acquaintances how marriage could change a man's opinion of what a wife was allowed to do.

She sometimes felt Horatio's eyes on her, and sometimes found her own eyes straying to his figure. His face, with familiarity, had grown even more appealing: It had a piratical cast now, hair grown shaggy and wild, the softness of land-living worn away by the strenuous life they now led. The sad cast to his eyes held something less of melancholy than before, as if that, too, had been burned away by this new life.

Up on his yardarm, Horatio gave a howl of exhilaration. His joy accentuated her own, making her own happiness at seeing land that much more intense. The day was suddenly brighter, the future more likely to bring success, troubles and trials losing their significance in the face of this small victory.

The silly man, he made her want to dance down the deck and meet him with a hug when he climbed down. It was a good thing she had her head firmly on her shoulders, or moments like this could make her forget her very sensible rationale for not marrying him.

Her joy faltered, the smile on her lips falling slightly. Deep in her heart she knew that whatever affection he felt for her, it was shallow and impulsive. It was not the soul-deep love that was necessary for a lifelong union, and for which she had a secret craving. Never mind what she had told him about friendship being enough in a marriage; she wanted the entire fairy tale, undying love and devotion, and she would not settle for less.

It was that which kept her from allowing any fondness of her own for him to grow beyond a gentle tendre.

At least, she hoped that she was keeping her emotions in check. She was the one who was the fool, if she was not.

Batavia Harbor

"How many guns, Ruut?" Horatio asked, gazing with trepidation at the fort and its massive walls. The flag that flew atop the fort was British, not Dutch as they had expected, and they none of them knew for certain what that meant. It could be a lie, for some reason he could not fathom. And if it truly was the case that the town was now under British control, how likely would its commander be to believe that their ship was British and not French? The *Cauchemar* was infamous, and it would not be inconceivable that a privateer who had taken on ships three times her size might try to take an entire port.

"Four, maybe five?" Ruut suggested.

"I suppose that might make a sufficient salute. Enough to give us some importance, but not so much that we sound arrogant. Damn, I wish we knew what the signals were," he said. Even now the fort was raising a series of colored flags, a code that he as an English ship should be able to answer with flags of his own. They had no code book aboard, though. Pity Chartier never managed to get his hands on one of those. The books had lead covers, and were the first thing to be tossed overboard when a ship was boarded by an enemy.

"Go ahead, fire the salute," he said. Ruut relayed the orders to Ulrich and Gianni, who set off the guns, packed only with gunpowder and wadding, in a steady cadence one after the other.

They waited tensely as the last echoing blast faded, and then a return salute came from the fort.

"They haven't sunk us yet," Horatio said, trying to be cheerful. "I suppose that's a good sign. Perhaps they won't shoot us, either, when we come ashore."

They were anchored out in the harbor, away from the long piers that already accomodated several boats, one of them what appeared to be an English warship. If they were welcomed, they would be towed into place somewhere along the pier, if they wished. First, though, he would have to go ashore and establish his credentials.

"You should be safe here until Ruut and I return," Horatio told Anne, as the one small remaining boat they had was lowered over the side.

"It looks safe enough, but it certainly smells bad," she said.

"Your nose is sensitive from having been at sea."

"I wish I could go with you," she said.

"Despite the danger?"

"I'd brave more than British guns to put my feet on

solid ground again, and to be able to walk more than eighty feet in a straight line. What I'd give to sleep in a bed that did not move! Or to eat fresh bread, especially if someone else baked it. I should like to lie upon the grass and stare at the sky, and feel the ground beneath me. I'd—"

"All right, all right!" he said. "If all is well ashore, I promise you will get your chance. I don't think there's much in the way of lawn or meadow here for you, though."

She shrugged and smiled the easy, quiet smile he had come to adore. She did not look much of a lady in her stained canvas sailor's hat, and her gown with its raw hem that ended above her ankles, the waist gathered in with a sailor's thick black belt. Neither did she look like a lady's maid.

His Anne was becoming something other than the quiet mouse of the *Coventry*. Her defensiveness had faded as she became familiar with him and with the others, and when she was frightened, like during storms, her reaction had been to throw herself into the job at hand, battening hatches and helping to take in sail. The reason might only have been that she knew every hand was desperately needed, but he still admired her pluck. She'd shown a wide-eyed, teeth-gritted determination, and the strength he had always known was in her was now beginning to show itself on the outside.

When he looked at her now, he did not know that there was a word to describe what he saw. She dressed like a female sailor, yet had the soft voice of a gently raised woman. Her feet were bare and callused, yet trod upon the deck boards with the same light grace as if she were wearing silken slippers. She was still quiet and reserved much of the time, yet had developed an easy camaraderie with the others, working beside them and managing to communicate even where, like with Gianni, the language barrier was too wide for most to leap.

His mouse had grown into . . . He racked his brain for a proper metaphor. A rat? A mongoose? A wolverine? No one was ever going to mistake him for a poet. "Mouse" would have to do, a superior and advanced mouse who would stand her ground instead of running to the shadows when trouble came.

"Do I get a kiss for luck?" he asked her.

She made a *tsk* sound and gave him an annoyed look from the corner of her eye.

He grinned, then leaned towards her and gave her a quick peck on the cheek before she could protest. Her hand was raised to push him away, but he was already leaving, joining the others farther down the rail, feeling jaunty and in altogether good spirits.

Ruut rowed, while Horatio sat in the bow of the small boat and looked with uneasy eyes at the fort. If Batavia had still been in Dutch hands, it would be a neutral port as far as the war with the French was concerned. He wouldn't have to worry what colors he flew. On the other hand, Batavia was also supposed to be a place from which the French launched themselves in attack on English East Indiamen en route to China. British was decidedly better, as long as his countrymen didn't mistake him for Chartier.

Horatio turned and looked back at the *Cauchemar*,

at the moment renamed the *Anne*. Anne herself was still at the rail, and she waved to him. He waved back, and took a moment to admire how their ship sat in the water, still sleek and elegant despite all it had been through and their lack of perfect care. On board, it was easy to forget how beautiful the ship was, how graceful its lines when seen from afar.

Gianni had shown some small skill with carpentry, and he had carved the new name boards for the bow and stern. It had seemed a sensible precaution to re-name the boat, a name like *Anne* carrying consider-ably less of a reputation and therefore less likely to get them into trouble than *Cauchemar*. The decision on the ship's new name had not been easily agreed upon.

"I don't want it named after me," Anne had pro-tested.

"Is good name," Ruut had said.

"You like *Monkey Boat*?" Kai had asked.

"It might better describe my sentiments," Anne had said sourly. "Or *Endless Work*."

"*Ann-gelina*, is good?" Gianni had put in.

"Nothing with 'Anne!' I do not want to be identified with this ship!"

"Do not fret yourself, my darling," Horatio had said, in as patronizing a tone as he could manage without laughing. "I do not believe anyone will confuse the two of you."

"*Lunatics Afloat*, that's what the name should be."

"*Eh?*" Gianni had said, the words too advanced for his vocabulary.

Anne had gone through a quick pantomime of her

157

meaning. Gianni had laughed, and then Horatio had suggested a vote, of which the outcome was a foregone conclusion. The *Cauchemar* had been rechristened as the *Anne*, no matter its namesake's protests.

He turned forward again, and focused on the town they were approaching. Decisions about the *Anne* were often made by consensus, but it was always understood—also, by consensus—that he was captain. He knew from his experiences in the East India Company how much men needed a figurehead to follow, needed to know that there was someone who was in control and would tell them what to do. When a man's life was in danger, as it was in the army or at sea, he wanted to be part of an efficiently working team headed by a skilled and experienced leader.

He might not be particularly skilled or experienced, but he was learning. This visit to their first port was as much a test as had been the navigation, or their first storm. He was going to do his best to live up to the expectations of his crew. And of Anne. Especially of Anne.

Asking her to marry him like he had had been a mistake both in approach and in sentiment. It had been an impulse that had him proposing, an impulse based not only on his fondness for her and a steadily growing desire, but on the shameful, vain wish to take the easy course to having her look at him in wonder and admiration. It was as if he'd said, "Look at me! I am grand, I am generous, I am offering my hand to a lowly maid." He flushed to even think of it.

He himself had not believed his words as they left his mouth. It was no wonder she had not, either. He had been an arrogant idiot, the only virtue to his proposal being that he sincerely meant to honor the vows he made to her. She had been right to refuse him, and he respected her for it.

Next time he asked, he would make certain she had no reason to say no. He would also do a better job of saying what was in his heart. He had a habit of hiding his feelings behind a smiling, joking face, protecting himself from pain while expecting her to give her own heart over to him. He would strive to do better.

Anne and he were meant to be married—why else would the Hand of Destiny have thrown them together? If they had met in England they would have passed each other by without a second glance, two people from different social worlds who had no reason to interact and thus would never discover how utterly perfect they were for one another.

Anne was his missing piece, his lodestone, the blacksmith of the steel in his spine. His impromptu proposal had been ill-advised and poorly considered, and not what he had expected to come out of his own mouth, yet there had been a truth beneath it that he had not at the time recognized. His heart had known, deep down where he could not see its workings, that Anne Hazlett was meant to be Anne Merivale. He was a better man when he was with her, and he loved her for that as much as he loved her for herself.

She needed him, too, and not just to pull her off of sinking ships or prod her into drugging pirates. She needed him to remind her of what a treasure she was, of how brave her heart and gentle her soul. She needed him to make her realize in both heart and head that she had more strength and intelligence in her than she knew.

Perhaps, though, she already knew about her intelligence. He had to admit, there were times he got the distinct feeling she believed herself smarter and more reasonable than he. She might not need any encouragement in that area.

He drew his thoughts back to the present circumstances, as they approached the dock and a man stepped forward, followed by two armed soldiers. The soldiers appeared to be British, but the last thing he wanted to do was prove Anne's opinion of him as an occasional idiot by getting himself shot before he even set foot on land.

He smiled, and called out a greeting.

Chapter Eleven

"Do I look all right?" Anne asked, nervously smoothing down her skirt with her free hand.

"Like a queen," Horatio said, and he patted her hand where it rested in the crook of his arm.

She tried to take reassurance from his opinion, and from what their crew had expressed after she had emerged from the captain's saloon in her newly altered finery, but it was difficult. It was not every day that a lady's maid was invited to dine with the lieutenant governor of Java. She had hastily basted a new hem into the gown, and darts to take in the bodice. She wore stolen jewels at her throat and ears, and wrapped around her wrist. She felt like a fraud, like a child playing dress-up.

She tried to distract herself looking at the sights—such as they were—of Batavia. She and Horatio were walking along one of the stone-paved streets, a canal on her left, Dutch buildings on their right. They'd passed through the warehouse section of town, and were now in a more residential area, if one wished to call it that. It had a flavor of Holland to it, with its canals and tall narrow houses whose façades rose in steps at the roofline. Almost, one could believe one-self to be in a Dutch painting like she had seen in the Godwyn home, rather than six degrees south of the equator on a wild island in the East Indies.

Of course, the heat and humidity would give away the location, if the buildings and canals did not. She snapped open her fan, yet another treasure gleaned from the chests of stolen goods in the hold. The sweat was trickling down the sides of her face, between her breasts, under her arms, in the small of her back—anywhere she could sweat, she sweated. She was not perspiring or growing rosy. She was leaking like a rot-ten row boat, and she was sure she would soon be seeing dark stains under her arms, marring the pale blue silk she wore.

She could barely stand to admit it, but after only one day in port she already missed being at sea, where except in the doldrums there was always a breeze to cool the skin. Here, the air was stagnant with heat and moisture, and whenever they passed through cool shade they had the annoyance of mosquitoes with which to contend, buzzing their high-pitched whine and leaving red and itching welts upon exposed skin.

The smells here were worse than aboard ship, as well, the stench of swamp, decomposing vegetation, human and animal waste, and the occasional nause-ating stink of rotting meat and grease all coming together to turn the air into a thick soup of odors that seemed to coat her throat and lungs with every breath.

If she weren't so hot, and so nervous she felt on the verge of throwing up, she would laugh at how eager she had been to come ashore. Ha ha ha. It did not even feel as if she were on solid ground: The earth moved and swayed under her feet, as if it were the deck of a ship. She had not found her "land legs," and stumbled as one of those illusory pitches caught her off balance.

"Are you all right, Anne?" Horatio asked, looking down at her with concern in his green-blue eyes.

She gave him a weak smile. "Of course. Splendid." She fanned herself a little harder, trying to ignore how her fingers and ankles had swollen with the heat. She felt like a boiled sausage.

"It shouldn't be much farther now."

Whatever her physical discomforts, she had to admit that Batavia was not completely without its interests, namely the native men who walked by, dressed in what appeared to be elaborately folded and gathered skirts, in prints of various color and design. With these skirts they wore high-collared jackets with a single row of buttons down the front, and narrow wraps of cloth on their heads. The attire bore some resemblance to that of a Scotsman in its components, but the effect was infinitely more exotic and conjured up images of Oriental potentates. She knew logically that these men were no more special than she and Horatio, yet with their ornate knives tucked into sashes and the intricate designs on their skirt-like wraps, they looked like they should be sitting on a pillow smoking a hookah rather than walking the dirt-dusted streets like ordinary people.

They rounded a corner, and up ahead they saw a house larger than its neighbors, with a small yard in front overflowing with flowers. A soldier stood at either side of the entrance, and the British flag flew from a pole attached to the front of the house several feet above the doorway.

"This looks like the place," Horatio said cheerfully. "Are you ready to be proclaimed a heroine?"

Her lips parted, but no words came out before they were at the door, Horatio presenting the invitation to one of the soldiers, and it was too late to protest. What, oh what had Horatio been telling people?

They were ushered into the stone-flagged great hall, the air marginally cooler inside. Her eyes were still blinded from the bright late-afternoon sunlight, and it took a moment of blinking before she could discern several large wooden carvings of native design arranged haphazardly against the walls, as if shoved there in a hurry. In the very center of the room sat an entire canoe. It was not what she had expected to see upon first setting foot inside the abode of an English lieutenant governor. Spicy smells of cooking reached her from elsewhere in the house, hinting at a meal that would be as foreign as the carvings.

"Captain Merivale, Miss Hazlett!" a man said, appearing in the doorway of a room off to the right. "It is an honor to meet you both." He came forward, taking her hand and bowing over it. "Stamford Raffles at your service." She looked at the top of his head in astonishment, not used to being treated so, and certainly not having expected the lieutenant governor to look and act like he did. For some reason she had expected a white-haired and red-faced old general, with a paunch and a bellowing voice. Stamford Raffles, however, was of medium height, with short, wavy brown hair and a fine-featured face. He looked young to be a lieutenant governor, and far more scholarly than warlike.

"Sir, it is I who am honored," Anne said softly, barely managing to find her voice.

"Nonsense! From what I hear, you are the heroine of the Seven Seas! I wish my wife were here—she would have loved to meet you. Now she'll just have to make do with my own version of the tale, and plenty unsatisfied she will be with that, I can assure you."

Anne turned wide eyes on Horatio. *What* had he been telling people? She knew that he loved to spin exagerrated tales for their entertainment aboard the *Anne*, but she had never expected him to do so amongst strangers. And certainly not with *her* as a character.

"And Captain Merivale," Raffles said, turning to Horatio. "I hear you are on a mission to establish new trade relations under the noses of the Dutch and the Portuguese. We have much to discuss, and I think I may have some information that will be of interest to you both." He rubbed his hands together and smiled, a charming, boy-like grin that reminded Anne of Horatio in its enthusiasm. "I don't think I've looked forward to an evening so much since . . . Well, since a month and a half ago when we landed and routed the Dutch."

"From what I gathered around town, it was an astounding victory."

Raffles made a dismissive sound. "There was hardly any fight to speak of. I almost felt the Dutch were happy enough for the excuse to leave, and good riddance to them. The atrocities of their government, the enslavement of the natives—" he cut himself off, looking at Anne and smiling. "But there will be time for such talk later. Come, you both are in need of refreshment."

He led the way to the back of the shadowed hall, giving Anne a chance to take a longer look at the astounding canoe. Raffles caught her looking at it. "Later I will show you the beginning of my Java collection, if you wish. I had to leave most of my things on Sumatra, but already I have found people here who are willing to bring me carvings and puppets."

Anne smiled and began to relax. Not only did Raffles not seem to know that she was a maid in lady's clothing, she doubted very much that he would care even if he did. If she was not mistaken, she thought she caught the hint of a less-than-noble upbringing in his bearing. Intuition told her that this was a man who had risen to where he was on his intelligence, not on his family connections.

She glanced up at Horatio. He met her eyes and winked, looking as enchanted as she with their host for the evening.

They were led to the garden in back, where a pergola covered in flowered vines shaded a table and chairs. The day was quickly turning to dusk, and as the light went so did a little of the heat, a meager breeze rising to take its place. A fountain sprayed nearby, its mist occasionally reaching Anne when the faint breeze shifted.

Raffles was happily naming the plants in the garden for them, dismissing those that had been Dutch in origin and exulting over the native species. Anne listened with half an ear, enjoying the setting and the company, the pineapple juice served to her in a tall glass, the quiet appearance and retreat of the native servants whom Raffles addressed in their own tongue. For the moment all was right in the world, her needs taken care of, no worries but when dinner might be served.

Horatio caught her eye, holding her gaze while he lifted his own glass to drink, and she smothered a smile. She could see he was amused by Raffles's botanical passions, and was paying little more attention to the lesson than she, herself.

"Not so frightening a pair, I don't think!" a man said, stepping out into the garden from the house, causing both Anne and Horatio to turn in surprise. "Hard to see how they could have chased the infamous Chartier from his own ship. Ha! Cowardly dogs, that's the French for you!"

"Captain Merivale, Miss Hazlett, allow me to introduce the Reverend Mr. Jenkins," Raffles said.

"Has he been boring you with his plants?" the reverend asked, mopping sweat off his smooth brow with a kerchief. The man was short, plump, and completely

167

bald. His age was unfathomable, his eyes deepset and dark.

"I would not have bored them if you had arrived on time," Raffles said. He turned to Anne and Horatio. "I did not want you to have to tell your story twice."

"I imagine it will improve with each recounting," Horatio said, making both the men laugh. Anne hid behind her glass of juice, embarrassed ahead of time for whatever role she would play in the story Horatio had concocted. The truth had had little of bravery or honor to it, and plenty of opium-induced disgrace. She could not forget that she had passed out in front of them all and had wept with fear and frustration— not that they'd seen that last part.

Dinner was announced by one of the soft-voiced native servants, and they went upstairs to dine at the heavy, carved Dutch table with its straight-backed, medieval-looking chairs. The meal was composed of large parts rice with several spicy side dishes of meats and vegetables, all served on Chinese porcelain that Mrs. Godwyn would have given both Pamela and her favorite lapdog to lay hands on, it was so delicate and beautifully painted. It seemed almost a sin to cover the graceful flowers and birds with food.

As soon as everyone was seated and served, Horatio began his tale, starting from that day on the deck of the *Coventry* when sails had been sighted on the horizon.

"Of course we knew they were pirates, and Miss Hazlett's traveling companion was terrified, but Miss Hazlett is made of sterner stuff. She said to me, 'If they're French pirates, then let them try to attack!

We'll show them what the English are made of. We'll give them a taste of our guns, we will! We've a ship of good English oak, and no French iron will be shattering our sides, you mark my words.' "

"Admirable!" the reverend murmured, as Anne choked on her food. The men looked at her in concern.

"Spicy," she explained in a hoarse whisper, her eyes watering as she reached for her glass of wine.

Horatio described the storm in deck-washing, lightning-striking detail, rumbling out the thunder and the crash of a mast hitting the deck. Anne's eyes grew wide in horrified fascination as he spoke of maimed sailors wrapped in ropes, pulled over the side. She knew Horatio had been down in his cabin through most of the sinking, knew that he could have seen none of this, yet it was so vivid she could believe he had.

"Miss Hazlett dragged her traveling companion to safety in the longboats, but then one of the other women cried that her child had been lost in the confusion. Miss Hazlett insisted on going back into the roundhouse to search for the little girl, the only man brave enough to accompany her the father of the child. Miss Hazlett finally found the tyke, huddled under the overturned cot in her cabin, terrified to within an inch of her poor little life. Just as she reached the girl, the portholes burst open, water flooding in."

Anne ducked her face down, picking at her food with her heavy silver fork. She cast a sidelong look at their dining companions and saw that neither was eating, too engrossed were they in the tale. Horatio paused to take a drink of his wine, and when the pause went on too long Raffles prodded, "Yes? The water was flooding in, what then?"

"And then," Horatio said, his voice catching. He stopped, and cleared his throat as if it had tightened with tears of emotion. Anne narrowed her eyes at him, thinking him a very bad actor. "And then she pulled the child free, handing her up to her father who was in the doorway that was now above her head. 'Save her,' Miss Hazlett said. 'Take her to the boats. Go! Do not worry about me!' And he went, leaving Miss Hazlett alone in the darkness, in a ship that would all too soon be her grave. She would willingly have died so that a tender innocent could have a chance to live."

"Incredible," the reverend murmured in awe.

Incredible, indeed.

Horatio continued on in the same vein, casting Anne as the heroine of the tale and himself and the others as her willing subordinates. He seemed to feel no need to claim the reverend's or Raffles's admiration for himself, and his downplaying of his own actions finally got to be too much for Anne to bear. To hear him tell it, he had been a helpless idiot while she commanded events like a field marshal. She forgot her inherent reserve amongst strangers and spoke her mind.

"He is not telling the story as it happened," she said, breaking into his account of how she had kept their spirits up aboard the flotsam raft. "I was miserable and frightened. Horatio was the one who kept us all believing that we would survive. He was the one who kept us hoping, not I, and I won't let him have you thinking anything different."

"Your modesty is commendable, my dear," the reverend said.

"It is not modesty, it is the truth. I cannot fathom why Horatio would paint himself in such a helpless light and me in such a courageous one. If not for him, I would have died two months ago, or been in danger of throwing myself overboard a dozen times since then." In her fire to correct their perception, she forgot to refer to Horatio as Mr. Merivale, and it wasn't until her impassioned speech came to an end that she saw the way Mr. Raffles and the reverend were looking at her, eyebrows raised, glances going between her and Horatio, as if assessing exactly how friendly their relations actually were.

She frowned fiercely and clamped her lips shut.

"I have asked Miss Hazlett to be my wife," Horatio said softly into the following silence. "I know that to men such as yourselves I do not need to state that I am a man of honor, and of course Miss Hazlett's is beyond question."

Raffles coughed, his cheeks coloring. "Of course. I would have thought nothing different."

"It is fortunate I am here, then, is it not?" the reverend said.

Anne blinked, a feeling of dread coming over her. "How do you mean, sir?" she asked.

The reverend smiled broadly. "Why, I can marry you!" He gestured towards Raffles. "With the lieutenant governor here as witness, I cannot imagine that any would question the lack of banns being called.

We can see you two wed this very night."

"But—" Anne said.

"You have taken my fiancée by surprise," Horatio said. "She had been assuming it would be months before we would have an opportunity to be wed. I don't think that she is quite ready to reconcile herself to the idea of being Mrs. Merivale forever after."

"It wouldn't do for you two to sail off without making your vows," Raffles said. "It would be quite foolish, really, when you have such an opportunity before you now. It could be months before you have another chance like this. And Miss Hazlett, my dear," he said, reaching over and taking her hand in a gesture of paternal care, "I would consider it a great honor if you would allow me to take the place of your father and give you away."

"That is most kind of you, sir, but I do think that tonight would be too soon, as Mr. Merivale suggests," she said, her voice an octave higher than usual. "And besides, I could not think of wedding without our crew present. They have become as family to us."

Raffles gave her fingers a squeeze and then released them, sitting back and looking satisfied. "Not to worry. We'll postpone the festivities until tomorrow, so that your crew may attend. You will spend the night here, under my protection, as befits a single young woman."

"We cannot leave our ship completely unattended," Horatio said.

"I will post soldiers on board during the wedding," Raffles said easily. "How I wish my wife were here! She would love this!"

"Really, we could not ask so much of you," Anne said feebly.

"Nonsense. As lieutenant governor, I insist. I do not believe I could in good conscience allow you to leave Batavia unwed."

Anne met Horatio's eyes, looking for help. He shrugged, then smiled as if helpless to change things. This was all still a lark to him, the search for the island, marriage to her, the taking of the *Cauchemar*, everything. He was probably thinking, "Why the hell not? I've got nothing better to do, at least not at the moment."

"I am not certain I wish to be married," Anne said softly.

"Of course you do," the reverend said dismissively.

"As I said, I insist," Raffles said, and this time there was no leeway or levity in his tone. "My wife would never forgive me if I let you continue on your way without a ring upon your finger and Mr. Merivale's good name added to your own."

Unwelcome understanding dawned: Raffles had the power to keep her on Java, or send her home again if she refused. She should have been able to predict this outcome, if she had thought about it. It was just barely acceptable for a single woman to travel alone with men if the alternative was death, but it would not do for that same woman to continue traveling in such circumstances by choice. If an offer of marriage was presented, she was expected to take it— and thank the heavens for her good fortune while she was at it.

"Then I suppose we have no choice but to accept

your generous offer. Do we, dear?" Anne said, looking over at Horatio and grinning with gritted teeth.

He looked wary, but covered it well enough. "It will be a tale to tell our children, how we were wed in Batavia. It's very romantic, don't you think?"

"Very," Anne said sweetly. She turned back to Raffles. "I will need to return to the ship for proper clothes tonight. I have a dress in which I would like to be wed, but it requires some alteration."

"I'll come with you both. We can go down to the docks in my carriage, and I will station the guards aboard as well. Your crew might appreciate the chance to leave duty behind for a short spell."

Anne pulled her lips back in what might pass for a smile. So much for any plans to slip away in the night.

"Here's to Anne Hazlett, my lady bride!" Horatio said, raising his wine glass.

"Hear, hear!" Raffles and the reverend said.

"And to my gentleman husband," Anne said, trapped with no escape. "May he reap what he sows."

"I say, that is a rather odd sentiment," the reverend remarked, his glass halfway to his lips.

"You think that only because you have not been married," Raffles said, giving a nod of appreciation to Anne. "Women know. Sow love and devotion, and that is what you shall reap."

The reverend grunted his approval and drank.

Anne met Horatio's eyes over the rim of her glass, and she silently promised him anything but.

Chapter Twelve

She could never have dreamed this. However strange her nighttime visions of the island, the red and gold kingfisher, the houses on stilts and the deep, dark green of the jungle, nothing could compare to what she saw at this moment, before the sun-faded front of the old Portuguese church.

Ulrich had borrowed a guitar somewhere, and true to his statement that he would be court poet and musician in her mythical kingdom he was playing it softly, some ancient Norwegian tune that she could not recognize but that seemed oddly apt to the proceedings.

Mango, in his admiral's uniform, was busy fighting the leash and collar that attached him to a nearby tree. It wasn't that they didn't want him to run away: that would have been fine. Keeping him from running *to* her was the problem. The overgrown rat with hands had gone on a rampage of destruction when confined alone in one of the cabins. Defeated by simian ill temper, they had reluctantly decided to bring him along. He had donned his uniform himself, once it was taken out of Chartier's chest and handed to him.

Ruut was Horatio's best man, and stood as stiff, formal, and stern-faced as if he were giving evidence in an admiralty court proceeding. There was pride to his stance as well, a hint of self-importance that was accentuated by the borrowed finery he wore. When the Dutch had been routed from town, more than a few possessions had been left behind, and it was among them that Ruut had found the green velvet coat and formal breeches he wore. He had to be sweltering in them.

Gianni was both florist and milliner. He had put together a veil with a crown of white and green jasmine, heavenly in its heavy scent. He had with great glee tramped through the small gardens of Batavia whacking down blossoms of huge size and brilliant hue, putting together for Anne a bouquet the likes of which no fair English maiden had ever seen. It had tendrils of vine and flower that reached the ground, and was so heavy she had to hold the mass of flowers cradled in her arms like a baby.

Kai was the strangest of them all. She had seen him and Ulrich whispering together, Ulrich using his hands to gesture and explain in the expressive Italian way that they had all begun to pick up from Gianni. When they were finished, Kai had come over to her and said quite plainly, "I maid of honor."

"A maid is a woman, Kai," she had said.

"I know. You see woman here?"

"No."

"I maid of honor."

Well, why not? "Thank you, Kai. That is very sweet of you."

She hadn't seen Kai again until a few minutes ago, when he had shown up at Raffles's house to walk with her and Raffles the short distance to the church. He was wearing formal wear "borrowed" from the absent Dutch, a lovely dark blue silk coat and breeches and frothy white shirt. His black hair was an inch long all over his head except for the long queue, which had been coiled atop his head and surrounded with bright blossoms. In his hands he carried a bouquet which was a smaller version of her own.

If not for the men's clothing and her own knowledge of his sex, she might have almost thought Kai a lovely maid of honor. Something about the flowers and the arrangement of hair emphasized the delicacy of his features and the softness of his skin, which Anne had never seen to need shaving. It was a marvel that the woman-hungry Kai would consent to looking effeminate himself, for her benefit. At least he had not gone so far as to wear a dress—that would have been too strange even for this gathering.

They had all taken the news of the impending nuptials with much greater equanimity than she had expected. They were neither surprised nor dismayed, and overall seemed to believe that the marriage was but a step in the natural course of events. The Englishman and the Englishwoman were to be wed. Of course! Who could have thought any differently? Their interest was centered more on what role they themselves got to play in the ceremony than in whether the wedding was a good idea to begin with.

She was little better than they were. By the time she had returned with Raffles to his house last night, she had been too exhausted to do anything other than fall into bed. She'd been certain that her racing thoughts would keep her awake, but heat, weariness, wine, and a comfortable bed all worked together to send her into a sleep of whose dreams she could recall nothing upon waking except for the flash of the kingfisher's wings.

No conclusions had been reached in her own mind, no comprehension of the change that was about to be wrought in her life. It was as if the shock of it had shut down both brain and heart, leaving only the shallow concerns of how to arrange her hair, and if her oversized shoes would stay on her feet. She had become Miss Godwyn.

Horatio was standing on the church steps beside Ruut and the Reverend Jenkins, dressed in black and an emerald embroidered waistcoat, his tall boots polished to a shine, his usually tousled hair subdued and parted on the side, giving him the look of a rambunctious boy forced to attend church. His true thoughts on these nuptials, she still did not know. There had not been a moment of privacy between them from dinner last night until now.

"Are you ready, my dear?" Raffles asked. He looked kind and wise, his features even softer through the veiling over her eyes. It seemed wrong that one so apparently harmless could cause such monstrous problems.

Her mother had once told her that there was always a choice, which was true. She could refuse to wed Horatio, and then Raffles would keep her here and put her on the next ship bound for England, for the protection of her honor. Or, she could go through with the wedding and continue her search for the island.

What was one little marriage as an obstacle, compared to pirates and shipwrecks? A marriage was a trivial thing, hardly life or death. What would it be but a ring upon her finger? She could take it off and pretend it did not exist, and it would be as if this day had never happened. No one need ever know that she had wed Horatio Merivale on an island in the East Indies. It was a lark, a game, a moment in a tableau.

"I wish my mother and father were here," she said. "And my brothers and sisters. Don't you think that siblings should see their sister wed?"

"And parents, too, my dear. We will send them a letter and inform them of the happy event."

A letter! Marvelous idea! So much for keeping this charade a secret. One could always hope it was lost, but the chances of that were slim when it would carry the seal of a lieutenant governor. On the other hand, at least her parents would know she was still alive.

"Come, your bridegroom is waiting."

"So he is."

Raffles nodded to Kai, who preceded them, and then Ulrich changed the tempo and tune of his playing to something grand and important, to herald the arrival of the glorious bride.

She didn't know whether to smile or look solemn as she walked with Raffles, her mouth settling somewhere in between. She probably looked like she was smirking. She and Raffles moved in a stately manner to the front steps, and then up them to join Horatio where they would be wed at the church door.

"You look beautiful," Horatio whispered to her while Raffles was stepping away and the others were taking their places.

"I'm sweating," she whispered back.

She did like her gown, though—that was one bright spot. It was a pale peach that flattered her skin, with a high waist and a narrow trim of ivory lace at neckline and sleeves. She had lost weight since the shipwreck, her breasts shrinking and her collarbone taking on a hint of definition where it had been invisible before. She felt sinewy, like an underfed chicken that spent too much time running about, but the gown made her look soft and feminine, and unlike a woman who hoisted sails or dragged slabs of salted pork out of barrels.

The service began, and she tried to concentrate on what was being said. Every three or four words, her attention would be distracted by the rustling of Mango over by the tree, by the shifting of Ruut in his sweaty suit, by the loud buzz of a cicada from the lintel of the doorway, its noise sounding as if it were from a monstrous machine, not a mere insect.

She felt that she could discern each of the hundreds of smells around her: the jasmine in her hair, the silk she wore, the faint whiff of mildew from her long-suffering stays, the soap on her skin, her own perspiration. She could smell Horatio: clean linen, sandalwood soap, boot polish, a trace of something alcoholic recently imbibed, and under it all a scent that was his alone, although she had no words to describe it. The world itself was fuzzy and indistinct through her veil, but the sounds and smells pressed in on her, imprinting themselves in her memory.

The reverend droned, his voice blending into the noise of the cicada. A rivulet of sweat began to creep its way down her temple. She was hot under the veil, trapped with her own breath and the heat of her body. She heard her name and forced herself to concentrate, repeating the words the reverend gave her, the sounds as meaningless in her mouth as if she had been speaking Malay.

And then Horatio was turning towards her, lifting her veil. She helped him, desperate to escape the confinement. He leant close, his mouth near her ear as he folded the netting behind her. "It will be all right," he whispered to her. "Trust me."

She shivered, and it was the feel of his breath on her ear that caused it, and the brief, light touch of his fingertips on the side of her neck as he pushed back the veil. And then he kissed her, softly, tenderly, a touch of affection that would not embarrass her by displaying lust in front of so many onlookers, although lust was what it stirred in her. She leaned forward after his retreating lips when the kiss ended, recalling herself only as her balance shifted and she was in danger of falling forward into him.

"I present to you Captain and Mrs. Horatio Merivale," the reverend announced.

A cheer went up in the small group, and then another. Raffles was grinning, pleased with himself. Ulrich was hugging Kai, Gianni was bouncing on the balls of his feet, and Ruut began to weep. Mango finally broke free of his bonds and went racing back and forth, cheeping and screeching, pausing only to bite Ruut lightly on the calf in a fit of monkeyish excitement.

Horatio put his arm around Anne, holding her close to his side in a comforting, almost brotherly gesture. "You're mine now, Mrs. Merivale," he said, squeezing her, and kissed the top of her head.

"Woe betide us both," she said.

"Nonsense. Chin up, Anne," he said, his voice at its most cheerful. "You must admit, this is all very romantic."

"And the Hand of Destiny arranged it," she said glumly.

"That's the spirit! Now throw the bouquet. I think Kai has his eye on it."

"Mango took one look at Mrs. Merivale and lost his heart to her," Horatio said, continuing the tale that he had begun the night before. They were in the garden of Raffles's house, crevets of burning wood lighting the growing darkness, the drifting smoke helping to keep away the mosquitoes while the flames drew moths the size of his hand.

What minor notables could be found in the newly English Batavia had come to enjoy the wedding festivities, the news of the nuptials, as well as of the exciting capture of the *Cauchemar*, the talk of the town.

The victory over Chartier was as nothing compared to the taking of an entire island, but the new residents of Batavia seemed to think an encounter with a notorious French privateer more romantic than their own ousting of the Dutch from Java.

"I didn't know that's what he was thinking when he came tearing across the deck, making that hideous *eeep eeep eeep* noise. I thought for certain he was jealous of the attention she was garnering from Chartier, and that the little beast was intent on dragging her overboard if he could manage the feat."

The monkey in question was lying drowsily in a pile of half-masticated papaya, an overturned wine goblet beside him. His hat was askew, his admiral's jacket smeared with frosting from the wedding cake.

"Ulrich tried to hold me back, sensing that Mango's true intent was love-inspired, but I could not be so objective. That was my lady love he was about to attack! I dove across the deck at him, tackling him, but I had no idea of the danger to be found in an impassioned monkey. He got my knife away from me, and threw it to Chartier."

There were at least twelve people listening spellbound, his own crew included. He'd been including them in his creative retelling of events, seeing their eyes light up at mention of their own names. They seemed to be enjoying his version of the truth, and the dramatic light in which they were being painted. He'd always thought that there was no reason to tell events exactly as they'd occurred, if a bit of embroidery could better entertain his listeners.

"Chartier was about to use my own knife to put an

end to my sad existence when Mrs. Merivale stepped forward, sighing pathetically as if the day had been altogether too wearying for her already. 'Capitaine Chartier,' she said, all weak and helpless, 'could you take me to my cabin? I'm feeling faint from the heat. And poor Mr. Merivale here, he is plainly suffering from madness, from drinking all that salt water. I did warn him against it.' And just like that, she saved my life yet again. She did not so much as cringe when the monkey climbed up onto her shoulder and wrapped its arms around her neck, enduring its filthy touch for the sake of myself and of our crew."

Approving looks were sent to Anne, who didn't notice them. She was gazing deep into her wine glass, as she had been for the last half hour. Horatio didn't know how much she had had to drink, but apparently it had not been enough to make her forget that she had been married today.

His mouse had no idea of how lovely she looked, he was sure of it. The veil had been removed, but the coronet of white jasmine and green leaves were still nestled in her hair, which had been put up in a braided chignon at the nape of her neck. Heat and the activities of the day had coaxed free some of her straight blond hair, and it framed her face now in dampened tendrils. Her cheeks were flushed, from wine or heat or emotion, he knew not which; he knew only that she looked tender and young, and more fragile than at any time before.

His storytelling was but a stall against their wedding night. It was plain enough that Anne was not happy to have been forced to become Mrs. Merivale, and he did not know what approach to take with her tonight.

He himself was pleased as punch that she was now his wife. Anne Merivale. He loved the sound of that.

He supposed there was something ignoble in having put up no protest to Raffles's suggestion that they marry when he knew it was not what Anne wanted, but there were limits to a man's nobility. One might as well ask a starving man to refuse a plate of roast beef.

At least he had made a gesture of considering her feelings, offering the excuse that she was not yet adjusted to the idea of wedding. Raffles and the reverend had smashed that fly of an excuse quickly enough, removing it from the ointment of his future pleasure.

In the back of his mind, he had known that a wedding was a possible outcome of taking Anne to dine with the lieutenant governor. He had heard about town that Raffles was a man of honor, and a single woman sailing with five men would be a situation begging to be put right. And then he himself had nudged events in the preferred direction by announcing that he had asked Anne to be his wife.

Oh, the deviousness of the male heart, intent on satisfying its wants. He ought to be ashamed.

He wasn't. He was as happy as he could ever remember being. He would be happier still if Anne could be persuaded to see that they were meant for each other.

He managed to draw out the telling of the story for another half an hour, then downed a last swallow of wine and summoned his courage. It was time to retire with Anne, and to try to make the best of whatever complaints she chose to throw at him.

For a brief moment he desperately wished it was already the morrow, the night of cajoling and soothing finished, with the happy result of Anne being content to be his wife.

He had a good imagination, he had to admit.

But at least she liked him, didn't she? He often made her smile, and he knew that she relied upon him, trusting that he would look out for her. She was probably not even aware of that herself, but he had seen it in the way she assumed he would help her when she asked, and the way she came to him when worried. Surely out of liking and trust could grow love.

The lust part, that at least there was no question of. He had seen in her eyes that she found him attractive, had sensed it when, over the past few weeks, she stood closer to him than was necessary, or found excuses to touch him, however briefly.

His mood lightened. He might not be able to fool himself into thinking that Anne would joyfully resign herself to being Mrs. Merivale, but on their wedding night he could show her that it was not the sorrowful sentence she seemed to believe. He could at least give her pleasure.

Tonight need not be eight hours of anger and tears, after all. Hurrah!

She was Mrs. Horatio Merivale. It was beyond comprehension.

"This is nicer than spending the night aboard the *Anne*, don't you think?" Horatio asked, as the servant left them alone in the bedroom of one of the Dutch houses. It had been prepared for their night together, vases full of Gianni's pilfered blooms on every surface.

Anne pressed her lips together in anxiety, saying nothing about their bridal bower. She couldn't believe she was having a wedding night, and with Horatio, of all people. The ring felt heavy on her finger, alien and obtrusive, reminding her of what was done. She had chosen it herself from the rings in Chartier's chest, her choice easy as this was the only one that had fit. The gold band was broad, the pale blue stone set in it the size of her thumbnail.

"I'm sorry now that I ever wished to sleep on a bed that did not move. God heard my wish, and saw fit to teach me a lesson in his method of granting it," she said.

The bed in question was low and wide, with only one thin mattress upon an underlying lattice frame. Netting draped from a ring above, to save their sweating skin from the mosquitoes, but allow in whatever breeze might chance upon them through the louvered balcony doors. Apparently even the Dutch had seen fit to make some accommodations to the heat of the tropics. Thick feather beds and heat-retaining curtains would be a punishment, not a luxury in this climate.

Horatio lit additional candles around the room, then pulled back the edge of the mosquito netting, looking in. "Gianni has been in here as well." He sniffed. "Jasmine, like in your hair."

At the reminder, she reached up and removed the coronet from her head, holding it in her hands for a moment, examining the small waxy flowers that were showing the first signs of wilting, although their fragrance remained strong.

She set the coronet on a table, then felt a rush of determination. "Horatio—"

"Anne—" he said at the same time.

They both stopped. She saw the hint of amusement in his eyes, the devil-may-care lightheartedness that charmed and infuriated her both.

"I don't know how you can be so cheerful," she said. "This was a great mistake, and if you don't realize it now, you certainly will later."

"It was a stroke of good fortune, is what it was, and I hope to help you recognize that soon enough."

"Then you've set yourself quite a task," she said, and walked to the other end of the room, pushing open one of the louvered doors to look out at the small, dark garden below, and the canal beyond it, the damp green scent of the water finding her even at this distance. The stars were scattered thickly overhead, their light echoed in the slow yellow-green flashes of fireflies in the garden below.

"I'm looking forward to it," he said.

Surprised, she turned to find him only a few steps from her, his crooked half-smile in place but the look in his eyes intense and serious. She took a step back, her eyes widening.

"Horatio, I have been thinking."

"This is no time for that. For shame, my dear," he said, closing the space between them.

"Horatio! I have been thinking that I have a way out of this dilemma we have gotten ourselves into," she said, stepping back again.

"The only thing we need get out of is our clothing."

She put up her hands, palms out. "Just because I married you does not mean you have the right to maul me!"

He stopped. "I have no intention of 'mauling' you, my darling. I should hope my lovemaking has more finesse than that."

"I was thinking, all we need do to escape this is to remain celibate."

"What?" he said, his voice pitching upward.

She had his attention, that was clear. "If we do not consummate the marriage, we can later have it annulled."

"That is a very bad idea."

"It's perfect!"

"No, it's absolutely the worst idea ever held by a woman in the history of creation."

"A man *would* say that. How many women have you asked?"

"Don't try to pretend to me that women do not want consummation as badly as men."

Anne gasped. "We never!"

"You just don't talk about it, is all. You keep it secret."

"Why, what utter rubbish! Are you implying that I—"

"I'm not implying at all. I know. You have the same hungers I do, Anne Merivale. I've seen the way you look at me when you think I don't see."

"Beastly man! How dare you?" The blush started at her chest, and rose in burning fire up her neck, over her face and into her hair. How had he known what

189

she was thinking? Oh dear God, how much did he suspect of her wayward thoughts?

"You've imagined my hand on your breast, haven't you? Perhaps even imagined that I lay beside you in your bed?"

"I'm an honorable woman, sir!"

"My honorable wife. I *like* it that you lust after me." He waggled his eyebrows at her.

She stared in horror at him, then when he gave his eyebrows another waggle she forgot her embarrassment and burst out laughing.

He pulled in his chin, his lips turning down. "Do you mock me, wife?"

"I'll mock you 'til sunrise, each night of our marriage. You had me fooled there, Horatio, I thought you were serious."

His playacting at affront vanished, and a truly devilish grin tilted his lips, his eyes narrowing like a cat finding its prey. "What makes you think that I was not?"

Her laughter gurgled to a stop. "But you *were* joking. Weren't you?"

He took her hand, and she let him lead her back over to the bed. There was nothing threatening in his movements, and she was so used to being in his company that she gave no thought to it when he gestured for her to sit on the bed where the mosquito netting had been pulled aside. They had sat beside each other many times, studying charts or splicing ropes, mixing tar or eating a meal. So she sat, and when he pulled off his boots, she kicked off her overlarge slippers and enjoyed the air on damp feet that had become accustomed to going bare.

"What are we going to do?" she asked.

"We're going to take the best from this, and leave needless worries for another day. Preferably a day that will never come," he added, taking off his jacket and tossing it across the room. It landed over the back of a chair. He untied his cravat, then pulled that off and tossed it as well. "Thank God, I can breathe again," he said.

She slanted a look at the opening of his shirt and the tanned skin now revealed, with its tantalizing dusting of dark hairs. Her dream of him lowering himself over her came back with muscle-weakening force, and suddenly he was no longer her friend and shipmate, but a man with whom she might lie entwined, flesh to flesh.

Awareness of his proximity shimmered over her skin in flushing waves, and her stomach sank down to her loins. She could lie with him this very night, and there was not a soul in the world who would find fault in her actions. They were married. God expected them to have sex. Her parents would expect her to have sex. Everyone in Batavia would assume on the morrow that they had had sex, whether they had or not.

Horatio was hers for the taking.

She leaned towards him, her eyes on that opening in his shirt, that opening that had been taunting her for weeks. She was vaguely aware that if she had not had so much wine she might very well be sitting on the other side of the room, but ignored the thought. It was no fun.

"Anne?" Horatio asked as she lowered her head in front of him.

She could feel the heat coming off his skin, smell that unique scent that was Horatio. The candlelight made a faint sheen on his damp skin, and she could see the pulse in the hollow at the base of his neck. Closer she came, until she was so close she could no longer focus her eyes. She shut them, and then with the tip of her tongue reached out and tasted that vee of salty skin.

Horatio jerked and gripped her upper arms in his hands as if to hold her away, but when her tongue flicked out again he kept her where she was, his hands on her arms so tight they hurt. His breathing was harsh to her ears, and she imagined she could feel the beat of his heart through the tip of her tongue.

She lifted her head and sat straight again, and he released her. "I've been wanting to do that for a long time," she said.

He looked at her as if he couldn't believe what had just happened: Christmas had come in the middle of summer. Sweetmeats were raining from the sky.

"That's all that I'm going to do with you upon this bed, Horatio Merivale. I may be drunk, but I am not going to consummate this marriage."

The sweetmeats went rotten, and Christmas proved a grave disappointment. "Don't play with me Anne, not like that. It's not worthy of you."

"I thought all you liked to do was play. Can I not serve you some of the same in return?"

"I never played with you in that way, and I never would. I have always been sincere in my caring for you, and would never have laid a finger on you if my heart did not agree."

He sounded so sincere, she wanted to believe him. Yet even if he was telling the truth, was it the truth only of this moment, and of those other impulsive moments, or was it a truth she could count on to be steady through time?

"Why don't you believe me?" he asked when she remained silent. "I can see it in your eyes. It's as if you want to accept what I say but choose not to. Why, Anne? What have I done to make you think me other than an honorable man?"

"Have you been in love before, Horatio?"

"A few times."

"I have never been in love. It came easily to you, didn't it?" she asked.

"Because it came easily did not mean it was of any less value, if that is what you mean to imply."

"And will you tell me now that what you feel for me is different from what you felt for those other women, that this time you know we were meant to be together?"

"You know I will."

"I would lay money you told those other women the same thing, and meant it when you said it, too." Even as he proved her right with his answers, she was saddened. She wanted to think that maybe he did love her, with the type of love that would last a lifetime.

"Are you jealous of them, those women in the past? I've forgotten them. They mean nothing to me."

She held open her palm to him, saying without words that he had just proven her case all over again.

He took her hand and held it between both of his, his thumb playing with the wedding ring on her finger. He met her eyes, his gaze steady, demanding that she listen. "I've forgotten them because none of them were the woman with whom I was meant to spend my life. You are that woman, Anne."

"I am your momentary passion."

She wanted to believe differently, wanted it so badly her heart ached, but the same excessive caution that kept her from doing so much else kept her from believing in him, as well. She needed more than promises that could so easily prove empty.

"You flit from one adventure to the next, Horatio, and for all I know from one woman to the next, as well. You were flirting with Miss Godwyn only moments before you began flirting with me. As I see it, the only reason you have paid so much attention to me is that there is no one else to be had out here. If we were in England—no, even if we were in India—you would not be sitting beside me pledging your devotion 'til death us do part. You would be dancing and flirting with a beautiful woman from a respectable family, and I would be invisible in the shadows."

He gave a sigh of frustration. " 'What if' could lead us to a thousand other endings than what we have here, but there is not a one of them I would trade for this. Stop being afraid. I know you are not without feelings for me, yet you hide from what you want. Even with your dreams of the island, you act as if you cannot accept them as truth. You think that admitting how much you want something will make it run from you."

"So I should just barrel ahead at whatever takes my fancy, like you do, and consequences be damned?"

"We would be having a lot more fun right now if you would," he replied, grinning.

She almost smiled, but there was too much he didn't understand about her. She felt as if he had not heard what she was trying to say, hidden beneath the words, had not seen what lay at the heart of her. "I'm not like that, and I never will be. It may be your nature to go where the wind blows you, but I can't live that way. I need something more solid beneath my feet, something I know will always be there."

His grin faded, and he lifted her hand, kissing her knuckles as if he were a courtier. "Sometimes you need to cross an unknown sea before you find shore. Take a chance, Anne. I may be the ground you are seeking."

It was tempting, so very tempting to give up good sense and trust herself to him, no matter that he was only a pretend captain of a stolen ship, foolish enough to sail in pursuit of her dreams of a jungled isle and a red kingfisher. But she was taking as much of a chance as her constitution could handle with this quest for the island—risking her heart on a man as unstable as her imagination was more than she could ask of herself. She was stronger with her heart protected than with it left open to Horatio's flirtatious whims.

"I can't risk that you are not," she said at last, tears tightening her throat. Why should doing what was logically right be so hard? Why did it feel so wrong? "I'm not as strong as you think I am. It is better that we remain as we are, friends. It is safer. I know you will not disappoint me as a friend."

"I will not disappoint you as a husband. I swear my life on that." He touched her cheek, then slid his fingers slowly into her hair.

A trembling of anticipation came over her, a will to let him do what he wished and take the decision from her hands. She let him draw her face closer, a desire for reassurance winning out over the warnings of the mind. A kiss was harmless enough, and a touch. There was nothing to lose in such a simple exchange.

His lips settled on hers, resting motionless for a long moment, allowing her time to take in the feel of his closeness: the smoothness of his lips, the warmth of his skin near hers, the barely discernable touch of his breath on her cheek. His fingers dug deeper into her hair, still coiled behind her head, and then his lips moved on hers, brushing lightly, nipping, then nudging them apart to allow his tongue to dip inside. His hand tightened in her hair, his kiss growing harder on her mouth as he gained access, and he began to lower her back onto the bed.

Her eyes widened, a fluttering of anxiety in her stomach. He lay half over her, one hand deep in her hair, the other at the bottom of her ribcage, the heat of his hand apparent even through her stays. His tongue rubbed against hers, an intimate contact like none she had ever known, causing a flush of desire.

The anxiety quieted and then disappeared, dissipated by her growing arousal.

He moved from her lips to the side of her face, then found that place where her neck sloped to meet her shoulders and fastened there. He sucked at her, his tongue working on her skin, and her loins contracted in pleasure. She dug her hands into his hair, pressing her chest up against his. She wanted more of him, more of what he was making her feel.

His leg went over hers, the top of his thigh pressing intimately against her. She raised the knee of her free leg, resting the sole of her foot on the thin mattress, using the leverage to shamelessly push herself against him. His hands went up to her hair, finding and tugging loose pins, his mouth moving back up to rejoin her own.

She felt her hair come free, his fingers acting as combs, spreading it out over the coverlet. Her own hands slid around to his back, tracing the line of his spine, then tugging at the material of his shirt, freeing it from his breeches and allowing her to put her palms to the skin of his back, warm and broad, the muscles moving beneath the smooth surface.

He pulled away for a moment, rearing back to pull his shirt off over his head. His chest was sculpted in broad, flat muscles, covered in an inverted triangle of dark curls of hair. Her lips parted, her dream of that chest against her own bare breasts coming back and mingling with the present. With the wine still blurring her thoughts, for a moment she could not discern present from dream and was surprised when he touched the neckline of her gown and she realized she was yet dressed.

He lowered himself again, lying half over her, his hand tugging at the drawstring of her gown. His cheek brushed hers, rough with the first hints of stubble, and she rubbed her cheek back against his, reveling in the feel that was so different from that of her own skin, that was so entirely masculine. She felt his breath on her ear and then his tongue tracing the whorls and then swirling gently against the center, making her squirm with a delight somewhere between ticklishness and pleasure.

His hands were still tugging at the fastening of her dress, and she reached up to help, untying the drawstring, then untucking the knot of her front-lacing stays and undoing that, as well as the tie of her chemise beneath. The moment they were undone he pushed her hands away, his own wide palm slipping beneath the material to cup her bare breast.

A barely audible moan escaped from the back of her throat, and she closed her eyes. No one had ever touched her there. Having Horatio be the first to do so made her feel vulnerable to him in a delicious way she had not expected.

His lips trailed down her neck, across her collar bone, then followed his hand as he pulled down the neckline of her clothes, the stays parting. He caught the end of her nipple between his teeth, biting gently, causing a bolt of pleasure to shoot straight down to her sex.

The trailing touch of his hand was on her raised leg, pulling up her skirts, teasing along the inside of her thigh. Her eyes opened, the anxiety coming to life within her once again. This was more than she had expected, more than a kiss. To have him touch her down there was to give him access to more of her than she was willing to share.

"Horatio, I'm not—" she started to say.

"Shhhh," he said gently, and came up and kissed her mouth, silencing her. "Your skin is so soft. It's like silk." His hand trailed upward and found her womanhood, his fingertips brushing through her curls, then stroking lightly over the sensitive center of her.

"I can't," she said, and closed her legs against his touch, her knee coming over to rest against his hip, trying to seal the entrance to her self. With her hands she pressed gently against his chest, a soft request that he stop. His hand stilled, caught against the most intimate part of her.

"I have dreamt of touching you like this," he whispered, kissing her again, then nuzzling the side of her face. "Your hair smells of jasmine. Do you know how beautiful you looked in your wedding gown? But nowhere near as beautiful as you are now, with your hair spread around you." He licked her neck, teasing.

With his hand motionless the threat was diminished, and her attention focused on his murmured words and his mouth on hers, on her neck, teasing at her earlobe. Her eyes shut halfway, and she let her hands explore the side of his chest, feeling the ridges of muscles overlaying ribs, the dips and planes of his body that felt so solid and hard against her own. She was aware as well of the firm evidence of his own arousal, pressed up against the outside of her thigh.

His hand between her legs began to move back and forth, in slow, gentle motions. She squeezed her legs more tightly together for a moment, then relaxed them as he continued and the sensations urged her to let him do as he wished.

"I love the feel of you," he whispered.

A sparkling warmth spread through her loins, and then she felt the tip of his finger dip inside her then retreat, and before she could find the breath to protest, his dampened finger was moving up her, parting her folds, then coming to dwell on the nub of her desire.

"You're wet. Do you know what that means, Anne, my love?"

"I don't want to know," she gasped.

"It means you are enjoying this."

She parted her lips to tell him to stop, but then his fingers slid down again, gathering moisture from her, and all she wanted was to urge him back, to keep doing what he had been. His fingers returned to stroke her again, his touch slick, the sensations building. Horatio moved his mouth back down to her one exposed breast, suckling at it, gently biting the nipple, and she grabbed his hair, holding him to her.

Something was building inside her, her body climbing towards some unknown peak, and with every touch from Horatio her hunger for him grew stronger. She wanted more than he was giving her, some deeper contact. She arched up against him.

"Horatio," she said. "Horatio . . ."

She didn't know what to ask for. Her hands went down to his shoulders, clenching him, her fingers digging into his skin and trying to speak for her.

"I know what you need," he said, coming up and playing his tongue in the hollow at the base of her throat. "I know what you want."

"Tell me."

Instead of speaking he moved his hand down, and in one smooth motion slid a finger deep inside her. She gasped, clenching her body against the invasion, and then he started thrusting gently, his finger inside her touching up against some hidden source of pleasure, the palm of his hand flat against her sex, moving with each stroke. Her thighs fell to the side, inviting him in.

"I want to be inside you."

"What—" she began to say, but then something miraculous overtook her. She tensed, her body sensing the peak she had been seeking was near, her muscles straining to help her reach it. She held her breath, afraid that so much as an exhalation would scare it away, and then came a throbbing wave of release that threw her mind back into the realm of dreams. Suddenly she was lying on the damp jungle floor, Horatio naked above her, their bodies together in a film of sweat. Around her insects called and buzzed, the leafy green an impenetrable wall of life. Tiny beams of sunlight pierced the canopy overhead, catching on leaves that shone and dripped with moisture, and in the air was the scent both of their own lovemaking and of the rich and mouldering forest floor, a sweet drifting of flowers weaving through it all.

The waves of relief subsided, the jungle fading. She opened her eyes to find that she was holding Horatio tightly in her arms, her thighs locked around his hand. He raised his head from the bend of her neck and kissed her as he slowly withdrew his finger from inside her. Her heart was still thudding in her chest, her muscles feeling both tired and wonderfully relaxed.

Horatio lifted himself up and began to fumble with the fastening of his breeches.

"Just hold me," she said, trying to pull him back down to her.

"There is more yet to come."

With the satiation of her desire came a slow return of her senses. "What are you doing?"

"Finishing what we have started," he said, and got his breeches undone. He slid them down and kicked both them and his linen undergarment off, and then was lying between her thighs, the firm, thick pole of his manhood against her.

"Horatio, no," she said, putting her hands against his chest and shoving. "We can't."

"Hush, my sweet," he said and kissed her cheek, his hands brushing back her hair and trying to soothe her.

"No, I don't want to go this far," she said, and squirmed under him.

He moved to the side, so that his erection was up against her thigh, his body resting only half over hers. "It's all right, Anne, my love," he said, kissing her brow, the corner of her eye. His hand made slow circles over her breast. "I won't push you, I promise you that. We'll go as slowly as you like."

She pulled herself out from beneath him, yanking down her skirts and rearranging her bodice so that her breasts were covered. She was still on her back, but there were a few inches now between them. She rolled onto her side and looked at him, reaching out to touch his startled face. "We can't, not if we want to have this marriage annulled."

"No one needs to know what we have or have not done in our own bedroom."

She almost laughed at the rationale, pulling her hand back and crossing it with the other across her chest. "We'll know. And what if there should be a child?"

"Then you'll be stuck with me," he said, reaching for her, hooking an arm over her hip and pulling her closer. He looked pleased with the idea.

"I won't be trapped," she said, holding him off with hands and knees, but finding it impossible to ignore the feel of him under her palms, and the firmness of his thighs against her knees. He was still erect—she could feel him against her leg, and it took all her willpower not to glance down and take a good look at him.

"I thought that was what a man was supposed to say." He lifted one of her hands from his chest and brought it to his mouth, kissing the knuckles, then taking her index finger into his mouth and sucking.

"It seems to me that marriage is even more of a trap for a woman than for a man," she said on a gasp, watching in fascination as he moved from one finger to the next, pausing at the sensitive skin in between, his tongue darting out to tease her.

"Don't talk that way," he said. "You make it sound as if all I want is to cause you misery, when the truth is anything but that." He swirled his tongue in her palm, then started to trail kisses down her wrist, to her forearm.

Her muscles were going weak, her legs relaxing, straightening out as if of their own volition. He pulled her closer, until his shaft was pressed against her lower belly. She felt a scandalous urge to rock herself against it, and her moistening flesh began to tingle again with the desire for more than this near contact through layers of gown.

He nibbled at the crook of her arm, and she wanted to give in to him, wanted to let him have his way for the sheer pleasure of what he could make her body feel.

With almost physical pain she pulled away again. "No, Horatio. This isn't right."

He ducked his head against her chest and made a low groan. "You're going to be the death of me, Anne Merivale."

She pushed farther away, and he let her go. She watched in some consternation as he kept his head down, his body still. She could hear his ragged breathing. Then all at once he rose up, startling her, her eyes widening at the thought that he might have his way with her after all.

But then he was off the bed, his back to her. He held his fists tight at his side, giving her a chance to watch the play of muscles across his back and arms, and to take a long look at the curves of his buttocks.

He gave another groan that was half a shout, then strode to the louvered doors that led to the balcony. He stepped out into the night, pulling the doors half shut behind him.

"Horatio?"

He didn't answer. She heard more groaning sounds coming from him, and more ragged breathing, audible even from across the room.

"Horatio, are you all right?" She slid to the edge of the bed and stood, uncertain of whether she should go to him.

"Just ... go ... to bed," he said between breaths. "Please."

She took a step forward. He sounded unwell. "Horatio?"

There was no answer, just more grunting and groaning and heavy breathing from the other side of the louvered doors.

Concern overcame her hesitation, and she hurried across the room, stepping out onto the balcony to see what ailed him.

He was hurting himself, doing some manner of damage to his manhood. He gripped it around the neck like a chicken he was trying to strangle, jerking on it, letting out cries of pain with each tug.

"Horatio, no, don't!" she said, and reached out to stop him, laying her hand over his. He was punishing himself, all on account of her. The poor man! That guilt could drive him to this!

"Go away!" he said, stopping, his hand beneath hers still in its death grip.

"Don't harm yourself this way," she said softly. "I don't want to see you in pain."

"Don't you?" he asked. Then before she could answer he grabbed her hand in his, putting his swollen member into her palm, closing his hand over the back

205

of hers and forcing her to perform the same strangling maneuver.

"Why are you doing this?" she cried, horrified, trying to pull away. When she couldn't, she reached out with her other hand, cupping the end of his penis in her palm as if she could protect the thing from the violence he was enacting. She felt a drop of dampness against her hand, the head of his penis moving now in slick circles on her skin.

Horatio's movements got faster, more frantic, and then he pulled away her hand that cupped the end of him. His body jerked, and something came out the end, where her hand had been. She stared, forgetting her hand still gripping his shaft, gazing in pure astonishment at the spurts of unknown substance that sailed out over the rail of the balcony to disappear into the garden below. The poor man. Something inside must have burst.

Horatio's fit came to an end, and he released her hand. "I'm sorry," he said, turning away from her.

She looked at her hand, then at his bare back. He didn't seem to be in pain. He seemed, in fact, much calmer than he had been moments ago. "What happened?" she asked. "You were hurting yourself."

His back shook with a silent laugh. "It was pain of another sort," he said, still not facing her. "And you helped me relieve it."

"You are better now?"

"Go to bed, Anne."

"It's just, I—"

"Please. Just go to bed. I don't think either of us really want to talk about this."

She bit her lip, undecided, but when he remained with his back to her she reluctantly did as he had bid. Back in the room she removed her gown and stays, keeping on her chemise, then crawled under the thin coverlet, staying close to her side of the bed. She closed her eyes and waited, listening for his movements within the sound of night insects, but it wasn't until more than half an hour had passed that he came back inside and blew out the lamps.

She didn't say anything, not knowing this mood he was in, and not knowing what could be said. The bed creaked as he got in on his side, but the lattice frame did not sag or roll her toward him. She remained perched on her side in the silence, opening her eyes to half-slits, trying to observe him in the dark.

She felt alone in the bed, as if a chasm lay between them instead of a mere foot of thin mattress. He was no nearer to sleep than she was, she could tell from his breathing and his stillness. She didn't know—had she been the one at fault, for allowing him to touch her and then stopping him? Or was he at fault, for trying to seduce her? And what had happened on the balcony—she didn't know what that meant at all.

None of that really mattered, though. At the moment, all she cared about was that her companion of two months was lying near her as stiff and alone as she herself was. It felt as if the comforting cloak of his presence had been withdrawn, allowing in a cold wind of winter that should be nowhere near this tropical clime.

Whether they were husband and wife, lovers, friends, or merely fellow knights errant on a futile quest, she did not want to wake in the morning with this same distance between them, making her heart ache with loneliness.

Stealthily, cautiously, she slid her hand across the intervening distance until she found his, then slid hers inside it, fearing all the while that he would brush it aside.

But he didn't. His head turned on the pillow, his eyes catching a glint of moonlight as he looked at her, and she felt him grip her hand and give it a gentle squeeze. He said nothing, but kept holding her hand until, reassured, she at last drifted off to sleep.

And when she woke in the morning, he was holding it still.

Chapter Thirteen

Married life was not all that he had hoped it would be. Granted, he'd been partaking of wedded bliss for less than a full day, but if one endeavored to begin a venture as one meant to continue, well, he must consider himself in dire straits.

He scratched at a mosquito bite on the side of his neck and stole a look at Anne, who was sitting beside him in the carriage that Raffles had put at their disposal, which was now carrying them down to the pier to reboard their ship. Her face was turned half away from him, as if the passing dull buildings were of absorbing interest. Her hands were clasped tightly in her lap, her posture stiff and ill at ease.

God only knew what demented demons she thought stalked his mind, from what she had seen him doing on the balcony. She plainly did not understand what he had been about, and for that he supposed he should be grateful. It wasn't the type of activity in which one wished to be observed by one's lady love.

Her innocence in sexual matters amused, annoyed, and aroused him all at once. He wished she were not a virgin so that she would be willing to share his bed, while at the same time he wanted to be the only one to ever touch her. He felt protective of her, and also he wanted to ravage her. And he was torn between wanting to laugh at the remembered look on her face when he had put her hand on his cock, and wanting with every fiber to feel that small hand wrapped around him once again, small and soft and damp.

He bit back a groan. He was going to have to persuade her to be his wife in all senses, and do so before he wore a whole new set of calluses on his hand. Masturbation wasn't much relief: He was still unsatisfied, a low hum of desire in constant course through his loins. Anne did that to him, the mere thought of her sending prickling arousal through his blood. The sight of her, or the scent—oh, those were pure torture, as they had been last night, holding her hand and wanting so much more.

When she had finally fallen asleep he had moved closer, careful not to disturb her, and pulled a tress of her jasmine-scented hair across the pillow to where he could lay his cheek upon it. It had been tempting to pull her towards him, but he had sense enough not to put such pressure on the fragile bridge she had built between them by taking his hand.

He'd been angry and frustrated when he had come to bed, at himself and at her, both. The mosquito-filled, swampy night air had done nothing to dispel his bad humor, and he had been busily berating himself for his mishandling of their wedding night, certain he had alienated her completely, when he had felt her fingers creep onto his palm.

For a moment he had been too surprised to respond, having convinced himself that she thought worse of him then than she ever had before. But that delicate hand, so tentative in the darkness, had spoken to his heart in a way no amount of words ever could. When he'd looked at her in the dark, her face just faintly visible, he'd seen again the mouse who needed him to be a hero, who needed him to be a better man than he thought himself.

He was helpless in the face of such trust and vulnerability. He would rather cut out his own heart and roast it on a stick than disappoint her expectations of him. He was well and truly in her power, in a way he never had been with any other woman. The passions roused by a pretty face or flirtatious manner were nothing compared to the soul-deep desire he had to give Anne everything she needed, and would ever need. He would conquer kingdoms for her, if it would keep her believing in him.

Which was not to say he wasn't still going to try to persuade her to his own way of thinking on the consummation issue. He knew they were meant to be together, and if she couldn't see it, he would just have to wear her down until she accepted it. It wasn't a plan with particular finesse or subtlety, but he was confident it would work. Eventually.

After all, their marriage been arranged by the Hand of Destiny.

The carriage was moving alongside one of the many dank and swampy canals, small insects hovering over its water. He reached over and took Anne's hand, giving it a squeeze. She looked at him, startled, and he grinned.

She frowned. "You have mosquito bites all over your face."

"Three or four, is all," he said, and tried to take her comment as a sign of caring rather than a remark upon his blotchy complexion. The bite on his forehead was particularly nasty, swollen an inch across. He'd tried to hide it with a lock of hair. "I'd forgotten how hungry the little buggers get. They seem to have a particular fondness for me."

Too bad that fondness was not shared by Anne—he wouldn't mind having her putting love bites over every inch of his skin, and they probably wouldn't itch afterwards.

"I never thought I'd say it, but I'm almost eager to go back to sea," she said. "No mosquitos, a constant breeze, and no Lieutenant Governor Raffles interfering in our affairs."

It probably wasn't a politic moment to express his own great pleasure at Raffles's interference. "Plenty of cockroaches, weevils, and rats, though. And don't forget Mango."

She wrinkled her nose. "I had been hoping he would run off into the jungle."

"He loves you," Horatio said, and as he said it realized he had never said those words to Anne himself. His grip on her hand tightened, and his heart thumped in his chest. He'd never said it to a woman, had always found a way around it, using words like 'adore' or 'admire.' A fresh sweat broke out over his skin as he felt the words rise in his throat. Could he say them to her? Could he open his heart so wide, when the reception was likely to be so harsh?

"Be that as it may, he is still a filthy monkey and it's a pity we didn't chuck him into Chartier's longboat," she said.

The moment of possibility passed. He could not declare his feelings to her in the midst of a conversation about Mango. It wasn't romantic. He tried to ignore the immediate sense of relief, not feeling it worthy of his feelings for her. Even without those specific words, "I love you," she had to know how he felt, didn't she? He had made it plain enough. He'd married her, for God's sake! Which reminded him:

"You're not going to tell the others about your plans for an annulment, are you?" he asked.

Her eyebrows rose. "I don't see why not. After all we've been through together, I think they deserve our honesty."

"Your honesty. It would not be my truth."

"Horatio . . ."

"Don't say anything to them. You saw how happy they were when we married," he said quickly, holding her hand now between both of his own. "I think it gives them a sense of stability, and it makes them feel more comfortable about you."

"What do you mean?" she asked, and gave a tug at her hand.

"I just mean that underneath the comaraderie, they are still men who have lived their lives with certain

213

ideas of what a woman should and should not do."

"I see no reason to live my life to their standards," Anne said, and this time succeeded in pulling free her hand. "If they have been uncomfortable in my presence, it is not my fault. I hardly had a choice in the matter. Would they prefer I had remained in my cabin and embroidered all day?" She paused, then narrowed her eyes at him. "Wait a moment. I have never had any inclination that they have been uncomfortable, and I'd think I should know them well enough by now to know that to be the truth. It's you who has been uneasy."

"That's nonsense."

She cocked her head to the side, still regarding him through narrowed eyes. He felt her gaze pierce right through his shields, delving into his inner workings. Her eyes widened, the treasure of information discovered, and he felt his stomach sink. "You're trying to find an excuse to have me pretend this is a real marriage," she declared. "You think you'll manage to trick me into staying in it."

Curses on the intuition of women! He was losing this argument, and fast. Time to change tactics. He leaned sideways, until his shoulder was pressing on hers, and tilted his head so he could whisper from the side of his mouth at her. "Don't tell anyone, but I always wanted to have a wife."

She leaned forward, turning so she could look back at his face. He let himself fall slightly into the space where her back had been resting. "I don't understand you," she said.

"Won't you let me pretend you're my wife for a

while? Please?" he asked, doing his best to look like a guileless idiot. "What harm could it do?"

She shook her head, but he saw the beginnings of a smile on a her lips. "You are completely mad, Horatio Merivale. You are an absolute lunatic."

"And you can pretend I'm your husband, lucky you! Come, it'll be fun, and everyone can go along thinking that we're blissfully in love. We don't have to disappoint them with the truth. You saw how happy they were at the wedding. You can't do anything about annulling the marriage at this point, anyway."

He could tell she was wavering, playfulness reaching her where reason had not. Or had part of her wanted to give in, all along? It was almost too much to hope for. "I'm not going to 'pretend' at consummation," she said.

"I should certainly hope not. I'll only have the real thing from you, Mrs. Merivale, or nothing at all."

"Or nothing at all," she repeated, then gave him a crooked smile. She shoved him upright and sat back, her shoulder fitting tightly against his. "I'll show you 'nothing' and make you sorry you ever agreed to this," she said, and he heard the first hints of cheer in her voice since they had been wed.

"Mrs. Merivale, I am sorry about nothing at all where you are concerned."

"You will be."

He could have kissed her. Although she had apparently overlooked it, agreeing to "pretend" to be his wife meant she would be sharing his cabin and his bed. Last night had been a fiasco, but there were infinite nights ahead in which to persuade her, and a thousand intimacies to be shared as they lived and dressed in the same confined space.

Familiarity might on occasion breed contempt, but it was far more often true that one liked what one knew, and was drawn to the familiar. Soon she'd be unable to remember what life had been like without him, and, if Destiny were on his side as he believed, that would be a positive thing. The future was looking bright, indeed.

"Company, Anne," Horatio said from the doorway between captain's saloon and deck.

Anne turned from the bunk where she was tucking in a freshly laundered sheet. "Who is it?" she asked, looking out the cabin's doorway, squinting at Horatio where he was silhouetted against the sunlight on deck.

"Raffles and someone else. Come to see that we're still happily married, I presume."

She snorted. "Come to gloat over his handiwork."

"As well he should."

She made another noise. "I'll be out in a minute," she said, and Horatio disappeared from the doorway. She finished making up the bunk, then went to the small mirror over the washstand and smoothed her hair back with her palm, frowning at the loose tendrils that hung straight alongside her cheekbones, instead of curling prettily or remaining in her braided bun as well-behaved hair should. It shouldn't matter how she looked, but despite the injury she felt Raffles had done her, she felt a certain admiration for the lieutenant governor and wished to leave him with a good impression of her.

She had only been back on board a few hours, just long enough to look over the supplies they had traded for, to take down the bedsheets hanging in the sun, put away the few things she had brought ashore, and to be introduced to the three disreputable-looking Dutchmen that had signed on as crew. Ruut had expressed his own distrust of the men, but there were no others to be had in port. These three were eager to leave the English-controlled town, but Ruut warned they would likely abandon ship the moment a Dutch settlement came into sight. She supposed they'd just have to avoid Dutch settlements. Unless, that is, the men became so disagreeable that they wished to be rid of them.

The atmosphere aboard had changed, and whether it was due to the marriage of she and Horatio or to the addition of the men, she could not tell. Both, perhaps. Everything felt unsettled, as if too many changes had come at once.

The desire for that return to unspoken harmony gave her another reason to be glad she had given in to Horatio's persuasions to continue the charade of being husband and wife. It felt simpler than trying to show their crew that she and Horatio were still no more than friends, with the constant pulling away from Horatio's flirtations that that would require, the constant public denial of affection, the constant effort to display an utter lack of attraction.

And Horatio had been right, however she had argued against it, that having her married to him would subtly put the men at ease.

Pretending to be a happy wife also meant that any fondness or desire she might truly feel for Horatio could be shown, without worry that Horatio would know it came from her heart. She could go to him on deck now, wrap her arms around his neck and give him a big smacking kiss on the lips, and he would think she was doing it for show alone.

She grinned at herself in the mirror. Not that she wanted to kiss him. But she could, if she wished, and without leaving her heart vulnerable. The poor, silly fool. He had no idea what he had gotten himself in for.

She left the cabin and the saloon, and stepped out into the bright sunlight on deck, only the quietest of internal voices warning that she might be the one who was the fool, and not he. She smothered the voice and allowed herself to be distracted by Mango, who screeched from his perch up in the rigging and came swinging down, then ran across deck and gripped her skirt with one paw.

"Kai, have you been chasing Mango again?" she asked the Chinaman.

"Missy?" Kai asked in deliberate innocence.

"He's going to get his revenge on you one of these days," Anne warned.

"Kai eat monkey first."

"I should think he'd taste as rotten as his disposition."

Kai raised one of his soft black smudges of an eyebrow, but Anne knew he had understood the gist of her meaning, if not every word. They went to join the others at the starboard rail, watching the approach of a carriage containing Raffles and a small dark man.

"Who that, Missy?" Kai asked.

"The dark man? I don't know." She put her hand to her brow as a visor against the sun.

And then, as she was staring, her red kingfisher appeared, flying from behind her out to the carriage, where it circled once. The dark man's head turned, watching the bird as it went by him and then headed back towards their ship, and Anne's mouth dropped open.

"Kai . . . Kai, do you see that red bird?"

"Bird?"

"By the carriage. Do you see it? A red bird?"

Kai squinted. "No bird, Missy." He turned to look at her. "Your red bird, dream bird?"

She didn't know how to answer that. How could it be her dream bird, if that dark little man could see it, too? Or perhaps it was coincidence that he had turned his head as if following its flight. "Maybe so," she answered Kai.

"If you see dream bird, maybe man good," Kai said.

"Let's hope so."

The carriage stopped a short distance from the *Anne*, and as it did so the dark man looked up to where she leaned over the rail. Their eyes met, and after a moment of staring, she saw recognition soften the features of the man, and he smiled.

He had stretched earlobes, weighted down with brass hoops that brushed his shoulders, just like the people in her dreams.

219

Anne stepped away from the rail, shaken.

The men came on board, and introductions were made, Raffles treating the dark man with regard. The stranger wore the same sarong and jacket as the Malays, and was barefooted. He wore nothing on his head, his black hair hanging straight down his back except where it was cut straight across his forehead in bangs.

"This is Imsa, from the isle of Sulawak," Raffles said. "He has been on *peselai* for the past three years, and has decided it is time to go home—"

" 'Peselai'?" Horatio asked.

"It means 'long journey.' It's a tradition in his tribe, and in many others, to go on a long journey and see the world before one marries."

"A tradition familiar to Englishmen."

"Mm, well, not so entirely familiar," Raffles said. "He is also expected to bring home a head or two from rival tribes, to show his manhood."

Anne's eyes widened, and she stared at this Imsa in alarm. A headhunter? Raffles had brought a headhunter aboard their ship? Imsa met her eyes, and she quickly looked away.

"Er, I do hope you are not going to say you've brought him aboard to help him fulfill his quest," Horatio said.

Raffles grinned, but it was Imsa who spoke, his voice surprisingly soft, and touched with humor. "You are not warrior, not make good head for spirits."

"I don't know whether to be pleased or insulted," Horatio replied. "I warrant my head is as good as anyone else's."

Imsa narrowed his eyes and looked Horatio up and down, then shook his head in refusal. Off to the side, Kai giggled, then went straight-faced when Imsa looked his way with a considering expression.

"If you don't want my head, then what is it that I can do for you?" Horatio asked, and Anne felt a twinge of pride in the matter-of-fact, level-headed way he was dealing with the situation. There was no bluster with Horatio, and none of the arrogance that in another man might have precluded him from even listening to whatever Imsa and Raffles had in mind.

"As Mr. Raffles say, is time go home. I like sail with you."

"He certainly surprised me with the request," Raffles said. "I hired him in Sumatra, and he's been with me for quite some time now. He speaks fluent Malay, in addition to English and his own native tongue, which is why I thought you might not reject the idea of his joining you. Although Imsa wishes to go home, he is in the unfortunate position of not knowing precisely where his island is. He has a sense that it is to the north-east of here, but deuced if we've been able to agree on where it might be on a map. Seems he wanted to outdo his fellow tribesmen by traveling off the island instead of simply across it, and now he's lost. Malay is spoken widely through the islands, so while he is looking for home, you will have the convenience of an interpreter."

"Why now?" Anne found herself asking, the question leaving her mouth before she even knew she was going to speak. She looked at Imsa as she asked the question, feeling a sudden need to know the answer.

"Signs," he said.

"Signs? What signs?"

Imsa linked his thumbs together, then flew his hands up above his head. "Birds."

"It's quite complex," Raffles said, clasping his hands behind his back and taking on the air of a lecturer. "His tribe, and many others throughout the region, have an entire dictionary of meanings for the appearance and behavior of numerous birds. They're seen as messengers from the spirit world, and although some signs are obvious for any to read, most can only be comprehended by those gifted in the language of the spirits. It's not quite as savage as it sounds, when you consider the mythologies surrounding crows and owls, robins and whatever else you find flying around the English countryside."

"You'll have me thinking nothing of headhunting soon, either," Horatio said. "Although, come to think of it, I suppose England has enough examples of heads on pikes to satisfy any native of Sulawak—and nevermind the French with their guillotine."

Anne listened to him with half an ear, her eyes on Imsa as she tried to digest what Raffles had said about birds. Messengers from the spirit world? Is that what her red kingfisher was?

"You are gifted in the language of birds," Anne said to Imsa.

He smiled. "Message sometimes very loud. Easy hear."

She nodded. That much she knew. She felt Horatio looking at her and turned to him, her mind still half lost in the spirit world of birds. "I think Imsa would make a welcome addition to our crew."

He tilted his head to one side, as if trying to read her. "If you have no objection, then I do not, either."

Anne heard Kai make a gurgling sound.

"Splendid!" Raffles declared. "Good, now that we have that taken care of, there is some news that I think you will be disturbed to hear. Last night I received word from the captain of a small merchantman that Chartier is in the area."

Birds and their messages were instantly forgotten.

"Chartier, here?" Horatio asked, incredulous. "How?"

Ruut, Ulrich, and Gianni crowded closer, questions pouring from their mouths in a babble of languages. Kai edged nearer Anne, and Mango gave an 'eeep' of distress, as if he knew of whom they spoke.

"Not here in Batavia, of course," Raffles said, "but in the South China Sea. He's gotten his hands on another ship, stolen it from some unfortunate soul. He's been waylaying vessels and searching them, ranting about his monkey and his "queen." And robbing the ships, of course, but from all reports he's in a hurry, taking only the stores and what wealth is easily portable, and then letting them go on their way. His victims say that he seemed quite crazed."

"The crew must have been picked up soon after we set them adrift," Anne said, reaching over and grasping Horatio's sleeve. "The poor people who picked them up, what must Chartier have done to them?"

"We should have chucked the lot into the ocean when we had the chance," Horatio said. "Damn. I never thought he would have been able to follow us."

"He didn't, precisely," Raffles said. "It sounds like he came through the Straits of Malacca."

"But how could he have known which direction to head?" Anne asked, and then realized she had herself to blame. She remembered telling Chartier herself that her island was east of Sumatra. She had thought she was making that up, but she had been saying what a hidden part of her had already known was true.

"I suppose it shouldn't be a surprise that he got into the South China Sea before we did," Horatio said. "We dithered about long enough for even a rowboat to outrun us, especially if they knew where we were going."

"Whatever the case, be on your guard," Raffles said. "That's quite a hornet's nest you've stirred up, and whatever he says about his monkey, I'll wager my best hat he'd like to have his ship back, as well. I doubt you'll receive as gentle treatment as the first time, if you cross his path again."

"Then we shall have to stay clear of him," Horatio said.

Anne gripped Horatio's forearm, needing the reassurance of his easy confidence, however spurious it might be. "You got us this far without encountering Chartier," she said. "There's no reason to think we can't continue avoiding him."

He looked down at her, his grin widening, his eyes crinkling at the corners. She could feel the strength doubling in him, see it in a subtle shift of posture, and for a moment was bemused that she could affect his mood so completely with a few simple words. After last night, she would not have thought that they were so closely in tune.

"And there's no reason to think the Hand of Destiny would put us in his path again, unless there was a very good reason for it," Horatio said.

"It's very romantic, to be pursued by a pirate," Anne said, smiling as innocently as she could at him.

He frowned. "Mrs. Merivale, in this instance I believe that romanticism is highly overrated."

She turned to Raffles. "Listen to the man! Married for one day, and already he is growing priggish. And here I thought I'd married an adventurer."

Her reward was an audible pat on the butt that made her hop forward, then go red in the face.

"You two make a lovely couple," Raffles said. "I don't know when I've seen a pair so well-suited." He smiled beatifically.

Anne restrained the urge to punch him.

"What are you doing in here?" Anne asked, appalled, sitting up in bed with the sheet clenched tight to her chest.

"I am about to prepare to join my wife for the night."

"I think not."

"Anne, you did agree that we should play at being husband and wife for the benefit of the others."

She narrowed her eyes at him. "This is what you had in mind all along, wasn't it?"

He gave her an innocent look. "Me? Am I so devious?"

"I wouldn't have thought so, but my opinion is undergoing alteration."

"Move over, my dear," he said, untying the collar and cuffs of his linen shirt. "It will be a tight fit, but I think we can share the cot quite comfortably."

"You are sadly mistaken if you think you're getting any closer to me than you are at this moment."

"The crew would think it strange if they knew we did not share the same bed. They think we are newlyweds, after all." He leered at her with an evil grin.

"Don't try to charm me, Mr. Merivale. And I don't give a monkey's flea if Ruut or Ulrich think it strange that you do not sleep with me. If your manly image in their minds is so important, you can sleep on the floor. I won't stop you."

"But it's hard," he complained.

"Then go sleep in one of the other cabins."

"I'd just as soon stay up and keep an eye on those Dutchmen on deck, as sleep in an empty cabin. Sleep was not the point," he grumbled.

"At least you admit it," she said, but was strangely gratified to hear him voice his desire for her.

"You are a confoundingly stubborn woman."

"You only say so because you can't have your way. If this is going to be what I have to put up with every night, we might as well tell the crew the truth. At least I'll be able to sleep in peace that way."

"Anne, you know I would never force myself on you, don't you? You don't need to fear that I'm going to take liberties with your person."

She raised a brow at him.

"Small liberties, perhaps," he said. "Would you mind so much?"

Well, no, she wouldn't mind so much, but that was

exactly the problem. "It's not a wise idea."

He pulled off his shirt and tossed it onto the wash-stand. Her eyes went to the smooth planes of his chest, the muscles, the hint of bone structure, the curling vee of hair, and then to his navel, surrounded with a fine, downy circle that disappeared into the waistband of his breeches. Her mouth inexplicably began to sali-vate, and she was possessed by the urge to lay her lips against that trail of dark hair.

"We could just lie side by side for a while," he said, softly. "Perhaps I could put my arms around you, and for a short time we could lie still and pretend that things were not as they are. It could be fun, pretend-ing."

She was tempted. Sorely, painfully tempted. What *would* it be like, to lie safe within a man's arms, and feel that he would keep you from all harm in the world? Is that what if felt like to be truly married?

"You don't want to share this bed with me," she said, regretting the words even as she said them.

"Yes, I do."

"This is not a good time," she said, each word care-fully enunciated, and gave him a meaningful look.

"Why not? What's wrong with it?"

She continued to stare at him, hoping his brain would reach the proper conclusion.

"Anne, what?"

"You know."

"No, I don't know."

"The moon is full," she said.

"What does the moon have to do with anything?"

"Ebbs and flows," she said, swishing her hand back

and forth through the air, eyes open wide, nodding as if by doing so she could get him to understand her. Her period had started a few hours ago, and she counted it as great good fortune that in those multitudinous stolen trunks of women's clothing there had been unused towels for this purpose, lovingly embroidered with the initials of their former owner.

"Yes, the moon and the tides. What of them?"

She was going to have to be blunt. "I'm not talking about the tide, Horatio. I'm talking about a woman's courses. I'm not comfortable with the idea of lying pressed up against you when there's blood—"

"But that surely shouldn't matter, if I but have my arms around you?"

"The flow is quite heavy. I'll have to change the cloths—"

"Oh," he said, interrupting, his cheeks coloring. "I see. Er, how long . . . Uh, is there anything I can . . . eh. Well. I'll leave you to it, then, shall I?" And he turned and left the cabin, stumbling like a boy who had just accidentally seen a female undressed.

Anne put her hand to her mouth and laughed.

Chapter Fourteen

South China Sea
Two weeks later

Horatio paused outside the cabin door, half afraid to knock. Anne might be sleeping, or might be in some state of dishabille. He hesitated a little longer, listening for sounds of movement from behind the louvered white door. Nothing.

He put his hand to the knob and turned, poking his nose through the narrow crack as the door opened, peering carefully through to see in what state she was.

Just as with his optimistic plans for his wedding night, his brilliant plan for slowly seducing his wife during the intimate hours they shared in the cabin had come to naught. Instead of reaching a stage of easy familiarity with Anne, where he could strip off his shirt and breeches while she sat on their bed and talked with him, he felt he was two steps behind where he had started.

For all his experience with women, there was plenty he had not known.

Women's troubles, for example. He could flirt with women, could kiss them and make love to them, he could dance with them and charm their mamas, flatter them on their dresses at a party and on the soft curves of their bodies when he had them in bed with him, but when it came to the inner workings of their womanly parts, he was at a loss. And he was not at all certain that he wanted to be educated.

Blood. He knew there was blood, and knew there were mood changes, but beyond that he knew nothing. He didn't know how much blood, or what she did with it—and that was how he liked it. When they knew each other better Anne might be willing to explain to him what went on, but that was one intimacy he would be content to leave to the future.

On the other hand, his ignorance had left him in some doubt of how essential it was that she have the cabin to herself, and he hadn't been able to pry into such a topic with her. Inquiring after the specifics of her courses had not fit in with his plan of seduction. One might as well inquire after an adored one's bowel habits. Some things were best left unknown.

He stuck his head all the way in the cabin and saw her lying on the bed, fully clothed. She was on her side, her hands up under her cheek, her eyes closed. She looked pale and tired, and distressingly small under the draping of her overlarge gown. Mango was curled in a ball at her feet, his head resting on her ankle as if he thought he were a house cat. Filthy bugger.

Just when he had thought the time must surely be up on her woman's courses, Anne had fallen ill with a fever. It had not been so intense that he need fear for her life—although the dreaded thought had remained at the back of his mind, making it difficult to eat or sleep—but she had been hot and unhappy, achy and sick to her stomach. She was now nearly recovered, the most visible effect of the illness the pounds she had lost.

Horatio felt a twinge of failed responsibility. It seemed a poor reflection on his performance as a husband that his wife had wasted away. Logically he knew there was nothing he could have done about it, but emotionally he felt he had subtly failed her. He would have to do what he could to fatten her back up, once they reached the island of her dreams.

"Anne, are you awake?" he asked softly.

Her eyes came open, her large pupils indistinguishable from the dark blue of her irises. For a moment there was no recognition in them, no consciousness, but then even as he gazed into her eyes he saw her returning, as if stepping out of a dream and back into the world of her living body. Something in those deep blue depths softened, the corners of her eyes crinkling in warmth and happiness to see him.

He felt his own heart flood in response. Such a quiet little thing, so easy for others to pass over, and yet she had become the center of his universe: the sun did not shine for him unless it first shone for her.

"I was dozing. I've become as lazy as Miss Godwyn."

He came into the cabin and sat on the edge of the swinging bed. Anne inched back, making room for him without shying away. "You've needed the rest," he said. Mango came awake and screeched in protest of his presence, so he shoved the monster off the end of the bed. The monkey continued his noisemaking from beneath the cot, but recent history had taught him better than to try for retaliation.

"I feel bad that Kai has had to take up my slack, plus helping care for me," Anne said, "although I have to say that I've enjoyed his company."

"I would have spent more time if I could have—" he started to say, but she interrupted him with a hand on his arm.

"I was hardly in need of such fuss. I rested easier knowing you were out there keeping an eye on those Dutchmen."

"Aye, the Dutchmen." He didn't trust the threesome. They did what they were bid, if reluctantly, and God knew the extra hands were welcome, but there were moments when he felt certain that the men were planning to do to him exactly what he had done to Chartier. And thank the generous Hand of Destiny, they had seen no sign of *that* terror of the high seas.

"Kai doesn't like them," Anne said, then frowned. "There's something strange about Kai, have you noticed?"

"Like what?" he asked. He'd been keeping an eye on both Kai and Ulrich, bothered by he wasn't sure exactly what.

"I'm not sure. I used to think he was being an inscrutable Chinese on purpose, for his own amusement, but I'm beginning to think there is something he is not telling us. He and Ulrich both. There's something between them."

Horatio could not help but think of unnatural acts between men too long at sea, and the moment he thought it he recalled Kai with flowers in his hair during their wedding, hugging Ulrich. He shook the thought off. "Don't worry about it. They may have their secrets, but they've been true enough to us."

"Don't tell me not to worry, Horatio Merivale," she snipped. "I'll worry over whatever I please—and likely come to a better conclusion than you. Don't start thinking that being technically my husband gives you the right to tell me what to think."

"Sorry!" he said. Women! Meek and gentle one moment, bite your head off the next. He supposed it would be ill-advised to point out that he did, indeed, have rights over her. No man who valued his future happiness would make such a mistake. "Are you sure you're feeling quite well?"

She glared at him a moment longer, then her lips twisted into a reluctant smile, and she relaxed. "I'm ill-tempered as a bedridden old man, aren't I?"

"Oh, not at all." He knew better than to say otherwise.

She opened her mouth to answer, but then her gaze shifted from him to somewhere over his shoulder. Her eyes widened, and she drew in a breath. "It's back!" she whispered.

He turned to look over his shoulder. "What?"

"The red kingfisher."

He stood up. "Where?"

She sat up, and swung her feet to the floor. He put out his hand and helped her to her feet. "It's gone out the door. Quick!"

Before he could help her further she was out in the main saloon, then headed for the bright rectangle of sunlight that was the door to the deck, Mango scampering at her heels, quicker off the mark than he. He followed close behind, feeling a surge of excitement. There had been no sightings of the red kingfisher since Anne had fallen ill. They had sailed past more than a dozen islands, but none of them had been "right." And whatever "right" was, only Anne knew.

For not the first time, he felt a passing moment of incredulity that he was steering his life on a young woman's fantasy. His father had always said he was foolhardy and impulsive, incapable of thinking before acting. Maybe so. But at this moment, he would gladly trade a thousand lives of plodding predictability for this one life of chasing dreams.

"This is it," Anne said, and the words did not do justice to her feeling of awe. Tears started in her eyes.

Dead ahead, a bank of towering thunderheads rose above the horizon. There was no island visible as yet, hidden as it was behind the curve of the earth, but they had all learned that such a column of clouds often meant there was land beneath. And in this case not just any land, but *her* land. Her island.

Twenty yards in front of the ship, the red kingfisher flew straight for the tower of clouds. She didn't need that sign to tell her what her heart already knew: This was her homecoming. The village on stilts would be there, the brightly painted boats, the girl upon the porch, the long houses in the jungle. This was it.

The last dregs of her illness fell from her body like drops of rain, leaving her clean and pure, ready for the new life that was ahead. The threat of Chartier was forgotten; her masquerade of a marriage; the three troublesome Dutchmen; even the deep, hidden ache of homesickness and thoughts of her family: All were washed away as she gazed at the towering clouds.

She was standing in the bow of the boat, holding tight to the base of the bowsprit as the ship rose and fell in the waves, spray misting her face and clothes. Her hair was down, and the wind caught at it, blowing it back from her face, lifting it to snap like a pennant behind her.

It was true. The dreams had spoken of what was real. An ecstasy of hope flooded through her, and she was suffused with the certainty that all would go right, that all was proceeding as it was meant to, and thus it would proceed forever after.

"This is it, you're certain?" Horatio asked, coming up beside her.

She nodded, too overcome to speak.

He put his arm around her shoulders and squeezed her close, planting a kiss on her temple. "I knew we'd find it! See? Didn't I tell you so?"

She was too surprised by his spontaneous embrace to protest it, and too happy, as well. She put her own arm around his waist. "You never doubted," she said, not looking at him. "Did you?" she added, almost an afterthought.

"Never for a moment."

She wondered if that were true, and if it mattered one way or the other. He had never let her see his doubts, if he had had them, and that perhaps stood for more than what his private beliefs had been.

Joyful warmth spread through her limbs, and to where her side was pressed up against Horatio. It was a moment of happiness shared, that asked for nothing more than it was. She felt none of the tense caution she usually did in his presence, as if she need be ready to defend herself from his advances; instead, it was the comfortable familiarity of friendship that had her relaxing against him.

She knew that the guard she had had raised against Horatio since before the wedding had been steadily slipping down during the past two weeks, as he had been forced to keep his distance. Funny, that. She had always assumed that it was relentless pursuit that won men the hearts of women; in her case, it seemed to be the slackening of tension that had her softening towards him.

Not that it meant she was ready to be Mrs. Merivale in all senses of the title. The man was still a better bet as a friend than as a husband: One could accept many more flaws in a friend than in a spouse.

She leaned her head against the side of his chest. Who'd have thought that she, Anne Hazlett, gardener's daughter and lady's maid, would ever be in the position of having a wellborn gentleman as her dearest friend?

Who'd have thought?

*   *   *

"How big is the island, Imsa, do you know?" Anne asked. It somehow had not surprised her when Imsa had come forward to say that this island she felt was her own was also the island he called home. Looks had been exchanged all around at that piece of information, and Ulrich had only needed to say "The Hand" for them all to nod in silent agreement.

She had wondered, though, if it might be more a case of Imsa joining them because he already knew where they were going. Or was that a form of destiny, as well? She pushed the thought aside. Thinking about it too hard just made things more confusing.

"Very big. I never see this side of island in my life," Imsa said.

"Then how can you know it is your island?" Horatio asked. They were on the quarter deck, their chart of the South China Sea weighted at the edges and spread across the deck, trying to decide which island on the chart corresponded to the one they could now see as a green shore backed by darker mountains. Mango crouched near her knees, reaching out with a paw to touch each drawn island on the chart in turn, in mockery of Horatio's movements. None of the islands seemed quite right, none fit exactly with Horatio's calculations. Imsa called the island Sulawak, but there was no such name engraved upon the chart.

The rest of the crew were huddled around them in what had become their usual forum for discussion, albeit with Kai keeping a certain distance from Imsa, as if fearing a sudden outburst of head-hunting. Ruut, at the wheel, kept one eye on the group and one on the Dutchmen, who were at work farther forward on the deck.

Imsa just smiled in response to Horatio's question. He knew in the same way Anne herself knew, and he probably knew a lot more besides, that he either could not or would not tell them.

"There is something we have not told you," Anne said to Imsa, feeling even as she said so that it was a waste of breath. His knowing eyes suggested he already knew what she would impart. "I have dreamed of your island for many years. I have dreamed that I was meant to call it home."

Imsa cocked his head to one side, the knowing look in his eyes fading, replaced by a hint of confusion.

She didn't want to continue, realizing suddenly how very presumptuous her next words were going to sound. And if her calling the island her home had surprised him . . . "I've dreamed I was meant to, er . . . be in a position of authority."

Imsa blinked, his frown deepening.

"She is queen!" Kai put in, ever helpful.

Imsa stared at her, incredulity on his face, and then he burst out laughing. "Queen! You, queen of Sulawak! A monkey-face, queen of Sulawak!"

"I say," Horatio put in. "She looks nothing like a monkey."

"You English! All same! Think world for you to take," Imsa said. "Ha! Sulawak is Sulawak, land of headhunters, not monkey-faces. You never be queen of Sulawak. We hang your head from roof beam before call you queen."

Anne felt her face heating, her neck, even her chest burning with embarrassment.

"Maybe I go to England," Imsa continued, "and say I am king."

"It's not quite the same," Horatio said.

"You not know Sulawak," Imsa said. "You know nothing!"

"Then tell us what we need to know, if you are so wise," Horatio countered.

Imsa shut his lips, glaring at Horatio, then shrugged. "You will find out."

"He know nothing," Ruut said from his place at the wheel. "He talk big, but know nothing. Your dreams real, Mrs. Merivale. They bring us this far, they bring us farther."

"Hear, hear," Ulrich put in.

"Not hang heads from roof beams," Kai said to Imsa. "Eat you before you eat Kai."

Imsa curled his lip at Kai. "We not eat people. You think we wild men? You think we have morals of Chinese?"

"Throw you overboard right now!" Kai shrieked. "Know you bad from first day. Not need you!"

"Hush, Kai," Horatio said. "No one is eating anyone, and we're all going to keep our heads upon our necks. Imsa, if there is something we should know, please tell us. You said yourself that it was signs that told you to sail with us, and you cannot think it mere coincidence that we have sought your home."

"If it his home," Ruut said. "Maybe he lie."

Imsa's face began to darken, and Anne felt certain he was nearing the breaking point of his control, such

239

as it was. She herself wanted this conversation to end, and end now. All her joy and certainty of such a short time ago had drained away under Imsa's derisive laughter. The slung taunts of the last few minutes had pierced her like a hundred needles, the tension invading her muscles, the voices of the others drumming on her ears until she thought she would scream.

One of the Dutchmen gave a shout, and a quick exchange followed in Dutch with Ruut. He turned to the group and the argument was temporarily forgotten, all eyes upon the big man at the wheel.

"Sail spotted," Ruut said. "It come this way."

Chapter Fifteen

"Give me the spyglass!"

Horatio handed her the glass, and she put it up to her eye, leaning against the rail for support. They were sailing along the coast of the island, seeking to either put it between themselves and the approaching sails, or to find a hiding place that, somehow, the other ship would miss.

But that wasn't what had caught her eye. It was the greyish-yellow smudge at the shoreline that had attracted her attention.

She twisted the barrel of the spyglass until the smudge resolved itself into what she had known she would see: a village of houses upon stilts, hovering above the edge of the water. The hairs stood on the back of her neck as she recognized the village from her dreams.

"This is the place I saw," she said, handing the glass over to Horatio.

He took it and looked at the village. "Extraordinary houses. What a curious way to live. I suppose they must be fishermen."

"I suppose, yes."

He continued looking, a frown drawing down his brow. Anne looked from him to the distant village, then frowned herself.

"Do you see any boats?" she asked. "Any people?"

"No one." He gave the glass back to her.

She took it, and, with growing puzzlement, saw that there were, indeed, no brightly painted boats bobbing amongst the stilts, no nets hanging out to dry, no person or animal moving on the porches or showing a face in a doorway. Where was the child of her dream? She scanned each doorway, each porch, and saw nothing but signs of abandonment. Here and there thin boards hung down from the porches, or patches of palm roofing and siding were missing. Her careful search of the waterline revealed the prow of a narrow boat, half sunk, protruding from the gentle waves.

She lowered the glass, the sense of wrongness churning her stomach. The village was dead, unlived in, and looked to have been that way for some time.

"What do you think happened?" she asked Horatio.

"I don't know. Attacked, maybe?"

"By whom?" she asked.

"The French are not the only pirates. Raffles said the Malays are a scourge in this region, along with a host of others. Or perhaps it was a tribe from inland.

I don't know. For all we know they may simply have moved on."

"I can't imagine anyone leaving built homes behind," she said.

"No, I can't either. We've no time to stop and look any closer, though."

The village was already falling astern, but in its place appeared something of even greater interest. The kingfisher was suddenly back with them, flitting straight towards a wide break in the jungled shore.

"In here!" Anne said.

"You took the words right out of my mouth," Horatio said, gesturing for Ruut to carry out the change in course.

It was a river mouth they saw, and towards which the red kingfisher flew, its sudden reappearance both comforting and alarming. If they needed help, then there was something of which to be afraid. Anne turned to look out to sea, and the pursuing sails had not changed their course. She felt in her heart it was Chartier who followed them.

The *Anne* glided slowly towards the mouth of the river, the waterway a good quarter of a mile across. The land to either side was low, mangroves growing to the narrow shoreline, hinting at a swampy interior behind their green-leaved shield. Some distance inland she could see the rise of foothills and mountains.

To their good fortune the tide was coming in, catching at their hull and sweeping them into the mouth of the river like a crab pulling food to its maw. Ruut gave the order for sails to be taken in, leaving up just enough that they could maintain sufficient speed to steer.

"Shouldn't we be making soundings?" Horatio asked Ruut.

Ruut shrugged. "We have time?"

"The kingfisher is still with us," Anne said. "Surely it would not lead us aground."

"Let's hope spirit birds take water depths into consideration."

Anne chewed her lip, herself worried. The kingfisher's intentions could be contrary to their own. It might think its job well done if they were grounded.

She looked out at the low bank to port as they cruised slowly by. Stubby palms were interspersed with the mangroves, and tall grasses higher than herself grew in muddy spots where the land had been washed away by the river's force. As she watched, something the color of mud and the size of a log ran down a bank and disappeared into the water with a splash.

"What was that?" Horatio asked, coming over to her.

"I believe it may have been a crocodile," she said, her throat dry.

"Truly? Saw lots of those in India."

"Did they . . . ever eat people?"

"We heard stories. They were a narrow-snouted variety, though. They fed primarily on fish. Nothing to worry about."

She had only had a quick glimpse, but she didn't think this crocodile had had a narrow snout. It had looked an altogether menacing creature to meet in the water, and she hoped she never had the pleasure.

The river curved in a long bend that brought them in nearly a full circle, then it curved again in the opposite direction, then again, thoroughly confusing her sense of direction. In which direction was the ocean now? She looked to the distant mountains to orient herself. They had traveled at least three miles, by her estimation, yet with all the turnings of the river she would stake her life on their yet being within a half mile of the coast.

Ulrich was up in the crow's nest, keeping lookout. "They are still coming," he called down from above.

Anne looked up at the masts, the sails now furled tightly against the yardarms. "Horatio, the sails," she said. "The masts. Will they be able to see them from the sea?"

He looked up, following her gaze, then looked at the height of the trees along the banks. "Let's hope not. The masts should be difficult to pick out against the backdrop of the mountains."

A shimmering of fear lodged itself in Anne's gut. Chartier could have seen their direction, and the mouth of the river was impossible to miss: He had but to sail upriver himself to catch them, for they had nowhere to flee. Their only hope was that the tide would turn before Chartier reached the river, for it would be nigh on impossible to come upriver against it. The banks had already narrowed to half their former distance, and tacking in a ship of any size would be difficult, and likely to send one into the swampy banks.

She tried to reassure herself with those thoughts, but the reassurance would not come. The tide would eventually come in again, and so would Chartier. And eventually the river would grow so shallow that they could no longer proceed, and then what?

"Mango, be still!" Anne snapped at the monkey, who was playing with the hem of her dress, pulling it over his head like a kerchief and making chirruping noises as if he were a woman gossiping. She yanked the material away, and Mango gave a cry of annoyance. "Don't you even think about biting me!" she warned.

Mango bared his teeth at her, then, choosing the better part of valor, scampered up a sheet into the rigging.

Horatio came and stood beside her, putting his hand on her shoulder. "We'll be all right," he said.

"I don't know how you can be so sure."

"We don't even know that it is Chartier," he said.

"It is." She felt his hand tighten on her shoulder, then relax. He didn't question her statement. "What are we going to do when they catch up to us?"

"*If.* If they catch up to us. The boat is well-armed. We'll take a stand and fight him off."

She blinked. She'd forgotten the cannon, the swivel guns, the arsenal of powder and pistols and cutlasses. She was so used to seeing them, she had ceased seeing them at all. "I've never been in a battle," she said.

"And I don't intend you to be in this one. It might be best to take you ashore before it begins."

She turned wide eyes on him. "Ashore? With the crocodiles?"

"Better a crocodile than cannon fire. The heart of the ship might be safe from shattered wood, but not from fire. Not from water, if they sink us. And certainly not from Chartier and his men, if they board."

It was a horrid picture he was painting. She could see in her mind's eye the jagged splinters of wood, piercing the flesh. The blood on the decks. The fire catching hold and consuming sails, as the stern of the ship surrendered to cannon fire and began to sink. Chartier's men swarming aboard, slashing with their blades, cutting open skin and lopping off limbs.

"It seems to me it might be better if we all went ashore, and left the boat to Chartier," she said, only half serious.

"Give up the *Anne*?" Horatio asked, appalled.

The idea suddenly seemed a brilliant, simple solution. "Yes! Why not? Lock Mango in a cabin, and leave the boat. Let Chartier have it. Let him have his cursed boat and monkey."

"He'll want his 'queen.' And he'll want revenge."

"I doubt he'll go far into the jungle to find it, and how would he ever track us? We have Imsa; he can lead us to safety. Why risk our lives?"

"We cannot give up the *Anne*."

"Why not?"

"It's ours. I'm not going to let some filthy French pirate have it."

"It's not important," she said, dismissing the boat. What did a tub of wood matter compared to their lives? "It's the island that's important, and we're here now."

Horatio looked pointedly around at the swampy jungle to either side. "Yes, we're here. But is 'here' exactly where we are supposed to be?"

"The kingfisher led us."

"Even if we are supposed to be in this river, how will we ever leave it? How will we ever leave the island without the *Anne*?"

"We'll find a way. The Hand of Destiny—"

"I'm not giving up the ship."

"You'd rather we risked being killed."

"We can't just run when we're challenged."

"Why not? It's worked fine up until now. This entire voyage we have chosen running over fighting."

"We're like a fox to the hounds with Chartier, can't you see that? Running won't stop him from pursuing."

"You know what happens to the fox," she said. "He either escapes or he dies. He never kills the hounds."

"It was a bad metaphor," he said. "We'll turn the tables on Chartier, and be rid of him for good."

"I think we should discuss this with the rest of the crew. They're going to be putting their lives on the line as much as you are, and I doubt they are as attached to this boat," she said, growing angry that he would not accept her point of view. "If I'm going to be safe on shore with the crocodiles, then I think they should be offered that option, as well."

"This is not a matter for a vote," he said, incredulous. "I'm captain of this ship, and the final decision rests with me. We are not giving up the *Anne*."

"The *Cauchemar*, you mean. It is Chartier's ship, no matter that we stole it from him. And if you're so certain your plan is the right one, why are you afraid to ask the crew what they think?"

"Why are you so set against seeing reason?"

"Reason? You call sitting in the middle of the river waiting to get slaughtered reason?"

"This is obviously something that only a man can understand," he said.

"Is it! Pardon me for using my fluffy little brain and seeing things differently. Apparently only a man could be stubborn enough, blinded by some twisted sense of pride and greed, to want to have cannon fired at him and risk the bloody death of himself and his crew, and risk, as well, leaving his wife—yes, his wife!—alone in a swamp with a bunch of man-eating crocodiles! And for what? For a stinking boat!"

"I'm not giving up the *Anne*."

She stared at him, and shook her head. "You just won't listen to any other point of view, will you?"

He set his jaw and did not answer. She felt her powerlessness against his opinion, if only because he was male. The crew liked her, they were her friends—except for the three questionable Dutchmen—but she knew that they would rather follow the lead of a man, and one who had been in the army. And she suspected, as well, that none of them would have the courage to admit they would rather be safely ashore than engage in battle on this narrowing river. They called themselves "men," after all.

She shook her head. There was nothing left to discuss.

Chapter Sixteen

The sun was setting over the jungle, tingeing the sky
with bloody crimson and the gold of greed, or so Horatio was sure Anne would have thought, if she had
come out of the saloon to see it. The clouds were
limned in the brilliant light, beautiful and eerie all at
once, the water of the river reflecting pink and blue.

The further inland they had gone, the taller the trees
along the banks had grown, until now some reached
over a hundred feet into the air, their branches draped
with flowered vines. In several places they had passed
stilt villages, each as abandoned as the one they had
seen outside the mouth of the river.

Ruut gave the order to weigh anchor, setting them
firmly in place before the reversing tide sent them
spinning back downstream. As dusk settled over
them, great crashing noises came from the forest,
marking the passage of monkeys half as big as a man.

He saw them, their fur a pale grey-brown, their bodies pot-bellied, their faces flesh-colored with, of all strange things, enormous noses smack in the middle as if they were some tree-bred species of human.

"Dutchmen," Imsa said, coming to join him at the rail, where they could see a troupe of the monkeys sitting in the branches of a tree, watching them.

"Your pardon?"

"They called Dutchmen, those monkeys," Imsa said.

Horatio laughed, although the sound was only half in humor. Imsa seemed to have little compunction about letting show his derision for those not native to the island.

"Better Dutchmen than Englishmen, I suppose," Horatio said.

Imsa grinned at him. "You see male, with big nose?" he asked, pointing.

Horatio nodded, realizing that the smaller monkeys had smaller, upturned noses. The females, apparently.

"Look between legs."

Horatio stared at Imsa, then turned back to the tree. Conveniently, the monkey in question had turned, and by putting the spyglass to his eye Horatio could get a good look at what Imsa wanted him to see. It was a red erection, stiff as a stick.

"Is always there. Like Dutchman," Imsa said, laughing as he sauntered away.

Horatio left the monkeys to themselves, having had enough of them. They had seen smaller grey monkeys walking in high-tailed troupes along the shore, long-armed maroon monkeys swinging in the branches, wild pigs at the shoreline, strange birds with a heavy horn sitting on their bills, graceful white cranes, and although he hadn't seen another of Anne's crocodiles, he had seen something halfway between that and a lizard, the creature six feet long and running along the bank in a windmilling gait that covered ground as fast as a man could run.

And then there were the sounds of the insects, so loud in places that their buzzing hum pounded against his skull, deafening him.

What the hell type of place was this island?

But thinking about the strange beasts in the forest was only a way of avoiding thinking about the situation they were in, and about the argument with Anne, which had left him feeling sick. He'd rather have Chartier appear around the bend at this very moment, guns firing, than go head to head again with Anne.

Some hero he was. He couldn't even face his wife.

But who had ever said marriage would be easy? No one. All the jokes he had heard over the years, all the plays, all the satires on married life, they had not been mere foolery: They had reflected the truth he had known too little to recognize, that marriage was filled with frustrations.

He had only to picture Anne's face, though, her deep blue eyes so full of hidden tenderness, to know that she was worth whatever he had to endure as her husband.

He loved her. It was as plain and simple as that.

But she was still wrong about the boat.

He was certain that they would win any encounter with Chartier. The boat was, after all, armed in the best fashion that the pirate, himself, could manage.

Doubt niggled at his mind. The ship had also been manned by a full crew of bloodthirsty pirates who had had practice at their job, not manned by a handful of pacific sailors.

Still, it made no sense to give up the ship. It was their home, it was their transport, it was their future income, it was their only way to escape the island. If Imsa was an example of the natives of the region, keeping escape an option was a decidedly good idea. Running off into the jungle was not.

And then, beyond logic, was that of which Anne herself had accused him: pride. For the first time in his life he was proud of what he had accomplished, proud to be Horatio Merivale, and leaving the ship without a fight, letting a Frenchman take it back without so much as voicing a single sound of outrage, that was beyond him.

No, he would not give up the *Anne*.

Anne couldn't sleep, her nerves drawn as tight as the anchor chain that held the boat against the pull of the current. It was well past midnight, and above the jungle to the east were silent flashes of heat lightning, too distant to do more than add to her tension.

The moon was a thin sliver, now and then visible between drifting clouds that revealed patches of star-studded sky. Along the shoreline flashed pale green fireflies, the only visible movements in a night alive with the sounds of jungle animals.

A rotating watch had been set, against the chance of Chartier having somehow caught up to them, as well as against the possibility of an attack from the shore. Imsa dismissed that idea, although in its place he suggested that the vacant stilt villages had been targets of Malay pirates, as she and Horatio had guessed. Some seafaring Sulawak tribes also were known to engage in pirating and raiding, but Imsa thought it unlikely they would attack a ship of the size of the *Anne*.

She was sitting on a capstan, Mango cradled in her arms as she scratched at his neck and chest. She'd taken pity on the beast, who had been a nervous wreck since the first wild monkeys were sighted earlier in the day. She'd thought Mango's relatives would be a source of curiosity for him, but on the contrary he was frightened. Her physical contact seemed to soothe him, and against all expectation she found that holding the monkey soothed her, as well. It helped distract her not only from the tension of waiting for an attack that might or might not come, but from her anger at Horatio, as well.

Her own fury had surprised her, and her willingness to show it. She was used to setting her jaw and holding in her anger, smothering it because to give voice to it would mean dismissal from her position. Even at home she had kept a calm face when crossed, for her parents had not been people to tolerate backtalk from their children.

It was because she felt safe with Horatio that she had raised her voice to him. She had known that he would not strike her, and he could not dismiss her. The only threat would be that he would cease pursuing her, cease trying to consummate their marriage. And maybe he still would stop.

They had only spoken briefly since the argument—or rather, Horatio had spoken, telling her what she should do if an attack should come during the night. He had said nothing about their disagreement, his voice expressionless as if she were a stranger.

She told herself she didn't care if he did lose some of his interest in her. Surely it was better to push him away, and surely it was better in any case to let her own opinion be heard, to let her true thoughts show. She was here because it was supposed to be *her* island. No queen worth her crown would sit meekly by and allow others to make foolish decisions.

He'd get them all killed, Horatio would, and probably not even have the grace to admit he had been wrong.

"Just like a man, isn't it?" she said to Mango. "All pride and no sense."

Her self-righteousness was some comfort, although not enough to erase the pain of the argument. Against her anger was an equally strong desire to go lay her head on his chest, to say she was sorry for any hurt she had caused, if not for the opinion she had expressed.

What was this pull she had, to always make things right between them? One would think she cared how he felt about her.

"I ought to be careful," she told Mango, scratching his chest until he wrapped his arms, legs, and tail around her forearm, gnawing playfully on her knuckles. "I might fall for the fool, and then where would I be?"

Somewhere behind her on the quarter-deck, a man

gave a cry that was cut short, followed by the sound of a body hitting the deck. Anne's hand froze on Mango, her head jerking toward the noise. Mango screeched and leapt from her arms, even as wide-eyed she made out the moving shadows of men coming up over the rail.

A shout went up from the other man on watch— Ulrich, she thought—and then the silence of the invaders was suddenly replaced by war cries.

The sound jolted her to movement, and with legs gone soft with fear she rose from the capstan and ran across the deck for the rail opposite the attackers, Horatio's instructions on her escape route blessedly sharp in her mind. She moved in a sea of shadows, familiarity with the layout of the deck and its hazards all that kept her from tripping on coiled ropes. There was a rope ladder attached to the rail, waiting to be slung over the side of the ship to the skiff that floated below.

The sounds of battle raged behind her, shouts and cries and the clash of steel. A pistol went off, and she heard Mango screeching. Voices cursed in English and French, Dutch and Italian. For a moment she thought she heard Horatio calling her name, and paused, her hand on the ladder that she'd just found.

Two men, fighting hand to hand, fell against the rail near her. Ruut, by the size of him, and someone else. They staggered away, falling to the deck and rolling, grunts and groans coming from she knew not which.

"Throw rope, Missy! Throw!" Kai said, appearing out of the dark beside her, his breath coming quickly. "Fast!"

She did as he bid, and climbed up over the rail and

down the ladder. Her heart begged her to run down the deck and find Horatio, to make sure he was all right, but to do so would be to call disaster onto both him and herself. She was a liability in an attack, and she had the wit to realize it and do her friends the courtesy of getting out of the way.

"Mango! *Mon petit chou, où es-tu?*" she heard Chartier call, the sound of his voice coming as a shock even though she had expected he was the one chasing them. She felt as if she had stepped into a waking dream. How could he really be here? How could this really be happening?

"Ma chère reine!" Chartier cried.

She nearly fell off the ladder, hearing him call for his queen. She shoved aside confusion about dreams and reality and focused on escape.

Kai was right above her, his feet nearly squashing her fingers in his haste to come down. As Horatio had planned, Kai would take her to the shore in the skiff and remain with her in case they were followed or ran into trouble.

She dropped into the skiff and moved to the plank seat as Kai dropped down after her. She unshipped the oars as Kai threw off the line.

Something flew off the boat, bouncing off Kai's back and landing in her lap. She screamed in surprise, and then when she lay her hands on the heavy thing, she screamed again, grabbing a human head by its long wet hair and flinging it overboard in a jerky motion of panic.

"A head! A head!" she cried.

"A head?" Kai answered, his voice rising to a pitch far above her own.

As they both looked up at the rail above them, another shadow launched itself, this time making a shrieking noise as it went. Kai threw up his arms, and when the thing landed it clung to him, making both she and Kai scream.

Kai pulled at the thing, and then Anne realized what it was. "It's Mango! It's just Mango!"

Kai kept struggling, and then suddenly the boat tipped to one side and turned over.

Anne went under, instinct guiding her to kick her legs, flashbacks of the night of the shipwreck filling her mind as the water swallowed her. Up and down became one, and water filled her nose.

And then her head broke the surface of the water, her shoulder hitting the edge of the overturned skiff. She scrambled and clung to the boat, coughing and gasping, and heard a similar noise from the opposite side.

"Kai?" she asked.

There was another cough, and then, "Kill monkey!"

Against all odds, perched atop the hull of the skiff, Mango hunkered like a half-drowned cat.

"Well, don't try to kill him now," Anne said. She tried to look around in the dark, tried to see how far the *Anne* was from them, but all was shadows.

"Move pretty quick," Kai said.

Anne looked up at the silhouette of the treetops against the dark sky, and saw that what Kai said was true: They were moving quickly, carried by the current. "We've got to get to shore."

"Kick," Kai said.

Anne obeyed, trying at the same time to hold tight to the boat. She didn't feel any change in their motion, didn't know if they were having any effect on their course. Her arms were already growing tired on the side of the boat, so she carefully let herself slide a little deeper in the water, rolling onto her back so that only her face was above water, her right hand in a death grip on the submerged gunwale. She used her free arm to paddle.

Her foot hit Kai's once, under the dinghy, but other than that she might not have known he was there. They were both silent, saving breath for the struggle to get to shore.

The blackness of the trees grew slowly closer, and then finally the bow of the skiff thudded up against the bank, even as she felt the mud come up to meet her from beneath. The skiff began to swing its stern with the current, almost coming over her before she could turn over and find purchase with her knees in the mud. She was too tired to drag herself more than halfway out of the water.

"Take boat up," Kai said.

"What?"

"Take boat up, out of water. Morning come."

It took her long seconds to understand: They had to take the boat up into the jungle, in case when morning came Chartier and his men were still nearby. Leaving the boat on the bank would be as good as an arrow pointing after them, and letting it float free would strand them.

She hauled herself out of the water, sinking several

inches into the mud with each crawled step. Mango was already ashore, his body a black shadow running back and forth against the pale mud.

She remembered the crocodile she had seen slithering into the water. There could be one three feet from her, and she wouldn't see it in this darkness. The thought failed to frighten her, as she had the skiff, Horatio, and the others to worry about first. The crocodiles would have to wait their turn.

The attack came as if out of nowhere. One minute the deck was quiet but for the sounds of the jungle, the next it was alive with the pounding footsteps of men, and the hair-raising whoops of those intent on slaughter. It was just that one cut-off cry that was their warning, and even as he pulled his pistol from his belt Horatio cursed his failure to see the attackers coming.

He could not blame those on watch, as he himself had been on deck and had not seen the approach. And admittedly, he was too intent on a battle plan involving two vessels waging war as if they were at sea to predict that Chartier could sneak aboard in the middle of the night. The power of the current had seemed protection against such a possibility.

He was paying for his mistake now, he and all the others.

Someone came to him, shouting, and he fired. The shadow dropped, the unfamiliar voice the only way he had known the man was foe, not friend. He grabbed the cutlass from his fallen attacker and took on the next shadow to come at him.

He felt the fear in his blood, the same as he always

had in battle, but recognized it for the boon it was, giving a burst of strength and agility to his muscles. Time slowed, each instant a decade long as he slashed and blocked, side-stepped and swung, feeling the bite of the blade in flesh and not allowing himself the luxury of dwelling on the reality of what he did. All that mattered was kill or be killed, kill or have one's friends killed, kill or lose one's wife and one's honor.

In a break between opponents he thought he saw the lightness of Anne's dress by the rail. He called to her, intending to tell her to go! Go, damn it! But then he was engaged again, the tide of Chartier's men seemingly without end.

Ruut was suddenly at his side. "Too many," the big Dutchman said on a gasping breath, swinging a cutlass himself.

It was what Horatio already knew. He didn't want to admit it, wanted to stay and fight. He wanted to find Chartier and slit open his belly. It was ignoble not to have the chance to face his enemy. He felt like he had been battling the Frenchman since the day they were picked up off the raft, and yet he'd never had a chance at a hand-to-hand battle.

"Must go!" Ruut said, an urgency in his tone that bespoke a weakening in his strength, and the realization that to stay longer was to die.

"The others?" Horatio asked.

There was no time for Ruut to answer. The fighting was too thick, the effort to protect oneself too intense. Horatio felt the sapping realization of defeat, the sinking knowledge that he was going to lose his ship, and he'd be lucky if he didn't lose his life as well.

He was willing to stay and die to keep the *Anne*, only he knew its namesake was waiting for him on shore—or at least, he prayed she was. That at least was one victory that Chartier wouldn't have. He had heard the Frenchman call for his queen and for his monkey, and while the pirate was welcome to Mango, he would never have Anne.

Horatio made a lunge at his opponent, then turned and ran for the rail, vaulting it one-handed and flying through the air, the river slapping him hard as he met it flat on.

It was as good a time as any to learn how to swim.

Chapter Seventeen

Anne huddled with Kai at the edge of the forest, wet and shivering, waiting for dawn. They were both too wary of the jungle to go inside it, and clung to the edge of the river as if it could protect them from the beasts that lurked in the dark.

The scattered clouds of earlier blew away, replaced by a solid bank of darkness that obscured the stars. It started to rain, at first a few scattered drops big as beetles, and then faster and more heavily, a pelting downpour that silenced the calls of the night creatures and turned the leaves of the trees into thousands of drums.

She and Kai pushed back until they were under the heavy leaves of a bush, Mango huddling in her arms, but after a few minutes the rain seeped through that meager shelter, and in desperation they crawled their way under the skiff, spooning together like damp dogs. The rain thundered on the wooden hull over their heads, and then the sound was joined by rumbling thunder from the storm. Flashes of light lit the narrow space between overturned gunwales and ground, hinting at the violence they could not see.

It was too noisy to sleep, and yet somehow Anne did, exhaustion taking her where her frantic mind would not. She awoke pressed against Kai's bony back, Mango on top of her, her clothes still damp, the side of her that was on the ground wet and muddy. She shook Kai's shoulder.

"Kai, wake up."

Kai groaned and shifted, then hit his head on the hull of the skiff as he tried to sit up. Mango made anxious sounds, then Anne and Kai together pushed the boat off, exposing themselves like the heart of a flower to the light of day.

With creaking bones and sore muscles they pushed through the thin layer of growth that hid the boat from the river, and stepped out onto the bank. There was nothing to see. There was no sign of either the *Anne* or the boat Chartier had used to follow them. All there was was a deep gouge in the mud where they had pulled ashore the skiff, and several sets of deep, incriminating footsteps leading up the bank.

"We've got to cover those," Anne said.

"Cover quick," Kai agreed.

They smoothed their tracks as best they could, then with their combined weights cracked a branch off a tree and lay it like windfall across the evidence of their passage. They were both covered with mud and sweat by the time they finished, and the cool, misty air of morning was already burning away under the equatorial sun.

"Tide come in," Kai pointed out.

"I know. What do you think we should do?"

Kai shrugged, standing listless, looking at the river as if it could tell him the answer. Anne looked closely at him for the first time that morning, and frowned. The boy looked preoccupied, a muscle in his jaw working. And then she saw a film of tears in his eyes, and he sniffed.

"Kai! What is it? What's wrong?"

Kai shook his head and turned away. "Nothing. Go sit in jungle. Maybe boat come upriver."

Anne cast another look at the swiftly moving water, realizing that Chartier's second boat could indeed appear around the bend at any moment. She called to Mango, who had scampered up a tree, then followed Kai back behind the sheltering screen of jungle.

Kai's upset had not lessened, though, and as Anne watched in surprise his jaw trembled, and then he broke down in sobs.

"Oh, Kai," she sighed, and took the boy in her arms, instinct guiding her. He came only to her nose, and she felt like she was holding a child instead of a man nearly grown. Kai was usually so full of fire and mischief, it unnerved her to see him this way, and the things she had not allowed herself to think about all night—what had happened to Horatio and the rest of the crew—came flooding into her own mind.

Against her will, she imagined Horatio murdered at the hands of Chartier. She imagined Ruut, Ulrich, Gianni, and even Imsa dead as well. Tears came to her own eyes, and soon she was sobbing along with Kai, all but certain that the two of them were all that was left of their brave crew. It was fitting that they were stranded at the edge of the jungle, thousands of miles from home, for it was but a reflection of how alone they were in truth.

"Ulrich," Kai said, his voice muffled by Anne's chest. "Ulrich!"

"You're afraid he's dead?"

The question prompted a fresh burst of tears, the depth of emotion surprising Anne enough to distract her from her own imagined loss. She knew that Kai and Ulrich seemed to have a special friendship, but this intensity seemed a little strange.

"Kai, we don't know that anything has happened to him, or to the others. Come now, let's not cry before we have to," she said, sniffing back her own tears.

"Need Ulrich," Kai said.

"Yes, I know you do."

Kai looked up at her, his swollen eyes accusing her of not understanding. "Need Ulrich. He is father."

"Father? Whose father?"

Kai stepped back, and his put his hand over his belly. "Father of my baby."

Anne stared. Baby? What baby? How could Kai and Ulrich have a baby? Then her jaw dropped as comprehension dawned. Before her eyes, Kai's boy's face reset itself in her perception, turning from delicate Oriental youth into the fine bones of a woman.

"You—" Anne tried, and could find no words. "You—"

"I need Ulrich."

"I'll say you do! Kai!" Anne said, then flailed about for words that she could not find. "Is 'Kai' even your name?" she finally asked, realizing she didn't know if 'Kai' was a boy's or a girl's name, in China.

"Yu Kai is my name," she said, her tone rising and falling on her name in an intonation that made Anne blink with the effort of remembering it. "I used to 'Kai,' though," she added. "Is easy for you."

"Why didn't you tell me?" Anne cried.

"Was not sure, about baby."

"No, not about the baby. Why didn't you tell me you were a woman? Good lord! When I think of all the time I thought you were a boy—I knew you had a secret, but I never imagined—Kai! I could just kick you."

Kai sniffed, the weeping for the moment stopped, a little edge of a smile tilting the edge of her mouth.

"It's not funny. You should have trusted me! All this time, I thought I was the only woman aboard. You could have saved me a lot of trouble in Batavia, let me tell you!" And suddenly all her minor braveries of the past few months seemed not so brave, not so large an accomplishment when compared to everything Kai—*Yu Kai*—had done, living as a male member of a foreign crew.

What were all of her fears, compared to what Kai's must have been, at the fear of discovery? What were all her demonstrations of strength and capability, when Kai had done so much more, and without the coddling she herself had needed?

She felt like an overly precious little girl, and almost

hated Kai for letting her see herself in such poor comparison.

It was Mango pulling on her hair that drew Anne from her deranged state, and his cheeping in her ear that annoyed her enough to turn her head in time to see movement on the river.

"Kai!" she gasped, forgetting her self-disgust and her anger for the moment. "Kai, the river!"

Kai stumbled with her to a bush, where they could peer out without being seen. It was a brigantine going by, all but a steering sail furled, a handful of dirty men on deck. The name on its side was *Temperance*, and Anne felt sorry for whoever the restrained individual had been who had previously owned the boat.

"What should we do?" Kai asked.

Anne squinted at her. "Your English is suddenly sounding much improved."

"Ulrich helped me, but best to keep quiet. People say many things near dumb Chinaman."

Anne snorted, but then wondered what she, herself, might have said in unguarded moments, assuming that Kai would not fully understand her. "I don't know which course is best. If we stay here, at least we won't become lost, and we can keep an eye on the river. We might learn something once the tide turns. And sooner or later, Horatio and Ulrich will come looking for us."

"Maybe later," Kai said, the quiet words implying that "later" might be never, if the men were dead.

Anne turned to look at their overturned skiff. It was shelter of a sort, but they had no food. Half of her argued that they should stay put, but the other half worried that Horatio and the others could be huddled in the jungle, wounded, in need of help. Or they might be held prisoner aboard the *Anne*, and in need of rescuing. Not that she had the faintest notion how she and Kai would effect such a rescue, but at least she could try. And at least, if they went back upriver, she and Kai would know what had happened.

And really, if they stuck to the bank of the river, they would run little risk of either missing their friends if they should come searching for them or of getting lost. So why not?

"What do you think of going to look for them ourselves?" Anne asked.

"Better than waiting," Kai said.

It was exactly her own thought.

Horatio woke to see Imsa weaving vines around the severed head of a pirate. A second bodiless head, already encased in a green cage, sat beside him. Horatio sat up quickly, ignoring the protests of his muscles.

"I had three," Imsa said, looking up from his work, his bloodshot eyes adding a creepy horror to his disappointed expression, "but it fall in water."

"I thought you didn't take the heads of Europeans," Horatio said, his voice hoarse as he took inventory and saw that the only blade was Imsa's, and out of his reach. The jungle around them was alive with the morning sounds of birds and monkeys, and the calls of things he could not name. He was alone with the headhunter.

"Take heads of warriors."

The implication was impossible to miss. "Then it is no wonder I still have mine," Horatio said, the defeat of the night coming back to him in full force. Not only had he lost the ship, he had likely lost most of his crew. Ruut and he had been separated after leaping overboard, and he did not know if the big Dutchman had made it to shore or had drowned. He had no idea what might have become of Ulrich and Gianni, and at least one of the hired Dutchmen had been killed.

The only saving grace was that Anne had gotten away. He had seen her climb over the rail with Kai close behind, and had to believe they had rowed to safety downriver. He dreaded what she must think of him now, although it could not be any worse than how he thought of himself.

"You warrior," Imsa said, surprising him. "You friend. I not take head of friend."

"Friend?"

Imsa paused in his weaving. "I make mistake?"

"No," Horatio said, unwilling to reject the friendship of a man with a severed head in his lap. The glazed eyes of the dead pirate encouraged him to be pleasant. "I just hadn't thought you cared much for any of us."

Imsa shrugged, and went back to work. "You like children—know nothing and with too much pride. Children need teacher, not hate."

"Eh. Well." He didn't want to know what type of teacher Imsa would make. He turned, looking around at the dense jungle. "Which way is the river?"

"This way," Imsa said, pointing. "And this. And this," he said, pointing in other directions.

"What—"

Imsa curved his hand through the air. "Bending."

"Oh." He felt like an idiot, and suspected that was how Imsa wanted him to feel. He may have been captain aboard the *Anne*, but here on shore Imsa was the one in control. "Which direction will bring us to the ship?" Horatio asked, trying to sound more patient than he felt.

Imsa raised his brows. "You want die?"

"I want to see my ship."

"Not your ship now."

"We'll see about that."

Imsa sighed, finishing up his weaving and setting the second head aside, then standing up. "Knowing nothing."

Horatio stood as well, stretching the soreness out of his muscles and keeping half an eye on Imsa's blade, which the headhunter was holding loosely in one small—but very capable-looking—hand. "There's nothing arrogant or ignorant about wanting to see if we can find Ruut and the others," he said, risking the show of annoyance. If Imsa wanted to cut his head off, he would have done so by now . . . unless carrying three heads was too much of a burden, and he wanted Horatio to carry his own for a while yet.

Imsa shrugged and grinned. "If we not find them, others will."

"Which is precisely what I want to avoid." He looked at Imsa for a few moments, trying to judge how straight an answer he would get to his next question. "Assuming Anne and Kai made it to shore, do you think they will be safe?"

"Safe from what?"

Horatio waited, tired of Imsa's verbal games. Who'd have thought that a headhunter could take pleasure in such obfuscation?

"Safe," Imsa said, swinging one head by its vine handle, "if they stay where are. We find them easy."

Horatio nodded. He wanted to find Anne first, but finding the others, who might be wounded or in danger, seemed a more critical issue. Anne had Kai to watch after her, and she had the good sense to stay wherever she had put ashore. She had to know he would come for her . . . unless her opinion of him had sunk so low she assumed him incapable of even that.

Imsa set off into the jungle, the heads dangling from one hand. Horatio followed close behind, knowing it would take little for him to become lost. Hell, he was already lost.

He kept his eyes on his footing, the wet layer of leaves concealing fallen branches waiting to trip him. He still had his shoes, thank God, although they were wet from the swim in the river.

It had been a miracle he'd made it to shore. Those first long seconds underwater, going overboard seemed no better than staying to have his innards spilled on deck. Then his kicking and flailing had brought him to the surface, and the instinct to paddle like a dog had kept him there. Thankfully, there had been no waves to sweep him under, as there had been the night the *Coventry* was wrecked.

Even as he swam, the shouts and cries from the ship had begun to die down, as Chartier and his crew ran out of opponents. As well as the fear of drowning, he had the fear the pirates would scramble into their longboats and come to shore to finish off him and the others.

Imsa had found him as he struggled onto the bank, and taking his hand had pulled him through the darkness and into the jungle. There had been no time to protest, and with the shouts of Chartier's bloodthirsty crew echoing over the river, he had been eager enough to escape.

His brave plan to face the pirates on the water had fallen apart before it got started, and all that was left to him now was the chance to pick up the pieces, and endure with good grace the derision that he had earned from the others. In his mind he heard his father's scornful voice, complaining what a useless son he had, one who had avoided both promotion and riches in India, but succeeded in getting himself shot within the first five minutes of battle.

Horatio shoved the thought aside. Yes, he'd failed, but he wasn't ready to crawl into a bush and die. Anne was waiting for him, and there were the others whom he might be able to help. He was no hero, but neither was he a coward who would slink away from those who counted on him.

Bugger his father. Bugger Chartier. And bugger Imsa, too, if the little man tried to take his head. He'd sit on him, and see how he liked it.

The thought broke the heaviness of his mood, and his native optimism began to show through. The situation was precarious, there might be tragedies of loss yet to discover, but he was alive.

And life was interesting.

*   *   *

"What do you think? Should we eat one?" Anne asked. She and Kai were standing near the base of an immense tree, its top lost in the canopy of foliage overhead. In the crooks of high branches ferns and vines grew, trailing down to the forest floor. Studded along those high branches were pinkish-yellow fruits, some of which had fallen to the ground.

She and Kai had frightened away a family of wild pigs that had been feeding on the fruit. Mango, once the last pig had barreled off through the undergrowth, had scampered to the fruit and begun eating.

"If Mango lives, then we eat," Kai said, and squatted down flat-footed, folding her arms over her knees.

"The little monster has a use after all," Anne said, watching the monkey. Her stomach growled, and she heard Kai's give an answering rumble. Mango picked up another fruit and gobbled it down, then yet another. "He'd better leave some for us."

"Bad monkey," Kai said.

Anne tried squatting down like Kai did, but her heels came up off the ground, and within a minute the position became too hard to hold. Kai raised one of her faint eyebrows at her, then smiled as Anne gave up and let herself fall backwards onto her backside. "I wish I could sit like that," Anne said. "It would save my bottom getting all wet again."

"Maybe if you try long time you can."

"Maybe."

They sat and waited, watching Mango eat the fruit. They were both tired and hot, their trek through the jungle not having gone as smoothly as expected.

Keeping close to the river bank had proved unfeasible. Mangroves made impenetrable barriers, their limbs reaching down into the soil like wooden prison bars. In other places there were patches of swampy ground that hinted at quicksand.

By necessity they had gone inland, and stumbled across a faint trail, its imprint on the ground so subtle that one had to follow it as much by intuition as by sight. They'd decided it was a game trail, but in both of their minds was the possibility that headhunting kin of Imsa might use the trail, as well.

They had used broken sticks to mark the place where they joined the trail from the jungle, so that they could find the skiff again. The trail ran close to the river in places—a hundred yards back they had seen the gleam of water through the foliage, and had tramped to the river bank to check their progress. There had been no sign of boats on the water.

Mango finally had his fill and sat cleaning his distended belly. He looked none the worse for his gluttony and, after exchanging an uncertain glance with Kai, Anne crawled forward and picked up one of the fruits.

"Let me taste it first," Anne said. "I don't want you risking anything, with the baby."

Kai pursed her lips, then nodded. While walking, Kai had told Anne the whole story of how she had gone from being a fisherman's daughter to a male steward, to Ulrich's lover, and now to a woman almost three months pregnant, her swelling breasts hidden under the vest she always wore. It had been enough to keep Anne from thinking about what they might find upriver, and the talking had seemed to distract Kai, as well. From the eagerness with which she spoke, Anne guessed the girl had long been anxious to share her secret.

Anne wiped the fruit on her gown, not sure which was dirtier. She was hungry enough not to care. She looked again to Kai, shrugged, then nipped her teeth through the skin.

Juice dribbled down her chin, and a heavy, fermented taste filled her mouth. The texture was like a plum, soft and overripe, while the skin was too tart and tough to eat. It didn't taste poisonous, not that she was sure she would recognize such a taste. She found another fruit, one not quite so squishy, brushed off a few ants, and tried it.

"Good?" Kai asked.

Anne made a face, and waggled her hand in a so-so gesture. "I think it's safe, at least."

Kai joined her in scrounging for the better of the fruit on the ground. Ants and beetles were dining on it, and some had been trampled by the pigs. At least it would assuage some of their thirst. They hadn't drunk water from any of the streams they had forded, with their waters clear but tinted brown like tea. Kai had explained the coloring was from the plants and trees, not dirt, but had been as uneager as Anne to taste it. Drinking the wrong water could make them deathly ill, and if they were going to risk it they'd risk it from quickly moving water, not that which was stagnant and warmed by sunlight.

She ate only two of the fruits, finding that despite her hunger she could not bear to eat more. The taste was too unfamiliar, and she found herself chewing with long teeth and a grimace.

Her hands and ankles were swollen from the heat, and she closed her eyes and imagined a pool of clear, cool water in which she could soak naked, her damp stays and grimy shift and dress discarded. As if an answer to the thought she felt an itch between her breasts, a tickle that might have been perspiration trickling down that small valley. She reached a finger absently down her cleavage to scratch.

And encountered something slimy.

Reflex was quicker than thought, and she scraped with her nails, pulling free and flinging away something dark and spongy. "Ugh!" she cried, and then saw that there was blood on her fingertips.

She yanked down her bodice as far as her stays would let her, tucking in her chin to look down at her chest.

"What?" Kai asked, flinging away the pit of a fruit.

Anne saw another of the dark things down between her breasts, and started to panic. "I don't know!" She reached and scraped the thing off her skin, but it fell farther down her stays before she could catch it. "Oh, God," she moaned, and started tearing at her clothes.

Beginning to look panicked herself, Kai scampered over and helped her pull her gown over her head, then tugged with Anne at her lacings. The stays were shoved over her hips to the ground, and then she flung the thin chemise off after it.

Kai sucked in a breath, her eyes going wide with horror. Anne looked down and saw her body dotted all over with the things, one of which was moving end over end up her thigh, stretched-out like an earth worm.

Leeches.

She whimpered, her hands shaking as she slapped at the things, one of them sticking to her hand, another leaving a dripping wound, another elongating to four inches when pulled by her fingers. Kai scraped and pulled and flicked with her, and then Anne saw one of the things on Kai's breeches, heading for the waistband.

"Kai! You too!"

The girl's face went pale, and she stripped as frantically as Anne had done.

They were dancing madly, flinging and pulling and checking each other's backs and most intimate places, their skin streaked with trickles of blood, when the sound of laughter came from the jungle. Male laughter, and not in voices that either had ever heard.

Anne froze, Kai leaning up against her, the both of them staring wide-eyed at the deep layers of jungle. She could see no one. Mango began to scream his warning cry, and then a group of four native men emerged from the foliage, nearly naked, their earlobes dangling to their shoulders and weighted by brass hoops, dark blue-green tattoos on their shoulders and chests.

They were carrying short swords in wooden scabbards at their waists, and long wooden spears. One had the body of a large monkey tied to his back with strips of some fibrous plant. He lay it down on the ground as he continued to laugh with the others, who began to dance around, giving girlish shrieks and slapping at their bodies.

Kai clung to Anne, shielding the front of her body from their view. Anne couldn't take her eyes off the men. They were shorter than she, their brown bodies undulating with muscle, their hair cut in the same blunt-banged style as Imsa's. They wore loincloths, and each had a bamboo cylinder on the hip opposite the scabbard.

A fruit flew down from the tree and splattered across the chest of one of the hunters, the action followed by gleeful monkey howls. Anne broke loose from Kai and scrambled for her chemise and pulled it on, casting a quick look up into the tree where Mango was plucking another of the fruits.

The hunters doubled over in laughter as their stricken compatriot stormed the trunk of the tree, shaking his spear at Mango. Mango jabbered, and pelted another fruit down at the man, who ducked and took the hit on his shoulder.

The men appeared distracted by the monkey. Kai had her breeches back on, and her shirt. Her eyes met Anne's, and then they both bolted down the path.

One of the men shouted in surprise, and then quicker than she could see him move he was blocking the path, his arms spread wide. He didn't touch either her or Kai, but gestured with his hands and a nod of his head for them to turn around.

She and Kai found each other's hands, and like young girls, hung tight for support as they obeyed and turned back towards their captors. She could feel the fine trembling in Kai's muscles, and remembered the fear the girl had of Imsa.

"I don't think they want to hurt us," Anne said under her breath.

Mango threw a rapid volley of fruit, missing most of his targets but getting one of the other men in the thigh. As his friends laughed, the man opened the canister at his hip and took out a long, thin dart with a cottony wad at the end.

"How do you know?" Kai asked.

"Wouldn't they have done so? Look at them. They're in too good a mood to do any harm." Kai wasn't showing any of the bravado that she had while a crewmember on the ship. The girl seemed undone by the absence of Ulrich.

"I think Imsa smile while chopping off head," Kai said.

The man with the dart slid it into the end of the spear he carried, then crouched down and raised the weapon to his mouth, the blade end pointing up into the tree. A vision of her little brother with a pea shooter came to Anne, and she suddenly understood that these were not simple spears: They were blowguns.

"No!" she cried, and as the hunter took a deep breath she lunged and pushed him over. He shouted and came back at her, then checked his attack. Anne ran to the base of the tree and called up to Mango. "Come sweeting, come down," she coaxed, and gave the whistle that she used just for him.

He jabbered and cheeped, hoarding a mass of fruit against his belly, then let them drop and scampered down the trunk, leaping the last few feet to land on her shoulder, clinging to her hair and barking angrily at the men.

The man who had tried to shoot Mango shrugged his shoulders and put his dart back in the carrier at his waist. One of the other men unsheathed his big blade, but before Anne had time to be frightened he had squatted down and started chopping at the ground, then moved over a foot and after careful observation chopped again. He glanced up at her and grinned, then with the tip of his blade picked his target off the moldering leaves and held it up for her inspection. It was a leech.

A few words flowed between the men, and one disappeared into the jungle. Anne cautiously gathered up her gown, but before she could get to her stays one of the men picked them up and tried to pull them on. The leech chopper watched and laughed, and then the one who had gone into the jungle returned with a handful of leaves and came over to where Anne stood beside Kai. He held the leaves out for them to take.

"Uh, thank you," Anne said. The man looked at her expectantly, his dark eyes alight. He made a gesture that suggested she should "go ahead," but "go ahead" and what, she didn't know. She cautiously took one of the leaves and raised it towards her mouth.

The man waved his hands, speaking quickly, then plucked the leaf from her fingers. He crouched down and gestured for her to raise the hem of her chemise. She cast a wild look to Kai, then obeyed. He pantomimed rubbing the leaves against her skin, but still did not touch her. Then he did it to himself, this time scrubbing the leaf hard and leaving a streak of green on his already greenish skin. She realized that his lower legs were coated with the stuff, and a quick glance showed that the others wore it, as well.

He found a leech on the ground, and pressed it against the leaf. The leech shriveled away.

Anne looked at Kai, then they both grabbed a handful and began scrubbing their legs with the leaves. Mango hopped onto the ground and went to examine the dead monkey, gingerly touching it and then bouncing away.

Anne tied her chemise skirts in a knot just above her knees, wanting to be able to see this time if there was anything crawling up her legs. The hunter was still playing with her stays, but she didn't ask for them back. In her chemise she was cooler than she had been all day.

The hunters were all but naked, and they seemed to have no interest in the shadows of her body visible through the dirty cotton chemise she wore. She rolled up her dress and tucked it under her arm. The hell with wearing it. She was lost in the jungle with headhunters and leeches, all but one of her friends lost, as well, or possibly killed by pirates: The least she had to worry about was her shocking state of dishabille.

The hunter who had been carrying the dead monkey made a teasing grab at Mango, who ran screeching back to her while the hunter hefted his catch back onto his shoulders. Kai came and put her hand in Anne's. They were ready to go.

Where, she had no idea.

Chapter Eighteen

"What the hell are they doing?" Horatio whispered, as much to himself as to Imsa.

"I do not—" Imsa began, but was cut off by the thundering boom of the cannon.

A dozen yards to their right the ball shattered a tree trunk. A cheer went up from the deck of the *Anne* as the tree creaked and then slowly toppled, branches crashing and breaking.

"Shit!" Horatio said. "He's a goddamn lunatic!"

"He shot tree," Imsa said, his voice flat.

Horatio was gratified by the headhunter's confusion: The man didn't know everything, after all. "That goes to show you what type of people the French are. If he can't kill us, he'll settle for an innocent plant."

"He hate you," Imsa said.

"I know. I stole his monkey." That, too, brought him a sort of savage satisfaction. Chartier might have his boat back, but Horatio knew that Mango was not aboard. The first thing he and Imsa had heard when they had reached the river bank was Chartier calling for his monkey.

There was a conference going on on deck, and when it finished ten armed men climbed down to the longboat that bobbed alongside the ship. The men rowed to shore, hitting the bank near where the cannon ball had shattered the tree, and all but two streamed ashore with the enthusiasm of sailors sighting a whorehouse, shouting and running and waving their cutlasses. The two with the boat quickly shoved off and rowed back to the ship.

The tide had turned again, and Horatio guessed that Chartier had decided to use his time stuck in the river to kill whatever and whomever he could. His men were too drunk and too loud to do anything but warn people and animals to flee, and it would be only the most stupid of creatures that fell prey to their marauding.

Chartier paced the deck, every few minutes stopping at the rail and staring into the jungle. "Mango!" the privateer called, cupping his hands around his mouth. "Mango!" And then, "Anne! *Ma belle!* Anne!"

The sound of his wife's name on the Frenchman's tongue was almost enough to make Horatio dive into the river and fight his way to the boat to strangle the man. Chartier would never again have Anne within his power—never!

The loathing he had felt for the man when he had been a prisoner had now trebled. In some rational part of his brain he knew that the man had done nothing for which he could be reprehended, if you accepted that he was a Frenchman and a privateer and that Horatio had stolen both his boat and his monkey.

Rationality had no part in hatred, though: Chartier was an integral part of Horatio's own humiliations and defeats, and he couldn't stomach the thought that Chartier had won.

A tenuous thought swept through him at that, too fragile to hold for more than a moment: If he had Anne, and if he had Mango, then Chartier hadn't won. *He* himself had.

But Mango was a filthy monkey Horatio would as soon eat for dinner as bear company with, and he could not believe that Anne would let him so much as put his arm around her after last night's fiasco. And there sat the ship of which he had so shortly been captain, once again under the command of its buggering master.

There was nothing to do now, though, but move forward. If the Hand of Destiny had any justice in it at all, he would have another chance at Chartier.

He had a brief conference with Imsa. There were no signs of Ulrich, Ruut, or Gianni, so the next thing to do was find Kai and Anne before the drunken pirates had the dumb luck to stumble upon them.

They moved downstream as the pirates moved deeper into the jungle, where they would soon find themselves coated with leeches. He had already found several on his own legs.

An hour of searching later, they had turned up neither Anne nor the Chinaman, nor had they found the skiff. Kai and Anne might be on the opposite shore, or might for some reason—lost oars, perhaps—have ended up miles downstream. Finding them on foot could be nigh on impossible: They needed a boat.

"We find village," Imsa said. "All village on river. All have boat."

"We saw plenty of villages on the river. They were all abandoned."

"We go small river, we find people. Pirates go large river, people move to small river."

"How will we find anyone?"

Imsa smiled. "If in England, in forest, you find village?"

"Eventually. But that's different," Horatio said, thinking of all the things he would be aware of that would direct him. Roads, trails, rivers, coppices, traps, all hinting at where to go or that there were people near.

"Is same," Imsa said.

Horatio looked around at the undifferentiated jungle. He would have to trust that Imsa could see things to which he was blind. They set off again, and Horatio tried not to notice the sound the pirates' heads made as they knocked together. They were beginning to smell, and were attracting flies.

"First man get no leeches," Imsa explained some time later, while Horatio paused to break the grip of one especially stubborn leech that had fastened itself to the back of his calf. "First man on trail wake them up. Second man is dinner."

"Thank you for explaining that. I feel so much better about our friendship now."

Imsa laughed. He was apparently not entirely without sympathy, however, and a short time later gave

Horatio leaves to use on his legs to help keep the creatures at bay.

They moved on, and after a timeless stretch of trudging Imsa stopped and sniffed the air. Horatio bent over, bracing his hands on his thighs, catching his breath. They had left the lowland jungle and had begun to trek through hills, following trails that only Imsa could see. The heat and humidity had been unpleasant enough on flat land, but the added strain of going up slopes with uncertain footing had drained him of his strength. He stared at Imsa's relaxed body, dry of sweat, and decided one had to have been born to this world to survive it.

A trickle of sweat ran down his nose and splashed onto the back of his hand. Half an hour back Imsa had grabbed a thick vine that hung from the ceiling of trees, and with a stroke of his blade cut it open. Water had dribbled out, and like an overheated dog Horatio had lapped it up. His mouth was parched again already, thirsty for another vine.

A large bee buzzed near his face, then dropped down to land on the back of his hand. Two more flew close, circling his head. He swatted at them, but they went no more than a foot before coming back.

This island belonged in a fairy story, being both beautiful and horrible at once. Some trees had wall-like buttresses fanning out from their trunks, anchoring them to the ground, and others grew as lacework *surrounding* other trees. There were sweet scents of flowers, and a few steps later the stench of things rotten and putrid. He had seen a beetle the size of his fist, cicadas as big as birds, and a dozen green and black butterflies dancing in the air above a patch of damp ground.

"Stop hitting bees," Imsa said.

Horatio brushed his hands through the air again. "I don't want to get stung."

"They drink sweat. They do not hurt."

"That's easy for you to say. You're not sweating. They're leaving you alone," Horatio complained as another half dozen bees joined the swarm already circling him.

Imsa gave him a patronizing look, then pointed in a direction that looked no different from any other. "This way. We walk, bees go."

"How do you know which way to go?" Horatio asked.

"Smell smoke."

It was as good a sign of habitation as any, although his own nose couldn't detect the scent amidst all the others of the jungle.

His worries for Anne, already at a steady simmer, had come near to boiling as the day wore on. The hope that they might be near a boat was enough to give him an extra burst of strength, and he straightened up.

"Lead on, MacDuff!" he said.

Imsa wrinkled his brow, then turned and led the way.

"Hah! Don't know Shakespeare! Don't know everything after all, do you?" Horatio muttered under his breath, as the bees drifted away one by one in obedience to Imsa's prediction.

They came free of the jungle, emerging onto the

side of a hill shorn of vegetation. Blackened stumps and raw earth made an ugly wound on the green of the jungle, and Horatio thought for a moment he was seeing the results of a wildfire.

The thought was quickly thrown out when he saw the three people lower down the slope, clearing the land of the charred remnants of forest. They wore circular hats three feet wide to shade them from the blistering sun that beat down on the exposed ground, and bent to their task with the efficiency of farmers familiar with hard work.

"Hill rice," Imsa said, by way of explanation.

"No paddies?" Horatio asked, curious. He had only known of rice grown in water.

"In Sulawak, only hill rice. You will like *tuak*," he added, grinning.

"I'm almost afraid to ask."

"Rice wine."

"Let's find Anne and Kai first, then worry about getting drunk."

Imsa shook his head. "You do not know people of Sulawak. You have rice wine before you have boat."

Imsa started down the hill, calling out a greeting in his own tongue to the workers. Horatio followed, and when he came up to them felt like a giant amongst pixies. None came higher than his chest, and all were as sleekly muscled as Imsa, even the man with grey hair. They looked him up and down, making "ohhh" sounds, yet seemed unsurprised by his arrival out of the wilds of the jungle.

He felt his appearance merited a little more astonishment than he was getting. He had to look strange to them—even in India he had caused a stir when traveling outside of usual British haunts.

Imsa was nodding his head as the three men talked, waving their hands in animation. Imsa began to laugh, said a long speech himself, then the men laughed, as well. They were having a fine time, which became finer when Imsa held up the pirate heads. That merited another round of "ohhh"s, much more enthusiastic than he had gotten himself.

Just as he was beginning to feel impatient and like a piece of the scenery, Imsa turned to him. "Their talking is hard for me, sounds different. Good luck, this tribe not at war with my tribe. We go to longhouse, no trouble."

"What about a boat?"

"We go to longhouse, drink *tuak*," Imsa said, amusement in his eyes.

Horatio bit back his impatience. The man was not one he could push, he'd learned that much today. He would have to try to appear calm, however strongly it went against his present inclination. He would have to keep away the image of Anne huddling wet and afraid along a riverbank, a crocodile swimming by in front and pirates shouting behind. Otherwise, he'd be tempted to steal a boat, and then it would be *his* head swinging from a net of vines.

A farmer led them to the head of a path and, gesturing, gave what must be directions. Imsa thanked him, and the farmer went back to work as they took the narrow path.

What he had assumed would be a five-minute walk stretched to half an hour through jungle, past fallow fields, and then finally along the banks of a river no more than two feet deep, running over smooth brown rocks and boulders. Only twenty feet wide, the river was shaded by trees that met overhead, the water looking cool and infinitely inviting. The light turned golden as the afternoon grew late, and the birds that had been silent during the heat of the day began once again to sing, and the cicadas' chorus of buzzes and drummings grew louder.

The path turned directly towards the river, and without pause Imsa stepped down the bank and into the water, wading across. Horatio followed, and as they neared the opposite bank their steps took them around a bend.

He stopped, the water pushing at his legs as he stared in shock.

Sitting on a low boulder in the middle of the stream, a beam of sunlight limning her in gold, was Anne. Her back was to him, but there could be no mistaking the long blond hair and pale skin.

"Anne?" His voice was not loud enough to rise over the sounds of the river, but she heard and turned.

"Horatio!" she cried, and was on her feet and sloshing towards him through the river. She either tripped or threw herself at him when she finally came near—he was not sure which—but suddenly she was in his arms, clinging to his neck, covering his cheeks and neck with kisses.

He wrapped his arms around her, holding her tight, his eyes shut as he tried to make sense of her presence.

"I was afraid you might have been killed," Anne

said, tears in her voice. "I was so worried. Or I thought you might have been lying in the jungle somewhere, bleeding, or being attacked by wild animals."

"Never! They don't like the taste of me," he said hoarsely, in disregard of leech bites and thirsty bees. "I was looking for you."

"You've found me." She released his neck and leaned back, looking at him, then hit him on the shoulder. "Don't ever do that to me again!"

"Do what?"

"Make me worry about you like that."

"You thought I couldn't take care of myself?"

"Chartier might have killed you while you were defending that stupid boat," Anne said, hitting him on the shoulder another time. He grabbed her hand to keep her from doing it again, his hold on her waist loosening.

"If I'd run the moment he appeared you would not have had time to escape," he said, and waited for her to tell him that if he'd abandoned the ship to begin with, escape wouldn't have been necessary. Or to say that if he'd done a better job of defending the ship, they'd be back aboard it at this very moment.

"I don't care. I'd rather that than—" she started, then cut herself off.

"Than what?"

"I didn't like being separated from you, is all," she said, and then, as if trying to make light of the admission, "You're my husband, after all."

"So you admit that at last?"

"We're supposed to pretend, remember?"

"I remember," he said, his mind turning over, unable to find the right way up. Anne seemed not to care a whit about the loss of the ship. Didn't she see how he had failed her?

"Kai is in the longhouse with Ulrich and Ruut," she said.

"What?"

Imsa splashed past them, grinning. Horatio stared at the headhunter's back, remembering the laughter he had shared with the field workers. He'd known.

"What in God's name is that smell?" Anne asked, then caught sight of the heads Imsa carried. Her hands tightened on Horatio's arms. "He didn't. . . ."

"He did. But Ulrich, Ruut? They're all right? How did they get here?"

She took his hand and pulled him over to the rock upon which she'd been sitting, then tugged him down beside her. The water came up nearly to his knees, but its gentle coolness was welcome after the hike with Imsa.

"It's safe to drink," Anne said.

With a cupped hand he drank, then washed the sweat and dirt from his face as Anne briefly explained that Ruut and Ulrich had been found by hunters alerted by the gunshots in the night. Ruut had dislocated a shoulder, and Ulrich had sustained a surface gash to his chest, but both had been tended to and were in good spirits. They didn't know what had become of Gianni, whom Ulrich had last seen below decks before the attack. The fate of the other Dutchmen was equally unknown, but it seemed possible that they had switched sides.

He rested his forehead in his hands, leaning on his

knees and feeling the water swirl past his legs. The ability to think was escaping him as both exhaustion and relief crept over his body. Almost everyone had made it to shore and been fine without him, which made the struggles and worries of the day seem almost comical in their pointlessness.

And now what was he supposed to do with himself? The ship was gone. Anne had found her island. What next? Where was his place? He had thrown away his position in the army, and he had lost his captaincy of the *Anne*.

He closed his eyes, hearing Anne's voice, the cicadas, the gurgling of the water, and the noise in his mind faded for a moment, leaving him only with an awareness of his love for Anne. It felt as if there was nothing left inside him, nothing except for that, tying him to her with a thousand golden bands.

His failures and successes were nothing next to that. They were but ripples on the surface of his soul, vanishing with the breeze. He loved her from the depths of his soul, and it was the greatest thing he had ever done.

He opened his eyes and noticed that she was wearing only her chemise, the wet bottom half of it transparent against her thighs as she talked about how she and Kai had met the headhunters in the jungle. Her wide neckline left the top half of her breasts exposed. She smelled of flowers and warm female skin, her skin dewy, the remaining sunlight picking out the fine golden hairs on her arms and tracing the line of her collar bone.

He'd never seen anyone so beautiful. She was more

at ease upon this rock in the jungle than she ever had been aboard the *Coventry* or the *Anne*. Her dreams had been right: This was her island, the home she was meant to have, with its oversized insects and trailing vines and nameless beasts of the jungle. Like a creature of that jungle, she belonged here and nowhere else.

And he did not.

Except for his bond with her, which made her world the only one in which he wished to live. Once, in another lifetime, he had seen her only as a lady's maid, a shadow behind her mistress and unworthy of a second glance. Now she was the queen of his soul. He would die for her, for loving her was life.

"And there's something about Kai I have to tell you," she was saying, but he wasn't hearing the words. She pushed her fingers back through her hair, combing through the silken strands with their sun-bleached streaks of white. The sun had brought out faint freckles across her cheeks and nose, and dusted her skin with tawny color.

He didn't know who he was supposed to be anymore, except that he was meant to be with her. A quiet faith stirred in his heart, that if he held to that truth all else would come right. Anne was his constant, his star to steer by.

"Anne," he said, interrupting her.

"Yes?"

He took her hand and clasped it between his own, then met her eyes. The deep sapphire blue reflected back jungle and sunlight to him, as if she were becoming part of this world in body as well as spirit. He would not let her disappear into it alone. "I love you."

Her lips parted, but no words came forth. He hadn't expected any. He leaned close and pressed his lips to her cheek. It was a gentle kiss that asked nothing of her but acceptance.

"I can't—"

"Shh. I wanted you to know," he said. "You don't need to say or do anything. Just know that it is the truth. It is the only truth I have."

Her eyes reflected her confusion. He released her hand and with his fingers brushed her hair back from her face, tucking it behind her ear. He felt a quiet stillness within him that accepted that she was not ready to return his love. He understood, as he never had before, that it was the loving of another that mattered most.

"Shall we join the others?" he asked, changing his tone to a light one, breaking the silence of her tension.

"They'll be glad to see you," she said, rising from the rock, still looking at him with uncertainty in her eyes.

"And I them. Is this longhouse the place you saw in your dreams?"

"It is like it."

He nodded, expecting no less. "What was it you were going to tell me about Kai?" he asked, following her up onto the bank.

She looked over her shoulder at him, giving a secretive grin like one of Imsa's. "I should let Kai tell you."

"If you prefer," he said, but it wasn't where his mind was. He could see the shape of her buttocks and thighs through the chemise, and it was becoming difficult to concentrate, his pure thoughts of love from moments before being swept up in a surge of desire that had nothing to do with passive acceptance of the situation.

He loved her, but he decided it did nothing to lessen the purity of that love to want to take Anne to his bed.

Life was looking bright again. He had heart for any fate, as long as he had heart for Anne.

Chapter Nineteen

"You'll have to take off your shoes," Anne said, her mind in a thousand places as she tried to take in what Horatio had said. She was leading him to the long-house, built on stilts a short way back from the river and backed by jungle. It was 300 feet long, the sloping roof made of dry palm leaves, floored in strips of bamboo tied onto an underlying frame made of wood. The structure was immense, but also gave the impression that a good wind storm would blow it away.

She was hardly seeing it, though, the oddity of it nothing compared to the oddity of Horatio having said he loved her. Not that he desired her, not that he wanted to marry her, but that he loved her. And she had seen in his expression that he meant it, with all of his being, without reservation.

"Am I supposed to walk up that?" Horatio asked, gesturing to the stairway that reached from the ground to the uncovered porch of the longhouse, some ten feet above the ground. It was a simple log, notched into steps, without a rail.

"It's not as hard as it looks," Anne assured him, nudging aside a chicken with her foot. The packed dirt under and immediately around the longhouse was alive with clucking chickens and domesticated pigs. Scrawny, ugly little dogs lay stretched out in the fading sunlight or wandered about looking for scraps.

A group of small children was watching them, giggling, from the porch, but she knew they would scatter as soon as she climbed the steps: One little two-year-old had burst into tears of fright upon first seeing her. Imsa had explained that her paleness and light hair made her look like a ghost.

Horatio grunted his disbelief. "You're shorter. It's easier for you to keep your balance."

"What nonsense. Take off your shoes. They don't like mud in their house, and you're less likely to fall through the porch if you can feel where you're stepping."

"You seem quite at home," he said, slipping off his shoes.

She paused. "You're right," she said, actively considering it, glad at least of distraction from the overwhelming thought in her mind: Horatio *loved* her. "I do feel at ease here. Strange, isn't it?" But not as strange as his truly loving her. It was as if she could feel a golden warmth stretching from his heart to hers, and with it a promise of eternity.

"I've seen stranger things in the past few months than your feeling at ease with a village of headhunters," he said. "This is what you dreampt of all along, after all."

"I didn't dream the headhunting bit. I don't think I'd have been quite so eager to go adventuring, if I had."

"I wonder about that."

"Oh, for heaven's sake, you're stalling," she said, lifting the hem of her chemise and climbing lightly up the log. The children had disappeared by the time she made it to the top. She turned and looked back down at him. "Go quickly and it's easier."

He put his foot on the bottom step and looked up at her uncertainly.

"Ruut fell twice trying to make it up, from what I hear," she said, "but finally succeeded on hands and knees. The villagers think it a very good joke, and will gladly act out the spectacle for you."

"You have a strange manner of motivation," he said, then raced up the log, arms out for balance, leaning first to one side and then the other, nearly falling, and then he was at the top.

She took his arm to steady him. "That was impressive, Mr. Merivale."

"I consider it my finest accomplishment in recent memory, Mrs. Merivale."

For the first time, she almost liked the sound of that name. "You do remember we are only pretending at that?"

"You may pretend, if you wish," he said, and pressed his lips to her brow, gently holding her neck in one broad hand. "It is true for me."

She closed her eyes, leaning against him, still feeling that powerful warmth that was his love. For a moment she was tempted to give in to that promise. Some part of her, though, still felt as if she was standing on a bank of shifting sand, and she could not release control of her heart until she had reached solid ground.

She had to know what this island meant to her before she could think of becoming his wife in the full sense. If she wished to stay here, and he wished to leave, what would she do then?

Horatio might not be any good at fighting pirates, he might be a lousy navigator and fond of singing racy songs out of tune, but he made her smile, and he believed in her in a way that she did not even believe in herself. And, as reckless and foolishly optimistic as he was, she had to admit she would never have made it this far without him. She'd either be dead, or back in service to Miss Godwyn, dreaming dreams that would be forever unfulfilled.

It felt good to have him close once more. She had grown used to him being always near while on board the ship, and had felt his absence like an ache while she had been wandering the jungle with Kai.

She stepped back, looking up at him with a feeling of warmth that echoed his own, and trying to hide the yearning she had to touch him, to feel his hands on her. "Come, Mr. Merivale. The others will be waiting to see you, and there are introductions to be made." She pulled him by the hand, gesturing with the other at where he should step on the uneven floorboards.

"What's that hole?" he asked, following carefully behind her.

"That's where Ruut put his leg through. They didn't think that was quite as funny as his falling off the log, from what I gather. They made him crawl the rest of the way across the porch."

"He must have enjoyed that."

She laughed. "He is still in a bad temper about it. The villagers don't seem to mind, though. I think they see him the same way Kai does: as someone to tease."

"Headhunters, teasing?"

"Just you wait and see."

Anne sat cross-legged on one of the many woven rattan mats on the floor of the inner verandah of the longhouse, her feelings a mix of unexpected comfort with her present surroundings and an almost painful longing to have Horatio within touching distance.

Forget touching distance. She wanted him touching her, even if it was only the edge of his leg against hers.

Dusk had settled over the jungle, and pitch torches had been lit, carefully placed to avoid setting the longhouse alight. Horatio had been given the same soap-producing leaves that she had, and had the chance to bathe in the river. They'd all been fed, bits of monkey and a great deal of rice and boiled, bitter green leaves that she could not identify.

Horatio was a few dozen feet away now, talking to Ulrich, Ruut, and Kai. She watched in anticipation as Kai spoke, finally telling both Ruut and Horatio her secret. Ruut made a loud noise, and Horatio sat back, as if hit. Anne smiled, enjoying the show.

This inner verandah stretched the length of the building like a long hallway, with the uncovered porch outside running down the left side, and a wall with doorways to private apartments running down the right. There were thirty such doors, and as people had returned throughout the day from hunting or farming, or bathing down at the river, she'd realized that there had to be over two hundred people who lived here, counting the children. Ruut and Ulrich had been given mats in front of the apartment of the healer, while she and Kai—and now Horatio—had places near the headman's home.

The headman, Ano, had seemed to welcome their presence, asking Imsa dozens of questions and showing the same curiosity as would any English villager of a stranger, if bold enough to ask. The age, marital status, number of children, home countries, and family backgrounds of all of them were inquired after, and the news that no one, as of yet, had any children seemed to be the worst mark against them.

The villagers were shy yet friendly with her, and as she sat quietly more than one woman had eventually come to sit beside her for a bit, trying to communicate. With hand gestures and nods of the head Anne managed to engage in basic conversation. Yes, he is my husband. No, I have no children. This is a lovely mat: Did you weave it? And they were curious about her hair and her chemise, and the dress that she had laid out on the outer porch to dry, after scrubbing it in the river.

Mango was unofficial ambassador to the children, letting himself be chased until he at last tired and came to her for protection. He was sitting now on a beam above her head, watching warily lest someone try to come pull his tail.

Horatio got up and walked back towards her. She smiled as she saw him suddenly remember to walk near the apartment doors, and not across the intervening mats that marked out private areas of public space. The rules of behavior in the longhouse came easily to her, from simple observation and common sense. Imsa had, more than once, raised his brows in surprise when she had done the right thing, like bend over to make herself smaller while walking near a person sitting on the floor.

Ruut, on the other hand, seemed incapable of doing anything right, and seemed unaware of most of his offenses. It was their good fortune that the villagers had a sense of humor.

Horatio was somewhere in the middle, stumbling but trying his best to be a polite guest in the home of these people who had, against all expectation, taken them in.

"I never even suspected," he said, sitting down beside her, and stiffly folding his legs into the same position as hers. Sitting with legs stretched out was another no-no, one that Imsa had had to instruct them on.

"She hid it well. And with her head half shaved like it was, who would ever have suspected?"

"Apparently Ulrich, the dog. We have to get those two married."

"I'm having a difficult time imagining Kai as a mother," Anne said.

"I can imagine her quite well, climbing ratlines with

a baby strapped to her back. Either that, or she'll let the little rotter crawl around as wild as Mango."

She laughed, wanting more than anything to lean against him and feel his arm around her shoulders.

The headman's wife, Lua, looked out her doorway at them, said something, and smiled before ducking back into her apartment.

"Are you going to start dressing like they do?" Horatio asked, nodding towards the doorway where Lua had disappeared. She was surprised he had restrained himself from commenting for this long. Her own eyes had about fallen out of her head when she'd seen their mode of dress, although she was becoming accustomed to it. Somewhat.

The women wore nothing more than a wrap of cloth around their hips, leaving their breasts and their legs below the knee bare for any and all to see. Most had heavy brass loops stretching their earlobes, and some had abstract tattoos on their legs and forearms. Their hair was pulled back into a bun of sorts, and most wore a thin band of either beads or woven cane like a circlet atop their heads.

"Only if you start wearing a loincloth. And you're a married man. You can't be ogling other women."

"Most are not ogling material," he said.

She had to agree. While the youngest women were lovely and nubile, those with children showed quite clearly the effects of childbearing upon breasts. It was not a welcome lesson in what she had to look forward to one day.

"What next?" Horatio asked, after they'd been sitting silent for a bit, watching the movements in the longhouse. "Where do we go from here?"

"Imsa says we can talk to Ano about that tomorrow. It would be rude to do so before that: Sociability comes first."

"That's a funny thing to hear from Imsa."

She slanted him a look. "Did you not get along while in the jungle?"

"Let's just say I think he enjoys having the upper hand. Playing assistant to Raffles may not have been as agreeable to him as Raffles thought. I think he believes his dignity was infringed upon, and he is taking his revenge."

"Being a servant is never as agreeable as the master or mistress thinks," Anne said quietly.

He was quiet a moment. "I'm sorry. I'd forgotten."

She touched his knee lightly. "It's nothing about which to apologize. There is nothing shameful in holding a position. You yourself were a servant to the East India Company. We are all servants to someone."

"Perhaps."

People were emerging from their apartments now, dressed in what had to be their finery. The men wore beaded headdresses with black and white feathers sticking out the top, and shaggy fur coverings over their shoulders. The women wore longer skirts now, bright red and white, woven in patterns of diamonds and standing figures. Some wore half-bodices of brass coils around their midriffs, and dozens of polished brass rings over their lower legs and forearms.

They came to sit near where she and Horatio sat, gracefully tucking their legs up beneath them. Some children ran around chasing each other, while others squatted in a semicircle and played a variation of jacks that involved throwing down stones while picking up others. One little girl, sitting in the lap of her mother, began a shy game of I-see-you with Anne, ducking her head and then peeking up again.

Ruut, Ulrich, and Kai came to join them, finding places in what was becoming a large oval, several people deep. Tarnished brass gongs were set up, and long narrow drums appeared, held across the laps of men who grinned with missing teeth when Anne met their eyes.

And then the Chinese earthenware jars came out. Imsa had warned her about them. Two or three feet tall each, the jars themselves were signs of an individual's wealth, and a sign of the worldliness of the owner, obtained through trade and handed down through generations. What they held was rice wine.

"Do I detect signs of a celebration?" Horatio asked softly.

"I think you do. It doesn't look much like anything you'd see in Bath or London, though, does it?"

He laughed under his breath. "I don't want to imagine my sisters in such garb."

Anne laughed, too, thinking of Miss Godwyn sitting petulantly in nothing but a hip wrap and a bit of vine in her hair, jealous of some other woman's beads.

Talking soon became next to impossible, as without warning the gongs started up, played by two young women wearing heavy loopings of beads over their chests. The sounds were foreign, without melody as she knew it, yet strangely entrancing. The drummers started in as well, the combined sounds thumping into Anne's breast.

Women with small wooden bowls began pouring rice wine and passing it around. Anne drank when a bowl came to her, and found it not unpleasant. Then the bowls came around again, and again, and more jars emerged from apartments.

The torch-lit scene, already alien, began to take on the aspect of a dream. Anne began passing the bowls by without doing more than touching her lips to the edge, not wanting to become more drunk than the slight buzzing feeling she already had.

A man in full regalia stood up and walked to the center of the circle, and in time to the beating of gongs and drums began a dance. He crouched, he stalked, he lifted his arms like those of an eagle, and slowly Anne realized he was telling a story through his movements.

When he was finished another man took his place, and then another took his, apparently without any pre-arranged order. The next one who stood up was wearing Anne's stays. The crowd, now seriously affected by alcohol, roared its approval.

The hunter crouched down and mimed eating something off the ground, making faces of disgust to the crowd's delight. Anne felt heat begin to burn her cheeks. The hunter scratched at himself, at his buttocks, at his head, and then at the space where his cleavage would have been. He pulled out his hand in amazement, and gave a blood-curdling screech that made the audience shriek in surprise, then people started collapsing sideways with laughter as the hunter danced around, trying to fling imaginary leeches off his fingers and off his body. He struggled wildly with the stays, finally flinging them off and stomping on them.

Anne ducked her face into her hands in embarrassment, hearing Horatio laughing beside her as he caught on to the story. As the pantomime continued she dared to look up and watch, and felt a smile tug her lips as the man played the part of hunters being pelted with fruit by Mango. The story ended with the pretend-Anne pushing over a disgruntled hunter to save the monkey, to the gleeful amusement of the audience who seemed to love seeing the man taken down a peg. The performer retired to shouts of approval and a bowl of rice wine.

The party wore on, the villagers growing progressively more drunk, even the children. Ruut was dared to drink more by a trio of tribesmen, then when Ruut refused, they pounced on him and held his head back while they poured the wine down his throat. He roared when they released him, and they ran off laughing like lunatics.

Dancing was still going on, women sometimes getting up now, moving in slow steps and floating their arms near their sides as if they were cranes, or reeds in the water.

A man pulled Horatio up and tried to teach him a song and a dance, making Horatio repeat his words and steps. The audience that was still capable of listening pealed their laughter as Horatio repeated words inaccurately, turning the meanings into God only knew what.

And on it went. A man pushed aside floorboards to vomit onto the ground beneath, the event followed quickly by the excited squealing of pigs come to suck up the treat. One hunter chased another with his sword, slashing in mock attack. A very drunk old man sat in front of Ulrich, speaking earnestly to him while Ulrich nodded as if in understanding.

The torches began to burn low, then sputter out, and people did the same, some returning to their apartments, others passing out where they lay. Ruut snored, at a volume to shake the rafters, while one long-enduring mischief maker tied bits of feather, bone, and fern into his hair.

"Let's get out of here," Horatio said, pulling her up by the hand.

"Where?"

"Anywhere. Out on the porch."

"Wait," she said, and bent down to roll up one of the light mats and take it with her.

They stepped carefully out onto the porch, Anne leading the way across the slats to the edge, where she unrolled the mat. Horatio sat with his back against a post, then when she sat near him he pulled her over to sit in front of him, between his legs, her back resting against his chest.

She gave in to the comfort of his body behind hers, relaxing against him and laying her arms over his where they held her loosely around her waist, both of them with their knees raised.

The edge of the porch was just beyond the edge of the mat, the river invisible somewhere below their line of sight, the jungle above the opposite bank a wall of darkness studded with the blinking, floating stars of fireflies. There was faint light from starshine and the moon low in the sky, and the night insects sang their chorus, a softer medley than that to be heard at either dusk or dawn.

"Are you terribly sorry about losing the ship?" Anne asked. He hadn't talked about it much, and it seemed somehow easier to ask him about such a thing here in the dark, and when she could not see his face.

His hands around her waist shifted, then settled again. "I'm more sorry about Gianni than the ship. I can only hope he's all right."

"Perhaps his former crewmates assumed he had been taken against his will."

"I hope he was clever enough to play it that way," Horatio said.

She was quiet a minute, not wanting to upset him, but still feeling the need to reach into his thoughts. "But the ship, what of losing it? I know how important it was to you."

"Don't."

She waited.

Behind her, he sighed. "There's nothing to say about it. It's gone. I'd rather not dwell on that."

"You're not upset?"

"Leave it, Anne. If I ever get the chance I'll take the ship back from Chartier, but I'm not going to waste time now thinking about how I turned everything bollocks upward."

"I'd be just as happy if Chartier sailed away and we never saw either him or his ship again."

"You really don't care that it's gone, do you?" he

asked, and she could hear the faint amazement in his voice.

"No. It got us here, and that's all I care about."

He wrapped his arms a little more tightly around her and kissed her hair above her ear. "But where is 'here?' "

"I don't quite know yet," she admitted. "These people are friendly enough, but they certainly don't look like they need me for anything. I'm almost afraid . . ." she said, trailing off, not wanting to voice the fear that lurked in her heart.

"Afraid of what?"

Now she was the one who was glad to have the anonymity of darkness. "I'm almost afraid that the dreams did not mean anything beyond this. What if all they did was predict that we would come here? What if there is no end to the story, except that we are stuck here and live out our lives in a longhouse like this?"

"You fit in so well, I'd almost think that was what you wanted."

She laughed, more an exhale of breath than anything else. "They are kind people, and I am beginning to like them, but that doesn't mean I wish to live as one of them. I don't want to work in a rice field, or have skulls hanging from my rafters. I want a proper bed, my own clothes, and I want to eat on plates, at a table. Most of the time, at least." She shifted her buttocks. "And a cushioned chair would be welcome."

"Now you are becoming much too demanding."

"What do you think it all means?" she asked. "Do you think there's more than this?"

"You've had no more dreams?"

"No. I wish I had some opium. That might help."

"You are altogether too fond of the stuff."

"Perhaps I can replace it with rice wine."

"God help me," he said. "I do think there is more to your dreams than what we see here. There must be. It wouldn't make sense, otherwise. You would never have left England if you had not had the dreams."

"I don't know. Maybe I would have. There has always been at least one rover in each generation of my family, one person overcome by wanderlust. No one expects it to be a woman, but there's no reason the urge to travel to distant lands should not be as strong in me as in a brother. Look at Kai."

"I've looked, and I still can't believe it." He pulled her a little more tightly against him, and with one hand began to stroke his fingers through her hair, their tips brushing against her scalp. The sensation was soothing and erotic at once, and she closed her eyes, letting one of her hands move to rest on his thigh at her side. "Trust that we'll find the answers to your dreams. I could never have predicted our path this far, so there's no reason to believe we can predict what is yet to come."

"You've never stopped believing in me, have you?" she asked, her hand playing along his thigh, exploring the hard, muscled contours.

"You are worth following. To the very ends of the earth."

The words sent a small shiver up her neck, bringing

to life a sense of wonder that this man could feel such devotion for her.

She was not drunk, yet she felt her inhibitions slipping away. She wanted to touch him, and wanted to be touched in return. She wanted more than fingers in her hair. She wanted to feel his hands on her body, telling her without words that he loved her.

She raised her arm and reached behind her, lightly touching the side of his face as she turned her head so that she could see him from the corner of her eye. He needed no further invitation, bending forward to kiss her, then taking her bottom lip between his own, pulling gently then releasing. He played with her lips, teasing, the kiss slowly growing deeper as she responded, moving her own lips under his guidance, until the position grew too great a strain on both their necks and he broke off the kiss.

Instead of moving her he moved his attentions to the side of her neck, kissing a trail down to her shoulder, stopping to nip with his teeth at the base of her neck, then pulling her once again back against his chest, his lips near her ear.

His hand around her waist moved up to her breast, cupping and molding the flesh that was free under the thin layer of her chemise. He pinched her nipple, and she felt a current of excitement run from it straight down to her loins. His other hand followed the sensation, stroking her belly, then descending between her legs and pressing in small circles, his large hand covering her entirely. She opened her legs wider to him, her raised knees falling against the support of his own raised legs.

He reached down to the hem of her chemise and tugged it up over her knees, letting it slide down her thighs to bunch at her hips. He trailed his fingers up the inside of her leg, brushing softly against her calf, dawdling at the tender space above the back of her knee, then moving lightly upwards over the soft curve of her inner thigh.

She braced both her hands on his thighs, squeezing, waiting to see what he would do next while silently urging him to touch her most intimate places. She wanted to feel his fingers delve into the concealing hair and dance upon that center of arousal that was tingling with anticipation. She could feel herself dampening with desire, her body begging for his attention.

His touch reached the very top of her leg, no more than an inch from where she yearned for it to be, but he changed course, drawing spirals on the back of her thigh. She rubbed her head against his shoulder, silently asking for more than this, as his other hand moved over her breasts.

She could hear his breathing growing heavy, and feel his arousal nudging against the small of her back. Neither of them spoke, and the silence and inability to see his face somehow increased her excitement. Before her was the jungle lit with fireflies, wild with unknown beasts, and behind her a longhouse full of people, one of whom might come out and see what they were doing. The slight threat of discovery was not enough to deter her; its presence only added spice to her impatience.

At last his hand moved again in the direction of her

desire, and as she held her breath in anticipation he finally touched her where she most wished, his fingertips tracing a line straight up the ridge of her moistening center. She raised her hands off his thighs and reached behind her, arching her back and gripping his shirt at the shoulders, opening her body in invitation.

He stroked her again, down this time, dipping the end of a finger into the core of her and then retreating, using her own moisture to wet her folds for his caress. She parted under his touch, a stroking that moved in time to the massaging circles of his hand on her breast. Deep in her throat she moaned, the sound like that of some savage creature calling in the dark. His stroking quickened, the movements growing, the sensations more intense.

His hand left her breast and came down to join its partner, and he slid one strong finger deep inside her and began to thrust. Her arms dropped back to his thighs and she rolled her head so that her forehead met the base of his throat, his heartbeat loud in her ear. She gripped his thighs and clenched the muscles of her body, urging herself towards the finish, unable to slow down.

The thrusting finger went deep, and then began to stroke her from within as his other hand worked her from without, the sensations coming at both ends of some hidden pole of desire within her. She gave a small cry and peaked at last, her opening around the base of his finger grasping and relaxing, grasping and relaxing in waves of contractions.

He held his hands against her as she finished, then

slowly withdrew them and shifted her to the side so that she was lying against his arm. He kissed her on the mouth, hard and intense, his tongue seeking and gaining immediate admittance. Her desire was both satisfied and lingered still, and she welcomed his tongue, rubbing her own against it and trying to suck him deeper into her mouth as her arms came up and wrapped around his neck.

His kisses moved down her throat to the flat space above her breastbone, and she was filled with the desire not for a repeat of her own satisfaction, but to give the same to him. She shoved herself upright and pushed him back, away from the post he had leaned against.

"What are you doing?" he whispered.

"It's my turn," she whispered back, shoving him down onto his back. She straddled his hips, feeling his arousal as a ridge beneath her sex, and despite her recent satisfaction she could not help rubbing herself against it. Beneath her he groaned, clasping her hips in his hands and moving her in a continuation of the motion. She bent forward and kissed him, and her hands went to work on his shirt.

She got the neck open and then pulled the garment off over his head as he lifted his arms. She moved up until she was straddling his belly, pulling her chemise up so that she could feel his bare skin against her still-moist center, her eyes closing with the pleasure of it as she moved in small circles, her hands flat on his chest. She ran her fingers through the slight matting of hair that covered him, her fingertips stopping to dwell on the smooth, soft pools of flat nipples that grew into miniature pebbles as she played with them.

She slid down his body onto his thighs and then unfastened his breeches, tugging them down and letting his sex spring free into the night air. Her eyes were adjusted to the dark and she could see it clearly, large and proud, reaching almost to his navel. She wrapped her hand around it, and it was as thick and silky as she remembered from their wedding night, the head half covered in the cowling of skin that moved back under her guidance, and that was wet and faintly sticky.

She remembered the way he had moved her hand on him, and suddenly understood what her shock had made her unable to understand before: He had been giving himself pleasure on their wedding night, not punishing himself. She felt somewhat silly.

Her hand tightened, and she moved it experimentally, trying to recreate the motion he had forced on her that night. He moaned softly. She moved her hand again, her hold tight enough that the skin sheathing him moved along with her hand, and was rewarded with another groan of pleasure.

She grinned, feeling her power over him, and set into a rhythm.

"Harder," he said under his breath.

Her eyes widened. She didn't want to hurt him. But when she tightened her grip even more and continued moving her hand, his hips started moving as if of their own volition, and with that encouragement she grew bold and sped her strokes.

He gasped and groaned, and she suddenly slowed, watching his reaction, then sped up again. Holding him in her hand was reigniting her own desire, her sex throbbing, her body recognizing that there was more to be done with him than this. And, absurdly, she felt her mouth begin to water as if her hunger for him was confused as to whether she should eat him or make love with him.

She rubbed her tongue against her palate, imagining the feel of the silky head of his shaft in her mouth. In the dark, in the wild, there was no reason not to indulge herself. Let him think her a savage if he wished. She scooted her body further down his legs and slid her mouth over the end of his member, instinctively covering her teeth with her lips.

He grabbed her shoulders, his fingers digging in as he held her, neither urging her forward nor pushing her back. The head was large and smooth in her mouth, and she moved her tongue over the slit at the end, tasting the salty wetness, pausing to delve more deeply there. She moved her tongue over him, sucking gently as if on a piece of hard candy, loving the texture and taste of him against the sensitive surfaces of her mouth. With her other hand she lightly stroked and played with the two full sacks beneath, and teased her fingers around the base the same way he had teased his fingers around her.

Her creativity began to run short, and she wasn't sure what to do next. He answered the question for her, releasing her shoulder to wrap his hand around the hand that still gripped him, urging her to resume the motion. She obeyed, rubbing him between the roof of her mouth and her tongue as she stroked with increasing speed with her hand.

Her jaw began to ache, and regretfully, with a long sucking pull, she took him out of her mouth.

"Anne," he groaned. "Please."

"My jaw," she said, putting her other palm over the head in poor substitute.

"Let me have you," he said.

There was a twinge in her heart, some small part of herself that wasn't ready for that final, irrevocable commitment. She intuitively understood that if she did as he bid, she would be doing it only to please him, not herself, despite the yearnings of her body. Her soul was not quite ready.

"No. This way," she said, continuing to stroke him.

Before she knew what was happening he had pulled her against him and rolled her over so that she was beneath him. She went stiff as he straddled her and raised himself up. As she started to protest he pulled her chemise up past her breasts, then moved up so that his knees were on either side of her ribcage. The protest died on her lips as curiosity overcame her.

He pressed himself in the shallow valley between her breasts, where it was wet with sweat, and then pushed her breasts from either side so that they held him in place, his thumb holding his member down into the narrow crevice. He began to move, thrusting as if he were thrusting inside her.

She brought her hands up over his, taking their place, her fingertips meeting in the middle over her breasts, where she could feel the head of his shaft sliding under them, then up to the exposed area of her breast bone. Her breasts were barely large enough to give him a valley, yet he groaned as he moved against her, bracing his hands now above her head.

She had never dreamt that a man could find pleasure in such a way. It required little of her but that she keep her grip on her own breasts, the sweat that had been trickling between them serving now as a lubricant for his motions. He was a shadow above her, moving against the backdrop of stars, and she was overcome by the wonder of what two bodies could do together under the mantle of night.

"Anne, Anne," he groaned, his movements quickening, his body growing stiff, and then he went motionless, one hand coming up to press hard over hers.

She felt a pulsing between her breasts, and the heat of warm fluid on her skin. He shuddered, then relaxed, moving off her and bending down to kiss her hard on the lips. He reached for his discarded shirt and used it to clean off her chest, then pulled her chemise back down over her and lay down beside her, cradling her in his arms and entwining his legs with hers.

She nestled against his chest, her arm around his waist, her hand stroking softly at the small of his back, sweaty with his exertions.

"Thank you," he whispered, and kissed the top of her head.

She smiled, the expression hidden against his chest in the dark. "It was my pleasure."

And it was.

Chapter Twenty

She was dreaming. Chartier stood before her on the deck of the *Anne* while around them tumbled the rage of hand-to-hand combat.

In her hand she felt a heavy weight and looked down to see that she gripped the hilt of a long head-hunter's sword, like she had seen them swing while dancing under the light of the torches and the influence of the *tuak*. Tresses of human hair from victims long dead dangled from the wooden haft.

Chartier grinned, his teeth spotty grey.

She lifted the sword using both hands and cocked her elbows, bringing the sword back over her shoulder ready for the stroke.

Chartier laughed.

With all her strength she swung the blade. It met the Frenchman at the neck, and his grinning head went flying off, blood spouting from severed vessels.

His body stood for a moment longer, then crumpled to the deck as his head thunked nearby and rolled to a stop.

She bent down and grabbed the head by the hair, hefting it high in victory, blood and bits of gore streaming down her arm. His expression in death was of wide-eyed surprise, unable to believe what had happened.

She woke herself screaming.

"Anne, what is it?" Horatio said, holding her by the shoulders.

Her eyes opened on semidark, the first blue-grey light of dawn creeping in at the edges of the inner verandah. Roosters were crowing loudly enough to wake the dead and drown out Ruut's snores, and there was the sound of movement in the longhouse as those without hangovers began to prepare for the day. She and Horatio had moved inside again last night, after the mosquitoes had found them and started to feast.

"Bad dream," she said. She shuddered, still able to feel Chartier's greasy hair in her grip, the grim determination to kill him, and the exultation when she had, lingering in her heart as if the emotions had been real.

"About the island?" he asked, pulling her close and combing his fingers soothingly through her hair.

"I think it was just from the festivities last night, and the rice wine. I don't think it meant anything." He was warm and very real in the half-dark, and even the hard flooring beneath them had seemed a comfortable bed with his arm as a pillow and his body heat as a blanket.

"Tell me about it?"

She grimaced. "I cut Chartier's head off. And what's worse, I think I intended to hang it from a beam in my house."

He chuckled, deep in his chest.

"It's not funny."

"I knew you belonged here," he said.

"It was a bad dream, that's all."

"Were you wearing one of those hip wraps?"

"You'd like that, wouldn't you?"

"You could chop off any number of heads if you wore one of those," he said. "I'd forgive you."

"Men. You're all savages."

"But I'm adorable, and you love me," he said.

She tucked her head against his chest, not answering. Then she reached over and squeezed his buttocks. "You're adorable," she agreed.

He kissed the top of her head and said nothing more.

Chapter Twenty-one

Two weeks later

Horatio dug the end of his pole into the river bottom and pushed off as a headhunter behind and Imsa far in front of him did the same. The long, narrow dugout canoe drifted forward against the current in the shallow, narrow river.

The quiet of their passage brought back to mind his long trip down the Brahmaputra after being shot, although he had been a motionless passenger then, lying in the bottom of a similarly narrow boat. Then, as now, long periods of time would pass in which nothing was said, the sounds of the natural world the only touch upon one's hearing. It left one's mind free to drift, and after a time thoughts were not of the future or the past, but only of the present. There were times he almost forgot he was separate from the river, the overhanging trees, and the shafts of sunlight in which dragonflies danced.

This island of Anne's, he had to admit, was growing on him.

Anne herself sat forward in the canoe, her blond hair shining in the periodic pools of sunlight, Mango sitting near her feet, playing with the hem of her chemise. Ruut, Kai, and Ulrich were in a second canoe, following behind. Five men from the longhouse were accompanying them, guiding the way into the interior. They had agreed to go as far as Gana Cave, which Imsa had explained was as far as anyone ever cared to go. The cave was not a place anyone went willingly.

And the cave was what they would have to pass through if they were to eventually reach the opposite coast. It went through the narrowest part of the steep mountain range that made up the spine of the island. The cave was supposed to be haunted, or magical— Horatio was not sure from Imsa's explanation which it was. Whichever the case, it was at the very heart of Sulawak and a place to be taken seriously. Horatio thought the taboo against venturing through it was more likely to stave off attacks from warring tribes from the other side of the mountain than to protect whatever spirits might dwell within.

When the time had finally come at the longhouse to talk about where to go next, the headman explained what they already knew: The coastal waters were aswarm with pirates, be they natives of Sulawak, or be they Malay, Chinese, Ilanun, European, or from one of the thousands of other islands in the region.

To combat this pirate problem, the Sultan of Brunei

had sent his uncle and a small army of Malays and Chinese to a village on the opposite side of the island, on the broad Kinanan River. Sulawak was technically owned and governed by Brunei, although all that that meant to its people was that taxes were imposed on trade, and yearly tributes of goods like antimony ore or rough diamonds were expected to be made. The sultan's uncle was the rajah of Sulawak, and no one had so much as a finger of respect for the ineffectual man.

European traders with their growing monopolies had interrupted trade routes that had been set for hundreds of years, and the result was displaced traders who turned to piracy for their living. And, Ano admitted, for the people of Sulawak sometimes piracy and coastal raids were simply the best way to find fresh heads to renew the spiritual strength of a longhouse.

Whatever the reasons, the piracy had gotten out of hand and made coastal living and trading impossible. Now that Sulawak needed the aid of a governing force like Brunei, all they got for help was a weakling rajah, too afraid to do anything but sit safely in the protection of his bored army and fret about the state of affairs.

The rajah would, however, have boats capable of seagoing voyages, so if Horatio and Anne and the others wished to leave the island, the rajah would be the person to go to see.

Imsa had not taken the news of the rajah's presence on the Kinanan with equanimity. The village at which the man and his army were staying was likely either his own, or one very near it.

Horatio had no clear idea what would happen when they finally reached this rajah, but he didn't need Anne to tell him that going to him was what they needed to do. Perhaps it was the mention of pirates that caught his attention: He was getting a sense that there was something to be done here on Sulawak.

Damn, but he hated pirates. Perhaps he could make himself useful and kill some. And they probably had a boat or two worth stealing, and then he and Anne would be free to leave or stay, as they wished, without being dependent upon the unknown rajah.

Anne. Glorious, beautiful, mysterious Anne. Some evenings they stayed with tribespeople in longhouses, but many afternoons when they stopped traveling for the day the headhunters built sleeping platforms a few inches off the ground, with loose roofs made of giant leaves to keep off the rain that more often than not came in the night. He and Anne had one such platform to themselves. They were in full sight of the others and unable to do more than lie close together, and his dreams as a result were filled with erotic imaginings.

Lying next to her made him ache in longing, the desire from the night carrying through the day. When he wasn't blank with absorption of the jungle and the river his mind repeated over and over their night on the open porch, and he daydreamed about what it would be like when she gave herself to him wholly.

If she turned around and offered herself to him right at this moment he would gladly drag her into the bushes and have his way with her. As it was, though, he derived a certain perverse, painful pleasure from the physical yearning to take her, and the energy he would so eagerly have spent in making love to her from sunup to sundown and every hour in between he diverted to poling the canoe upriver.

"When I was a bachelor I lived all alone," he sang.
"I worked at the rover's trade;
And the only, only thing I did that was wrong
Was to woo a fair young maid," he sang.

Anne turned around to give him a look, one eyebrow raised. It was an old song, and he suspected she knew what the next verse was going to be.

"One night she knelt close by my side,
When I was fast asleep.
She threw her arms around my neck,
And then began to weep.

She wept, she cried, she tore her hair,
Ah me, what could I do?
So all night long I held her in my arms,
Just to keep her from the foggy, foggy dew."

She joined him for the next verse, and then Imsa and the other headhunter started to sing along, following the simple melody if not the words. Behind him he heard Ulrich add his rich voice, his boat mates following.

For the next half hour they poled upriver, headhunters, a Chinese, and Europeans singing an old English song in the middle of the jungle. He would have laughed, but he was enjoying himself too much to pause to do so.

Anne sat and stared, almost not believing what she was seeing. The river ended in a wall of limestone. The river did not narrow, did not lessen its flow or grow more shallow. It simply ended, water flowing straight towards her out of a wall of solid rock.

Horatio and the others poled the canoes to the bank, and she accepted his help out of the boat, her muscles creaking from long sitting and her buttocks both sore and wet.

One of the headhunters spoke, and Imsa translated. "River is under rock. You see cave mouth, after long time no rain and water low," he explained.

"That's not the cave opening we'll be using, is it?" she asked, only half joking.

Imsa exchanged words with the headhunter, who pointed up the side of the vertical mountain. Anne peered upwards, but all that was visible was vegetation.

"Gana up there," Imsa said. "At other end of cave is place you see river, far below in rocks of cave. I have seen. I find Kinanan from there."

The headhunters unloaded the canoes of their group's belongings. There wasn't much: a few *parang*—as she had discovered the short sword used for everyday tasks was called—with wooden scabbards, sleeping mats, rice, dried fish, a pouch of the dried leaves that made soap when mixed with water, and three tall baskets meant to be worn strapped to the back, to carry it all in.

The goods had not come free. As generous as the villagers were, they were not so wealthy as to be able to give up their hard-earned rice and *parang* without a bit of trade to compensate. The hunter who had fallen in love with her stays had agreed to trade for them; two other hunters wanted the skiff that she and Kai had hidden; and Imsa had reluctantly parted with one of his precious heads.

Anne gave her dress to Lua, but instead of more rice or dried fish, the garment gained her one of the red-and-white hip wraps, to Horatio's amusement. Imsa explained that it was a more valuable trade than she might think, for the material had prayers woven into it in the stylized figures and plants. Lua also gave her a pair of heavy brass ankle bracelets that she liked, although it felt awkward to walk in them and she had tucked them into Horatio's basket along with the skirt for safe-keeping.

"It looks awfully steep," Anne said, as in single file they followed one of the headhunters the short distance to the base of the mountain.

"Climb is not bad part," Imsa said, hearing her.

"Then what is?"

"You see."

She frowned at him.

"Now you see what I had to put up with when I was alone with him," Horatio said.

Imsa gave Horatio a wicked grin. "I tell you what in Gana, and climb be hard for you. You not want to go."

"Well *that* doesn't encourage me any," Anne said.

"What is in cave?" Ruut asked, looking worried and on the verge of a bad temper.

331

Lisa Cach

"I won't let Kai take any unnecessary risks," Ulrich said.

"Tell," Kai demanded of Imsa, crossing her arms over chest. "Tell, or I'm not going."

The headhunter sighed, seeing he wasn't going to get away with not telling this time. He fluttered his hands around his head. "Bat."

"Oh," Anne said. "That's all?"

"Many bat."

"It's a cave. I would have expected that," she said. "We do have bats in England, you know."

"They should be sleeping, shouldn't they?" Horatio asked. "They won't bother us if we don't bother them."

Imsa shrugged, and Anne got the feeling there was something he wasn't telling them. The mutinous look on his face said that he wouldn't be saying anything more, though, so she gave it up. She'd find out soon enough, and there was no way around whatever was waiting in the cave, anyway. Maybe the bats were extraordinarily enormous, or glowed in the dark. In any case, Imsa didn't look overly distressed, so she assumed they would be safe.

On the other hand, she had never seen Imsa distressed about anything, so that was no gauge.

The hunter picked a nearly vertical path up the mountain that required hands and careful, cautious placement of feet. Anne tied her chemise above her knees to keep her feet clear. Horatio climbed behind her, as Ulrich climbed behind Kai, to catch them should either slip. She could hear Ruut behind them all, cursing and grouching and occasionally sending a stone plummeting down the mountainside.

The hunter went steadily upwards, not pausing to let them rest, and despite the fatigue growing in her muscles Anne labored on, afraid that if she did stop she would lose sight of the exact path the man had taken. Sweat trickled down her forehead and between her breasts. She was grateful for the calluses that the months going barefoot had given her.

Mango had no trouble at all, scampering ahead of even the hunter, then pausing to look down on them as if to show off his superiority and marvel at their awkwardness.

Then at last she was over the lip of the near-cliff they had been scaling, finding herself crawling through ferns into the open maw of the cave. She stood up and turned around, then parted her lips in awe.

The entrance was twenty or so feet high, and dripping from its roof were limestone stalactites as much as twelve feet long. The inside of the cave beyond a few feet was in darkness, but looking outwards the stalactites gave the impression that she was standing inside the mouth of some monstrous behemoth of the sea, its teeth bared to the green world of the jungle that grew even up the side of the mountain, branches and vines a brilliant green as the sun illuminated them from behind.

She had never seen anything quite so beautiful and eerie at once.

The others climbed over the lip one by one, Ruut at the last. He flopped onto the ground and lay spread-eagled, the hem of his shirt hiking up his belly to reveal a leech attached to the pale white flesh. "I not goat of mountain."

Five minutes of body searches followed, but only Ulrich had a leech, which he flicked into the cup of one of the strange pitcher-like plants that grew nearby.

A whiff of ammonia distracted her from her contemplation of her own leech-free body. She wrinkled her nose, turning around and facing the blackness of the cave.

"Bat dropping," Imsa said.

"Is that what you meant, before, about what we wouldn't like?"

"Many bat dropping."

She looked at her bare feet. She was not going to enjoy walking through that.

A headhunter opened a container that had live coals embedded within, and soon he and Imsa had lit the torches that had been carried up in their packs. The hunter handed a torch to Horatio, then said something to them all.

Imsa translated. "He wish good luck, and someday want see again."

"Why does that sound like he doesn't expect to?" Horatio asked, but the hunter had climbed back over the lip of the cave and was gone.

No one answered. They all stared at the black maw of the cave. In the quiet, beneath the soft crackle of the torches, a faint high-pitched chittering could be heard. Anne shuddered.

"Do you know the way through?" Horatio asked Imsa.

He shrugged. "No wrong way, one passage."

Still they hesitated.

"How far?" Kai asked, her hand protectively over her belly.

"Not far," Imsa said.

"You're sure?" Anne asked.

Imsa looked at her for a moment, and she thought she saw a hint of nervousness deep in his black eyes. It was not reassuring. "No."

It was Ruut who broke them out of their hesitation as he finally stopped playing with the leaking spot of blood on his belly. "We go, or we stand here like sheep?"

Anne raised her brows in surprise.

"Dinner on other side of cave," Ruut said.

It was as good a motivation as any, she supposed. "We go."

Imsa shrugged, and in single file they entered the cave.

The floor was damp beneath Anne's feet, and she felt something wet drip onto her scalp. She cringed, then touched the spot on her hair and was relieved to feel that it was water. The smell of ammonia grew stronger, making her and the others cough, and beneath her feet the ground grew squishier with, she feared, a combination of the water that dripped through the limestone and the droppings of the bats. She could feel the stuff oozing between her toes.

Their passage was slow, Imsa leading the way and lowering his torch so that they could take note of drops in the floor, or stones in their path. The cave was a vast cavern, not the narrow hall that Anne had expected.

After several minutes Imsa stopped, and the group gathered for a moment to check that everyone was all right. The opening behind them was out of sight, and there was no sign yet of the opening on the other side.

"Many dropping," Imsa said, and lowered his torch to the side of where they were standing. The flame illuminated the base of what looked to be a hill, and then Anne saw that it was covered in thousands of insects, some narrow and silvery-grey, but others a golden brown and as big as her thumb. They looked like fat, giant earwigs, with a dozen legs, and pincers at the front of their heads. She shuddered, holding her skirts closer to her legs.

Imsa stepped onto the base of the hill of droppings and thrust his torch upwards. The hill was not the low mound she had thought: It was a mountain, taller than she was, its surface shimmering and undulating with tiny creatures. Her eyes rose above it into the unreachable heights of the cave, and she heard again the chittering of what had to be hundreds of thousands of bats.

It was as if they had descended into Hell.

Mango put his paw on her leg, and she jumped. "Mango! You'll have to find your own way, sweeting. I'm not going to carry you and risk you setting me off balance." She could imagine nothing worse than falling into one of those mountains of bug-covered guano.

Imsa started off again, and Anne followed, Horatio behind her with his torch, then Kai and the others. There was a noise from the back of the group, and she paused to turn and look, as did Horatio.

"I drop torch," Ruut said.

Ulrich, who was in front of him, went back to help him find and relight it while Kai stayed by Horatio. Anne turned forward and called to Imsa, who was now nearly twenty feet ahead. "Wait, Imsa!"

He stopped, raising his torch. She took a few steps toward him, then noticed something glowing a faint blue-white a few feet off to her left. It was on the ground, giving off the same glow as foxfire she had seen on rotten wood in the forest at home. If someone with a torch had been closer she might not have noticed it at all. She heard Ruut grumbling, heard Horatio ask Kai how she was faring, and then she stepped towards the glowing spot to get a closer look.

Her foot sank into softness, and she lost her balance. Her arms flew out for balance, but still she fell, keeping her lips shut against a scream lest she end up with a mouthful of guano.

She hit the soft ground, and it gave way beneath her, sucking her down into a hole, the guano and insects rushing with her like water through a drain. She shut her eyes and curled into a ball, her arms over her head as she rolled and dropped and slid in the heavy, rushing, powdery stink, her body bouncing off walls of rock and spilling over short drop-offs.

After an eternity she came to rest, half on stone and half on the soft final wave of guano that had carried her. The sound of chittering bats had been replaced by the rushing of water, echoing loudly. She carefully unfolded from her fetal position and opened her eyes to blackness.

"Horatio!" she screamed.

Her voice reverberated off the stone walls, giving her the sense that she was in a space much smaller than the cavern had been. "Horatio! Imsa! Help!"

She waited, listening, ears straining. There was no reply. There was no light of torches. She looked behind her at where she assumed she had come from, and there was only darkness. A panic began to rise within her, and on hands and knees she climbed up the slope of guano that had brought her here. It met a roof of stone. Whatever passage had been there was blocked now.

"Horatio!" she screamed again, and coughed as guano dust was sucked into her throat. "Horatio!"

She felt something crawling under the hair at the back of her neck and screamed, her hands clawing at her hair and finding it full of wiggling insects. The ammonia fumes burned her nose and throat, and she stumbled again and fell, rolling down the guano onto the stone floor, coming up against a boulder. She scrambled up onto her feet, crouching down low, pulling at the bugs in her hair, screaming uncontrollably.

It was the night the *Coventry* had foundered all over again. She was alone in the dark, no one to help her. She would die if she was not rescued. There was no way out, no way to rise to the surface. She was suffocating.

Horatio had come. Where was he now? He would never be able to find her down here, never be able to dig out that mountain of droppings that had followed her down the long chute to this hellish grave.

She was alone. And she was in utter darkness.

Her cries died off as her throat wore out, and then it was only the rush of water and her own heavy breathing and coughing that she heard, echoing off the stones.

The mountain that was the heart of her dream island had taken her, had swallowed her as if that cave opening had indeed been the maw of a giant beast, only she had been too ignorant to recognize that she was walking straight into its gullet.

It had her now. A slow certainty grew in her that the stones around her were aware of her presence, and were watching. The mountain was alive, and it was waiting to see what she would do next.

Either that, or it was waiting for her to die, her body rotting away to become part of the very soil and earth of this wild land.

Her breathing steadied, her strange conviction of the mountain's awareness giving her the option of choice. She didn't want to die here. She didn't want her grave to be a mound of stinking bat droppings and dung-eating insects. She didn't want the journey of over half a year to end with her alone in the dark. Her life could not be meant to end that way. The Hand of Destiny, for all its perverse sense of humor, could not have been this cruel.

The rushing of the water intruded upon her contemplation, and she turned her head toward it in the dark. The river. The underground river.

She knew where it came out: under the wall where they had left the canoes. To follow it in that direction would be to invite a drowning. But Imsa had said you could see the river from the other entrance to the cave.

She got onto all fours and began to crawl towards the sounds, the rock hard on her palms and knees, but no worse than the bruises she already felt forming on her body from her tumble. It took no more than two minutes, and she was at the edge of the water. It was as cold as ice, moving swiftly and pulling at her fingers when she touched it. She plunged her hand in and felt for the bottom, relieved to find that here it was only a few inches under the surface.

The fear had not left her. This cave in the bowels of the mountain had infused terror through every vessel and muscle of her body, sending her senses stretching out into the darkness, but she would not sit still and let it have her. If no one else was going to save her, she was going to have to save herself.

She started to move upstream on the rocky shore, but then her questing hands met with a wall of rock. She was on a narrow beach, but beyond that point the beach ended and the river apparently traveled through a tunnel. She put her feet in the icy water and stood, the current rushing over her ankles and threatening to cut her feet out from under her. She ran her hands along the rock wall for guidance, and began the slow trek upriver.

"Anne! Anne!" Horatio shouted, scrambling with the others at the place where she'd last been seen before the mound of guano collapsed. Mango shrieked and leapt about, as frantic over her sudden disappearance as Horatio himself. He dug with his hands at the guano, the others joining in except for Kai, who had been forbidden by them all due to her condition.

"What happened? Where did she go?" Horatio accusingly asked Imsa, obscurely feeling that this was somehow the headhunter's fault.

Imsa's face was uneasy in the torch light, his hands right alongside Horatio's as they dug. "I not know."

Horatio knew she was under the mountain, knew she was still alive. He could almost feel her, and almost feel her terror. He was afraid that she would suffocate before they could find her. He didn't want to think that they might not find her at all.

"She was right here," Horatio said, as if the statement could refute what had happened. "Anne!"

There was no answer. There was not even the faintest echo of her voice. It was as if she had been swept from this plane of existence, as if she had never been.

"She was *right* here," he said again. Imsa said nothing, and as Horatio looked at the headhunter, he thought he saw unspoken words in his eyes. "What is it? What do you know?"

"This is Gana Cave."

"What do you mean? You're not going to say something about spirits, are you?"

Imsa shrugged, and looked down. They all continued digging, the powdery guano sliding back into the hole they made almost as fast as they dug it out. Ulrich emptied out his basket pack and tried using it as a scoop, but the weave was too wide to hold the dust.

"It makes no sense," Horatio said, more to himself

than to the others. "No sense. She brought us here. Why?"

Imsa did not try to answer, and the others remained mute, engrossed with digging, although Horatio could see that it was an impossible task. An entire mountain of dried droppings had rushed down into the ground. That would not stop him, but it put an edge of wild desperation to his movements, making his limbs jerky with panic.

He paused to wipe sweat from his brow with the back of his arm, and that's when he saw it. The red and gold kingfisher. It glowed with its own internal light, illuminating nothing of its surroundings as it sat and watched him from several feet away. Horatio stared.

The kingfisher took flight, then alit some thirty feet along the passage.

"Imsa."

Imsa looked at him, then turned to follow his gaze. It was Kai who spoke, though, her voice small and breathless. "I see it."

"I see," Ruut said.

"The red kingfisher," Ulrich said.

"We must follow it," Imsa said, standing.

He didn't want to leave the hole, but the kingfisher was too much to ignore. It was Anne's guide, and if it was here he could only assume that it meant to tell them something. He was vaguely aware that he should be questioning its appearance, that he should be in awe the same way one might be in the presence of a ghost, but all he cared was that it was linked to Anne.

They gathered up their torches and followed.

*   *   *

Her feet were numb, and she had stumbled and fallen more times than she could count. The riverbed was smooth limestone, peppered with pebbles and the occasional stone large enough to trip her. She didn't know how long she had been moving upstream, and the blackness and the constant rushing roar of the water had sent her mind into a different state, somewhere beyond reality.

It wasn't a dream state: It was more like when she had eaten the opium, her mind disengaging from her body and exploring thoughts and images untied to her surroundings. Her fear had become a dark hum in the background of her consciousness, serving to push her forward where weariness might otherwise have had her stopping.

All around her she could feel the mountain, its massive presence above her and reaching deep into the earth, far below where she walked now. In the utter dark it felt as if her soul had expanded beyond her body, stretching with her senses to touch her surroundings. And her surroundings, in turn, touched her. She was passing through the heart of the mountain, but it, as well, was passing through her with the force of the river, washing out the bits of her that it did not want and leaving behind nothing but the pure essence of who she was.

There was no sense of being Anne Hazlett Merivale, adventuress and lady's maid. Such descriptions were merely decorative, describing the surface like paint on a medieval sculpture. What she was as she moved through the dark was fear and strength, smooth stone and cold water, a fragile body and a will of iron. This path through the darkness was hers to walk, alone.

Ahead she saw the faintest hint of light, a lessening of blackness to deep charcoal. She kept her slow and steady pace and moved towards it, the charcoal spreading and growing lighter as she approached. The wall beneath her fingertips sloped away from the river, and she found herself looking up a wide opening to a patch of grey light at the top. Enormous boulders tumbled upon each other to make a rude stairway fit for giants.

She climbed up onto the first low boulder and drew up her knees, wrapping her hands around her chilled feet to try to restore feeling to them. They felt dead against her hands, her toes barely moving when she tried to force them to obey. She was too impatient to wait for them to warm, the imperative to move forward still pushing her. She turned to the boulders and climbed, and despite her numb feet scaled them like Mango up a tree.

Her impatience grew as the oval of grey light grew larger and the sound of rushing water lessened, still loud but with distance to it now. Then she was at the top, crawling out onto a flat boulder and raising her face to meet the astonished gazes of Horatio, Imsa, and her friends.

They were all around her before she could even make sense of their presence, and she found herself smothered not only in Horatio's arms, but the arms of the others.

"I'm all right," she tried to say, her voice muffled under the combined mass of bodies. "I'm all right!"

"What happened? You disappeared. We dug for you, and then the kingfisher appeared," Horatio babbled, making little sense.

"We all saw it," Kai said.

"Saw me fall?"

"Saw the kingfisher," Horatio clarified. "After you disappeared. What happened?"

"The floor of the cave gave way, and I fell down some sort of chute. I ended up by the underground river. The passage I'd come through was blocked by guano, so I had to walk up the river to get out." It sounded so simple when she said it, and so practical as to make fear sound foolish. "You saw the kingfisher?" she asked, that bit of their story finally penetrating her consciousness.

"When we were digging," Horatio said. "It appeared and led us here."

Her gaze shifted to Imsa, who was looking at her with a mirror of what she thought might be in her own eyes. Her awareness of the mountain as the living, beating heart of the island came flooding back to her, and she felt almost faint. Her fall had not been an accident. Had she escaped on her own, or had she been let go?

Mango was pulling at her hem like a child in need of attention, and she opened her arms and let the little bugger climb up and beg a ride. His warm fur was a primitive comfort under her hands, and his eyes reflected no more need from her than touch, leaving her mind free to try to grasp what had just happened.

They were only a short walk from the exit of the cave, the mouth here forty or fifty feet high, opening out onto what looked to be a paradise after the hell of the cave. The cave had sloped steadily downward, and they stepped out of it not onto a ledge as at the other end, but straight onto the side of a jungle-covered hill, the plants and trees richly green and dappled with sunlight. She had to look back over her shoulder to prove to herself that Gana Cave was still there, deep and dark.

"Anne, hold still," Horatio said, his voice tense.

"What?" she said, setting Mango down.

"Hold still. There's something on you." He reached slowly towards the side of her head.

She knew without him saying what it had to be: one of those horrid bugs that fed on droppings. A small rush of revolted fear went through her, then as quickly washed away. It was just a bug. She reached up to her own hair before he could, and combed the thing out of her hair, then held it in her hand to examine it in the light of day.

Its legs feathered against her palm, and the yellow-brown creature was no prettier now than it had been in the torchlight. She made a face, and tossed it into the bushes. "Any more?" she asked.

Horatio was blinking at her in surprise, but complied and examined her all around. Kai started to examine herself, but it was Ulrich who groaned when he found several of the things clinging to his own clothes. Ruut suddenly erupted into a frantic dance, slapping all over his body.

"Oh, God, Anne," Horatio said hoarsely as he found several more of the bugs, and of the small silvery-grey ones, as well, all either clinging to her chemise or tangled in her guano-fouled hair.

"You've got one, too," she said.

His face lost some of its color under the dusting of guano dirt. "Get it off me," he groaned.

She smiled crookedly and obeyed, flicking the thing off into the air. "It's just a bug. Boys are supposed to like bugs."

"These aren't normal bugs."

"All the better, I would have thought." She looked at his beleaguered expression, his clothes and hands as filthy as she knew her own to be, and she started to laugh.

The others looked at her, pausing in their own frantic searches for monstrous scaly creatures, and she laughed harder. She did not know when there had ever been such a group, who had survived shipwreck and pirate battles, encounters with headhunters and the storms of the high seas, and yet could be made pale by a few bugs that they could crush between their fingers.

For the first time, she was the only one who was not scared.

"Anne, are you all right?" Horatio asked, his expression concerned.

"I am," she said, gasping for breath. "I am better than I've ever been."

Chapter Twenty-two

Anne sat naked beside a shaded stream outside the mountain and watched a red kingfisher hunting for its breakfast. It wasn't *her* kingfisher, just a regular creature of the wilds. It seemed strange that she herself hadn't seen her guide since setting foot on the island. Perhaps it felt that she was no longer in need of it.

After the exertions of climbing to Gana Cave and enduring the passage through it, they had unanimously decided to give themselves a day for rest and cleaning up. No one wanted to keep going with clothes that were permeated with bat guano, and when silvery bugs had been found in the dried fish it had been tossed away and Imsa declared he would go hunting. The head he had given to the longhouse had earned him a blowgun and quiver of darts, and this morning he had looked glad of the opportunity to get away from them for a time.

She assumed he would come back. He hadn't talked to her since her adventure in the cave, but she sensed his view of her had changed somehow. She had always felt that he expected something of her, or knew something about her that she did not, but also that he did not take her quite seriously, regarding her with some of that patronizing amusement with which he regarded the others. Now, though, he seemed almost uneasy around her.

If she were Horatio, she'd revel in this mysterious awe she now aroused in Imsa. As it was, though, she just wished someone would come sit down and tell her what it all meant.

It would happen in time, she supposed. The Hand of Destiny seemed to have its own ideas about how to reveal its plans.

She leaned back onto her hands, her legs stretched out before her. Her sleeping mat was rolled out beneath her, protecting her skin from the ground. Her chemise, washed as well as the tattered thing could be, was spread on a bush to dry. Her hair was half-damp from its recent washing—the third since the previous afternoon—and her body felt relaxed and comfortably cool. For once she wasn't covered with sweat, and despite some bruises and stiffness from Gana Cave she felt better than she had during much of the two-week canoe trip.

She'd learned at the first longhouse that the riverside was the coolest place to spend the day, and today she planned to take advantage of that fact and loll here all afternoon, as she imagined did the others, up or down stream a short distance and taking advantage of the rare opportunity for privacy.

Now all she needed was Horatio. The past two weeks, sleeping pressed up against him, all she had been able to think about was their night on the porch, and the way he had touched her. She had found herself rubbing up against him, trying to grind her sex against his through their clothes, but each movement sent their rickety sleeping platform to creaking in a pattern that she knew would be all too obvious to their companions. Her only comfort was the rare occasion when, spooning against Horatio's back, she could under the cover of darkness reach around and tuck her hand into his breeches, holding the silken shaft of his member in her palm.

She lay back on the mat, closing her eyes against the dappling of warm sunlight that touched her face, and rested her palm over her stomach. She ran her hand lightly over her midriff, feeling the smooth contours of her flesh and the hard rises of hipbones that had once been mere foothills to her rounded belly. She had lost even more weight since Batavia, and she hoped she hadn't become too bony to be appealing. She missed her soft layer of padding, but at the same time there was something of pleasure to be found in this stronger, sleeker self. She felt more capable of handling whatever physical challenge came her way than she ever had before.

She heard a soft movement, a shift in the air from the jungle behind her, and smiled to herself. She sensed that it was Horatio, and knew as well that he had stopped to gaze upon her.

She moved her hand up to her breast, cupping the small mound, massaging, then playing with her nipple until it grew hard between her fingertips. She heard his breathing quicken.

She sent her hand back down her torso, pausing to dip into her navel, then bent her leg and reached down to caress the inside of her thigh.

There was a guttural throat-clearing behind her. Her hand stopped where it was, and she opened her eyes, tilting back her head until she could just see Horatio behind her, upside-down, wearing nothing but his torn breeches, his tanned chest broad and infinitely touchable in the shaded light. He was looking off to the side, trying, apparently, to give the appearance of being a gentleman.

Her courage at playing the forward wench faded a bit, and she rolled onto her belly, rising onto her forearms so that they just barely covered her breasts. She crossed her ankles and, raising them into the air, swung her feet back and forth like a schoolgirl lying on the grass reading a book.

"Hello, Mr. Merivale," she said.

He looked back at her, his eyes widening when he saw what few moves she had taken to cover herself. "Mrs. Merivale."

"What brings you to these dark woods?" she asked, watching as his eyes drifted to her exposed derrière.

"I was looking for my demure young wife. Have you seen her anywhere?"

"Nowhere, sir, but I am quite alone if you wish to stop awhile and keep me company." She let her fingertips brush along the outside of her breast, drawing his eyes.

"I don't know if my wife would approve."

"I promise not to tell."

"Maybe you could help me," he said, coming to sit down beside her on the mat.

"Yes?"

He trailed a finger over the hill of one buttock, making her shiver. "My wife, she seems to welcome my touch, but she hesitates to take the final step."

"Perhaps she has been frightened."

"Of what?"

"Perhaps she doesn't know what will happen, if she lets you take her."

"What would she like to know?" he asked, his fingertips swirling in the small of her back, then tracing up her spine. He combed her damp hair over her shoulders, out of the way, and bent down to place a warm kiss at the base of her neck.

She felt a rush of warmth run down to her loins. "Tell her what you would do."

"How I would take her?"

"Tell her. Tell me."

"If I found her here like this, I'd kiss my way down her back," he said, doing so, pausing in the small of her back to scrape lightly at her skin with his teeth.

She shivered, letting her legs drop down to the mat and uncrossing her ankles. "And then?"

"I'd kiss and fondle her buttocks, like I've wanted to do every time I see them in front of me, moving beneath her chemise. You have no idea what the sight of a woman's backside can do to a man."

"What does it do?" she asked, as he held the mounds in his hands, massaging them lightly, kissing their tops and then delving his tongue into the first short space of cleavage between them.

"It makes me think of coming up behind her and lifting her gown. Of bending her forward until I can take her, while she stands with legs spread."

She caught her breath, the words making her body contract in eager response. "It doesn't sound very romantic."

, "You're wrong, there," he said between kisses that went down the backs of her thighs. She parted them slightly, inviting his attentions elsewhere. "It's very romantic. While I take her, I touch her *here*," he said, and with a fingertip touched for a moment upon the peak of her exposed folds. She tilted her hips, trying to expose herself more fully, but his fingers trailed away, down the inside of her thigh.

"That's what I think about," he said. "But if I had her here like I have you, I would work my way down her legs to her ankles and her feet. She has pretty feet."

"Feet aren't pretty."

"They are." His fingers found the sensitive place between her ankle bones and her Achilles tendon, digging in and massaging. The touch sent waves of pleasure up into her belly, and she dropped her head and arms onto the mat, lying flat so she need do nothing but enjoy his touch.

"And she has such dainty little toes. I could eat them in one bite," he said, raising a foot up and sucking one of her toes into his mouth.

She giggled into her shoulder, trying to pull her foot

away, but not trying very hard. He sucked her toes one by one, tickling her between them with the tip of his tongue, making her laugh even as she felt herself growing wet from his ministrations.

"And then I'd work my way back up her legs," he said, gently putting her feet down and using both hands and lips to come slowly up her legs, pausing to dwell on the space behind her knees. When he got to her sex he held his mouth close but not touching, and breathed on her so that she could feel the hot moistness of his breath. She parted her thighs further, silently begging for his touch, but he moved past, up her spine, and then was lying on his side beside her.

"And then just when she thought she'd never get what she really wanted, I'd touch her here," he said. His fingers at last went to her, one tip just barely going into her and then moving down with the other fingers, down towards her front, pulling wetness along with them.

She sighed, legs going wider still, her hips moving up and down as he stroked her slowly.

"I'd be remiss if that was all I gave her, though," he said, his voice low and close to her ear. "There's a whole other side of her that I have yet to explore."

"Don't stop," she said, feeling his hand slow on her. "Please don't stop."

"She might be getting impatient, but perhaps that is good for her. It's a delicious sort of impatience, after all," he said, and took his hand away.

She moaned and clamped her legs together, trying to rub them against each other and recreate some of the same sensation. Then she felt his touch on her hip, urging her to turn over, and she obeyed, letting her arms lie bent above her head, leaving her body open for him to do with as he wished.

"She has perfect breasts, soft, with dark little nipples that ask me to taste them." As he spoke, he bent his head to her breast, the warm wetness of his mouth closing over the peak. She felt his tongue swirl around it, and then with gentle suction he pulled away, letting her hard nipple slip from between his lips. He ran his tongue along the bottom curve of that breast, then bent his attentions to the other.

"I wouldn't want the rest of her to feel neglected, though," he said, pausing between licks up the side of her breast. His hand softly caressed the top of her thigh, moving slowly inward with each passing sweep of his fingertips. Again her thighs parted, and she shifted her hips towards him, as if she could coax him to hurry his way to her center. His fingers grazed the inside of her thigh, then brushed lightly over her sex, barely parting her curls.

"When I touch her here," he said, brushing his fingers back down and then pressing the tip of one against the entrance to her core, hard enough that she could feel and yearn for it, but not so hard as to enter, "I feel how she wants me. She's slippery with desire," he said, swirling his fingertip in a tiny circle and then stopping. "But do you know what else she does? Her sex sucks at me."

In response to his words she felt her inner muscles contracting in pulses against the place where he pressed, as if she could draw him into her body. She tried to lift herself against his hand and was rewarded by him stroking slowly up her folds as his head bent again to her breasts.

His hand left her, and he kissed his way down her belly, dipping his tongue into her navel while the shifting posture of his body told her he was removing his breeches. He tossed them aside, then continued his descent, nudging her legs farther apart so that he could lie between them.

"What I like best, though, is to taste her."

She felt him part her, using his fingertips to brush back the concealing hair, and then after a long moment of waiting the tip of his tongue touched on her entrance, tasting and taunting, then traveled up the length of her. He repeated the motion, on either side of her nether lips, then up the center again, making her writhe as much with impatience as with pleasure. Then his mouth fastened over her and his tongue took careful control. Her writhing stopped as every ounce of her being focused on the movements of his mouth.

Again a finger pressed against her opening, and the hint of the penetration she desired made her legs tense, and she felt ecstasy approaching, her hands fisting as she held her breath, urging on the peak even as she wished to prolong the moment.

And then he stopped, pulling his mouth away, and she let out a cry of frustration. He rose up, coming to lie over her with his weight on his elbows, his hard manhood lying pressed against her, and when she opened her eyes he was gazing down into her eyes.

"Anne."

She didn't need him to ask the question, for her to answer. "Yes."

He kissed her gently on the lips, and she brought her arms down and instinctively took hold of him, guiding him towards her entrance. When the head of his manhood was seated against her, she withdrew her hand and wrapped her arms around his back.

The first thrust was shallow, no more than an inch, but still she gasped. She felt herself stretching, her body forced to open, the feeling bordering almost on pain.

He withdrew slightly, then thrust again, harder, going deeper. She looked up at him in question. His jaw was tight, his brow drawn with tension, but when he met her eyes he managed a reassuring smile. "Trust me."

On the third thrust he buried himself fully, and she felt herself completed in a way she never had before. She was stretched and full, and at the same time open to him in a way she never had been before, in a way that went beyond the physical. They were joined together, heart, body, and soul.

He began to move, slowly at first, and then with increasing force and speed as she relaxed beneath him. He lifted himself up onto his arms, forcing her to loosen her hold on his back, then pinned her hands under each of his and slowed his pace, looking into her eyes as he thrust slow and deep. With each downstroke her eyes half closed, then opened again as he pulled away. She began to move with him.

As soon as she did he stopped. Still embedded deep within her he took her legs and pushed them toward her belly, making them bend, then he grasped both her ankles together and placed them on his right shoulder, so that her thighs were tight together. She felt her swollen sex exposed beneath them, squeezed between her thighs, penetrated by his manhood.

He leaned forward, his belly against the backs of her thighs, and started a series of shallow thrusts, two, three, four, then plunged deep, making her gasp, then back to the shallow thrusts that made her ache for their successor. She rolled her head to the side, letting the sensations take her, loving having him in control of her body, leaving her no task but to accept the pleasure he gave her.

"Anne," he said.

She opened her eyes and looked at him, and he slowed and deepened his strokes, then reached down and pressed his thumb against the centerpoint of her desire. The waves of pleasure broke over her, and she kept her eyes open, allowing him to watch as the waves moved through her.

He parted and lowered her legs, settling back between them, and with one more thrust reached his own release. She saw him try to keep his eyes open, but the sensations were too strong and he clasped her to him, saying her name again and again as he found release within her, pulsing as he did between the tight walls of her flesh.

He relaxed on top of her, and she wrapped her arms tight around him, her own body still throbbing with the aftereffects of their lovemaking. He slowly pulled himself from within her, then rolled to the side and pulled her against him, his arm around her waist. She found herself nestled against his chest, her legs entwined with his. He kissed her brow, and she closed her eyes, falling into a dreamy half doze.

She was wakened when he spoke. "What changed?" he asked softly. He was lying on his back now, and she was tight against his side, her bent leg lying over his now-soft member.

She raised her head and looked at him, but he had his eyes closed. "Why did I finally say yes?" she asked.

He nodded.

"I realized I didn't need you."

She felt the muscles tense all through his body, and hurried on, realizing how clumsily she had phrased that. "In the cave. I had to save myself, I knew you couldn't come do it for me. And I did it, I took care of myself. It made me realize that whatever happens with you, wherever you go, whether you someday leave me or you get killed chasing pirates, I'll be all right. I can rely on myself. I don't have to look for my security in someone else."

"I don't make you feel safe."

"It's not about you," she said.

"I should think it damn well was about me," he said, his eyes coming open as he sat up, forcing her to sit up as well, breaking the close contact of their bodies. She lay her hand against his chest.

"It's about something inside me," she tried to explain. "It wouldn't matter who you were, or what you did, you would never be able to make me feel safe. I had to find that within myself."

"What use is a husband if he can't keep his wife secure? What other purpose does he have?"

"Horatio, what are you talking about?"

"You said it yourself: You don't need me."

"I didn't explain myself well. I need you more than I ever have. It's just that I had to find my own strength before I could be free to love you." She clasped his face between her hands, forcing him to look at her. "I love you, Horatio Merivale."

But in his eyes, instead of the joy she had hoped to see, she saw instead the look of one who is lost.

Chapter Twenty-three

Ten days later

Imsa's longhouse was larger and richer than any they had been to before, and the welcome they received was on a higher level as well, as Imsa had been gone for years and was, it quickly became apparent, the son of the headman.

There were two longhouses in a large clearing set back from the river, and a third building that Imsa later explained was usually for the single young men, but had been turned over to the visiting rajah from Brunei and his guard. Smaller structures dotted the available space, and in front of each lounged Malay and Chinese soldiers. Horatio estimated that there must be at least two hundred such troops, and wondered at the strain their presence must be putting on the village. Down on the river were several large oared boats, but nothing that looked worthy of a long sea voyage.

The unseen rajah and his soldiers were ignored by the villagers, though, while they celebrated Imsa's return. The jars of rice wine were rolled out, a pig went to its squealing death, and brass gongs appeared for the torture of their eardrums.

Horatio smiled and nodded and accepted drink after drink of rice wine, while the women sang and carried Imsa's treasured pirate head up and down the verandah, then fed it tidbits of food and scattered grains of rice on its pate. The soft matter had mostly either rotted away or been devoured by birds and insects, but Horatio imagined that he could still vaguely see the astonished expression of the pirate, wondering how he had come to such a pass.

One young woman in particular looked very happy to see that Imsa had returned, and looked fair to bursting with pride that he had brought a fresh head and exotic visitors, to boot.

Would that Anne looked at him in such a way. Perhaps he should try taking a head or two?

She looked more beautiful than he could ever remember seeing her. She was wearing the red and white skirt that Lua had given her, riding low on her hips. She had taken Imsa's parang to her chemise, cutting it down to a short shirt that reached barely to the bottom of her ribcage, then taking strips of cloth and wrapping them around her breasts so that the hem did not float up in every stray breeze and expose her. The brass rings were around her ankles, and she wore her hair pulled back from her face and tied with a bit of rattan vine, stray tendrils of hair framing her face.

He could hardly keep his eyes off the inches of exposed belly and her navel, but it wasn't just the revealing outfit that had him thinking she looked extraordinarily beautiful. It was something from within her, some confidence that had not been there before. It gave her a steadiness, and a serene glow that even Imsa's relatives and friends seemed to recognize, treating her with a reserve and respect that they did not show any of the rest of them.

He feared she would slip away from him. If she didn't need him, then why would she stay?

Despite all his best efforts these past three weeks to talk himself into believing that it did not matter that he had lost the *Anne*, that he had tried his best and that was all that mattered, still a part of him did not believe it, and Anne's statement of not needing him had only brought the conviction that he was a failure back to the surface of his mind. He tried to act his usual self, tried not to show how useless he felt, but all the time he was wandering in a sea of emptiness. Anne was still his guiding light, but with every day that her calm strength grew he felt as if he were drifting farther and farther from her beloved shore.

Dimly, almost below the realm of conscious thought, he realized that it was something he had to find an answer to on his own. She might not have cared if Chartier took back his ship, but eventually she would care if she sensed he did not believe in himself.

It still did not make sense to him, her finding that she loved him at the same time she found she did not need him to keep her safe, and he found it hard to believe or to accept. He wasn't going to argue with her about it, though: He'd happily let her continue to feel herself in love with him, and with any luck he would become worthy of it before she figured out any differently.

Some hours later, the impromptu welcome-home feast consumed along with yet more jars of rice wine, the tribe settled down into a large oval and awaited the evening's entertainment. Anne sat by his side, her legs tucked neatly at her side, her shoulder touching his. He put his hand down beside hers, and she intertwined her fingers with his own.

"Would you like me to fetch you more rice wine?" he asked in a whisper.

She nudged him with her shoulder, making a face of comic disbelief.

"I think I'm almost developing a taste for it," he said. "We can send some back to England and see if we can create a market for it. We'll be rich! We'll have exclusive trading rights to Sulawak rice wine."

"As long as I don't have to drink any more of the stuff," she whispered back. "It's burning a hole in my stomach." She smothered a small ladylike burp, and he grinned.

"I'll know to begin worrying you've become a head-hunter yourself when you start to like it," he said.

"God save me from that day."

"You said you'd never dress like them, either."

"Are you complaining?"

"Never!" he whispered fervently, and sneaked a

peek at her bare belly. "Hell, no, I'm not complaining."

Mango scampered up and sat himself in front of Anne, leaning against her folded legs. Horatio met the little monster's eyes, and they glared at one another, each daring the other to break contact first.

"For heaven's sake, he's just a monkey," Anne said, laughing under her breath.

"That's what he's made you think," Horatio said. "But I know better."

Mango hissed and bared his teeth at him, taking a crouching, defensive posture with hackles raised.

"Oh, stop it," Anne said. "Both of you." She elbowed him at the same time she nudged Mango with her knee.

Horatio exchanged one more narrow-eyed glare with the demon, then allowed himself to be diverted by the headman, Ensa, who was standing up dressed in a short bearskin cloak and beaded headdress of black and white feathers. He started to speak, and quiet came over the group. Imsa sat down on the other side of Anne and translated for them, Kai and the others sitting nearby and leaning forward to hear.

"He saying who you are and where from," Imsa said. "And how you come here."

Ensa kept talking and talking, and Horatio looked at Imsa. "That's all he's saying?"

"He like tell story," Imsa said, and shrugged.

The village apparently liked to hear stories as well, sitting rapt as their leader talked, eyes turning frequently to their small group as if seeking confirmation for whatever unbelievable fact they were hearing.

Horatio decided that this was his type of headman.

Then Ensa sat and another man stood, this one much older and tattooed all over his arms and chest and back, his stretched earlobes holding a dozen rings each and lying against his collar bones. His eyes were rheumy and he moved with the stiffness of the aged, but he had a presence that made Horatio feel that he should mind his manners and pay attention.

"He is holy man," Imsa said. "He tell story."

"What story?" Anne asked.

"Very old story." The man started to speak, and Imsa again translated, only this time he took care to repeat in detail.

The story was, that in the time when the gods still lived on the earth, there was a great chief who fell in love with the spirit of the river, who appeared as a beautiful woman. Together they had a daughter, but soon after she was born the river spirit flowed away and did not return.

The daughter grew into a woman as beautiful as her mother had been, and like her mother she could not stay in one place. She desired to go to the sea, and so one night she slipped away and took a longboat down the river.

The chief was heartbroken that his child had gone, and he thought never to see her again. But a kingfisher came to him, and said his daughter would return, and at the next full moon she did.

At that point Horatio felt a chill go up his spine, and felt Anne's fingers tighten on his.

The story continued that the daughter said she had gone to the sea, and seen wondrous things. She had fallen in love with a man with skin the paleness of moonlight, and had lain with him. He had left her, though, and now she had come home to bear her child.

The child came, a boy with light skin and hair the color of wood. Over the years the boy grew, growing taller than any other man in the village. The chief loved him, but all others treated him warily, seeing the trace of the foreign lover's presence in his skin and hair, and knowing that his grandmother had been the spirit of the river.

And like his mother and his grandmother, the boy wanted to go to the sea. The chief wanted him to stay and to take his place when he died, but then the red kingfisher came again, and he knew he had to let the boy go where he wished.

"I will not return," the boy told his grandfather. "The bird spirits have told me so. I do not know where I will go, but I will travel far upon the sea. Someday, like the rains bring water back to the rivers to flow again to the sea, a child of my line will return to this village and bring you help in your time of need. For my grandmother was the spirit of the river, and she loved you."

The boy, now a man, left the village never to return. And the old chief died and one of his other sons took his place, and the generations passed one after the other, and always they waited for the descendent of the river spirit to return.

"One day, she did," Imsa translated.

The holy man turned and looked directly at Anne.

Chapter Twenty-four

"I still don't believe it," Anne said. She was sitting as close to Horatio as she decently could, on the inner verandah of the longhouse. It was morning and people were moving about, and she hoped not paying attention to her. It was a vain hope, though, after last night.

"I don't know what to think," Horatio said. "It seems too neat a story. Imsa must have told them about the kingfisher and your dreams. They may have concocted that tale to force us to help them get rid of the rajah and his soldiers."

"It's very clever of them." She bit her lip, thinking, aware that part of her wanted to believe the holy man's story. "Still, there are the dreams I had."

"But were they meant to draw you 'home,' or were they predictions of the future?" he asked. "You've wondered that all along."

"You're not helping."

"I know. I'm as confused as you are. We've been blaming events on the Hand of Destiny, only half believing it, and here when we're given a clear answer we still don't trust it. Perhaps it doesn't matter what the truth is."

"It matters to me."

"There's really no reason that it should, when you think about it," he said. "Our fate is what we make it. If we try to help them, then the story was as true as any story can be. Does it really matter if we chose it or it was fated?"

"I just want to *know*."

"Do you think it likely you have a headhunter for an ancestor?" he asked, a tinge of humor in his voice.

She was quiet, frowning.

"What is it?" he asked.

She gave a quick smile, and the hint of a laugh. "An old family story. A family joke, more of. Unlike most families, mine has moved around a lot through the years. We don't have ancestors going back hundreds of years in Stowe-on-Tyne. It's more like fifty years."

"The roving spirit of the river?"

"There's more. The family tendency to wander is said to be the fault of an ancestress who worked in a tavern near the wharves in London, back in the time of Queen Elizabeth. She had a liaison with a foreign sailor."

"No."

"Yes. A sailor who, as sailors do, sailed away before the child was born, never to be seen again." She looked at him, the possibility catching firm hold of

369

her mind. "I really *could* be the descendent of a head-hunter."

"With that type of story, any one of us could. Kai could be, or Ruut. There could be descendants in half the ports of Europe."

"But I came back."

"You want to believe it," he said.

She smiled. "It's more interesting than being a lady's maid."

"You haven't been that for a long time." He waggled his brows suggestively. "I'm not entirely averse to being married to a savage, myself, although I'm not sure my family would approve."

Kai and Ulrich came and joined them then, and a few moments later Ruut too eased himself to the floor.

"You want my head?" Kai asked.

Anne made slashing motions through the air.

"Yes, you more scary than Imsa," Kai said, mischief in her eyes.

"What happens now?" Ulrich asked.

"Apparently an audience has been arranged with the rajah," Horatio answered, "and then heaven only knows what." Silence greeted that statement, as they considered possibilities. If they were like Anne, their minds were as blank on what to expect as her own. How could they possibly make the rajah leave?

"Imsa's head," Kai said into the silence. "I know why it so important."

"The pirate head?" Anne asked.

Kai nodded. "Men, they marry only after they bring home head."

Anne's lips parted in surprise, and then she began

to laugh. "That girl who was watching Imsa yesterday, that must be who he intends to marry. No wonder she looked so happy!"

"Imsa has a sweetheart?" Horatio said in disbelief.

"Why not?" Anne asked. "He has a certain appeal, when he's not being smug."

"I not see it," Ruut said.

"Me, neither," Ulrich agreed.

Imsa walked up to them just then, his faint brows drawn down in a suspicious frown. They stared at him for a breathless moment, then fell over laughing. Imsa's frown deepened, his eyes narrowing, and they laughed harder.

"Why you laugh?"

"She is lovely girl," Ruut said. "You be very happy."

"We bring flowers to girls in England," Horatio said. "Heads tend to be messy, and don't smell half so sweet."

"You have many babies," Kai said. "One, two, three, four . . . they cry very loud all night, keep you awake."

Anne wiped the tears from the corner of her eyes. It was childish to make fun of Imsa for having a sweetheart. She knew that. She looked up into his glowering face, his earlobes hanging low with their brass rings, his *parang* at his hip. He looked quite savage. And embarrassed.

"She make good wife," Imsa said.

They started laughing all over again.

The Rajah Budru sat stiffly in a black velvet jacket, green silk trousers, and a sarong of gold brocade, the hilt of a kriss protruding from his sash. He was a small man, soft looking, with a discontented face. He spoke words of welcome as Horatio executed his best formal bow and Anne curtseyed beside him.

"We are honored to be guests of Your Highness," Horatio said. "We have heard much of your great wisdom and just rule." The formality of the occasion reminded him of India, and he knew well enough the type of flattery that was expected. The rajah smiled tightly and gestured for them to be seated in the chairs facing him. They did so, the others in their crew sitting on the floor behind them, while Imsa kneeled to the side, serving as translator.

Strains of queer, stringed music began, coming softly from behind a screen, and then Malay servants appeared, carrying trays of tea and long rolled leaves of tobacco. Anne gave him a wide-eyed look when the tobacco came to her, and he gave his head a bare shake. He doubted she would be expected to partake: It was unusual enough for her, a woman, to even be here.

The rajah shifted in his seat. He was looking impatient with the formalities, and as Horatio surreptitiously examined him, he realized that the man might not be entirely well. There was a faint sheen of sweat on his face, visible even in the shaded interior of the building, and his skin had a certain paleness to it that might have been the result of either illness or lack of sunlight.

"You are English," the rajah said, his words translated by Imsa. "How do you come to be here?"

With an internal sigh Horatio launched once again into the story of their journey, answering the questions that Rajah Budru occasionally interjected.

Rajah Budru's eyes turned to Anne as Imsa translated, and Horatio thought he saw a speculative, hopeful glow begin to shine in their dark depths. When the story was finished, the rajah fidgeted for a bit, chewing the inside of his lip, then spoke in a burst of words that Imsa translated with more formality and care than he used in his own speech.

"As you may know, although I am the rajah of Sulawak, my home is in Brunei. I am only here because of the piracy that has gotten out of control. My subjects need my protection."

Horatio mentally translated that to mean: My subjects are not providing the income they are supposed to.

unately, the pirates are clever and tricky. They are cowards who run instead of staying to fight. They are a small problem, a pest, yet like a mosquito they are difficult to swat down.

"To make matters worse, three weeks ago two foreign ships appeared off the shores. I believe these are the ships of your enemy, the Frenchman Chartier. You brought this man to the waters of Sulawak."

Horatio felt his mouth go dry.

"This Chartier, he sank three of my best boats."

Horatio tried to swallow, but couldn't.

"I think this is a problem you brought to Sulawak, so it is a problem you must solve." Rajah Budru folded his hands, looking pleased with himself.

"He is still offshore?" Horatio asked.

"One of my captains believes he is looking for something. They sail up rivers, they send out landing parties. They cause chaos. And the ships are too well armed for us to fight, so we stay here and wait for them to leave. Only, I think he will not leave as long as you are here."

Horatio began to speak again, but Rajah Budru held up his hand, the sweat now visible in beads on his forehead.

"I have been on Sulawak for too long. I miss my home. You can understand that, yes?" he asked, then went on without waiting for an answer, Imsa struggling to keep up. "You will capture this Chartier and his ships, and give one of them to me so that I may sail home in comfort. The other I will leave with you, so that you may control the piracy that is destroying Sulawak."

Horatio sat stunned. "You wish us to remain here?"

"You have brought trouble to Sulawak, so it is only right that you correct it. It is what you were meant to do. The story of the river spirit says so, yes?"

"Yes, I suppose . . ."

"The pirates that cause the trouble, half of them are from Sulawak. They may listen better if the one who rules over them is of their own race."

Horatio looked at Anne. Whatever the legend may have said, whatever the truth might or might not be, she was as blond as sunlight and still looked far more the Englishwoman than a headhunter, nevermind the anklets and native skirt. Rajah Budru was grasping for an excuse to dump the responsibility of Sulawak onto someone else's shoulders.

"We had thought to ask you for passage to an English port," Horatio said, testing the man. A rough wooden house in the middle of the jungle must seem a horrid exile to a man accustomed to the rumored splendors of Brunei's court. And if Rajah Budru was feeling ill, his discontent would be all the greater, his eagerness to go home all the stronger.

Rajah Budru's eyes showed a flicker of alarm. "You cannot leave. You must capture this Chartier. You took his ship once before. You can do it again."

"It would be very dangerous. If the man could best Your Highness's boats, then what chance do we have? No, it might be best for us to wait here, or deeper in the jungle, until he gives up and leaves. It might take a very long time . . . a very very long time, but I think that might be the safest course."

"You do not want to do that," Rajah Budru said. "You want to fight the pirates."

"Why do I?"

The rajah put his lips tight together, then said, "Because if you do, then I will give the government of the island to you. All the moneys, all the trade, you may have it if I am given one of Chartier's ships and can go home. You and your wife will be Rajah and Ranee of Sulawak."

Imsa made a choking sound as he translated, and Horatio heard Anne draw in a breath.

"I think maybe that is a very poor exchange," Horatio said. "I do not see any wealth to be had, nor any trade."

"There is some mining," the rajah said. "And it is a great honor, to be a rajah. Your countrymen will bow before you! Sulawak is a wonderful island, with gold and diamonds maybe, in the mountains. Emeralds. It could be very rich. But I need to go home, I am not well, and it would be unkind of you to refuse me."

"The Sultan of Brunei would not object to such an arrangement?"

"If you can bring prosperity to Sulawak, he will be happy. He is my nephew, and I will talk with him."

Horatio's heart was beating rapidly in his chest, and he hoped his excitement did not show on his face. "Let me talk with my crew. Perhaps we can be of help to you."

The rajah smiled.

"I not believe it," Ruut said, staring at Anne.

"I not believe it," Imsa said.

"I am stunned, myself," Anne said, sitting on a stone by the river, Mango beside her. She could feel her legs quivering, her hands shaking when she did not hold them clasped together. They had all felt the need for privacy for this conversation, and had decided on a short walk up the river to find it.

"The Hand of Destiny truly did guide us," Ulrich said in wonder.

"You doubted that it did?" Horatio asked. "It was your idea in the first place."

Ulrich shrugged. "It was good to talk about, it made the bad things not so bad. But maybe I did not believe in it as much as I pretended."

"We do it, yes?" Kai asked. "We take the ships?"

"Do we?" Anne asked, looking to Horatio, but she already knew the answer. There was only one answer to give, when fate had provided an opportunity such as this.

"Yes." He grinned the crooked grin that she loved, and there was a mischief and a light in his eyes that had been missing since he had lost the *Anne*. "The only question is, how?"

Anne scratched the back of Mango's neck, the answer having formed itself in her mind as soon as Rajah Budru had suggested they capture Chartier. "We offer him what he seeks," she said.

"The monkey?" Horatio asked.

"And me."

Chapter Twenty-five

Anne dug her paddle into the water and pulled with all her might. Mango crouched in the bow of the small dugout canoe, protesting every stray splash of water that hit him.

"Quit your complaining," Anne said, switching sides and paddling again.

Mango gibbered a response.

"There were no paddles small enough for you," she said. She was talking to distract herself from the ship towards which she paddled, and from the half-dozen boats that were entering the sea behind her, emerging from the mouth of the river. They were crammed bow to stern with headhunters, Malays, and the odd Chinese soldier, all dressed in the loincloths and headbands of the natives, armed with spears and rifles.

Her little canoe was surprisingly heavy in the water, moving slowing through the small waves. She prayed she did not capsize. She'd been given lessons in swimming over the past few days, and thought she could at least keep herself afloat should she overturn, but a quiet pool in the river was not the open sea.

"Help!" she screamed towards the ship. "Help me! *M'aidez!*" It was the *Cauchemar* before her, still a couple hundred yards off. She wondered if they could hear her. "Help! Help!" She put her paddle back into the water and pulled, and risked a glance back over her shoulder.

Rising above the jungle was a thick plume of grey smoke, rising, she knew, from an immense bonfire set purposefully to lure Chartier here from wherever he had been raiding. There was nothing like a fire to draw human attention and pique the curiosity. The plume was growing steadily less visible as the day died, the sky to the west turning to peach and pink, painting the underbellies of clouds.

The boats of the headhunters—both real and pretend—were still a fair distance behind her. They would be pacing themselves to stay the right distance behind her, gaining only slowly. Horatio was in one of the boats, his skin darkened with a vegetable stain. The effect had been marginally more believable on him than it was on Ulrich and Ruut.

Horatio hadn't wanted her to play this part in the attack, but it was her plan, and it was the simplest way to approach the ship in force.

She heard shouts from the *Cauchemar*, and waved her hands above her head, then put her paddle alongside her knees and picked up Mango, holding him above her head. "Help!" she screamed again, then put Mango down and resumed paddling, as if afraid for her very life.

And she was afraid, but instead of letting it paralyze her like the night the *Coventry* had foundered, or reduce her to tears and the need to drug herself like when she had put the opium in the stew aboard Chartier's ship, this time she used it to power her muscles and propel herself towards the *Cauchemar*.

Courage was not being unafraid: It was being afraid and mastering it long enough to do what needed to be done. She was not helpless. She was not weak. She need not let the world have its way while she sat back and accepted.

She *wanted* to be a ranee. And damn it, she was *going* to be a ranee. Sulawak was meant to be hers, and she would do what she had to in order to get it.

"Help! Help!"

"Mango?" she heard floating to her over the water. "*C'est* Mango?"

"*Oui!*" she shouted back. "*C'est Mango. Et Anne! M'aidez! Les sauvages, ils nous attaquent!*" It was a pretty poor line, but she didn't know how to say anything much more complicated than "the savages are attacking us," and get her point across.

"Mango!"

She supposed that showed her where she rated: below the monkey.

There were shouted orders aboard the ship, sails trimmed, cannon no doubt being loaded. She slowed her paddling, letting the headhunter boats gain even more ground on her. As they closed in, Chartier would be unable to fire without risking sinking his monkey.

Wild war cries rose up behind her, and she turned to look, seeing those not rowing raising their spears toward the sky in threatening, blood-mad thrusts. They sent a chill up her spine, and she turned back to her paddle, moving a little more frantically than she'd intended.

She knew they were not after her, but still . . . They were unnerving.

"Vite! Vite!" Chartier shouted. She could make him out now, jumping up and down, waving his hands. It must be killing him to see his monkey so close, and yet in such danger. A longboat was being lowered over the side, to come fetch her, she assumed. There was no sign of the second ship, the *Temperance,* which was good luck, at least for the moment.

She was fifty yards now from the *Cauchemar.* She slowed her paddling, letting herself sag as if she were exhausted. And truth be told she was getting tired, the rush of fear notwithstanding. Mango recognized his home, and the man on deck, and began to leap about, cheeping and gibbering.

The canoe drifted almost to a stop, and she heard the eager cries of the men behind her. On the deck of the *Cauchemar* a sailor at a swivel gun took aim, others lifted weapons in preparation to fire, and sailors climbed down the side to the longboat that was now in the water. She was sitting in the middle of what was about to become a sea battle.

The fear in her stomach sank to new, nauseating lows, and she decided she had gone far enough. Fear had a purpose, after all. It saved one from stupidity.

She dug into the water and backpaddled this time, sending the canoe drifting backwards as the boats full of men came up even with her, then in a rush of splashing paddles and thudding chants passed her by. With a few sweeps of the paddle she managed to turn the little canoe around until it faced shore, and then she pulled for all she was worth.

Behind her, headhunters and pirates met in an explosion of gunfire and shouts. She shuddered, not wanting to think about what was happening to the men on both sides, but finding it impossible not to. Horatio was there, and her friends, and when she had drawn away from the immediate danger she could not help turning to watch.

The headhunters were swarming up the sides of the *Cauchemar* likes insects on a dead animal. Some were knocked back, falling into the water, and others gained the top rail and flung themselves into the battle on deck with sword in hand.

She picked Horatio out, seeing him for a moment, his dark head moving quickly through the throng. Then others blocked her view, and she caught her breath and sent a prayer heavenward that he be all right.

She hated that he was aboard that ship, in very real danger of losing his life. She wanted him on shore, safe. She wanted him in one piece. But she wanted him whole in more than just body, and the only way she would get that was if he took back the ship. She'd seen that when his eyes had lit up when they'd decided to try for it. However well she might think of him, however much she might love him, he would not believe it or accept it unless he could prove his value to himself first.

Somehow, Horatio's sense of who he was had gotten tied up in Chartier and the *Cauchemar/Anne*. She didn't like it, but she recognized that there was something similar in it to what she had gone through in Gana Cave. If he had to best Chartier before he could accept her love, then she would not deny him the chance.

She could barely stand to watch any longer, and knew she should be going. If by some chance Chartier were to win this battle, she would be no help to anyone if she were sitting within his easy reach.

She paddled back to shore to where Kai and others from Imsa's village were waiting, Mango frantic in confusion in the bow of the canoe.

"Sorry, sweeting," Anne said. "You're stuck with me." She could only hope that when the day was done, Mango wasn't *her* only companion, as well.

Kai came forward from the edge of the jungle, and helped her drag the small boat up the sand. When it was secure they both turned and stared back out to sea.

She was too far away, and the light too dim now to see what was happening aboard the *Cauchemar*. While paddling she had caught the sounds of fighting, carried by the wind across the water, but she was either too far away now to hear anything, or the rush of the surf was too loud. Or the battle was over, and who the winner they would have to wait to discover.

She felt Kai's hand slip into hers. Both their hearts were with the men on that ship.

Horatio fought his way towards the poop deck, where Chartier was shouting orders to his embattled crew and using a cutlass to fend off attackers. His sole focus was on reaching the Frenchman, and he was nearly oblivious to the headhunters around him, hacking and goring with a ferocity that belied their small statures.

A pirate came at him. He fended the attacker off with his borrowed sword, and a moment later two tribesmen took the man down. He climbed up onto the poop deck, for there his prey was waiting.

"You!" Chartier cried, recognizing him.

"Yes, me, you damn bloody Frenchman!" Horatio shouted. He attacked.

Chartier parried the blow with his own blade. "English dog! Pig! Thief!" He struck back, his movements strong, the skill of them taking Horatio by surprise. No matter that he was a lunatic, Chartier knew how to handle a sword.

"You call *me* thief?"

"You steal my boat," Chartier spat, swinging, his blade scraping across Horatio's as it was raised in defense. "You steal my queen," he added with another blow that Horatio barely managed to deflect. "And you steal my monkey!" With his third blow, Chartier knocked the sword from Horatio's hands.

Chartier grinned, then laughed, raising his cutlass for the *coup de grace*. "You will not have the chance to steal from Philippe Chartier ever again!"

Horatio saw his sword, out of reach. He saw Chartier, savoring his victory. He saw himself, dying a failure, everything his father ever said about him true, and Anne left alone, knowing he had failed her. He recalled all the things this man had done. The men he'd killed, the way he'd had Horatio beaten that first day they'd met. And now the Frenchman was going to win. After all his wandering Horatio had finally found meaning and happiness in Anne, and in the end he was going to fail her.

Fury ran like acid through his veins.

"Raaaaa-argh!" he cried, and launched himself bodily at his enemy. The man's eyes went wide, his sword arm motionless as he was taken by surprise. They both went down, the cutlass knocked from Chartier's grip as the two men hit the deck.

"I'll take your monkey," Horatio said, smashing his fist into Chartier's nose. "And your boat," he said, wrapping his hands around the man's neck. "And the queen was never yours." He choked Chartier while pounding the man's head against the deck, ignoring his punches, and then the frantic digging of the dying Frenchman's hands against his own.

Chartier began to pass out, and Horatio released him, rising to his feet and snatching a belaying pin from the rail. Chartier coughed and gagged, his wig to one side, his scraggly, oily hair plastered to his skull. Blood ran down his face from his broken nose.

A few well-placed strikes with the belaying pin, and Chartier would be dead.

It wasn't satisfaction enough.

Ulrich climbed up onto the poop deck, his sword dripping red. "Horatio?"

Horatio did not take his eyes off Chartier. "Yes?"

"We have the ship."

"Good."

A silence stretched, broken only by the diminishing coughs of Chartier as he regained his senses. "Er . . ." Ulrich said. "What are you going to do with him?"

Horatio smiled with hatred, and, as Chartier began to reach for his fallen cutlass, he conked him on the head with the belaying pin, knocking him out. "Put him in chains below deck, of course."

The French pirate lay like a puppet without a master. For a long moment Horatio stared at him, unable to reconcile the present reality with the demonic dimensions his nemesis had taken on in his imaginings. He nudged Chartier with his foot, and the man's body moved as any other would, mere flesh and bone.

He turned then, and saw for the first time the carnage on deck. The boat had become a slaughterhouse, and most of the bodies were of pirates. If Anne ever knew how much blood had poured across this deck, she would ask him to burn the thing.

But he could never do that. Anne would be ranee, a queen, but a queen could not rule without the strength of her army and her navy. She needed him, whether she thought so or not. He had earned his place by her side, and the accomplishment gave him a savage sense of pride.

He was almost tempted to cut off Chartier's head to hang from his own roofbeam as a trophy to remind him of this day.

"Trouble," Ulrich said, and pointed over the port rail.

Horatio looked, and his grin faded. His self-congratulation had been premature.

The *Temperance* was coming round the headland.

"In Su-la-wak there lived my wife,
And I will love her all my life," an off-key voice sang.

Anne lifted her head off her arms. She was lying next to a small fire, on the jungle floor, along with Kai and the tribespeople who had stayed to wait with them.

"I'll go no more a-roving,
Without you, fair maid."

Horatio stepped out of the forest, his body bare except for the loincloth, his skin streaked with brown dye. He grinned at her, teeth white in his darkened face. She was on her feet in an instant, throwing herself into his arms, holding him tight against her as she felt his arms settle around her back, his cheek coming down to rest atop her head. Sobs of relief wracked her body.

"It's all right," he said softly. "It's all right."

She dug her fingers into his back, never wanting to let him go.

"We have both ships," Horatio said. "Those of the crew that surrendered are locked up in the hold of the one Rajah Budru will take home. He can go back to Brunei as a hero."

"I don't care," she said. All she cared was that he

was back, safe. But then there was one question she had to ask: "Chartier?"

"I could have killed him. I almost did." He was quiet for a moment. "Let Budru take him home as a prize, and do with him what he will."

"I'm glad," she said softly. She was dimly aware of Kai and Ulrich engaged in a similar reunion, and Ruut and Imsa were safe, as well.

"I have a surprise for you," he said.

She lifted her head. "I don't need any—" she started to say, and then saw someone unexpected from the corner of her eye. She turned her head, and gasped. "Gianni!" she cried.

The solid little Italian held out his arms as if to show himself off. "Yeeees, Gianni!" he said.

She abandoned Horatio and flew to the little man, hugging him, hardly believing he was still alive. "How?" she asked.

He tapped his head and nodded, grinning. He'd tricked them.

Anne went back to Horatio, and took both of his hands, looking up into his eyes. "You have the *Anne* now. The world is yours, if you wish to explore it."

"*We* have the *Anne*," he corrected. "And the only world I wish to explore is yours."

"You want to stay?" she asked, tears starting in her eyes.

"Whither thou goest, my love." He pulled her into his arms, and kissed her softly on the lips. "And besides, where else can I be an oriental potentate?"

She slapped him lightly on the side.

"That's no way to treat the future rajah of Sulawak."

"Just remember that it is the descendent of a goddess you hold in your arms."

"As if I could ever forget."

Epilogue

Two years later

Anne stood on the verandah of her new Malay-style house, with its doors and windows, chairs and tables and real bed. Her feet were bare on the smooth wooden planks, but she wore a proper dress of pale blue silk, the fabric so fine that it lifted in the slightest of breezes. Mango perched on the rail beside her, eating fruit.

The first few huts of this new settlement dotted a clearing to the west, and the sounds of building echoed across the intervening space. Kai and Ulrich had a small house at the near end of that clearing, where they lived with their mischievous little daughter. In Kai Anne had found a friend nearer to her heart than her own sisters, and they spent most days together.

Ruut and Gianni lived aboard the *Anne*, unwilling

to give up life at sea for the comforts of shore. They visited as frequently as they might, but always at the end of a few days there was an anxiousness in them to return to the ship. The sea was their home.

The yard in front of her sloped down to the river, where a pier extended into the water, a sloop and several smaller boats moored at its side. Horatio was disembarking from the sloop: He had rendezvoused with the *Anne*, which had been to Batavia for supplies and now lay at anchor farther down the river, restocking the arms of one of the new forts they had built to control both native and foreign piracy. The jewels and goods that had been aboard the *Cauchemar* had by consensus been sold, used to fund their struggling government.

He started up the path from the pier and saw her. "News from home!" he said, waving letters above his head.

She ran down the steps and across the rough grass, but instead of letting her have the letters Horatio hooked her with his arm and swung her around, pulling her against his chest. "A kiss first?"

She gave him a quick peck on the cheek and reached for the letters.

"My lovely queen, that will not do," he said, and pulled her close.

She felt the pressure of his firm body against hers, and was reminded that it had been almost a week since they had had time or energy to indulge each others' desires. She relaxed against him, and tangled her fingers in the hair at the base of his neck, pulling his face down to hers.

She led the kiss as much as she followed, and as it deepened she felt the liquid sensation of desire settling into her loins, the letters almost fading from consciousness. Almost, but not quite.

"Now give them to me," she said playfully, breaking away and pulling the treasures from his hand.

He didn't try to take them back, instead walking beside her as she carefully opened the first. She knew he was as hungry as she for news, and as anxious about what the letters might hold. It had been over a year since their last piece of mail from home, and much could happen in that time.

She scanned her mother's writing, looking for words like *illness* or *death*. What caught her eye instead was *marriage*.

"Oh, heavens," she said, laughing.

"What is it?"

"Miss Godwyn. She has married a man forty years her senior." Anne knew from a previous letter that Miss Godwyn had survived the shipwreck and, upon arriving in Cape Town, had chosen to return to England rather than continue the journey to India.

"Why on earth did she do that?"

"Apparently he promised never to take her aboard a ship." Anne read further, then broke down into giggles, gasping as she read aloud, " 'When she visits Suffington Hall no one is permitted to mention either your or Mr. Merivale's names. She flies into a fit if one does, the reminder that her lady's maid has married a gentleman and become queen of a small country being more than she can bear.' "

Horatio started laughing, too. "I don't think she'd

be half so jealous if she knew it was a country that operated in the red."

"Perhaps not. But she'd have every reason to be jealous of my marriage."

"Sometimes I wonder at how I was lucky enough to get you," he said, his smile tender as he took her gently into his arms, the letter caught between them.

"It wasn't luck," she said. "It was Destiny."

"And very romantic."

Author's Note

In 1839, the young Englishman James Brooke sailed his yacht the *Royalist* to the small settlement of Kuching, in Sarawak, on the island of Borneo. Sarawak was ruled by Rajah Muda Hassim, the uncle of the sultan of Brunei. In return for Brooke's help putting down a rebellion in the interior, Muda Hassim gave Brooke governorship of the state, then returned to the comforts of the royal court in Brunei.

James Brooke became Rajah Brooke, founding a dynasty that lasted more than a hundred years. He spent much of his rule eradicating piracy and discouraging the practice of headhunting.

Sarawak is now part of Malaysia.

⤙the Mermaid of Penperro
LISA CACH

Konstanze never imagined that singing could land someone in such trouble. The disrepute of the stage is nothing compared to the danger of playing a seductress of the sea— or the reckless abandon she feels while doing so. She has come to Penperro to escape her past, to find anonymity among the people of Cornwall, and her inhibitions melt away as she does. But the Cornish are less simple than she expected, and the role she is forced to play is harder. For one thing, her siren song lures to her not only the agent of the crown she's been paid to perplex, but the smuggler who hired her. And in his strong arms she finds everything she's been missing. Suddenly, Konstanze sees the true peril of her situation—not that of losing her honor, but her heart.

___52437-6 $5.50 US/$6.50 CAN

Bewitching the Baron
Lisa Cach

Valerian has always known before that she will never marry. While the townsfolk of her Yorkshire village are grateful for her abilities, the price of her gift is solitude. But it never bothered her until now. Nathaniel Warrington is the new baron of Ravenall, and he has never wanted anything the way he desires his people's enigmatic healer. Her exotic beauty fans flames in him that feel unnaturally fierce. Their first kiss flares hotter still. Opposed by those who seek to destroy her, compelled by a love that will never die, Nathaniel fights to earn the lone beauty's trust. And Valerian will learn the only thing more dangerous—or heavenly—than bewitching a baron, is being bewitched by one.

___52368-X $5.50 US/$6.50 CAN

Dorchester Publishing Co., Inc.
P.O. Box 6640
Wayne, PA 19087-8640

Please add $1.75 for shipping and handling for the first book and $.50 for each book thereafter. NY, NYC, and PA residents, please add appropriate sales tax. No cash, stamps, or C.O.D.s. All orders shipped within 6 weeks via postal service book rate. Canadian orders require $2.00 extra postage and must be paid in U.S. dollars through a U.S. banking facility.

Name_____
Address_____
City_____State_____Zip_____
I have enclosed $_____ in payment for the checked book(s).
Payment <u>must</u> accompany all orders. ❑ Please send a free catalog.

The CHANGELING BRIDE

LISA CACH

In order to procure the cash necessary to rebuild his estate, the Earl of Allsbrook decides to barter his title and his future: He will marry the willful daughter of a wealthy merchant. True, she is pleasing in form and face, and she has an eye for fashion. Still, deep in his heart, Henry wishes for a happy marriage. Wilhelmina March is leery of the importance her brother puts upon marriage, and she certainly never dreams of being wed to an earl in Georgian England—or of the fairy debt that gives her just such an opportunity. But suddenly, with one sweet kiss in a long-ago time and a faraway place, Elle wonders if the much ado is about something after all.

___52342-6 $4.99 US/$5.99 CAN